Abode of Misery

An Illustrated Compilation of Facts, Secrets and Myths of the Old Charleston District Jail

David C. Scott

BUILDING ART
P R E S S

ISBN: 1451512023
ISBN-13: 9781451512021

TABLE OF CONTENTS

Author's Preface

Why a Book about the Jail?

Photo by author

The Charleston District Jail Today

.

Where are the books about The Old Charleston Jail?

I've asked the city's merchants, librarians and preservation groups that question. "There just aren't any," has been the usual answer. In a city of bookshelves sagging under the weight of Charleston-related histories, the jail exists only in the occasional anecdotal reference or, more often, in sometimes fanciful oral history passed from one person to the next.

And yet this dour, sinister-looking landmark was the loathed but mandatory residence of many thousands of unfortunates over 137 years of operation. From the time it was erected in 1802 until it was closed in 1939, real persons were locked inside. Life for most was grim, indeed.

I first passed through the arched, brick entrance of the jail on a chilly night in late 2007 and immediately was trans-fixed. The event that had opened its doors was an exhibition of College of Charleston student art but, for me, the jail itself stole the show. A few bare light bulbs strung here and there only served to make shadows darker, more mysterious and threatening. Huge iron cellblock doors, heavy and rusting, groaned when disturbed but revealed little more than dark-ness beyond their thresholds. I vowed to find out as much about the building as I could.

The next day I began searching for more information but found only scraps. In fact, local residents seemed barely aware of the jail's existence. The only printed work devoted exclu-sively to the jail that I found was in the Charleston County Public Library. It is a spiral-bound collection of pen-and-ink drawings and poetry self-published in 2001 by artist Robert Grenko of Walterboro, SC. Grenko, whose primary interest is in low country rice plantations, had stumbled across the old prison and couldn't resist producing intricate renderings of its moody architecture. He has kindly permitted me to repro-duce some of them in these pages.

Courtesy of Robert Grenko

Grenko depicts the arched entrance, and a staircase

Grenko's emphasis being more aesthetic than historic, text was limited to poems and brief comments. Moving as it was, I hungered for more facts but could find little else.

There are a few good reasons why jail history has been hard to come by. One is the general inaccessibility to the building itself. It was closed down, locked up and mostly unoccupied from 1939, when it ceased operating as a jail, until the late 1970s when it briefly was made a museum. After that venture folded, public access has been limited to occasional social events and nightly "ghost" tours.

More challenges lurk in the scarcity of verifiable information and the difficulty in rooting out and compiling the reliable material that does survive. It appears that whatever official records may have been kept have been lost or destroyed. A few administrative references to the jail and its inmates may be found in court ledgers, death records and grand jury reports but log books, mug shots and other jail-specific documents remain undiscovered.

How many persons were incarcerated there and who were they?

How many died within its walls by disease, accident, execution or otherwise?

What was day-to-day life there really like?

Since the official record pertaining to such questions is silent, how might answers be found?

Libraries and archives are an obvious place to look but there are drawbacks. The digital record, while occasionally intriguing, is incomplete. Microfilm versions of old newspapers yield tantalizing nuggets but seldom are conveniently indexed. That means finding worthwhile items requires countless hours squinting into the blurry screens of contrary microfilm viewers.

Many news clippings were trimmed so closely that they often don't include the exact name of the publications in which they appeared or precisely when. Over the years, Charleston enjoyed a flourishing community of newspapers, some of which merged facilities and names along the way, further complicating the task of identification.

Maddeningly, discoveries can create more questions than answers. A jaw-dropping, jail-related story might command ink in one day's, turn-of-the-century newspaper, then vanish from subsequent editions. Was the story quashed by political pressure or did fresher, breaking news simply squeeze the jail story out of the paper?

Also frustrating is the fact that too many interesting, jail-related tales referenced in a particular book, article or by a person frequently lack reliable corroboration. Lots of jail stories are tantalizing but did the events to which they allude really occur? For example, were thousands of inmates "baked alive" inside its impossibly hot cellblocks? Were prisoners mercilessly shut inside stone "coffins" in the basement as punishment? Some swear these accounts are true but are unable to provide believable proof to back them up beyond "I heard it somewhere."

None of this whining is a bid for sympathy from the reader. I'm simply suggesting that factual information about the Charleston District Jail can be as elusive as the phantoms many visitors claim brush against them during visits there. I like a good, scary story as much as the next person but I prefer my thrills to be factual.

So, permit me to state up front what I hope this book represents. First, I don't claim that it is the exhaustively complete, end-all/be-all, final word on the Charleston jail. I did the best

I could with two years of digging but hope others will bring forth additional contributions to the jail's history.

Rather, this is a first and serious attempt to assemble all of the currently known, jail-related information in one volume. I've tried to make it interesting, but not at the expense of facts. Source notes are included and if I have reason to be suspicious about a legend, I explain why.

The fact is that thousands of men and women (and not a few children!) endured the awfulness of this place and most have long been forgotten. Whether hardened criminals justly confined for breaking the law or victims of innocent circumstance, they were locked away and suffered greatly. Now, only traces of them remain. Some of their names were recorded in newspaper articles and court ledgers while others wrote about themselves in diaries and journals. A few even drew pictures, including some scratched in plaster that can still be seen in some of the cell-blocks to this day.

Much of the material I came across has been reproduced verbatim and edited only to remove extraneous content or make clear an unfamiliar term or historical context. Sometimes archaic spellings and vernacular have been preserved in the interest of authenticity.

It should be noted, though, that included are recollections by writers with a point of view who, in some cases, waited years to commit their notes or memories to print. Such delayed storytelling can produce versions of history that, while essentially true, are subject to a bit of embellishment. This may particularly be the case of prisoner-survivors of the Civil War, who published books and articles detailing their experiences, sometimes many years after the fact. The nature of the conflict and the hardship many of them experienced may produce understandably subjective accounts.

In anticipation of the scrutiny of academics, professional researchers and other experts, apologies hereby are offered for omissions, distortions and errors in fact. These largely will be the result of vague, incomplete or contradictory citations in the written record. Flawed interpretation on my part is a possibility, as well.

However, I earnestly welcome additions, corrections, alternate perspectives and related suggestions, both for revisions of this volume as well as for the benefit of those who might build on it to produce more comprehensive works. In fact, anyone taking umbrage at my puncture of a particularly cherished story or myth is encouraged to come forward with countervailing evidence. If your version is verifiably more factual, I cheerfully will admit my error and supply the correction to a future edition.

Also, if readers are in possession of jail-related facts in the form of records, manuscripts, illustrations, photographs or artifacts, please contact me at dc_scott@mac.com. Let's get this story right.

The Charleston District Jail is more than a curious, old house of detention that provides giggly shivers for those who visit in the dark of night. Sights and sounds there can be both moving and unsettling. The mystery is intoxicating. The questions are numerous. If you ever have the opportunity to walk its halls, stand in its cellblocks and find yourself wondering what really happened there, you might understand why this book was created.

DCS
Charleston, SC September 2010

Epigraphs

"... what must be the effect upon us, whose vision cannot extend beyond the dismal walls which surround this abode of misery..."

Capt. Willard W. Glazier, Union prisoner
Charleston District Jail, 1864. [1]

**"When I enlisted in the army,
Then I thought t'was grand,
Marching through the streets of Boston
Behind a regimental band.
When at Wagner I was captured,
Then my courage failed;
Now I'm dirty, hungry, naked, Here in Charleston jail."

"Down in Charleston Jail"
Composed by Sergeant Johnson of the
54th. Massachusetts (colored) Infantry
while a prisoner at the Charleston jail, 1864 [2]

**"A man's ambition must be small to write his name on the jail-house wall"

Graffiti scratched into the plaster
of a cell in Charleston District Jail,
probably 1920 to 1930

Introduction

A Place Shrouded in Tragedy

Photo by author

On a July afternoon in 1864, the high brick walls that boxed the yard of the Charleston District Jail probably choked off what little breeze might have stirred beyond them. Their height cast broad shadows across the space but even the shade would have offered little relief from the hot, fetid air trapped inside.

The yard (actually, a rather generous term for a barren plot upon which grass seldom grew) was likely crowded. Groups of gaunt, sallow-looking men — and a few women — would have sat or moved among rows of dirty, tattered tents pitched alongside the base of each wall. Youngish guards, perhaps shrugging rifles from one aching shoulder to another, may have gazed at the scene, more bored than concerned.

It was a time of war and there were two kinds of captives at the jail. One group was composed of ordinary civilian convicts, doing time or awaiting trials. They occupied the building's cells at night but were permitted to wander the yard during the day. Some tended to swagger a bit, as if to confirm that they, at least, knew the ropes.

In the other group — by far the largest — were Union soldiers that had been captured on countless Civil War battlefields. They were there because the Confederacy lacked cash and had far more captives than its hastily constructed stockades could handle. In Charleston, prisoners of war were warehoused among its thieves, murderers and prostitutes already resident at the District Jail. And since the jail building itself was already full, most wound up in its filthy back yard. The mix was decidedly uneasy. What resentments festered, however, mostly were dulled by the heat, tedium and their shared plight.

Another noonday meal — such as it was — had passed. Curls of smoke from dying cook-fires rose to join wisps from clay pipes lit by the fortunate who had them. A few men drew cracked and oily decks of playing cards from their uniform pockets. Others resumed long-fought skirmishes with the hated "graybacks" (lice) and other vermin that squirmed over every square inch of the jail yard ground.

It was here that 26-year-old Michigan Cavalry Lieutenant Samuel Harris said he saw a Confederate soldier murder a child.

"One day I was standing near a door leading into the jail," Harris wrote years later. A Reb soldier was standing guard at the door to keep us out. A colored boy, about fifteen years old, who was errand boy to the jailer, came down the hall and looked out of the door. The guard ordered him to go back. The boy started to go and had got to the foot of the stairs about ten feet from the door, when the guard drew up his gun and deliberately shot the boy through the lungs. He gave one cry and fell to the floor dead."

Drawing by Sam Wilson

"...the guard drew up his gun and deliberately shot the boy..."

Jailers, hearing the shot, hurried to the scene. The guard complained that the youth, while complying with the letter of his order, had laughed in the process, which drove the soldier to exact a penalty. The jailers huddled and, apparently satisfied that this perceived impudence justified summary execution, quickly exonerated the guard. By the time the blood at the foot of those stairs dried to black, life in the yard had returned to what it had been.

"This man, or rather brute," Harris wrote, "was placed on the same post in the afternoon. We immediately called the officer of the guard and requested him to remove that man from guard in our camp, as we were afraid he would kill a Yankee as quick as he would a n— if he imagined any of us were laughing at him. The officer respected our wishes and removed him from amongst or even about us, as we saw no more of him during our stay in the jail yard." [1]

Death was no stranger here, to be sure. Prisoners' lives could be claimed by disease, injury, old age, suicide and hanging. But this victim, Harris said, was neither criminal nor POW. His bad fortune was simply to find himself inside the walls of the Charleston District Jail.

There are places so thoroughly steeped in wretchedness that, for some, simply crossing their thresholds is enough to evoke a disturbing uneasiness. Horrendous things happened in these places and it is as though the suffering was so dark and so intense, it can still be felt years after the fact. One of these places is in Charleston, South Carolina.

Today, the Charleston District Jail is a grim, cracked skull of a building that frowns on an otherwise pleasant street just three blocks from the bustle of tourist commerce along Lower King Street. Its towers and walls are pocked and feeble, its gates and window bars rusting away. A skin of stucco is slowly crumbling to reveal the ordinary and ancient brickworks that lie beneath.

Construction was completed late in 1802 and it was operated as a jail from 1803 to 1939. To many confined there, it was a place of inestimable human misery. Thousands passed through its doors and gates to await trial, serve time, cope with deprivations small and large, suffer agonizing hardship, die and, on occasion, give birth.

To the persons in charge, it was an ever deteriorating, over-crowded embarrassment for which there was never enough funding. They struggled with faulty construction that made escapes tempting. The place was stifling hot in the summer and achingly cold in the winter. Approval for repairs or enhancements could drag on for years, if approved at all.

Overcrowding was the rule rather than exception. Over the years, various segregations by floor and cell kept black from white, women from men and the truly dangerous from more benign offenders. But all shared deprivation, filth and desperation. It sometimes confined children, too; some the result of petty crimes and others because parents were incarcerated and there no other place for them.

The surrounding neighborhood was among Charleston's worst. Dilapidated hovels shared unpaved streets with brothels and bars. Poverty was rife. Crime festered. Officials sought solutions and began considering plans to level the area and start over.

Official hangings in the jail yard ceased after the last one in the summer of 1911 and its gallows eventually was disassembled. It continued to house prisoners for another 28 years, but a certain measure of the horror of the place began to ebb. A compassionate jailer who did the best he could with what he had even provided special roast pork dinners for inmates at Christmas and Thanksgiving.

By the late 1930s, the neighborhood's fate was sealed. Much of the area was to be razed and a government-funded housing project for low-income whites erected. The efforts of preservationists saved the jail building itself from demolition but bricks from its once-towering walls were used in some of the neat and tidy houses of the development.

After the last prisoners were transferred out of the jail in September of 1939, the building was locked. It sat unused except for storage and occasional service as temporary office space. A wading pool for neighborhood children was dug in its yard and, for several years in the 1950s, a church operated a kindergarten on one of its upper floors.

Today, the wading pool and kindergarten are long gone. The housing project is still quiet and orderly and many of the jail's cellblocks have been outfitted as classrooms for a building arts college. Jeans-clad students busily come and go and workmen can be seen attending to the seemingly unending job of shoring up its walls and foundation. Despite the sprucing-up and student activity, the jail still feels stubbornly foreboding.

The building itself is closed to tourists during the day but the brave among them can return after dark for candle-lit "ghost" tours. Some claim that supernatural forces within sabotage photographs, create cold spots and otherwise have their way with paying customers. And who is to say otherwise? Many, who ordinarily reject notions of "haunted" houses, admit sensing something disturbing within those walls. They say there's an eerie feeling, a heavy presence, a palpable sense that remnants of something unpleasant linger in the shadows.

For those whose interest in the jail concerns its history, a visit can provoke a host of questions to which there are few reliable answers. Many of the records that may have been kept remain undiscovered. First-hand accounts of life there exist in newspaper articles, journals and books that are widely scattered among various libraries and archives but many reports are incomplete or otherwise unsatisfying.

Still, these disparate sources, when aggregated, reveal how and why the jail was built, some of its more unusual uses, how its occupants fared and why it was eventually shut down.

This book seeks to trace the history of the jail, based on as much factual information as the author could assemble. It includes many verbatim accounts by eyewitnesses. Material generally is organized in chronological order, segmented by topic, but is also summarized in several spots for readers desiring uncluttered access to the most compelling of them.

Section One — "Jail History, From Beginning to End" - starts off with a section of brief answers to many of the most frequently asked questions about the jail. Following is a comprehensive chronology of the jail story highlighting early Charleston's need for the jail, why it was built on Magazine Street, how the building changed in appearance over the years and some of the calamities that have befallen it. It describes activity at the prison from the day it opened in 1802 through its last days in 1939. Finally, it reveals why the jail was closed.

Section Two — "The Devil is in the Details" takes a closer look at some of the more notorious aspects of inmates' lives and, sometimes, their deaths. Specific prisoners are identified, as are the crimes for which they were locked away. Jail escapes and executions are examined as well as the man who served as jailer for most of its final 27 years. A chapter on archeology includes photos of artifacts found in and around the jail and graffiti prisoners left behind on its walls. Then, a chapter touches on the belief by some that the jail is home to lingering spirits who occasionally make themselves known to visitors.

Section Three — "Preserving the Jail" offers more detail on what happened to the jail building once it was closed and of the efforts to keep it standing, even as its high wall was cut down amid controversy. How a college came to own the jail and what it is doing to prevent the 137-year-old building's collapse rounds out the story.

Listed on the National Register of Historic Places, the Charleston District Jail is unique both in its history and in the extent of its preservation. In many ways it is a kind of living textbook for serious students of architecture and those of social reform. In greater numbers, though, are the many visitors that stop, stare and simply wonder why such a sad, pain-burdened place ever existed. The best answers discovered to date, follow.

SECTION I

JAIL HISTORY, FROM BEGINNING TO END

Photo by author

A view from the jail yard

CHAPTER 1

SEPARATING FACT FROM FANCY – 22 THINGS VISITORS TO THE JAIL WANT TO KNOW

True or false? Forty thousand persons suffered horrible deaths at the jail. Prisoners routinely were tortured, raped and beaten by unspeakably brutal guards. Human bones have been found inside but their discovery has been suppressed. The wheeled cage in the jail yard was a paddy wagon that dates to the 1700s and was regularly used to deliver to the jail criminals scooped up from the city's streets.

Though frequently accepted as accurate notes of jail history, all of the above are just plain wrong.

To be fair to the perpetuators of these and other myths related to the Charleston District Jail, research-based material is scarce. That which does exist is hard to come by or remains undiscovered. Also, there is a rich oral tradition of storytelling associated with intriguing places like the jail and some of what is offered as fact comes ladled from a long-simmering kettle of legend, speculation and embellishment. The temptation is to entertain. It is not surprising that dark rumors, misinformation and distortion persist.

This is not to say that portions of the jail's reputation are unearned. Its ancient appearance is foreboding, its purpose, unsavory. It was, to be sure, a profoundly dreadful place in which to be confined but perhaps its truths are as disturbing as the fictions created about it.

As for the veracity of a given story or legend, is not out of the question that genuine historical support for certain notions disclaimed here has been overlooked by the author. If this proves to be the case, evidence will be offered in future editions of this book.

In the meantime, and for the convenience of those eager to quickly focus on popular jail assumptions and curiosities, here are some of the most frequent queries and their most reasonable answers. More detail and source references about many follow in subsequent chapters.

1. How old is the jail?

The original building — which looked nothing like it does now — was completed in late 1802 and began accepting prisoners in January 1803. Prior to that, lawbreakers, debtors and even witnesses were kept in a number of city guardhouses, lockups and other buildings rented for the purpose. These included a wood frame building once located in the same block as today's structure. This "gaol" was converted into a workhouse when the structure at Magazine and Franklin was erected.

The present jail's first iteration was a 100-foot by 50-foot rectangle of bricks that still exists as part of the core of the present structure. Remodeling and expansion in 1855 added twin stair towers on the front and an eight-sided cellblock at the rear. All were coated with a veneer of stucco-over-brickwork, scored to create the impression that the jail had been built with large, stone blocks. An appearance of massive strength was the goal.

Incidentally, it was never a "city" jail, despite the fact that even today it is often labeled as such. While city and even federal prisoners frequently were kept there, it was a state-financed "district" — and, later, a "county" — facility.

2. Why was it made to look like a dark fortress?

It was thought that a gloomy and forbidding structure would instill fear in would-be wrongdoers and deter crime. A frightful appearance was also to contribute, however subtly, to the penalty prisoners were expected to pay.

By the 1800s, penal reform in America had mostly moved beyond physical mutilation and public "shame" punishments —

like the stocks and pillory — to deprivation of freedom. But this removal from the general populace should be, some felt, decidedly unpleasant since the emphasis remained on punishment rather than rehabilitation. A medieval, gothic-like style for jail buildings was popularized in Europe and adopted in many US prisons, many of which resembled Charleston's but are now gone.

In 1855, architects John H. Seyle and Louis J. Barbot, also of Charleston, gave the jail its arched facade, towers, octagon and general battlement look.

3. Didn't Robert Mills, architect of the Washington Monument, design the jail?

No, but he did create an addition that no longer exists. Twenty years after the jail was built, Mills, a Charleston architect responsible for the Washington Monument and the US Treasury Building in Washington, was commissioned to create a wing to the original building. This four-story rectangle of individual cells jutted off the rear (southeast) corner and, according to Mills himself, had been "made fireproof." It measured 18x51 feet. Though this addition had been torn down by the 1850s, Mills' name continued to be associated more broadly with the entire jail until evidence surfaced in the late 1970s that suggested otherwise. However, remaining to this day in the jail basement is a section of distinctive brickwork that hints that at least a portion of it might have been part of the Mills addition.

4. How many prisoners was the jail designed to house?

No reliable reference has been found to suggest precisely how many inmates the first building was expected to accommodate. Written references to prisoner counts range from 60 to 600, the latter being during the Civil War when Union POWs greatly swelled the usual number. The majority of them spilled over into the jail's yard where they outnumbered the tents made available by the Rebels. A number of modifications were made over the life of the jail to address issues of overcrowding.

5. How many persons died in the jail and what were the causes?

Without official records, it is impossible to arrive at an exact number but it is undoubtedly not the 40,000 some claim. The jail was officially in operation for 137 years. To reach 40,000, mortality would have had to average nearly 300 deaths a year, or about one each day. Based on available death records and newspaper accounts, this seems preposterous.

The Charleston County Public Library's bound copies of "City of Charleston Health Department Death Records" pertain to some of those early years, beginning in 1819. Besides name, age and manner of death, many include a category that lists the place of residence at the time of death. "Charleston Jail" appears only occasionally.

For example, in a 1938 Post and Courier interview with long-time jailer Capt. William J. Bennett, he said, "In the last twenty-seven years, only five prisoners have died at the jail. Two committed suicide and two were sick when brought to the jail. The other died suddenly."

Furthermore, it appears that executions were relatively rare. The last one was in 1911, the year Bennett took over. And while, again, an official record is missing, only a couple dozen references to jail yard hangings have surfaced. Newspapers of the day aggressively covered such events but their news stories number no more than a few in any given year.

Most in-jail deaths probably stemmed from disease, injuries sustained before incarceration or natural causes and it is likely the majority occurred in the jail's first 65 years. During the Civil War, thousands of captured Union troops flowed through the jail and its yard. Many were already wounded or ill when they arrived, forced to live with little shelter or appropriate clothing and failed to receive adequate rations or medical treatment.

6. Haven't human bones been found there and kept secret?

Among the many bones found inside the jail, mostly in the area that once served as its kitchen, none have been human. All bones found must be, and are, analyzed by County officials to satisfy both moral and legal requirements.

Rumors of the discovery of human remains at the jail crop up from time-to-time, most recently when a ghost tour participant directed a flashlight beam through a window and onto a collection of bones lying on a table. Workmen had found them while remodeling. These, plus numerous others discovered at the bottom of a long-neglected corner of the old kitchen area, were examined by Charleston County Coroner's consultants and found to be from cattle, hogs and squirrels.

Photo by author

What a ghost tour participant saw through a window

Interestingly, bones have been found in crevices high up the basement's original brick walls. It is thought that foraging rats carried them there.

7. What was it like to be held prisoner in the jail?

By nearly every account, confinement in the Charleston District Jail ranged from dreadful to abominable. The record suggests this was due to lack of protection from the weather, the constant presence of vermin and less-than-ideal rations, rather than regular physical abuse or torture at the hands of guards (See below, "10. Were prisoners regularly tortured by their guards?"). While cruelty may have existed from time to time, only a few reliable accounts of intentional mistreatment survive among the first-hand documentation.

Most complaints pertained to the extreme heat and cold, unsanitary conditions, poor rations and overcrowding. The majority of these came from Civil War POWs. Most Union captives were kept in the yard of the jail where conditions were the worst. There were never enough ragged tents and it was regularly reported that the very ground was alive with lice and other pests.

Apart from obvious hardships, prisoners were mostly idle and constantly fought boredom. Some have written that they played various games like cards and checkers and even baseball. A few left their names, pictures and other scribbles on the walls of the cellblocks. Some hatched escape plans that occasionally were successful. Union inmates during the Civil War write that they were entertained watching the shells fired by comrades on Morris Island that passed over their heads — and occasionally landed nearby.

Clearly, though, the life of a Charleston District Jail prisoner — in any era — was a hard one. Over the prison's operational life, even its jailers complained repeatedly to supervisory boards of the hardships endured by inmates. Their requests for more space, badly needed repairs and additional funds were rarely successful. Even as late as the 1930s, conditions remained grim. One eyewitness interviewed for this book, who, as a young boy, managed to sneak into a cellblock, describes seeing a sobbing female inmate in rags and horrendous filth.

8. What kinds of prisoners were held in the jail and who were some of them?

The jail and its yard confined pirates, murderers, thieves, prostitutes, conspirators, petty criminals, debtors, slaves and Union soldiers, to name a few. Interestingly, some held there committed no crime at all but, rather, were witnesses to crimes by others. It was an early custom to confine everyone involved, including innocent bystanders who saw the offense, so that all would be available for the trial. Those jailed for owing debts and other non-violent offenses were kept separate from common criminals in so-called "gentlemen's quarters," generally on the ground floor.

Prisoners were black and white, male and female and were segregated except when permitted to roam the jail yard. Union POWs kept there during the Civil War frequently expressed disgust over forced proximity to civilian criminals, particularly prostitutes.

Other mentions of women prisoners include those giving birth inside cells as well as deaths of infants incarcerated there with them, probably because there was no other place for the children to go.

While official records of those confined presumably were kept, none have turned up in recent years. Identities of specific inmates mostly come from transcripts of trials, newspapers, personal journals and a number of these are included later in this book.

The names of specific individuals range from the notorious to the obscure. Among the most famous were convicted husband-and-wife highway robbers John and Lavinia Fisher, kept in the jail until their hangings, several blocks from the jail, in February 1820. Stories told about the Fishers and their deaths seem particularly subject to exaggeration but the written record uncovered so far does not sustain the bulk of them. (Please see the next item in this section.)

In an even more sensational case, four white men served from six months to a year in the jail for involvement in what was believed to be a conspiracy by blacks to rise up against their bondage. Allegedly hatched by ex-slave Denmark Vesey, who had bought his freedom with money won in a lottery, the rebellion was to include the murder of slave owners and seizure of the city of Charleston. However, two slaves against the plan apparently tipped off their masters and it was thwarted. Of the scores of blacks arrested and held at the Work House, 35 were hanged at several Charleston-area locations but not at the jail. None of the white men were executed.

The vast majority of prisoners held no celebrity at all. They were petty criminals or people who made their mistakes at the wrong time in the wrong place, like teenager Gracie Tonsey, who was sentenced in 1908 to 30 days for being drunk and disorderly on Queen Street.

The names of many others can be found in subsequent chapters of this book, among them Union soldiers held there during the Civil War and a few of the persons executed in the jail's yard.

9. Wasn't the country's first woman serial killer, Lavinia Fisher, hanged with her husband in the jail yard?

One is hard pressed to locate any verifiable, published proof that Lavinia Fisher killed anyone. Nor was she executed at the Charleston District Jail, although she and husband John were confined there, apparently for about a year. Both actually were hanged, according to the Charleston Courier of Friday Morning, Feb. 18, 1820 near "... the lines, on the Meeting-Street Road..." for the crime of "highway robbery." Murder is not mentioned.

Still, no presentation of the jail's early times seems quite complete without some richly dressed up account of how Lavinia met her end. These fact-deprived stories speak of the unearthing of decomposed corpses of scores of victims.

Supposedly Lavinia, the serial murderess, is ravishingly beautiful in her wedding gown and defiant at the gallows. "If you have a message for the devil, give it to me for I'm on my way to hell," storytellers claim she told onlookers. One persistent legend is that John was hanged just before Lavinia, making her a widow and therefore no longer protected by a law prohibiting married women from being executed.

But according to the handful of newspaper reports published at the time, Lavinia was hysterical and had to be nearly dragged onto the scaffold. And while husband John, it was reported, met death with "great firmness," Lavinia's screams were terrifying and demonic. Both wore plain white garments (perhaps spawning the "wedding gown" legend) and both were dropped through the trap door at the same time. (For more on the Fishers, see Chapter 8.)

10. Were prisoners regularly tortured by their guards?

There is no solid evidence to support this allegation.

Certainly jail life from 1802 to 1939 could be astonishingly harsh, if not downright inhumane. Poor conditions were mainly the result of an overcrowded, poorly constructed building that received little in the way of financial support from the state. Without question, some inmates died from jail-related injuries or disease and executions were conducted there until 1911. There are references to whippings in the jail yard, as well, and these probably were a short-lived carryover from Colonial notions of punishment.

Extraordinary cruelty among inmates and their captors, if it occurred, probably was in the jail's earlier years. The construction of the jail was part of a societal movement away from mutilation and infliction of pain on convicts, following the new path of simply keeping lawbreakers shut away from the community at large. Perhaps the change in thinking was gradual enough to allow older, harsher methods to persist but it doesn't appear their use was widespread.

Responsible persons of the community — grand jury panels, religious leaders and concerned others — regularly visited the jail and reported what they saw to county officials and sometimes to the local press. While often bemoaning unsanitary and markedly uncomfortable living conditions for inmates, no surviving and verifiable account suggests extreme and sadistic punishments occurred.

The same cannot be said for the jail's neighbor, the Work House. Exclusively for blacks (mostly slaves), punishments meted out there were barbaric. It was said to be the home of the infamous "treadmills" (large, slave-propelled wheels for the grinding of grain) and the so-called "crane of pain" (a ceiling-to-floor rope stretcher to facilitate whippings).

It has become popular to associate the jail with these devices but there is no reliable proof that either was used in the jail. The Work House was torn down after heavy damage from the earthquake of 1886.

Photo by author
**Despite this display at the jail, there is no proof
a "crane of pain" was used there**

Several references can be found to cells buried in the jail yard in which inmates were locked, presumably to penalize bad behavior. Additionally, whippings were still being carried out in the yard of the jail but it appears these were court-ordered sentences for specific crimes rather than routine jail procedure. The Charleston Courier reported on July 12, 1858 that:

> **James Kennedy...convicted of stealing a gold watch valued at $100...sentenced to be imprisoned one week, and then to receive upon the bare back, in the Jail yard, twenty stripes; afterwards to be imprisoned one week, and then discharged.**

By all accounts, though, the jailer in charge from 1911 almost to the jail's closing in 1939 did his best to provide humane treatment of his charges. He frequently asserted that beatings by guards were strictly forbidden. Instead, he said, unruly prisoners were denied small privileges such as cigarettes or food from the outside. The worst punishment might be a period of solitary confinement. Most years he provided special meals on holidays like Thanksgiving and Christmas.

11. How were individuals executed at the jail?

Officially sanctioned execution was by hanging in the jail yard. The records that remain, mostly from newspaper accounts, describe some of these deaths. However, unlike modern-day depictions that drop the noose-bound victim through the trap door of a wooden platform, the Charleston jail's method jerked the condemned from the ground and into the air by means of a heavy weight dropped into a hole near the gallows pole.

From the Emmett Robinson papers, Courtesy of the South Carolina Historical Society

How men were hanged in the jail yard

This procedure may have been copied from the one used on the decks of ships moored in Charleston Harbor. It required only a pole, a rope, a weight and the space it takes for an appropriate drop.

Colonial accounts of hangings place some on the decks of ships in the harbor, in the vicinity of the Battery and, according to Robert Stockton, in the Charleston News and Courier on Dec. 29, 1975, "… on the Charleston Lines, the War of 1812 fortifications which gave Line Street its name, and which were still standing at the time."

Interestingly, however, the hangings of husband and wife John and Lavinia Fisher on The Lines (noted above in No. 9) apparently involved the more traditional platform gallows since reporters at the time described the need for the condemned to climb a set of stairs and said that both were dropped through a trap.

It is unclear when executions began in the jail yard but it is thought two men, Richard Dennis and Joshua Nuttler, were hanged there in 1805, just three years after the prison was opened. Many executions were witnessed by hordes of on-lookers who crowded into the jail yard. Apparently it was not uncommon for children to be among them. Those unable to gain admittance sometimes rented space atop neighborhood balconies and rooftops so that they could see over the high yard wall. In later years, efforts were made by law enforcement officers to limit the number of persons permitted inside but newspaper accounts of some of the last executions performed there still reported large attendance.

12. Where are the jail gallows now?

The gallows apparatus in place by 1911 was disassembled and removed sometime after it was used a final time that year to hang Daniel Duncan, who had been convicted of murder. Whether the gallows pole and machinery were destroyed or found service elsewhere is not recorded but the heavy weights used may still be buried somewhere in the jail yard. A newspaper article published in 1932 said the weights would be offered to the Charleston Museum but current representatives of that institution say there is no record of them having been received. Given the fact that they probably weighed at least several hundred pounds, it is possible they were simply left in the last hole in which they dropped and covered over with dirt.

Over the years, there were at least several versions of a crossbar-topped gallows pole planted in various spots around the yard. While no known photographs of any Charleston jail gallows have surfaced, several engravings made during the Civil War show one between the rear of the octagon and the back wall. One prisoner described it as a "permanent fixture" but others tell of tearing one down and burning it for firewood.

Reporters covering several famous executions there in the early 1900s place that era's gallows on the east side of the octagon. And one intriguing reference says that a man named Pierre Matheseau was hanged in front of the jail on January 29, 1813.

13. Did anyone ever escape from the jail?

Yes. Poor construction and lack of funds to correct it created opportunities too tempting for some inmates to ignore. But in cases for which there are historical references, most escapees were captured and returned to the jail. In fact, some of a group who fled when the earthquake of 1886 split a section of the jail yard wall, gave themselves up once their initial terror over the tremor subsided.

One long-time jailer liked to boast that no prisoner ever successfully escaped during his watch, meaning that those who did manage to break out eventually were recaptured and returned.

14. When did the jail close and why?

The last prisoners were escorted out the front door on September 16, 1939. Overcrowding, lack of adequate funding and structural deficiencies of the then 136-year-old building conspired to force its closing. The general environment was considered so unsafe and inhumane that few mourned closure. However, protests were lodged by preservationists over proposals that it be razed. Eventually it was decided to keep the main structure more-or-less intact. However, a plan was devised to lower its wall to admit more light onto a playground intended for the neighborhood. Ultimately, most of the wall was reduced to a height of four feet. Some estimate the original wall was 20 feet high.

15. Were slaves ever held in the jail?

Some were kept in the jail's yard, just prior to being marched to the market to be sold. In the words of Basil Hall, British naval officer and author, who visited the jail in March 1827:

> In the court-yard of the jail, scattered about were no fewer than 300 slaves, mostly brought from the country for sale, and kept there at 20 cents, or about ten pence a-day, penned up like cattle till the next market day.

> The scene was not unlike what I suppose the encampment of a wild African horde to be - Men, women and children of all ages, crowded together in groups, or seated in circles, around fires, cooking their messes of corn or rice. Clothes of all colors were hung up to dry on the wall of the prison, coarse and ragged, while the naked children were playing about quite merrily, unconscious...of their present degradation, and their future life of bondage.

> On the balcony with us, stood three or four slave dealers, overlooking the herd below, and speculating upon the qualities of each. The day was bright and beautiful, and there was in this curious scene no appearance of wretchedness, except what was imparted to it by rejection from our own minds.

16. Why are there cracks and splits in the jail yard walls near its entrance?

Most of the bricks, mortar and masonry that make up the jail are more than 200 years old. A devastating earthquake in 1886 damaged the building so badly that the top floor and a two-story tower that had been atop its octagonal rear section were removed. Also, general neglect has taken a toll. Some cracks visible in the front wall along Magazine Street are inhabited by expanding vegetation that probably exacerbates the severity of these breaks.

A remarkable photograph made in 1886 or soon after is one that shows a vertical crack in a wall just west of the front entrance. The crack may still be seen today.

Courtesy of US Geological Survey

Photo by author

1886 photo (top) and one shot today show earthquake crack

The general stability of the structure has been carefully examined and continues to be monitored by experts. Since the late 1990s, many repairs have been made and a sophisticated, laser-based device regularly checks targets installed on exterior walls to check for even the slightest change in position.

17. Is everything at the jail authentic to it?

The keys sometimes seen hanging in a hallway are not the originals. They were donated to the jail by a person who responded to a newspaper ad that solicited jail-related artifacts. It was hoped that the keys actually might work in some of the building's old locks but none did. Student craftsmen at the American College of the Building Arts, current owner of the jail, actually made a workable key for the massive front door lock. The original may still exist but its location is unknown.

Photo by author

These keys are an iconic symbol of the jail but not authentic to it

Many deteriorating portions of the building's floor and ceiling have been replaced and some doors and other interior fixtures have been added to accommodate modern uses of its rooms. The heavy, locked doors to cell blocks are original but the cell cages were removed when it ceased operation in 1939. The outlines of where they stood, however, can still be see on the floor.

Certain iron bars and gates are said to have been lent by the penitentiary in Columbia, probably when, for a time in the1970s, the jail was operated as a "prison museum."

18. What about the "paddy wagon" that sits in the jail yard today?

The iron-latticed vehicle rusting in the western part of the yard may have been brought to the jail as part of its use as a museum (see item above). It is unlikely that it ever was a fixture at the jail prior to that time.

Photo by author

This 1921 steel convict car is a modern addition to the jail yard

Horse-drawn convict cars, which were much too heavy for ordinary pick-up and drop-off use, were actually used to confine and house prisoners working in the countryside on various public works projects like road repair and clean-ups. Typically these cages-on-wheels were hauled to the work sites and left there for days or weeks at a time. Many were outfitted with crude toilets, heating stoves, canvas drapes and insect screens that could be lowered to cover the sides.

The convict car parked at the jail was manufactured by the Manly Jail Works, a Dalton, Georgia company that still exists as Manly Steel. The company has a copy of the original sales ledger entry. According to company president Judson Manly, 79, it was sold for $890 (that included an $80 commission to the sales agent and shipping by rail), on April 9, 1921 to the Sanitary and Drainage Commission located on John's Island.

"That particular car was designed to accommodate 12 persons," said Manly. "It was outfitted with oversized wheels, probably because of the sandy soil over which it would sometimes be pulled. But, even empty, a car was too heavy for ordinary hauling."

Lighter, more nimble vehicles, sometimes known as "Black Marias" were the vehicles that delivered prisoners but none associated with the Charleston jail are known to exist.

Since the convict car on view in the yard today was used in the Charleston area, there's a good chance that Charleston District Jail prisoners were among those who spent time in it at various work sites.

19. Is the Charleston jail mentioned in "Porgy"?

It seems likely that the prison described as "…no better, and no worse than many others of its period…" by DuBose Heyward in his 1925 novel "Porgy," is based on the Charleston District Jail. Heyward spent years in Charleston studying black culture. His portrayal (that he later adapted into a stage play and, George Gershwin, into the opera "Porgy and Bess") includes the imprisonment of the character Bess in a "County" facility. The District Jail was, at the time, Charleston County's official jail.

20. Are there any living persons who visited or were incarcerated there?

Operation as a jail ceased about 70 years ago so any surviving former inmates would be quite elderly at the time of this book's original publication. None have made themselves known to the current owners of the building. However, several persons interviewed by the author visited the jail prior to its closing and remember what they saw and experienced. These include the granddaughter of a long-time jailer, a man whose grandmother owned a store that sold rope to the jail hangmen and a retired South Carolina senator who, as a youngster, fetched cigarettes for inmates when they lowered tiny baskets from some upper reaches of the jail.

21. Who owns the jail?

The American College of the Building Arts, a school that educates and trains artisans in the traditional building arts, purchased the jail on February 25, 2000 from the Charleston Housing Authority. The school paid a token $3 and pledged to stabilize and restore the building and use it for community and education purposes. Within months it launched an "emergency stabiliza-tion" program that included interior installation of huge steel support towers. Other preservation efforts include regular laser monitoring of cracks in the jail walls, replacement of the roof and ongoing repairs. The College uses many of the rooms of the jail as classrooms and regards the building as a "living laboratory" for the kinds of craftsmanship and preservation it espouses.

The College leases portions of the jail to Bulldog Tours of Charleston that conducts nightly "Haunted Jail" excursions, advertising "This is quite possibly the scariest place you will ever go. The experience is NOT recommended for small children or men that cry easily."

22. Is the jail haunted?

Many visitors report feeling a certain "presence," perhaps due to the grim environment and their knowledge of the jail's history. Others more open to the notion of the paranormal describe hearing and seeing ghostly evidence. Some have tried to detect or measure what they consider to be "unnatural" phenomena but the results are inconclusive, at least in the judgment of persons of a more skeptical nature.

Twenty thousand chill-seekers each year take the nightly "ghost tour" of the jail and the number has increased every one of the past three years of the tour's operation. Some snap photographs that include circular "orbs" of light that they claim are manifestations related to the spirit world but which look identical to artifacts produced by particles of dust on sensitive camera parts.

Several persons working for the current owners of the jail have reported unusual phenomena, including the late evening sighting by one man of a full-figured, somewhat ashen apparition near a basement door.

For many, resolution of the ghost issue may require a personal experience — which believers claim the jail's "ghosts" will be only too happy to provide.

CHAPTER 2

FOLKS AFOUL OF THE LAW – CHARLESTON DECIDES IT NEEDS A JAIL

Earliest Charleston, like other struggling new world settlements, faced a dilemma: What should be done with individuals who refused to conform to generally accepted principles of behavior?

In other words, what punishments are appropriate for murderers, thieves, rapists, brawlers, blasphemers, drunks, con-artists, assaulters, profaners, prostitutes, cheaters, counterfeiters, adulterers, debtors, runaways, idle persons and any one else caught afoul of the Lord and the law?

Colonial answers were swift and included public humiliation, mutilation or even death. Whipping and branding were common. So were painful hours in stocks or the pillory — wooden frames with holes that held fast head, hands or feet. The notion of simply locking lawbreakers away in cages came much later.

Charles II of England in 1663 had bestowed the chartered territory of Carolina - which originally stretched from the bottom of Virginia to the top of Florida — to eight supporters in his court who became known as the Lords Proprietors. This octet bankrolled and dispatched sailing ships packed with settlers that eventually arrived on the eastern border of the continent of North America.

For some, the journey led to a natural harbor off a coastal peninsula in the center of this vast holding and named it after their patron, "Charles Towne." Its potential as a hub of commerce was soon recognized and the population swelled.

"Carolina primarily attracted farmers and artisans of modest means," Alan Taylor in his book, *American Colonies,* wrote, "At least a third of the early Carolinians began as indentured servants, procured in either Barbados or England." [1]

Charles Towne, renamed "Charleston" a dozen years later when it was moved to the center of the peninsula, was a temporary jumping-off place as well as a home to princes and paupers, alike, although the latter were in decidedly much greater numbers than the former. Besides the wealthy, colonists ranged from clergy to seekers of fortune, from laborers to merchants, from farmers to builders. And, there were many black slaves.

Human nature, as well as hardship, guaranteed that among them were some destined to upset the proper order of things. Those charged with maintaining civic peace operated in the context of Colonial thought and rule which was thick with religiosity. The menu of transgressions could be quite lengthy.

Punishable offenses ran the gamut from indolence to murder and everything in between, including the owing of debts. Those judged guilty, it was agreed, must pay a price. But what should the price be?

EARLY PUNISHMENTS RARELY MEANT CONFINEMENT

Depending on the perceived severity of the offense, Charles Towne's first criminals were fined, physically abused or killed. Only occasionally were they confined for any length of time. Incarceration usually lasted only as long as it took to stage a trial or administer punishment.

For example, Stede Bonnet was convicted of piracy November 10, 1718 and sentenced to death. Despite his pleas for clemency, a pledge to eschew thievery on the high seas and an offer to have his arms and legs cut off to ensure the fact, Bonnet was hanged December 10 at White Point (the vicinity of today's Battery) just 30 days after his sentence was rendered. [2]

The concept of locking the convicted away for specific terms, especially lengthy ones, is so prevalent now that it's easy to assume it has always been so. But the creation of jails and penitentiaries as we know them didn't become commonplace until the 1800s, more than a century after Charles Towne's birth.

In his book *Crime and Punishment in American History,* Lawrence Friedman wrote " ... loss of liberty was not a standard way of making criminals pay ... Nobody in the Colonial period had yet advanced the idea that it was good for the soul, and conducive to reform to segregate people who committed crimes, and keep them behind bars." [3]

Since religiously minded Colonials equated crime with sin, Friedman says, they believed very immediate and public punishments would promote remorse and, except in the case of horrific offenders, lead to a fast lesson in morality and a speedy return to productive society.

Records of the nature of Colonial punishments in the southern settlements, particularly Charleston's, aren't as numerous as those that have survived in the North. However, it seems reasonable to assume there were similarities. Relatively minor offenses were satisfied via the payment of fines while more serious affronts earned whipping, branding, other grotesque forms of mutilation and hanging. These "shaming" punishments almost always were administered in public.

Sometimes the punishment did not seem to fit the crime. Odd loopholes were exploited by those educated or clever enough to game the system. Friedman's book cites an example. "In North Carolina, in 1702, Thomas Dereham was convicted of manslaughter; he beat William Hudson to death 'with a Certain Weapon Commonly Called ... a Catt of Nine tayles.'" Dereham's price was the branding of the letter "M" on his left thumb, not by any means pleasant, but arguably not in keeping with the fact that he had taken a man's life. His salvation had been that, in court, he demonstrated an ability to read from the Bible and was thus "Savd by his Book," returned to daily life, albeit indelibly marked. [4]

As a rule, punishment of slaves was more severe than that of whites. According to Taylor in *American Colonies,* their importation from Barbados to colonies like Carolina was accompanied by a fiercely abusive slave code, designed to keep them in line.

"Deemed property," Taylor writes, slaves had no legal or political rights, not even to venture into court when especially abused. Considered dangerous, they were closely watched and brutally punished for the slightest misstep.

The master could drive and punish his slaves in any way he liked, for there was no penalty for whipping, torturing, maiming, castrating, or even destroying his own property. Barbadians developed the practice of 'putting a man to dry': placing defiant slaves in an iron cage hung from a tree, there to die slowly of hunger and thirst as a warning to others. In 1694, for the crime of stealing a pig, judges had a black man sliced into quarters for public display. Regarding such conspicuous deaths as in the public interest, the government compensated owners for the value of their executed slaves. [5]

ATTITUDES REGARDING PUNISHMENT BEGIN TO CHANGE

Despite harsh measures, early Colonial masters became increasingly dismayed to find that crime and rebellion continued to flourish. And, in time, new attitudes evolved. Some in Europe were, by the late 1600s, seriously rethinking penal approaches, concluding that hard work in a controlled environment might be more effective in suppressing misbehavior.

In his book, *Punishment and Reformation — A Study of the Penitentiary System,* Frederick Howard Wines wrote in 1895 of a very early movement in the Germanic states to create "workhouses" or "houses of correction." Wines quotes the founder of one such institution, as observing "…that the exposure of petty thieves and prostitutes in the pillory tended to make them worse instead of better." [6]

Through the 1700s, the approach to criminals began to shift from immediate, public but mostly short-lived punishments to the notion of long-term incarceration. This, they thought, served the dual purposes of rehabilitation of the criminal and separation of them from law-abiders.

This is not to say that physical punishment ceased - particularly in the southern colonies like Carolina. Friedman writes:

In the South, there was a fierce debate over the penitentiary system. South Carolina, perhaps the most conservative state in the slave belt, never built one. Whipping and shaming punishments (and the gallows) stayed on the books in South Carolina. The very arguments that made the prison system seem preferable in the North, did not work in South Carolina, where "face-to-face contact remained important and where honor was accorded great protection." The more "primitive" punishments, in other words, survived in this more primitive section of the country. Here were the fewest cities, factories, mines. Traditional punishment suited this almost feudal social system: the honor code, shame and humiliation, corporal punishment. And for slaves, bodily punishment was considered most effective, and, in fact, downright indispensable. [7]

Still, the continued existence of crime and criminals and the gravitation toward longer-term solutions ultimately led to jails and prisons. According to Nick Butler, Special Collections Manager for the Charleston County Library, there may have been as many as a half dozen in various parts of the city. Old maps suggest that at least one sat in the block bounded by Back (now Franklin), Magazine, Queen and Mazyck (now Logan). As early as 1685 it had been set aside as public land. Previously it had been a cemetery for blacks, variously labeled "The Burying Ground" and "The Old Church Yard."

One early jail was described in 1766 by Anglican cleric Charles Woodmason of Charleston in his book *Carolina Backcountry on the Eve of the Revolution,* under a heading "Close and Stinking Gaol":

A Person would be in better Situation in the French Kings Gallies (sic), or the Prisons of Turkey or Barbary, than in this dismal Place - Which is a small House hir'd by the Provost Marshal containing 5 or 6 Rooms, about 12 feet square each and in one of these Rooms have 16 Debtors been crowded - And as the Heat of the Weather in C.T. in Summer is almost intolerable, What must the Situation of Prisoners then be? They often have not Room to lye at length, but succeed each other to lye down - One was suffocated by the Heat of this

Summer - and when a Coffin was sent for the Corps, there was no room to admit it, till some Wretches lay down, and made their wretched Carcasses, a Table to lay the Coffin on.

Men and Women are crowded promiscuously - No Necessary Houses to retire to - The Necessities of Nature must be done by both Sexes in the presence of each other. And this shocking Confinement debarres (sic) unhappy Persons from receiving Visits from their Friends and Acquaintances, prevents the Clergy of all denominations from visiting of Criminals, thro' fear of Infection.

And how terrible is the Reflexion, that many of these unhappy Persons are sent there, and are suffered for Nothing? Arrested by those who owe to them, instead of their being indebted to others - Or confin'd for simple Assaults - for a small fray occasion'd by Liquor, or in Passion - where they must lye 5 or 6 Months till Sessions - and when Sessions comes, then no Prosecutor. They are discharg'd by Proclamation - No Redress for this severe Punishment - Loss of Health - Strength - Fame - Credit - Complexion - Oft-times the Reason and Understanding - The Attorney General shows that (there) was just Cause of Commitment - and thus he is discharg'd paying of his fees! This dismal picture that could be drawn of the Sufferings of Prisoners in this Place, would melt ev'ry Eye - affect ev'ry Heart, and exceed all we have related in the History of foreign Countries. [8]

Another writer, Francois Alexandre Frederic, known as the Duke de la Rochefoucault Liancourt, offered observations on his visit to the Charleston jail in his book *Travels Through the United States of North in the Years 1795, 1796, and 1797:*

I have visited the prisons of Charleston, which, it is asserted, are the best in the State of South Carolina; they form one single building, which is several stories high. The rooms are pretty spacious and airy, but few in number. Debtors are in a separate room. Felons, either imprisoned on suspicion or convicted, are confined with the police-prisoners and all are treated on the same footing. They are all in irons; a dreadful treatment, but which is the necessary consequence of the smallness of the prison, and of the facility of plotting mutinies. The prisoners are permitted only to walk about in their room; the prison having no court, where they might take exercise. The jailor is allowed one shilling a-day for the board of each prisoner … [9]

1794 - CALLS TO BUILD A PROPER JAIL IN CHARLESTON

Numerous official voices were raised by the 1790s, arguing that Charleston needed an adequately fortified structure of incarceration. According to a Grand Jury report published in the South Carolina State Gazette and Daily Advertiser of August 14, 1794, found by News and Courier reporter John Bennett in 1939:

At a court of General Sessions at Charleston, Monday, 19th May, 1794, the Grand Jury presented as a very great grievance the dirty, filthy and unwholesome state of the rooms in which prisoners are confined in gaol; also the yard around the same, by which means they are liable to malignant disorders which would easily be communicated to the inhabitants of the city.

We present as a grievance the bad state of repairs the gaol is in at present; viz., the roof being very leaky, the gate insufficiently strong, so as to keep the prisoners save should they get out into the yard; also, there being sheds adjoining the walls, which would enable them to make their escape, and recommend the same to be taken away; and further recommend an additional wall in front the gaol.

We present the want of a good gaol for the District of Charleston, as the present house used as such is

> **insufficient to hold the prisoners frequently confined therein.**

> **We present also the keeping of witnesses in gaol from one court to the other as a great injustice to said witnesses.**

Bennett went on to say " ... that the protest of the Grand Jury was not without effect (as) testified (to) by an additional follow-up item in The State Gazette for Thursday, September 4, 1794":

> **A New Gaol for Charleston: Commissioners are appointed by Act of Legislature for the purpose of receiving sealed plans and specifications, also for erecting a New Gaol; and advertise for proposals from any capable and responsible workman to construct the said Gaol building to be not less than 48 feet square and 3 storeys (sic) high.**

Bennett's story concludes that he was unable to find follow-ups to the Gazette report. He wryly concludes:

> **It would appear, perhaps, that the only visitors to the city interested in the gaol and its additional walls were those destined to occupy the said gaol and to view the walls from the inside, a prospect not calculated to attract travelers to town. 10**

But by this time sentiment for long-term confinement of Charleston's unruly was gaining favor and eventually approval was obtained from the state for the erection of a more substantial jail.

CHAPTER 3

CITY BLOCK OF SADNESS – WHY THE JAIL IS LOCATED ON MAGAZINE STREET

As Charleston's population grew, so did its criminal class. Minor offenses were still satisfied by fines but public punishments for more serious crimes were giving way to confinement. Besides making the convicted "pay" through deprivation of freedom, it was hoped that rehabilitation might be induced through hard work and penance.

There were other social unfortunates that required shelter and supervision. These included the indigent sick, the mentally infirm, orphans and the poor. Early Charleston kept these individuals in a variety of buildings all over town. Even private citizens were enlisted to lease space in their homes and outbuildings.

Understandably, this hodgepodge approach proved unsatisfactory. Security was an issue and conditions were deplorable. More appropriate accommodations were needed.

Ultimately the Charleston District Jail still standing today would, in 1802, be built at 21 Magazine Street. As early as 1685, the block bounded by Back (now Franklin), Magazine, Queen and Mazyck (now Logan) had been set aside as public land. Previously it had been a cemetery for blacks, variously labeled "The Burying Ground" and "The Old Church Yard."

By 1740, the city had erected there a storehouse for gunpowder and arms, a military barracks, a "work house" and a "poorhouse," the latter an accommodation to the growing numbers of impoverished in the city.[1]

A map published 1739 by W.H. Toms called "The iconography of Charles-Town at High Water" shows the locations of the magazine and a work house in the corners of the plot.

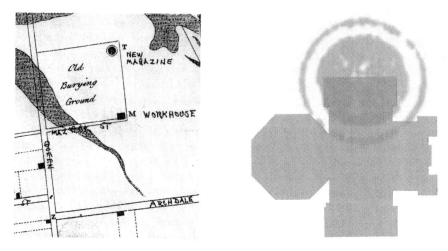

Courtesy of the American College of the Building Arts

1730 map on left shows round Magazine; at right is outline of where jail eventually was built (in both, north is to the right)

When the city was incorporated in 1783 by an act of the State Assembly, the parcel officially was reserved as a "public square" to be owned by the City. This ground was host to a series of hospitals, poorhouses, workhouses, jails, an insane asylum and an orphanage.

Over the years, these structures were built, made over and repurposed until they deteriorated and were torn down. The city eventually disbursed its more miserable souls across a wider area. Today, the Charleston District jail and neighboring "Old Marine Hospital" are the only remnants of this collection.

THE POORHOUSE

In her documentation for the 1995 Historic American Buildings Survey (HABS) of the jail, historian Christine Trebellas said that local churches initially assumed responsibility for the indigent but were soon overwhelmed. In desperation, they tried to hire private citizens to take the destitute and despairing into their homes. At some point it was obvious that "private dwellings rented for the sick and poor were inadequate, dilapidated, and costly." [2]

The solution, as proposed by the Charleston District Grand Jury, was the construction of a building to house the poor, and, for good measure, "...to punish idle and disorderly people..."

A vestry committee of St. Philip's church agreed. This poorhouse, it said, was to provide "a controlled environment to regulate the morals of the uninhibited."

As a result, the State Assembly authorized erection and maintenance of such a facility and it was completed by 1738. But within 30 years, a second structure was built because it was felt that the old poorhouse and hospital, with its "putrid smells, filthy, crowded rooms and indiscriminate mixing of poor widows, prostitutes, and thieves, was unfit for human occupancy." The older building it replaced, Trebellas wrote, then became a place of confinement and correction for fugitive seamen, runaway slaves, vagrants, and disorderly people. [3]

Since both buildings were authorized as "houses of correction" and occupants might be held for weeks or months at time, the concept of extended incarceration became fixed in Charleston.

Interestingly, one of these two structures was spectacularly destroyed in May of 1780, during the Revolutionary War, just after the surrender of Charleston to the British. Trebellas said that by then this public square "contained a 'pest house,' a prison or house for the insane and the poor, an arsenal, barracks for soldiers, and a powder magazine. When the city surrendered, the British ordered the citizens to relinquish their weapons and deposit them at the arsenal. They carelessly gathered '... guns, fowling-pieces, rifles, muskets, pistols, all crammed to the muzzle with the remaining cartridges of their late proprietors...cartridge-boxes, powder-horns, all recklessly into one heap. The result was an explosion which shook the city to its foundation.' The blast destroyed the magazine, the poorhouse, the guardhouse, the barracks, and the arsenal, and killed most of the soldiers and civilians in the area. Several bodies were hurled against the neighboring Unitarian Church on Archdale Street." [4]

Two hundred persons were killed, reports said, as the blast also ruined six private homes and a brothel.

Evidence suggests that the magazine that blew up stood precisely on the same spot as the today's jail building now stands.

The destroyed poorhouse was replaced with one on Logan (then known as Mazyck) Street, between Magazine and Queen. Paupers were the occupants of the three-story, brick structure while individuals judged insane were kept in a separate outbuilding until, said Trebellas, they could be transferred to the "lunatic asylum" in Columbia.

German nobleman Karl Bernhard described the, by then, 40-year-old poorhouse and asylum, in his book *Travels Through North America, During the Years 1825 and 1826*:

> **The poor-house, an old building raised by subscription, contains one hundred and sixty-six paupers. It will only admit such poor persons as are completely disabled. Those who can labour a little can obtain the employment they desire, and then receive good attendance and proper support. The sick were taken care of in a distinct infirmary, where each had a separate bed. The healthy slept upon the floor. I enquired why the sick were not provided with iron bedsteads in place of the wooden ones they occupied? and was informed that it was from apprehension of the prevailing severe thunder-storms.**
>
> **Connected with the Poor-house is a Magdalen Asylum, which provides shelter and care for thirty unfortunate beings...I saw under an open shed in the yard where the poor walked about, the dead cart, and close by it numbers of empty coffins piled up together...** [5]

Trebellas' report said that by 1852, overcrowding at this poorhouse was alleviated by the relocation of its occupants to a former factory building on Columbus Street. The former poorhouse became " ... 'The Bettering House' or the 'House of Correction' for the confinement of vagrants, transient lunatics, and convicts sentenced by the mayor's courts."

THE WORK HOUSE

The mid-to-late 1700s also saw the establishment of "work-houses," originally in Europe and soon in America. While generally intended as a place for the poor to live and "work" to support themselves, the Southern workhouse tended to be exclusively for the "correction" of misbehavior of black slaves.

Charleston's first seems to have been known as "The Sugar House." In fact, early records and references suggest the term "Sugar House" may have applied at different times to several sites that served to administer corrections, hold runaway slaves or provide a workhouse environment. Trebellas found the first known Charleston reference to The Sugar House on a 1780 map of an unlabeled area resembling the city's public square.

Its euphemistic name aside, the place was one of horror. John Lambert, a traveler and author in the early 1800s, toured a Charleston Sugar House and wrote:

> **For common offences (sic), they (slaves) are flogged at home by their masters or mistresses, or sent to a place next to the jail in Broad-street, called the Sugar House, where a man is employed to flog them at the rate of a shilling per dozen lashes. I was told that a lady once complained of the great expense she was at for flogging, and intended to contract with the man to flog her slaves by the year! [6]**

Trebellas said a workhouse was established on Magazine Street early in 1802 - next to the newly completed District jail. Many persons still called it the Sugar House and, in the 1820s, it became the notorious home to a pair of fearsome devices — the "crane" (tour guides call this the "crane of pain") and the dreaded treadmills.

Karl Bernhard, the previously referenced nobleman who described city square's poorhouse and asylum also paid a visit to the Work House. There he saw about 40 slaves, both men and women that had either been arrested by police the night before or had been sent there by their masters.

Bernhard's first describes the Work House technique for the crane:

> The house displays throughout a remarkable neatness; black overseers go about every where armed with cow-hides. In the basement story there is an apparatus upon which the negroes, by order of the police, or at the request of their masters, are flogged. The latter can have nineteen lashes inflicted on them according to the existing law. The machine consists of a sort of crane, on which a cord with two nooses runs over pullies (sic); the nooses are made fast to the hands of the slave and drawn up, while the feet are bound tight to a plank. The body is stretched out as much as possible, and thus the miserable creature receives the exact number of lashes as counted off! [7]

Walking to a building in back, Bernhard then saw:

> ... two tread-wheels in operation. Each employs twelve prisoners, who work a mill for grinding corn, and thereby contribute to the support of the prison. Six tread at once upon each wheel, while six rest upon a bench placed behind the wheel. Every half minute the left hand man steps off the tread-mill, while the five others move to the left to fill up the vacant place; at the same time the right hand man sitting on the bench, steps on the wheel, and begins his movement, while the rest, sitting on the bench, uniformly recede. Thus, even three minutes sitting, allows the unhappy being no repose. The signal for changing is given by a small bell attached to the wheel.
>
> The prisoners are compelled to labour eight hours a day in this manner. Order is preserved by a person,

who, armed with a cow-hide, stands by the wheel. Both sexes tread promiscuously upon the wheel. Since, however, only twenty-four prisoners find employment at once on both wheels, the idle are obliged in the interval to sit upon the floor in the upper chambers, and observe strict silence. [8]

Bernhard, apparently disturbed at this perceived bit of inefficiency, offered a helpful suggestion:

To provide against this state of idleness, there should be another pair of tread-wheels erected. The negroes entertain a strong fear of the tread-mills, and regard flogging as the lighter evil! Of about three hundred and sixty, who, since the erection of these tread-mills, have been employed upon them, only six have been sent back a second time. [9]

Even esteemed, Charleston-born architect Robert Mills (who, as will be noted later, contributed a section to the jail's evolution) applauded the treadmill as a good way to keep slaves obedient while relieving their masters of the burden of having to administer punishment themselves. In a win-win endorsement, Mills wrote:

Such a mode of correction has been long a desideratum (Editor's note: something wanted or needed) with many of our citizens, who heretofore have been often induced to pass over faults in their slaves demeriting (sic) correction, rather than resort to coercive measures with them, who now will, without doing violence to their feelings, be able to break their idle habits, and subject them to a discipline that promises, morally, as well as physically, to be beneficial to them. [10]

This and other period references suggest Mills was perpetually sunny regarding Charleston's methods of incarceration and discipline.

Trebellas wrote, "A new and vastly expanded Workhouse, designed by Edward C. Jones, was constructed along Magazine Street, from the corder of Mazyck (now Logan) to the (present day) Jail." Judging by surviving photographs, the building was enormous and its appearance resembled the Gothic architecture of its neighbor.

A photograph for the U.S. Geological Survey shows the Work House as it appeared sometime after the earthquake of August 31, 1886. Damage can be seen to the top of right tower. The jail is at its right, in the distance, obscured in this shot by a tree.

Courtesy of the US Geological Survey

Work House on Magazine Street; jail towers can be seen at far right, obscured by trees

Writer and social observer F.C. Adams wrote in 1853 that the Work House had just been "erected upon a European plan:"

> It is very spacious, with an extravagant exterior, surmounted by lofty semi-Gothic watch-towers, similar to the old castles upon the Rhine. So great was the opposition to building this magnificent temple of a workhouse, and so inconsistent, beyond the progress of the age, was it viewed by the 'manifest ancestry,' that it caused the mayor his defeat at the following hustings...What is somewhat singular, this magnificent building is exclusively for negroes. [11]

The very culture of slavery and its obscene excesses kept racial tensions high in Charleston. Revolts and rumors of them created fear in the minority white population. Heretofore, the correctional horrors of the Work House had been a private, for-profit enterprise but eventually the city took control. In addition, according to Trebellas:

> The city also created an official slave market, run by the new master of the workhouse, which was to remedy the problems of Charleston's growing slave trade. All public slave sales were then conducted at the newly created market, while slaves awaiting the auctions were held at the Workhouse (Editor's note: And sometimes in the yard of the jail). [12]

However, Trebellas wrote, by the time of the devastating earthquake of 1886, the Workhouse had become the "Colored Hospital" and was so heavily damaged that it was taken down and never rebuilt. [13]

THE JAIL

Within the above-described city's public square, a two hundred foot parcel at the northwest corner specifically was to be reserved for a "gaol" (a British term interchangeable with the word "jail" and identically pronounced).

The imposing, medieval-looking structure still standing on Magazine Street actually looks nothing like the first jail built on the block. The first one was just east of the present structure (where the workhouse once stood) and its beginnings were much more humble.

As previously mentioned, colonial Charleston's earliest jails appear to have been numerous and scattered around the peninsula. Nick Butler, Special Collections Manager for the Charleston County Public Library, has said that his research suggests that over the years "there were four or five and maybe as many as seven or nine" in a variety of locations.

Also, according to historian Trebellas, early Charleston's provost marshal leased private dwellings to serve as jails.

> **Black and white criminals and debtors were imprisoned together in these small, rented rooms," Trebellas wrote. "Many criminals escaped because the rooms were often left unguarded. The large number of fugitive slaves, unruly indigents and criminals in Charleston concerned citizens, who felt that the lack of a well-built, secure jail was responsible for the breakdown of law and order. [14]**

But despite legislation leading to the establishment of poorhouses such authorization for a jail did not materialize, so confinement of criminals in rented buildings continued.

Wretched conditions and a steady increase in the numbers of arrests kept the clamor for a proper jail alive and, eventually, overcame officials' concerns about cost. Trebellas found that one official noted that South Carolina was the only British colony that had never built a prison. [15]

Finally, in 1770, money officially was appropriated for a construction of a permanent jail. Trebellas said the "act not only appointed commissioners for the project, but also chose the location and plan of the building, and authorized the commissioners to hire workmen for its construction."

It was to be erected on the south side of Magazine Street, near the poorhouse (which was torn down after it was severely damaged by the earthquake of 1886).

Builders William Rigby Naylor and James Brown, who had just completed the city's new guardhouse, were awarded the construction contract.

Trebellas said this first iteration was roughly square and "resembled a dwelling house" and was only 45-feet by 40-feet. In back was a detached kitchen. A plat from 1783 includes what appear to be garden plots in the rear of the jail yard, perhaps to produce vegetables "to help defray the cost of the convicts upkeep," wrote Trebellas. [16]

The Duke de la Rochefoucault Liancourt, who toured parts of the U.S. while in exile during the French Revolution, in 1795 actually saw this first jail and wrote:

> I have visited the prisons of Charleston, which, it is asserted, are the best in the State of South Carolina; they form one single building, which is several stories high. The rooms are pretty spacious and airy, but few in number.
>
> Debtors are in a separate room. Felons, either imprisoned on suspicion or convicted, are confined with the police-prisoners, and are all treated on the same footing.
>
> They are all in irons; a dreadful treatment; but which is the necessary consequence of the smallness of the prison, and of the facility of plotting mutinies. The prisoners are permitted only to walk about in their room; the prison having no court where they might take their exercise. The jailor is allowed one shilling a-day for the board of each prisoner, for which money he gives him a pound of bread every day, and meat three times a week. [17]

It's not clear in what year that first jail had been erected but it was approved in 1770, shown on plats by 1783, viewed by the Duke about 1795 and ultimately converted from a jail to a workhouse by 1802. It possibly operated for 20 to 30 years before its deterioration was deemed harmful to prisoners. A leaky roof promoted the following Charleston District Grand Jury pronouncement:

> The Situation of those now confined is truly distressing and shocking to humanity; the noxious damps have compelled the removal of some to hospitals; and in the opinion of the Jury, unless speedily removed to a more wholesome habitation many of them must be number with the dead.

Mortal danger wasn't the only issue, either, according to Trebellas:

> The lack of a northern jail wall enabled the convicts to communicate with people outside the building. Rather than fearing inmates would escape, the Grand Jury appeared to be most concerned that outsiders might provide the inmates with liquor. The Jury's January 1793 presentment complained that the lack of a wall allowed prisoners to have "a communication with the people in the Street who supply them with spiritual Liquors & by which means they get Intoxicated and become very unruly as we are informed by the Jailor." [18]

In 1783, the city was incorporated and given control of the area bounded by Queen, Magazine, Franklin (formerly Back) and Logan (formerly Mazyck) Streets for public use but reserved a 200-square-foot parcel therein that previously had been set aside for a jail. Actual construction was delayed for years. Cost was an issue and there was confusion and apprehension over penal reform, all of which was having an effect on the design of new jails.

Trebellas pointed to a significant movement in Pennsylvania "...which abolished the punishments of death, mutilation, and whipping for most criminal cases in the state in 1786. Imprisonment replaced corporal punishment, while solitary confinement supplanted capital punishment."

An articulation of these reforms was most apparent in construction of the Walnut Street Jail in Philadelphia that, Trebellas said, " ... grouped convicts according to their crimes and provided separate cells for those sentenced to solitary confinement."

While the original plans for the Charleston District Jail are lost and we don't know who designed it, it seems apparent that the Walnut Street jail influence is reflected in the Charleston structure. Trebellas wrote:

The structure (in Philadelphia) had an 'imposing' two-story facade on Walnut Street and two wings extending into a yard surrounded by a stone wall. Large rooms in one of the wings housed debtors and those convicted of misdemeanors, while the other wing accommodated more serious offenders. The upper two floors of the new building contained a cellblock with sixteen cells for those sentenced to solitary confinement.

Trebellas said that Charleston commissioners charged with building the jail used Philadelphia's as a model and sent a letter that espoused many of ideas behind the Philadelphia jail to the governor of South Carolina. [19]

Finally, in 1794, commissioners appointed by the state - John Blake, Edward North and Timothy Ford - advertised in the Charleston Gazette for artists and workmen to submit proposals for a new jail. But more time passed as they reviewed submissions that, while acceptable, cost more than the state had allocated. All agreed to delay construction for several years since it was felt that criminal code reformation would add even more to the price.

However, it was noted by the Grand Jury of the Charleston District that the old jail continued to deteriorate and that it hoped concerns could be resolved as quickly as possible.

During this time, other considerations surfaced. One plan involved bypassing Charleston altogether and building a penitentiary in Columbia but the availability in Charleston of better materials and less cost scotched that idea.

Eventually, it was decided that the jail would be 100 feet by 50 feet (which are the approximate dimensions of the existing building's central cell block - the first part of the jail to be built).

Estimated cost was $45,000, with the state providing $15,000 of the total and the rest obtained by selling stock. Still the project languished as bureaucrats wrestled with how, when and to whom the stock would be sold. Nonetheless, construction apparently began sometime in 1800. [20]

The New Jail Opens for Business

In November 1802, the commissioners handed a heavy, brass key to the governor and suggested that the new jail, though not completed, should receive prisoners. However, costs had exceeded estimates. Outbuildings had yet to be built. Furthermore, construction of a wall around the yard, a well and a privy hadn't been included in the original price so none of these existed, either.

Still, the Charleston commissioners recommended occupation and the state agreed. By late January 1803, inmates were transferred to the new jail from the old one next door, which then became the Work House.

None of the early surviving accounts specifies the number of prisoners the modest, three-story design was expected to accommodate. But, almost immediately, complaints about its construction and doubts about its suitability were lodged. The mortar in the new building was barely dry when Sheriff Thomas Lehre, in the fall of 1803, wrote:

> ...the Criminal apartments are much in want of Sashes, or Shutters, to keep out the inclemency of the weather. Sundry out Offices, and a high wall is also wanted around the same, which would add much to its Security...Great hardships are endured by Debtors and criminals, especially the latter, by being confined, several together in small apartments in a loathsome prison, particularly in the summer Season for want of fresh air and exercise.
>
> In addition to the above they are compelled to answer the calls of nature, in the very same Rooms, where they eat, drink and sleep which in a climate like ours, creates

such a stench as is enough to poison them, indeed in many instances it totally destroys their appetites. [21]

A year and a half later, little had been improved and additional concerns were raised. The list included:
 – Unprotected windows admitted wind and rain
 – Neither the wall, nor the privy had been built
 – The swampy ground was "filled with stagnant and putrid matter"
 – Prisoners were escaping because of weak windows and walls
Concerns about cost were unabated. Pleas to the state for further funding came to naught and the jail sat incomplete for many months. Even the wall was not built until December 1805 – almost three years after prisoners had been moved in. [22]
Serious and unrelenting complaints about the condition and maintenance of the building would continue for all of the jail's 136-year operational life.

CHAPTER 4

FROM BRICK RECTANGLE TO OMINOUS CASTLE - HOW THE BUILDING EVOLVED

A MODEST BEGINNING

The looming, castle-like edifice still standing at 21 Magazine Street originally was much smaller and less elaborate. Over the years, it would evolve in size and appearance. Alterations were made to remedy poor construction, to accommodate more prisoners and also reflected changing notions of what a jail ought to look like.

While no plans or drawings are known to exist, today's predecessor apparently was an unadorned three-story rectangle of bricks and mortar measuring 100 feet by 50 feet. Its ground floor of stone included a kitchen. Second and third story floors were wood. The ceiling of the upper-most "apartments" was of thin pine boards. Stone steps - probably the ones that still exist just inside the Magazine Street entryway today - led to the original front entrance, although there were several other gated doors that provided access in other spots, as well.

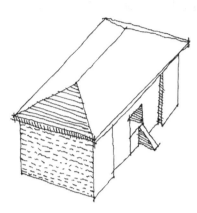

Courtesy of The American College of the Building Arts

Photo by author

**Jail's first iteration was a 100 x 50; steps seen today
just inside may be originals**

From the start, the jail's construction was criticized as being shoddy and incomplete. Modifications — even the most meager — proceeded at a glacial pace. In many instances, years might elapse between approval and actual completion of a given repair or improvement.

Early on, the jail's roof both leaked and was easily pried apart by inmates trying to get out. Sheriff Nathaniel G. Cleary was among the first of a long line of officials to express concern over the health of his prisoners, as well as the insecure nature of their confinement. In his formal complaint to the state legislature in 1812, he wrote:

> **That in its present situation and condition in points of health and Security is truly deplorable and unsafe, it is injurious to the health and Comfort in as much as whenever there falls a heavy rain which is very frequently the case, the rooms are all wet and remain so for several days from the open and untight (sic) State of the roof: It is unsafe and insecure in this particular that the ceiling nearest to the roof which is of thin pine boards or plank which can be Cut through by prisoners and after they get thru this ceiling it is a very easy matter to penetrate the covering and from thence let themselves to the Ground and in this way make their escape.** [1]

But the roof wouldn't be repaired for another five years. In 1817, state approval and $3,000 finally were obtained to repair slate on the roof, as well as add a railing to the front steps leading into the building. The railing shows up on an invoice for a variety of items labeled "for Repairing Charleston Gaol" dated December 20, 1817. But there are unexplained notations to the effect that the railing wasn't fully installed until two years later.

In any case, the bill, which sets the railing price at $259, also lists door plates, hinges, nails, rivets and sliding bolts as items installed. Total cost for all was $417.14. [2]

THE MILLS ADDITION, A PIAZZA AND OTHER IMPROVEMENTS

By 1821, some were clamoring for a larger, more secure jail and an addition was approved.

The "Mr. Mills" of 169 East Bay, who was named as a coordinator of the project in a Charleston Courier advertisement requesting proposals, was, in fact, architect Robert Mills. Robert Mills would later have a hand in designing many famous national projects, including the Washington Monument and the US Treasury Building. At the time, he was Commissioner of the Board of Public Works for South Carolina.

According to "Internal Improvement in South Carolina 1817-1828," written in 1938 by David Kohn, the state paid Mills $1,000 for his design work. Also compensated were carpenter J. O'Neal and bricklayer I. Gordon. [3]

Mills' own description of the addition, apparently completed in 1826, was published in his "Statistics of South Carolina and said:

> **There has been lately added to it a four story wing building, devoted exclusively to the confinement of criminals. It is divided into solitary cells, one for each criminal, and the whole made fireproof. A spacious court is attached to the prison, and every attention to cleanliness is paid throughout, which is highly creditable to those who have charge of the institution. Very general good health is enjoyed by the prisoners.**

Mills added that the jail, itself, was "very roomy and comfortable."[4]

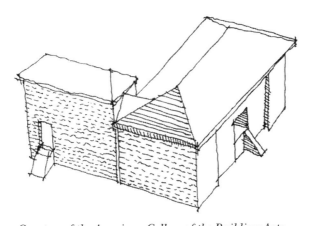

Courtesy of the American College of the Building Arts

Mills wing added to southeast rear in 1826

Christine Trebellas' research for the Historical American Buildings Survey (HABS) found sketches of Mills' addition on several old maps which clearly show it jutting squarely off the rear, eastern portion of the existing building (along with a curious, additional appendage on the west side, referenced below).

Trebellas said the annex was one story taller than the original building and measured approximately 18-feet by 51-feet. She said its design arranged windows and doors to maximize air circulation. She said Mills also recommended that a belfry for an "alarm system" (Note: perhaps as simple as a bell on a rope) be placed atop the prison and that the caretaker's apartment be placed so as to overlook the most important parts of the jail. [5] (This latter recommendation was incorporated about 30 years later — see "How the Medieval Facade and Octagon Came to Be" later in this chapter.)

The same year, 1826, a nine-foot wide piazza was added, although its placement is open to conjecture. Some research suggests it was placed it parallel to the rear of the jail building but it may have been placed opposite Mills' so that the three structures — the rectangular jail and its two "wings" — formed a "U." [6]

These wings may be indicated on a map published in 1855 by A.H. Colton.

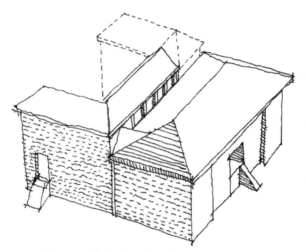

Courtesy of the American College of the Building Arts

Courtesy of the American College of the Building Arts

Detail from 1855 map seems to show both "wings" (in upper left corner of square)

One traveler described standing on the piazza when the yard was filled with slaves being readied for their march to the market and subsequent sale. [7]

During the 1820s and 1830s, repairs and modifications continued. There are reports in 1824 that workmen plastered and painted the building and added a garden to the jail yard. Two cisterns were built in the jail attic and it is likely that the pair that still remain there are the originals.

Photo by author

Cisterns in the jail attic were probably added in the 1820s

By 1851, both the original jail and the "wings" were deteriorating. The structure was almost fifty years old and some felt constructing a new jail building was in order. The Grand Jury at the time floridly reported:

> ... defects of the Jail have not arisen from a neglect of proper repairs of the same, but indicate such radical errors in the original plan and construction of the building much increased by the ordinary wear and tear of such a building in constant use through a long course of years - as cannot be even partially remedied, except by such thorough alterations as would involve a large pecuniary outlay, which might be more advantageously appropriated towards the thorough renovation of the whole establishment, on such approved plan as enlightened experience and modern improvement will suggest, in the arrangement and construction of such a building. It is therefore recommended that a new Jail be built. [8]

Much discussion ensued and more requests were made. The state legislature indicated tacit approval for a new structure but, ultimately, remodeling won out, almost certainly in an effort to cut costs. Both "wings" — including Mills' — were torn down but the core rectangle of the original building was kept.

Various public officials, writers and visitors have left us descriptions of what the building and its yard looked like at this time. For example, in his *Travels Through North America*, the Duke of Saxe-Weimar-Eisenach, Karl Bernhard in 1825 noted that the jail walls and floors were made of oak. The jailer, he said, lived on the ground floor as did "gentlemen" prisoners, described as those who had some community standing or could afford bribes.

On the second floor, said Bernhard, were less prominent debtors or minor criminals and these occasionally were permitted to stroll the jail yard.

Captive on the third floor were the hardened types convicted of dangerous crimes. Some were chained to rings installed in the floors of the cells, Bernhard said. [9]

In 1853, a writer concerned with social issues wrote a novel that is generally recognized as providing an accurate description of the Charleston jail. F.C. Adams in his "Manuel Pereira" mentions a high brick wall surrounding the building and double rows of iron bars on the windows. He described an iron-barred entry door that led to the ground floor containing the jailer's quarters on the right and four small debtors' cells and a kitchen on the left.

Another iron door, he said, led to stairs to the second floor where eight or nine cells of varying sizes contained an astonishing collection of offenders including "refractory seamen", persons accused or convicted of assault and battery with intent to kill, deserters, arsonists, murderers along with the unfortunate witnesses to Charleston crime.

The worst of the lot found themselves on the third floor which, according to Adams, was dubbed by prisoners "Mount Rascal." On either side of a vestibule were large, grated doors with heavy iron bolts and bars, which opened into "dark, gloomy cells".

Adams also said certain other inmates were confined outside, in back of the building:

> **In the yard were a number of very close cells, which, as we have said before, were kept for the negroes, refractory criminals, and those condemned to capital punishment.**

Physical evidence of these outdoor cages has yet to be found but several written references to them survive including some that suggest they were actually below ground level. The inference is that these special cells, exposed to the elements, were used as additional punishment for hard cases. [10]

How the Medieval Facade and Octagon Came to Be

Faced with a redesign of the existing jail, rather than a fresh start, planners had at least three goals. First, they wanted additional space to deal with overcrowding. Second, they hoped to correct structural flaws that provided too many opportunities for escape and exposed inmates to harsh weather. Third, they wished to make their prison more intimidating in appearance.

These challenges fell to Charleston architects John H. Seyle and Louis J. Barbot.

When completed — probably by 1859 — the Seyle and Barbot version of the jail was four stories high. The two towers that still flank the front were even higher. At the rear, an eight-sided block of cells was built, topped by a two-story structure called a "ventilation tower" but that also may have been used to confine prisoners. [11]

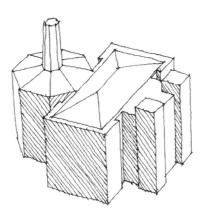

Courtesy of the American College of the Building Arts

The tower facade and octagon were added about 1859

The result certainly expanded capacity and the whole building was made more secure by strengthening walls and ceilings. Their design included a layout popular in European jails in which jailers could see corridors and cellblocks more clearly and thus monitor inmate movement. This feature was based on the growing popularity in Europe of prison layouts that positioned supervisors so that inmates could be observed at all times. Trebellas wrote:

> **By situating the Jailer's Quarters immediately above and opposite what had been the front door to the jail, the designers gave the Warden symbolic and visual domination over everyone who came or left the facility. One might imagine the impact of entering the Jail, mounting the stairs to the Second floor, and, on glancing back prior to entering one of the gang cells of the Main Cell Block, realizing that you had been watched, unawares, the whole time.**

While specifics as to the inclusion of jailer's quarters in the Seyle and Barbot design have not survived, it may be surmised that they were. Certainly in later years, jailer William J. Bennett and his entire family occupied space toward the front of the jail but it is not recorded if his predecessors did likewise. It is likely that at some point jailers or their designees were on-site 24 hours a day and these rooms were almost certainly where they stayed.

However, in subsequent years, overcrowding remained an ongoing problem and escapes, some successful, continued.

Seyle and Barbot probably came closest to satisfying their third task — that of making the building appear more frightening. The very distinctive and ominous appearance of the front of the jail that survives today was much in vogue among prisoner designers, particularly in Europe. The authors of one research paper that examined the jail's architecture wrote that, "During the reform period, prison architecture not only developed highly specific typologies, but also stylistic standards. It was generally agreed that the style should not be ornate, but appearance was much more than a matter of economy and security...the style was not only to be appropriate to the purposes of a jail, but to play an active part in accomplishing the function of imprisonment, deterrence." They then cited a quote from *Encyclopedia Londinensis* written in 1826:

The style of architecture of a prison is a matter of no slight importance. It offers an effectual method of exciting the imagination to a most desirable point of abhorrence. Persons, in general, refer their horror of a prison to an instinctive feeling rather than to any accurate knowledge of the privations or inflictions therein endured… The exterior of a prison should, therefore, be formed in the heavy and somber style, which most forcibly impresses the spectator with gloom and terror.

Photo by author

A foreboding appearance was the aim of jail 1850s jail additions

The report added that, "The most common choices were Greek Revival or a castellated style with Gothic details." The latter approach was followed to the letter in Charleston. In fact, Barbot had previously worked for a firm that designed the Gothic Revival style county jails for South Carolina jails in Walterboro and Orangeburg. Both still stand today and are similar in appearance to Charleston's, though not nearly as elaborate. [12]

Also probably added at this time were distinctive "quoins" (cornerstones) that, in the case of the jail, were decorative but were thought to lend a sense of strength and solidity to the visual effect.

Intimidating criminals was a goal but of equal or greater concern were ongoing public fears of slave uprisings. Kenneth Severens, in his book *Charleston Antebellum Architecture and Civic Destiny*, writes:

> **Better police and fire protection were ongoing, yet by no means constant, concerns during the antebellum period. City officials had vacillated between shrill hysteria and indulgent indifference concerning real and imagined black conspiracies. The Vesey plot of 1822 (Editor's Note: Free black Denmark Vesey was hanged along with 34 other blacks accused of plotting an uprising against Charleston whites) had led to the building of the Arsenal, the remodeling of the District Jail, and the installation of a treadmill for the punishment of slaves at the Work House. The increased abolitionist agitation about 1835, as well as a rash of major fires, coincided with the monumentalizing of Meeting Street and the building of the Guard House at the Four Corners. Yet anxieties over slavery persisted, although often suppressed within the context of other events. [13]**

When viewed from a distance, the Barbot and Seyle treatment bespoke fearsome impenetrability. It was as though they had stacked massive blocks of granite to form indestructible walls topped with battlements. Windows and doors bristled with heavy iron bars and the whole seemed coldly unmerciful.

However, it was partly sham.

Lacking funds and a convenient or economical source of stones of sufficient size, stucco was smeared over brick and scored in a giant rectangular pattern, creating an impression of stone block construction. Whether this approach was actually intended to fool anyone is open to conjecture. It was, however, a design technique then popular in many American cities, including Charleston.

In any case, this faux block skin eventually began falling away. It continued to dissolve as erosion and earth tremors took their toll, particularly on the sides and at the rear.

The redesign was attacked almost immediately. The new iteration received harsh criticism from Grand Jury visitors in June 1859 who cited poor layout and inadequate ventilation. The group recommended that the whole thing be razed and rebuilt! [14]

Nevertheless, other than the addition of a new stove in January 1860, it appears that little else changed. Shortcomings in structure, layout and amenities were dramatically exacerbated when the jail's population was swelled by trainloads of captured Union soldiers during the Civil War, from 1861 to 1865.

Significant structural change didn't come for another twenty years - and that was due to a cataclysmic event.

Horrendous Earthquake Claims the Entire Fourth Story

Just before 10 p.m. on August 31, 1886, the largest earthquake to ever hit the southeastern United States took only one minute to create unparalleled devastation. It left scores dead and 2,000 buildings damaged, including the Charleston District Jail. (See Chapter 7 - Bad Food, Bad Blood and an Earthquake: The Jail's Final 75 Years)

According to an article in the Charleston News and Courier published four days after the quake, an examination of the jail after the quake revealed that:

> **The damage to the Jail, in Magazine street, is well nigh irreparable, and parts of the building will have to be taken down and rebuilt. The massive brick walls, in some places nearly three feet thick, yielded to the quivering earth like so much glass and the walls are filled with gaping cracks, many of which extend underground. The main building and "tower" are seriously damaged and the walls badly cracked, but can probably be repaired. The jailer's apartment, facing on the**

street, is a tottering ruin, and will, no doubt, have to be condemned. The ventilator, or high cupola, on the top of the "tower," is badly shattered, and will also have to be taken down. [15]

After the quake, prisoners were temporarily housed elsewhere while damage was accessed and repairs were begun. It is unclear from the record just when they were returned but it appears that the building was still four stories tall and "in need of repairs" two years later in 1888.

By the 1890s, the fourth floor of the building, including the uppermost portions of the two front towers, was removed, as was the ventilator that had been above the octagon. Also, what had been a 20-foot-high wall surrounding the sides and back of the jail property was reduced to 15 feet. [16]

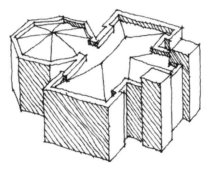

Courtesy of the American College of the Building Arts

Photo by author

An entire floor and the octagon tower were removed; at bottom is the octagon today

At some point — the record doesn't reflect precisely when — the original wood flooring of the upper floors of the main cell block was replaced by a "shallow brick jack arch system" in which arches made of bricks were built between steel joists with rods (the "jacks") supporting the arches. Atop the arches was placed rubble and oyster shell fill.

Modern examination of these components reveals that the steel was milled at the Carnegie Steel Company of Pittsburgh. The entire system, unlike the previous wood-based one, was non-combustible but not fireproof, as it was thought to be when built. Certain components of the steel beams could rapidly lose strength if flames exceeded 800 degrees Fahrenheit, threatening collapse. Fortunately, the building never was tested by a major fire.

An Annex is Built in 1932 - But Torn Down Seven Years Later

While there is little surviving documentation regarding significant modifications between the 1890s and when it was closed as a working jail in 1939, physical evidence remaining in the building today point to the installation — sometime — of amenities such as electricity, indoor plumbing and a limited heating system.

In 1932, construction of an annex to address overcrowding was approved. The Simons-Mayrant Company of Charleston successfully bid $5,883 and construction began on June 10 of that year. An article in the June 10 edition of the Post and Courier said:

> **The building will be fifty-five by twenty feet and two stories in height. Members of the jail commission believe that approximately 100 to 125 additional prisoners will be accommodated in this annex.** [17]

However, in a follow-up published August 28, estimates had fallen a bit:

> **With the completion of the new annex, the jail now can handle comfortably approximately 200 prisoners. There are now 153 inmates in the jail. The new annex accommodates seventy-five prisoners. And the old**

building, while constructed to accommodate approximately 140 has housed as many as 160. At such times, however, it was greatly overcrowded.

...In the new annex all prisoners will sleep in two large rooms in hammocks, instead of on the cots provided in the cells of the old structure. The main jail building also has been improved, principally in the kitchen. The jail, however, still uses prisoners as cooks. There also are no provisions made for the handling of women prisoners, who will be lodged at the Charleston police station and in other jails as heretofore. [18]

A photo that appears to include a portion of the annex appeared in the Charleston Yearbook of 1940 and apparently was taken just before it was razed in March 1939 - just seven years after it had been constructed. [19] The teardown was a precursor to the over-all fate of the jail. After 137 years of patchwork repairs, under-funded renovation and unrelenting criticism, it was decided the jail's service would end.

From the Charleston Yearbook of 1940

Jail annex behind the octagon is visible at far right in this rare photo

THE JAIL IS CLOSED

The jail's fate was sealed when local officials secured federal funding for construction of a housing project to replace slums in the jail's neighborhood. Early discussions included demolition of the jail building, but it survived, mostly thanks to preservationists. Lack of funds to cover the cost of removal was probably a factor, as well.

Its wall, however, was another story. Already cut down from a height of 20 feet to 15 feet after the earthquake of 1886, most of it would be reduced another 11 feet so that sunlight could enter the jail yard where a playground for housing project children was planned. Bricks left over once the wall was reduced were used in construction of homes in the development. [20]

On September 16, 1939, the remaining prisoners were moved to the state penitentiary in Columbia and to a prison farm on North Charleston Boulevard. A newspaper account said, "A truck is expected to arrive here about 11 a.m. from the state penitentiary to return there with six white men, thirty negro men and three negro women, sentenced at the March term of the court of general sessions." An unspecified number of additional inmates went to the farm where, it was noted, "A suitable place for the detention of white women prisoners also is needed." The jailer and his crew were to be assigned to the farm. [21]

And, with that, operation of the jail ceased.

Jail equipment, including the cells themselves, was removed and may have been installed in what was to become the new jail, a former immigration station under the old Cooper River Bridge, on the Charleston peninsula side. Sheriff Joseph M. Poulnot turned over the empty, 137-year-old Magazine Street building to the Charleston Housing Authority. It was promptly locked up and essentially unused (except for storage) and unchanged until the 1970s.

THE NEW JAIL

On August 1, 1941, a lengthy Charleston newspaper article described the new facility as an "Up-to-Date Bastile" that comfortably could accommodate 185 prisoners, and 200 if needed. Two rooms were provided for city chain gang prisoners ("... one for each race...") as well as separate sections for federal prisoners and women. It said the kitchen extended the width of the building, was equipped with a new stove and utensils and that its cook was a man serving an 18-month sentence. All was heated by steam, could be air conditioned and was fireproof.

The article said the county sheriff had tried for years to persuade authorities to replace the deteriorating, old building on Magazine Street and had been " ... humiliated when the government refused to allow its prisoners to be detained (there)." The new facility was deemed acceptable by the government and it resumed paying to keep its inmates there, generating revenue that would help maintain the jail. [22]

CHAPTER 5

DEPRIVATION, INJUSTICE AND VIOLENCE: THE JAIL'S FIRST 60 YEARS

There was never a good time to be a prisoner at the Charleston District Jail but surely its earliest years were among the worst. Agonizing deprivation and extreme discomfort were routine.

When the first prisoners were locked up in 1802:

— No well had been dug on the property from which fresh water could be drawn.

— No toilet facilities existed — not even an outdoor "vault" or privy.

— There was no central system to provide relief from temperature extremes.

— Rain and wind plagued inmates through a chronically leaky roof and glassless windows.

— Meals were meager, sometimes consisting of little more than bread and water.

— Sentences of confinement were sometimes accompanied by physical punishments such as whipping and branding.

Some prisoners, perhaps understandably, regarded the newly opened jail as their worst nightmare. The jail's supervisors were unhappy, as well. County commissioners, the sheriff and the jailer, issued protests, complaints and pleas to state officials for improvements. Officials were especially concerned with the absence of a wall to help keep prisoners in and keep out those who wanted to consort with them.

Even when improvements were approved, it took years to get the projects done. In the meantime, prisoners bore the brunt of the delays.

Detailed, written accounts about the jail's first six decades are rare. The scraps that do exist provide a glimpse into life there. Here are a few:

1802 – No Water, No Well, No Wall

Even the officially appointed commissioners "for building a Gaol in Charleston" noted insufficient funds kept them from providing several items that had been included in the original plan; namely digging a well for badly needed fresh water, erecting a privy and building a wall around the yard.

These were critical, health-related deficiencies. Water surrounding the swampy lot was stagnant, foul and useless. This forced the jail to rely on the collection of rainwater or deliveries for its supply.

Absence of indoor toilet facilities or even an outdoor latrine meant that inmates were forced to urinate and defecate in buckets in their cells — and live with the results until the "slops" could be removed.

Lack of a high, sturdy wall, besides facilitating escapes and interference from outsiders, kept prisoners from exercising. This, it was argued, further endangered their physical and mental health.

These deficiencies were specifically named in a letter the commissioners wrote November 11, 1802 and sent to then-Governor John Drayton. However, they warned that remedies would be costly.

> **Should your Excellency think proper to apply to the Legislature for a further grant of money for the purpose of effecting what may be necessary on the premises surrounding the Gaol: We beg leave to inform you that agreeable to the present extravagant price of materials & workmanship, a wall of twelve feet in height above the surface surrounding the Lot of two hundred feet square, a well, & a brick building & arched vault for a**

Necessary of ten feet by twenty feet square, could not be built & finished for a less sum that $9000. [1]

The sheriff, perhaps hoping to offset any monetary fears aroused by the commissioners, chose remarkably flowery language to appeal to the governor's sense of compassion:

The New Gaol, the key of which you sent me this day, is not compleat (sic) for want of a Well, a Vault, and a Wall round the Lot, however, … I presume to be authorized by Law, or a Resolution of the Legislature to occupy the same. The benevolent disposition that your Excellency has uniformly manifested upon every occasion, towards your fellow Creatures, particularly those in distress, furnishes me with most pleasing hope, you will in due season lay before the ensuing Legislature, the different matters contained in this Letter. I am with the highest consideration, Sheriff Thomas Lehre. [2]

Provision eventually was made for a protective wall, a water well and an outdoor privy, but it took years. In the case of the wall, it wasn't until December of 1805 that the state assembly appointed men to superintend its construction and it is not clear when it was actually completed.

Whatever well was dug apparently was of little use. By 1826, water from it was deemed "unfit for drinking" and two cisterns for the collection of rain and storage of water were installed in the attic. [3]

When the first privy appeared is unknown but one is actually depicted in engravings created in the 1860s. [4] When indoors — which apparently was most of the time — inmates were forced to rely on the pails in their cells. The extent of their access to outdoor "sinks" or "vaults" is not recorded but soldiers held in the jail yard in the 1860s wrote that they were poorly maintained and offensive.

There was little protection from extremes of heat and cold. It appears some cellblocks might have been equipped with fireplaces, but it is unknown when they were used or how effective they might have been. Installations of window coverings, stoves and electricity were slow in coming.

1819–Jail Time Could Include the Lash and the Brand

The concept of lengthy incarceration, versus early colonists' inclination to administer immediate physical punishments, was relatively new and still evolving as the newly built jail was completed. Physical penalties, some quite severe, remained and were recorded in local newspapers.

There were two, officially sanctioned physical abuses still being mandated by the courts for both men and women. Whipping is mentioned as having been administered in cases from the 1820s and as late as the 1850s — in the market and in the yard of the jail. One Charleston newspaper account published in 1858 said a man who had been convicted of stealing a gold watch was to jailed for one week, lashed "upon the bare back" in the jail yard, then released. [5]

Also, certain sentences required a particular letter of the alphabet corresponding to the crime be seared into the skin with a red-hot iron.

According to research collected by the late Emmett Robinson and archived at the South Carolina Historical Society:

> **Branding was done either by the sheriff or the jailer in the presence of the court.**
>
> **Three letters, "T", "M". and "F", were used in (South Carolina) brandings. These were burned into the victim's thumb, cheek, or in rare cases, his forehead. The letter "M" was used exclusively for malefactors guilty of murder or manslaughter. "T" marked the thief, and "F" was used for the freymaker (NOTE: rioter).**
>
> **The depth and severity of the burn might well depend on the victim's quickness of speech, for sentences sometimes required that the sheriff hold the hot iron in place "until the words 'God save the State' could be pronounced three times" by the unhappy culprit.**
>
> **...Some brandings were punishments in name only. A jury would convict a man of a crime and at the same**

time ask that he be granted mercy. In such cases the judge might order the sheriff to apply a "cold iron."

Brandings, like public hangings, were well attended. Since they took place in court not so many people would watch the proceedings, but crowds gathered nonetheless. [6]

In one recorded case, Martin Toohey, convicted in 1819 of manslaughter, was held in the Magazine Street jail while awaiting his execution. The court also ordered him to be branded. A story published in The Charleston Courier, February 13, 1819, lists several persons to be punished, including Toohey and at least one woman:

The Court of Sessions and Common Pleas for this District, adjourns to day...and the following penalties were imposed on the culprits by the Hon. Judge Nott, who previously addressed them in a very interesting and appropriate manner. We hope to be favored with his remarks, and trust that their publication may tend to retard the alarming progress of crime among us.

Martin Toohey for Manslaughter, was branded with the letter M. in the left hand.

Lionel Uniacke, Daniel James and John Robinson, for Grand Larceny, were branded with the letter T.

Elijah Libby, for Petit Larceny, was sentenced to receive, on the 19th inst. fifteen lashes.

M. Miranda, for the same offence, (sic) thirty lashes, J. Smith, twenty lashes, and Dorothy Quin, five lashes.

As it happened, Toohey eventually escaped from the jail but quickly was recaptured and executed on May 28, 1819. [7]

1825–CHARLESTONSHERIFFSAYS37½CENTSPERDAYPER PRISONER NOT ENOUGH

By 1825, at least some official voices were decrying draconian methods embedded in South Carolina's justice system.

Charleston Sheriff Nathaniel Cleary, who was responsible for the jail for a number of years in the 1800s, authored a fascinating reforms petition to the State Senate in October 1925, according to an abstract maintained by the on-line Digital Library on American Slavery:

> "...our Criminal Code stands before you a patched, rusty and uncouth edifice, in most of the feudal tyranny, superstitious cruelty, and sombrous (sic) ignorance of its remote origin." For example, he states, fifty-one crimes can result in capital punishment, and branding is still a punishment listed on the books, thus showing that the laws should undergo "a radical, thorough and instantaneous reformation."

However, as a consequence of fears of insurrection harbored by Charleston whites, blacks got short shrift in Cleary's plea. The abstract notes:

> In addition, Cleary seeks larger appropriations to prevent the "ingress and return of negroes and persons of color into this state." Averring that this job requires the "utmost vigilance and activity among his deputies," Cleary is of the opinion that, unless he commits more resources to it, the problem will persist.

And, Cleary said funding for jail operations was woefully inadequate:

> The sheriff also seeks to improve the fee structure, speed of the legal process, compensation for sheriffs who testify before a grand or petit juries, and jail allowances. The 37 1/2 cents a day allowance for each prisoner, for example, is barely enough to provide

food, much less blankets or clothing. Moreover, allowances for imprisoned debtors should be granted from the time of their arrest. Recently, the time in jail for insolvent debtors was extended, he states, but "there is not regulation of any avail for the support, from any quarter whatever, of an insolvent while in prison... before it is proven that he is at all in debt." [8]

1825–"Upon the whole...an unfavorable impression" of the Jail

Traveler and author Karl Bernhard, cited elsewhere in this book, described individuals and conditions he observed during his 1825 jail visit:

The prisoners are too much crowded together, and have no employment. The atrocious criminals live in the upper story, and are immured two together in a cell, without ever being permitted to come into the open air. This is allowed only to those dwelling in the first story, consisting of debtors, and persons who are imprisoned for breaches of the peace.

... In the upper story there is a negro confined, who, implicated in one of the late conspiracies, had not committed himself so far as to allow of his being hung; nevertheless, his presence appeared so dangerous to the public tranquility that he is detained in prison till his master can find some opportunity to ship him to the West Indies, and there sell him.

Photo by author

Jail's basement left "…an unfavourable impression…"

In another room was a white prisoner, and it is not known whether he be an American or Scotchman, who involved himself by his writings deeply in the last negro conspiracy. The prisoners received their food while we were present: it consisted of very good soup, and three-quarters of a pound of beef.

Upon the ground floor is the dwelling of the keeper, who was an Amsterdam Jew, and the state-rooms in which gentlemen, who are lodged here, receive accommodation for money and fair words. The cleanliness of the house was not very great; upon the whole it left an unfavourable impression upon me. [9]

1828 – ONE MONTH'S JAIL EXPENSE = $29.25

Official reports regarding jail activity are exceedingly rare but one discovered suggests menial tasks around the jail in 1828 apparently were the responsibility of hired blacks. A invoice prepared by Sheriff Samuel Hymans that was included in a jail committee report includes these ledger entries:

January

Negro Hire for Cook & 2 other negroes to clean & attend the Gaol & Prisoners $20

Cash for Vegetables, Rice & Salt for Soup for Criminals $5

Oil for Lamp in Gaol $3

Sweeping Chimneys .44

Broom & Brushes .81

Total $29.25

Subsequent months' expenses included "Tubs for Prisoners, $2.50; "House and Yard Brooms, 75 cents and "3 Cords Wood & Carting, $15."

But, in addition to expenses, the invoice listed reimbursement to the jail for the expense of housing prisoners that couldn't pay fines. Sentences for petty crimes often were a choice between a fine or jail time. Indigent offenders unable to pay were locked up and the expense of their confinement was sought from the State.

To Gaol fees for Wm Bason - swore off his fine in Gaol from 29 June to 10th July $5.04

To Gaol fees for Dexter Fields swore off his fine from 26th July to 3 August in Gaol $3.91

Total $8.95

Grand Total for the Year $ 440.45

Samuel Hyams, gaoler, to the S. C. Senate praying for payment of account with the itemized statement of said account. Penal System, Petitions, 1829 Charleston District [10]

1830 – "...INSANE PERSONS AS WELL AS CRIMINALS..."

Surviving records mention an "insane asylum" that once existed in the block bounded by Magazine, Logan, Queen and Franklin. But there are also some suggestions that some of the mentally ill were confined in the jail. A traveler and author identified only as "S.G.B.", visited both City Hall and the jail in the early 1830s and his (or her) observations were included in The Monthly Religious Magazine, Vol. XV," 1861:

I was led ... to visit the City Hall and the Jail. In the former building I was shown the pillory, the instrument of a punishment antiquated elsewhere, and, I hope, since abolished in South Carolina. The pillory consisted of a platform, supporting upon upright beams a sort of yoke, with apertures for the head and hands; and in this frame the culprit was to be exposed to the view and to the insults of the crowd.

In the Jail, the presence of my companion procured me a general inspection of the building. It was spacious, and appeared to be neatly kept. I found that it was used for the confinement of insane persons as well as criminals. The impression of this was painful, but the fact was no uncommon one, thirty years ago, and before our people in general had had their attention strongly directed to the claims of the victims of insanity by the philanthropic labors of Miss Dix (Note: Probably Dorthea Dix, a crusader for the compassionate care of the insane).

The writer then met a prisoner whose offense apparently was the distribution of anti-slavery tracts:

After our general view of the prison, the keeper observed 'Perhaps you would like to see a prisoner who has lately been sent here; he is from the North....' With these words he led us to a room of comfortable dimensions and well lighted, where a young sailor rose to meet us. His name was Edward Smith, and he had been arrested for distributing incendiary pamphlets. His account of it was, that, on leaving Boston, some person had given him these pamphlets and asked him to circulate them in Charleston, and that he had done so without knowing their character.

The book was "Walker's Pamphlet," the first publication, I think that was made in Boston on the subject of slavery. I have heard the pamphlet described as of a highly incendiary character, but cannot vouch for the truth of the account. I asked him some questions, in the hope of being useful to one whose appearance made me think he had been rather indiscreet than criminal; but my introducer showed great uneasiness, and soon cut short the colloquy. I afterwards saw by the papers that Smith had been found guilty, and sentenced to a long imprisonment. [11]

David Walker was a free black man who grew up in North Carolina and lived, as an adult, in Boston. He was an active abolitionist.

According to Hasan Crockett, a professor of political science at Morehouse College in Atlanta, the piece, called *Walker's Appeal* "...chastised the bondage of enslaved blacks and implored them to 'Arise! Arise! Strike for your lives and liberties. Now is the day and hour." Crockett said it was considered particularly dangerous because it was enjoying wide distribution. He wrote:

When the pamphlet reached the South it represented one of the slave owner's greatest fears, blacks (not whites) writing and reading about abolition. As a result, southern governments reacted swiftly to Walker's

Appeal. South Carolina, Georgia, North Carolina and Louisiana immediately passed harsh laws, some requiring the death penalty, against possession or distribution of Walker's Appeal, or similar materials. (Although I [Hasan] found no evidence of anyone receiving the death penalty because of the Appeal.) [12]

1852–INMATES INCLUDE FREE BLACK SAILORS, CHILDREN

The jail was always an integrated facility. As has already been noted, slaves were temporarily kept in its yard before being marched to the Market Street area to be sold.

Prior to the American Civil War, slavery was legal in 15 states, including South Carolina. Blacks in bondage were subject to various rules and codes over which only their owners had say. However, free black persons were not subject to those laws and, in theory, accorded the same rights as whites.

An egregious exception pertained to free blacks aboard ships that anchored in Charleston's harbor. Because of white fears of black insurrection — numerous plots were rumored or thwarted — it was thought best to minimize the influence of these free, black outsiders by locking them up.

By far, the most detailed description of mid-1850's life at the Charleston District Jail is provided by Francis Colburn Adams in his 1853 novel "Manuel Pereira". While the book uses a fictional character to level a withering political broadside at perceived injustice, its detailed descriptions of jail life seem historically accurate. At the time Adams wrote, the building was still the primitive, three-story brick structure described earlier in this book.

In Adams' story, Manuel Pereira is a free black Portuguese sailor seized from a British vessel that had docked in Charleston. Under a law enacted in 1822 to protect the white citizenry from slave rebellions, all free black mariners arriving at South Carolina ports were to be immediately imprisoned until fines were paid and they departed the port. Adams considered this an affront to basic human rights and hoped to arouse public support for repeal of the law, in part by describing the deplorable conditions to which such men like his character Pereira were unfairly subjected.

Adams lived in Charleston when he wrote "Manuel Pereira." While the story strongly promotes a particular point of view, the descriptions of the jail seem consistent with other contemporaneous accounts and thus generally are accepted as fact-based:

> The jail is a sombre-looking building, with every mark of antiquity standing boldly outlined upon its exterior. It is surrounded by a high brick wall, and its windows are grated with double rows of bars, sufficiently strong for a modern penitentiary. Altogether, its dark, gloomy appearance strikes those who approach it, with the thought and association of some ancient cruelty.

> You enter through an iron-barred door, and on both sides of a narrow portal leading to the right are four small cells and a filthy-looking kitchen, resembling an old-fashioned smoke-house. These cells are the debtors'; and as we were passing out, after visiting a friend, a lame "molatto-fellow" with scarcely rags to cover his nakedness, and filthy beyond description, stood at what was called the kitchen door. 'That poor dejected object,' said our friend, 'is the cook. He is in for misdemeanor — one of the peculiar shades of it, for which a n— is honored with the jail.' 'It seems, then, that cooking is a punishment in Charleston, and the negro is undergoing the penalty,' said we. 'Yes!' said our friend; 'but the poor fellow has a sovereign consolation, which few n——s in Charleston can boast of — and none of the prisoners here have — he can get enough to eat.'

Adams' narrator, after giving the emaciated inmate some tobacco, continues his journey through the corridors and stairways of the jail.

On the left side, after passing the main iron door, are the jailer's apartments. Passing through another iron door, you ascend a narrow, crooked stairs and reach the second story; here are some eight or nine miserable cells — some large and some small — badly ventilated, and entirely destitute of any kind of furniture: and if they are badly ventilated for summer, they are equally badly provided with means to warm them in winter. In one of these rooms were nine or ten persons, when we visited it; and such was the morbid stench escaping from it, that we were compelled to put our handkerchiefs to our faces. This floor is appropriated for such crimes as assault and battery; assault and battery, with intent to kill; refractory seamen; deserters; violating the statutes; suspicion of arson and murder; witnesses; all sorts of crimes, varying from the debtor to the positive murderer, burglar, and felon.

Adams' narrator then decries the fact that two of the worst offenders – one who committed a murder and another who attempted it — were "deputy jailers" who supervised other prisoners. They were not, though, permitted to carry cell keys, he said.

Then, continuing his descriptive tour, he wrote:

From this floor, another iron door opened, and a winding passage led into the third and upper story, where a third iron door opened into a vestibule, on the right and left of which were grated doors secured with heavy bolts and bars. These opened into narrow portals with dark, gloomy cells on each side. In the floor of each of these cells was a large iron ring-bolt, doubtless intended to chain refractory prisoners to; but we were informed that such prisoners were kept in close stone cells, in the yard, which were commonly occupied by negroes and those condemned to capital punishment. The ominous name of this third story was "Mount Rascal," intended, no doubt, as significant of the class of prisoners it contained.

It is said that genius is never idle: the floor of these cells bore some evidence of the fact in a variety of very fine specimens of carving and flourish work, done with a knife. Among them was a well-executed crucifix; with the Redeemer, on Calvary - an emblem of hope, showing how the man marked the weary moments of his durance.

At this point in the story, Adams offers more clues as to the nature of specific offenses and sentences. Perhaps, surprisingly, some being confined were children:

We spoke with many of the prisoners, and heard their different stories, some of which were really painful. Their crimes were variously stated, from that of murder, arson, and picking pockets, down to the felon who had stolen a pair of shoes to cover his feet; one had stolen a pair of pantaloons, and a little boy had stolen a few door-keys. Three boys were undergoing their sentence for murder.

A man of genteel appearance, who had been sentenced to three years imprisonment, and to receive two hundred and twenty lashes in the market, at different periods, complained bitterly of the injustice of his case. Some had been flogged in the market, and were awaiting their time to be flogged again and discharged; and others were confined on suspicion, and had been kept in this close durance for more than six months, awaiting trial.

Adams' account suggests even petty criminals might wait many months before their cases were heard due to courts that, "…sit seldom, and with large intervals between." During these times, he said, "Prisoners seem mere shuttlecocks between the sheriffs" who expect favors from those for whom they expedite hearings.

We noticed these cells (on the third floor) were much cleaner than those below, yet there was a fetid smell escaping from them. This we found arose from the tubs being allowed to stand in the rooms, where the criminals were closely confined, for twenty-four hours, which, with the action of the damp, heated atmosphere of that climate, was of itself enough to breed contagion. We spoke of the want of ventilation and the noxious fumes that seemed almost pestilential, but they seemed to have become habituated to it, and told us that the rooms on the south side were lighter and more comfortable. Many of them spoke cheerfully, and endeavored to restrain their feelings, but the furrows upon their haggard countenances needed no tongue to utter its tale.

Among the most acute deprivations, according to Adams, was the quality and quantity of food provided to prisoners:

The allowance per day was a loaf of bad bread, weighing about nine ounces, and a pint of thin, repulsive soup, so nauseous that only the most necessitated appetite could be forced to receive it, merely to sustain animal life. This was served in a dirty-looking tin pan, without even a spoon to serve it. One man told us that he had subsisted on bread and water for nearly five weeks - that he had lain down to sleep in the afternoon and dreamed that he was devouring some wholesome nourishment to stay the cravings of his appetite, and awoke to grieve that it was but a dream. In this manner his appetite was doubly aggravated, yet he could get nothing to appease its wants until the next morning.

To add to this cruelty, we found two men in close confinement, the most emaciated and abject specimens of humanity we have ever beheld. We asked ourselves, "Lord God! Was it to be that humanity should descend so low?" The first was a forlorn, dejected-looking creature, with a downcast countenance, containing little of the human to mark his features. His face was covered with hair, and so completely matted with dirt and made fiendish by the tufts of coarse hair that hung over his forehead, that a thrill of horror invaded our feelings. He had no shoes on his feet; and a pair of ragged pantaloons, and the shreds of a striped shirt without sleeves, secured around the waist with a string, made his only clothing. In truth, he had scarce enough on to cover his nakedness, and that so filthy and swarming with vermin, that he kept his shoulders and hands busily employed; while his skin was so incrusted with dirt as to leave no trace of its original complexion. In this manner he was kept closely confined, and was more like a wild beast who saw none but his keepers when they came to throw him his feed. Whether he was kept in this manner for his dark deeds or to cover the shame of those who speculated upon his misery, we leave to the judgment of the reader.

Adams said freedom to roam the jail's yard was a privilege reserved for lesser criminals and debtors but that stubborn, unmanageable prisoners, those awaiting execution and blacks were held in special jail yard cells. "These cells seemed to be held as a terror over the criminals, and well they might," wrote Adams, "for we never witnessed any thing more dismal for the tenement of man." [13]

If these outdoor cells were the same as those referenced in other accounts, they were installed below ground level.

1852 – Jail Offers "Safe Keeping" of Slaves

According to Frederic Bancroft in his 1932 book "Slave Trading in the Old South," the jail was used to warehouse slaves:

Most of them were brought by coast or river packets. If not locked up in one of many warehouses near the wharves, they were most often driven up Queen Street to Ryan's "n— jail" or on the somber and still impressive Charleston Jail, there on Magazine Street.

Bancroft's account includes the text of ad he found in the Charleston Courier, Jan. 7, 1852:

> **NOTICE. — NEGROS** (sic) (either singly or in gangs), will be received in the Charleston Jail on as favorable terms as elsewhere, for safe keeping. Accommodations roomy. — **JOSEPH POULNOT, Jailor** [14]

1857 – First Drawing of the Jail to Appear in Print?

A detailed engraving of the jail rendered from its west side appeared in an 1857 edition of "Ballou's Pictorial Drawing Room Companion," a 19th century periodical based in Boston. By the time this drawing was made, the jail had been remodeled by Barbot and Seyle and included the castle-like front facade and octagon of cellblocks topped by a tower, all surrounded by a high wall.

Courtesy of the Library of Congress
Earliest depiction of the jail?

The picture was accompanied by this text:

In our present number we give several illustrations of Charleston, one of the finest cities of the South, and the metropolis of South Carolina, drawn expressly for the Pictorial by Mr. Kilburn...The first of our views represents the Jail and Marine Hospital, at the corner of Magazine and Franklin Streets. The buildings on the left are occupied as the jail, and in the rear is seen a portion of the Charleston work-house; the marine hospital is on the right. [15]

Several observations may be made about this picture. First, the view is looking east. Magazine Street runs parallel to the front of the jail, shown in the left of the picture. Franklin extends along the western wall, on the right.

The building on the right, just to the left of the trees, is the Marine Hospital, which still exists today. The Work House, shown at the far left, was razed after an earthquake in 1886. While the artist likely took a fair amount of license, the area is shown as being considerably more rural than it later became. In the picture, a family of blacks - probably slaves - has paused on a wide thoroughfare upon which horsemen traverse.

It is difficult to say definitively, but in addition to the arched doorway in the wall just below the jail's front entrance, there appear to be two more entrances in the wall, shown here right above the head of the horse on the left.

It appears supports were being employed to shore up the western portion of the wall but that Barbot and Seyle's renovations are fully in place. This is also a depiction of the building at its remodeled, four-story height (the two front towers were even higher). These upper floors and the tower seen in back would be removed after the 1886 earthquake.

1859 – JAILER AND SON INJURED IN PRISON BRAWL

Many articles about the Charleston prison refer to quarters inside the jail, in which the jailer could reside. Over the years, these were located in various parts of the building and some were said to be securely separate from the cellblocks. That, however, apparently didn't entirely eliminate danger. An article in the Monday, March 21, 1859 edition of the Courier reported the jailer, his son and a jail watchman were savagely attacked. Headlined "Affray in Jail," the article said:

> During Friday night, the Watchman on duty for the Jail of Charleston District, in this city, had his suspicions aroused by unusual noises proceeding from Room or Cell No.3, which was occupied by John Gurley, under sentence of imprisonment for larceny, and E. Holden, in custody awaiting trial for burglary. Having his attention thus attracted and directed, the Watchman heard a conversation between the two prisoners mentioned, in which his name and the name of the Jailor, Mr. John L. Milligan, were distinctly heard. Being thus convinced that an attempt to escape was in immediate contemplation, the Watchman communicated with the Jailor, and they together proceeded to the cell, suspected and watched it for some time.

> At 6 o'clock A. M., on Saturday, the usual hour for visiting the cells, the Watchman and Jailor opened this room, and were immediately attacked with violence; the Watchman by Gurley, and the Jailor by Holden - who had prepared for the purpose a brickbat, covered and slung in a shirt sleeve. Mr. Milligan received a blow with this with such force as to bring him down. Recovering promptly he defended himself by presenting a revolver, one barrel of which he fired without effect. Before the weapon could be used further Gurley seized the pail of water in the cell, and dashed it over the pistol hand of the Jailor. Another pistol in the hand of the Watchman was fired accidentally during the struggle, and the ball inflicted a slight flesh wound on the forehead of Master Milligan, a son of the Jailor, who had gallantly hastened to the scene of danger on the first alarm, and exerted himself with

a courage and presence of mind very creditable to a lad fourteen years.

After some continued struggle the prisoners were secured and remanded to confinement, and examination was given to the wounds received. It was found that Mr. Milligan had received a very severe concussion on the brain. He has since suffered considerable pain, but at our latest accounts on Sunday evening he was in a hopeful condition for recovery as soon as could be expected. [16]

CHAPTER 6

"ALIVE WITH VERMIN": JAIL LIFE DURING THE CIVIL WAR

"I think it was the nastiest, dirtiest, filthiest, lousiest place I ever was in." So said Union Lt. A. O. Abbott of his confinement in the Charleston District Jail. It was the summer of 1843. "The ground was literally covered with lice. The next morning after my arrival there, I killed over fifty on my shirt alone, and my case was not an isolated one." [1]

During roughly four years of the Civil War, between 1861 and 1865, the Charleston District Jail was enlisted as part of the South's effort. The jail was said to have held as many as 600 Union prisoners of war on a given day [2] but the total number that flowed into and out of its gates is unknown.

Already decaying and overcrowded with inmates serving civilian sentences, the lockup suddenly was inundated with army captives. Totally unprepared for the influx, there was not enough shelter, not enough to eat, no protection from vermin, disease and the elements nor apparent relief from despair.

The South's resources were stretched thin on practically all fronts. POWs quickly overwhelmed existing prisons, some of which were already over capacity. The jail actually was only one of several holding areas in and around the city. Soldiers also were held at Castle Pinckney in the harbor, a racetrack north of town (now Hampton park, near today's Citadel) and at various hospitals and other buildings.

Most who wound up in Charleston were being shuttled to and from larger prison facilities like Andersonville in Georgia and Libby Prison in Virginia. Stays in the jail could be just a few days or many months. Already horrendous jail conditions were continuously made worse by hordes of new arrivals. Many were sick or wounded and some of them died there.

Most, however, survived and some wrote of their experiences in journals and newspaper articles. Nearly all bemoaned harsh, miserable conditions and many expressed disgust at their captors' behavior as custodians. It should be noted that passions on both sides ran white hot. Certainly the hatred of mortal enemies colored some of these accounts. But, beyond the rhetoric, surely there was a lot of truth in these snapshots of day-to-day life. The POW's told how they ate and how food was prepared, how they passed the time, how white soldiers were treated compared to blacks and how they coped with hardships.

In sum, soldiers' recollections offer a richly detailed picture of life at the Charleston District Jail during the war. A selection follows, mostly in the captives' own words.

From the Battlefield to the Jail

Typically, capture meant a move back from the front lines though a variety of stockades, guarded camps, prisons and other facilities. Trains handled most of this movement and, for some prisoners, these journeys provided deep and abiding impressions of the South. Lt. Abbott's introduction was typical. After his capture, he was held briefly in a stockade in Savannah, and then moved. In his "Prison Life in the South," published in 1865, he wrote:

> ... a train of freight cars was backed down to us, and we were ordered on board, forty being assigned to each car. These cars were old and filthy, and had been used for transporting coal, the bottoms of the cars being covered with about two inches of dust. I asked one of the Rebel officers for a broom to sweep it out, when he replied, "The Confederacy were not able to furnish brooms to sweep cars for Yankee prisoners;" so into the dirt we had to go, and make the best of it...

It is one hundred and four miles from Savannah to Charleston...

As we neared the city, we could see some of the fortifications on the land side; yet they were empty, and, for the most part, without guns. In crossing the Cooper River, we could see Castle Pinckney in the distance, and, for the first time since we left Richmond, could hear the fire of our own guns. As we entered the city, about 1:30 P.M., the streets were fairly crowded by the negroes, with a slight mixture of the whites... [3]

About his approach to the city, captive John McGregor said:

The journey from Richmond to Charleston was a dreary one. If I am any judge, the country is very poor in many respects. The negroes lived in huts; and their masters lived in houses, which were set upon posts five or six feet from the ground. In many places the hog sty was underneath the house. [4]

WHAT PRISONERS FOUND WHEN THEY ARRIVED

Taken off the trains, POWs were marched from the depots to the jail. The Charleston Mercury on September 14, 1861 reported the arrival of one group:

Yesterday the Yankee prisoners of war, who had been expected on Thursday, reached the city at an hour when most of our citizens were probably still slumbering in their beds...At 5 3/4 A.M. the order to form was given, the train having been signaled...Cadets, (under command of) Capt. Chichester, were specially detailed to receive the prisoners from the cars...The corps...proceeded through Washington, Calhoun, Cumming (Coming), Beaufain, Mazyck and Magazine streets to the jail... [5]

Pennsylvanian Graham McCamant Meadville, in his "Sixteen Months in Rebel Prisons by the First Prisoner in Andersonville" recorded a lively, if somewhat disconcerting, conversation with one of the Rebels who was part of his escort to the jail in 1863:

> Arriving at Charleston there was...waiting to receive us, over a Company of soldiers to take us into town... The Company was mostly Irishmen. One young fellow, a son of Erin's fair Isle, said to me:
>
> > "Hello, young fellow, duz yez know what we are going to do wid yez?"
> >
> > I answered: "No and we don't care."
> >
> > "Take yez out and hang yez," was his reply.
> >
> > "You dare not do it if you will give us a chance to fight," I said.
> >
> > "He shut one eye and squinted the other and laughing said: 'Divil the hair of your white head will we harrum, lad. '"
>
> Then the order was given to march and we halted not until we reached the gates of our first prison, Charleston Jail, and then began a prison life of sixteen months and ten days. [6]

In his book "The Capture, the Prison Pen, and the Escape," Willard W. Glazier, Captain New York Vol. Cavalry reports that his group's walk to the jail was observed by war-weary citizens who lined the route. Some, but not all, vented their anger with name-calling:

> The citizens turned out in crowds as we marched down Coming Street, and, as usual, we listened to the stereo-

typed billingsgate (Editor's Note: vulgar language) of the Southern chivalry. We were entirely satisfied that "familiarity breeds contempt," as we listened to their course (sic) comments on the "damned Yankees," "northern blue-bellies," "baboons," "Lincoln's monkeys," etc. Many, on the other hand, in the interval of our short halts, expressed sincere regrets at our unfortunate situation, and, rather quietly, to be sure, assured us of their faith in the ultimate triumph of the Government. It was rather surprising to find so many of this class in the cradle of secession. There were just enough of them to save from utter ruin that treason-polluted city. Our destination was Charleston jail-yard, the grand receptacle of all Union prisoners in Charleston. [7]

From Glazier's "The Capture, the Prison Pen, and the Escape"

One of several variations depicting life in the jail yard

Glazier's book included a detailed picture of the jail yard. The drawing is one of at least six variations that apparently were produced at the time and widely published, including one attributed to "Lieutenant F. Millward" in the February 18, 1865 edition of Harper's Weekly. The one Glazier used does not provide attribution. In each, the jail yard and the Work House (at the right) are similarly rendered but the position of tents and the number soldiers change. Also, the weight box at the base of the gallows shown in Glazier's is missing in some renditions. Whether or not each copy was done by the same artist or a series of them is not known.

Another account of first jail impressions was written by George W. Shurtleff, Brigadier-General, United States Volunteers, whose "A Year with the Rebels" is included in Lawrence Wilson's book "Itinerary of the Seventh Regiment, Ohio Volunteer Infantry":

> **Early in September an order came to transfer thirty officers to Charleston, South Carolina, to be placed in Castle Pinckney, a dismantled fort in the harbor... Reaching Charleston early in the morning, we were kept waiting for hours, that our march through the city might be witnessed by the people. When we finally moved we were escorted by a brass band, a troop of cavalry in gala attire, and thousands of citizens, men, women, and children. We were paraded through the streets of the city, and when we finally came to a halt, it was not at Castle Pinckney, but in front of the city jail. We filed into the jail, climbed the dark and dirty stairs, and passed along a dingy hall with grated cells on either side. Five of us were thrown into one of these cells. The first sight that caught our eye through the only window was a huge gallows, and I said to Major Potter, "There's our castle, and it is a veritable castle in the air."** [8]

Captain John G. B. Adams, 19th Regiment Massachusetts Volunteers was taken prisoner at the Battle of Cold Harbor in April 1864. He and his fellow captives hoped their transfer to Charleston meant they would be traded for Confederate soldiers being held by the North. Adams dark mood turned even more so when they soon learned otherwise:

> Disheartened, hungry and tired we arrived in Charleston. We did not know why we had been sent there but in every heart was a hope that it might be an exchange. They marched us through the city down into the burned district. As we halted on one of the streets a woman on the sidewalk said to me, "I don't think they will put you way down under the fire." This was the first intimation I received of what they intended to do with us, but it soon became known that we were to be placed under the fire of our batteries on Morris Island. The noble qualities of the southern chivalry were being shown to us every day, yet this was the most cowardly act of all, - to place unarmed men under the fire of their own guns. We continued the march to the jail and were turned into the yard. [9]

The Harsh Realities of Confinement

As groups were marched west down unpaved Magazine Street, their first glimpses of the gray gothic towers and looming walls of their destination almost certainly gave them pause. Remodelers of the 1850s had specifically employed a harsh, stern medieval design to intimidate lawbreakers and the Rebel Army no doubt hoped it would generate similar misgivings among Union captives.

Prisoner Graham McCamant Meadville said arrival for him included a meal but an unwelcome change of attire:

> We were placed in cells and the doors locked. About four o'clock, as nearly as I can tell, we were taken out into the yard and given rations – corn grits, fresh beef and salt; a big kettle and wood to make a fire to cook the rations.

That night General Beauregard issued new clothing to us...We were ordered to take off our Union blue and put on pure Rebel gray-the common butternut. Of course we were like the man who ate the crow, we didn't like it but had to do it because Bure said so and what he said, had to go. [10]

Some Charleston newspaper reports suggested accommodations were quite agreeable, albeit from a Southern point of view:

The Zouaves were detailed for guard duty at the jail. The Yankee officers, thirty-four in number, were placed in three good airy rooms (NOTE: "rooms" may refer to cells), on the second floor of the jail. The privates, to the number of one hundred and twenty, occupied twelve rooms on the uppermost story of the building. None of the rooms contain any furniture, but the prisoners all had their blankets, and seemed at no loss to make themselves tolerably comfortable. [11]

The manner of distribution of prisoners among the jail's four stories was provided by the author of a New York Times article published in 1891:

The Jail's First Floor

Of the four floors of the jail, the first was occupied by criminals, black and white, with all the intervening shades of color to be found at the time in all the Southern cities. The men charged with the graver offenses were kept closely confined in cells, but the ordinary, every-day thieves were permitted to have an outing in the yard once a day under the delusive impression that they were getting a change of air. I talked with a number of those white criminals, not one of whom but stoutly declared that he was innocent of the offense for which he was arrested and that he was convicted on perjured testimony, and I found that without exception they were in favor of a vigorous prosecution of the war, and were certain that in the end the Yankees would have to succumb to Southern valor. Indeed, some of these fellows affected to regard with contempt the ragged men who slept in ragged tents in the filthy yard and in the shadow of the gallows. It assailed the last fortress of one's manliness and pride to be patronized by these outcasts and to have a burglar looking down on you with an air of lordly superiority.

On the Jail's Second Floor

The second story of the jail was occupied by Confederate soldier, officers, and enlisted men, who had either been convicted of offenses against the rules and regulations of the Southern Army, or who were impatiently or nervously awaiting trial. There were fully a hundred of these unfortunate men, and, in the main, they were not bad fellows. Some of them were veteran soldiers, and keenly felt their humiliation, but the majority were (sic) heartily glad to be in prisons rather than the front.

On the Jail's Third Floor

On the third floor were confined a number of our colored soldiers who had been captured at Wagner and different points along the coast. They were lean, dirty, and ragged; not a few had repaired their trousers and coats with pieces of canvas purloined from the tents in the yard, and the effect was very odd. Our colored comrades were not only "the innocent cause of the war," but they were also the cause of the suspension of the cartel agreed to for the exchange of prisoners. Yet I never heard a decent Union soldier say a word against them, and I can bear evidence to the fortitude with which they bore their privations and their simple but unwavering faith in the ultimate triumph of the Union cause. Often after 9 o'clock at night, when by the rules we were confined to our quarters, I have been aroused from a doze by the singing of the colored prisoners. At such times the voices, coming down from the upper floors of the jail, sounded very sweet, and there was a certain weird, indescribable sadness in the minor-key melodies that told of camp meeting days and the religious hope that seemed to be confined exclusively to these poor fellows.

On the Jail's Fourth Floor

To give completeness to the heterogeneous character of the inmates of this jail, I must add that the very top story was occupied by deserters – deserters from the Confederate Army, who grew more and more numerous as the war progressed...were by all odds the most degraded creatures in this wretched place. They kept aloof from the military prisoners, not from a sense of shame, for they were incapable of that, but because they feared the manly indignation of soldiers whose cause they had betrayed... [12]

Uncharacteristically, a Union sailor sent there in 1863 reported he enjoyed relatively roomy accommodations, according to a passage in "The Story of a Strange Career being the Autobiography of a Convict" by Michigan author Stanley Waterloo:

We were taken to the top floor and had an entire corridor to ourselves. There being about sixteen large cells, twelve feet square, we had plenty of room – in fact, each of us could have had an entire suite to himself had he desired it.

Much to my surprise, a single mattress and blanket were sent up to me by some of my former acquaintances. I considered it only proper that such good fortune should be shared... so we used the mattress for a pillow, and, by sleeping "spoon fashion," we made the blanket cover us all. I may now state that it was the only time that we had a blanket during our imprisonment. In all of that part of the building there were no furniture of any description. We had to utilize the floor for all purposes. Our food consisted of cold boiled rice, and was brought to us twice a day in a tin pan. Table etiquette was dispensed with for the time being, and our fingers had to be used for disposing of the food. The evening of the seventh day some of the provost guard took us to the railroad depot en route for Columbia. [13]

WHY THE JAIL'S YARD WAS DESPISED

Since the jail building itself was already jammed with ordinary prisoners and deserters, most Union captives resided in the hated yard of the jail. According to their accounts, they were exposed to the extremes of the weather, battled vermin that infested the ground and were overwhelmed by the stench of overflowing latrines.

In a book written after their release, Union captives Asa B. Isham, Henry M. Davidson and Henry B. Furness provided their observations:

...we were turned into the jail yard, a filthy, lousy place, with an insufficient supply of water, and what little there was of it was unfit for use, by reason of its brackishness and warmth. There were a few "A" tents, not nearly enough to afford shelter to all. There was a tent next to the gallows in which an enlisted man from Andersonville was dying of yellow fever. The mess of six to which the writer belonged was assigned to this tent. We sat down upon the outside until the breath left the body, when the corpse was removed and we took possession of the quarters, lying upon the ground, as no boards or bunks were furnished. Our old comrades, who had preceded us from Macon, had been paroled, and were in occupation of Roper and Charity hospitals, where they had good quarters and could procure some of the necessities of life. Many of those who came with us from Savannah were also paroled and sent out to the hospitals - among whom were four of our messmates.

The jail yard was surrounded by a brick wall, twelve feet high(sic), upon two sides, and by the work-house and jail upon the other two. The privy-vault was over-flowing; we were cut off from the sea breeze, and the sun poured down his fiercest rays upon a sandy soil, producing a stifling atmosphere and heat almost over-powering. Occasionally, a sort of whirlwind would play over the yard, filling the air with fine dust and sand, adding to the misery of our condition. [14]

Lieut. Alonzo Cooper, 12th N.Y. Cavalry published in 1888 an account of his stay in the jail. Cooper and his comrades had been captured at Plymouth, N.C., and, after stints at Andersonville and Macon prisons, wound up in Charleston:

This jail yard itself was filthy to a fearful degree, and was enough to create an epidemic. An old privy occu-pied the south-west corner of the ground, the vault of which overflowed into the yard and emitted an effluvia that would be certain to create disease, even in an otherwise healthy locality. We petitioned to have this nuisance abated, and after a week or more, upon the recommendation of Dr. Todd, who was the attending physician, and who tried to do all within his power to render our situation more bearable, some men were sent in one night to tear down the old privy and clean out the vault.

This took all night and most of the next day, and during that time, Charleston jail yard was the most revolting place that civilized humanity ever occupied and lived.

As I have said, there were only fifty 'A' tents to accommodate six hundred officers and, as not over two hundred and fifty could possibly be crowded into these, there were three hundred and fifty officers without shelter of any kind, and as the weather part of the time was rainy, the suffering among those was fearful and a frightful mortality must have ensued, had we been compelled to have remained there much longer. As it was, I have no doubt that the germs of disease were planted there that afterwards cropped out in some form, and perhaps in many cases resulted in broken constitutions, and even death.

Cooper said that another ongoing hardship was the lack of wood to fuel cooking fires.

In our extremity we broke up the lumber of the old privy that had been torn down, and tried to cook with that; but as the pails we used to cook in were mostly without covers, and the old lumber was so thoroughly permeated with the filth it had so many years covered, that the rations thus cooked were too revolting to the stomach to be eaten.

The ground of the jail yard was a sandy loam, and the yard having been occupied by prisoners for a long time, was actually alive with vermin, with which we were soon supplied to an extent that was discouraging to those who had any ideas of cleanliness.

In the center of the yard was a gallows, which had evidently been erected for a long time, and had probably done considerable service. This was a post about twenty-five feet high, with a horizontal arm extending out about eight feet; at the extreme end of this arm and also at the top of the post where the arm joined it, there were pulleys for a rope to run through. A weight at the end of the rope running down the posts, acted as a drop to elevate the body of the victim from the ground

and lifted him towards the end of the extending arm.
This gallows we cut down and used for fuel. [15]

Nineteenth Regiment Massachusetts Volunteer Captain Jack
Adams had been taken to the jail after being captured at the
Battle of Cold Harbor in July 1865. In an account preserved in
"The Patriot Files" (an Internet site "Dedicated to the preserva-
tion of military history"), Adams said:

> One day the rice was so poor and so full of bugs
> that we refused to accept it and held an indignation
> meeting. We drew up a petition to General Jones, the
> rebel officer commanding the department, asking, if
> the rebels could not or would not issue rations enough
> to keep us alive, that our government might be allowed
> to do so. The next day they sent in the same rice, and
> as the petition did not satisfy our hunger we ate it,
> bugs and all, to keep from starving. Another day they
> issued nothing but lard. What they thought we could
> do with that I never learned, but I drew two spoonfuls
> on a chip and let it melt in the sun.
>
> We had no change of underclothing, no soap to wash
> with and were covered with vermin. We hunted them
> three times each day but could not get the best of
> them. They are very prolific and great-grand-children
> would be born in twenty-four hours after they struck
> us. We made the acquaintance of a new kind here,
> - those that live in the head. We had no combs, and
> before we knew it our heads had more inhabitants
> than a New York tenement-house. After a hard scratch
> we obtained an old pair of shears and cut each other's
> hair close to our heads.
>
> We were growing weaker day by day; were disposed to
> lie down most of the time, but knew that would not
> do, so resolved to walk as much as possible. We craved
> vegetables, and scurvy began to appear, sores breaking
> out on our limbs. One day a naval officer bought a

watermelon. As he devoured it I sat and watched him, the water running out of my mouth; when he had finished he threw the rind on the garbage pile, and I was there. I ate it so snug that there was not much left for the next.

Our home was under a window of the jail. Sometimes it would rain all night and we would have to sit crouched against the walls. [16]

The elements could be a particularly ferocious enemy to those forced to endure them in the jail yard, Glazier wrote in his diary.

September 20. - I find myself weak and exhausted this morning, with blood feverish and my system racked with pain, the result of yesterday's suffering; for it was one of the most wretched days that I have passed since my capture.

Nothing could have been more lovely than the morning, but the sky was soon overcast with dark clouds, and one of the most fearful thunder-storms broke forth that I have ever witnessed, followed by a severe and drenching rain, which continued during the day and night. We were without shelter, or wood to build fires, and were obliged to exercise constantly to keep from chilling.

At night, as there were no signs of the storm abating, we sent a committee to wait upon the jailer, to obtain permission, if possible, to go inside the jail, as there a number of unoccupied cells, but were refused admission without a reason being given.

Before morning the yard became flooded with water some four or five inches deep, and with our garments drenched and our limbs benumbed with cold, we were

compelled to walk through this flood, in order to keep
the blood in circulation.

There were a few small out-houses connected with the
jail, formerly used as sinks, and which were in the most
loathsome and filthy condition; yet into these a small
portion of the prisoners crowded themselves, and
were partially protected from the storm, but suffered
almost as severely from the obnoxious vapors, as we
from the drenching rain. [17]

Captain Adams vividly recalled the yard:

We found the jail yard a filthy place. In the centre was
an old privy that had not been cleaned for a long time,
and near it was a garbage pile, where all the garbage
of the jail was deposited. A gallows occupied a place
in the rear of the yard. The wall surrounding the yard
was twenty feet high, so that no air could reach us and
the hot sun came down on our unprotected heads. [18]

WHAT PRISONERS ATE AND HOW THEY PREPARED IT

Isham, Davidson and Furness in "Prisoners of War and Military
Prisons" said the quality of the food supplied by the jailers and the
cooking of it once it was received, were particularly challenging.

The ration was scanty, and very poor in quality. The
issue was as follows for ten days; corn meal, five pints;
flour, three pints; rice, two quarts; beans, black and full
of bugs, three pints; two ounces of bacon, and a small
quantity of salt. We only had such cooking utensils as
we had purloined and brought with us from Savannah.
The issue of wood was scant; not enough to permit us
thoroughly to cook our provisions. [19]

An unidentified captive recalled rations for a New York Times
piece published in 1891:

The rations at the Charleston jail were not only limited, but they were very bad. The cornmeal was musty, and we had to cook it as best we could in a number of rusty skillets. Some of the more ingenious of the prisoners added water to the meal and let it stand till it fermented, when it formed a sour, vile-smelling drink which they called "beer." The bacon issued to us was very little and very strong. it was as rusty-looking as the skillets, and the rancid taste asserted itself in the throat for hours after it was eaten. The cow peas were not at all bad. They were said to be "nourishing," and I ate them for that reason, but I never hankered for them if I could anything else to stay my hunger. [20]

Even drinking water posed a problem. The jail was located in a swampy area of brackish, polluted water. It's unclear when the two cisterns still on view in the jail's attic were installed but even if available during the war, they apparently were inaccessible to jail yard prisoners. As the unidentified prisoner of "With Gun and Caisson: Scraps from the Notebook of an Artilleryman" put it:

…an artesian well supplied us with water for washing. We drank rainwater, as all the citizens did, and every roof and parapet in sight was thickly set with broken bottles to protect the unused watershed from the turkey buzzards. [21]

And from A.O. Abbott's *Prison Life in the South*:

A single pump, in an artesian well in the jail-yard, was the only means of getting water, except after a rain, when we could get it out of our old cistern. The well was nearly dry after 2 o'clock P.M. each day, for it was affected by the tide. The water was brackish, and to many a fruitful case of sickness. [22]

Rations provided by the jail sometimes were augmented with items obtained from outside its walls. In *Prison Life Part 1 of*

Delaware County by T.B. Helm, 1881, food was sometimes delivered from home:

> The prisoners got some things from the North, though not a tenth part of what was sent. Before a box was brought into "the prison, a man would take an ax and knock the box in, to see that nothing contraband was inside. Sugar, coffee, butter, canned fruits, would all be smashed" together into one confused mass. [23]

Prisoner Joseph T. Darling of Company F., First Maine Cavalry, wound up in the jail yard in 1864 and benefited from a family visitor.

Occasionally, inmates were allowed visits from relatives and Darling's sister, who feigned loyalty to the South but whose heart was really with the North, one day delivered a leather valise which, when opened, delighted Darling.

> What a sight for a soldier prisoner to look at! A nice boiled ham, a nice beef roast, a boiled beef tongue, biscuits, cakes, butter, cheese, preserves, a bottle of wine, salt, pepper, ginger-snaps, tea, coffee, sugar, etc., etc. I had now been in Charleston prison six weeks, and had become so emaciated and weak because of improper and insufficient food, that I could not walk up stairs in an upright position. I had to use my hands and go on 'all fours.'

> Food was issued to us at 3 o'clock p.m., and consisted of cornmeal of the very worst and coarsest sort. We were given nothing to cook it in, nor could be find anything in the prison or yard. Finally, they sent us in some old rusty frying pans which we had to scour out with a piece of brick before we could use them.

> Mr. Simpson, a great tall, red-headed old rebel, was prison commissary. My comrades chose me as their commissary to draw and distribute their rations. But

the boys made a sorry mess of it, cooking their meal without salt or fat. In a great city by the salt sea, yet we could get no salt! Those who had money could send out and buy it. A few days after our arrival, I discovered a great round iron pot in one of the underground cells, from which we were separated by an iron grate. I asked Mr. Simpson if we could have it. He told me it was broken, but I assured him that we could fix it, so he got the keys, unlocked the old door and turned it on its rusty hinges, and two of us went down and got it.

One of the three legs was broken, and a three-cornered hole had broken out with it. I took a piece of pie wood and made a plug as nearly the shape of the hole as I could, and leaving it long enough outside for a leg, I drove this in from the outside, then poured in a bucket of water, and the wood swelled and stopped the hole completely. This made a splendid pot to cook mush in. Mr. Sims had ordered a cord of pine wood for us, and when the rations came again, we scoured the old pot with brick, and I made mush for fifty-two men. I had a small bag of salt which my sister had brought, and some of the boys had bought some, so we had salted mush that day. But what a feast for me and my chum! A slice of ham, a slice of roast beef, a biscuit, and a dish of tea with sugar in it - the first good meal since we were captured.

We had a few sick boys in our company, and straight mush was not very palatable, so I fixed up something nice for them every day. When my sister left, she gave me a roll of Confederate bills, two hundred dollars in all, equal to about twenty dollars of Uncle Sam's greenbacks. With this I could buy flour, milk, salt, and such things as we needed, so I was able to share in part with all of the boys.

Preparing food required a good deal of creativity. Pots, pans, grills and utensils were fashioned out of whatever inmates could scrounge. Darling said:

> ... I saw a large iron spittoon in one of the cells and it took my fancy, so I asked the commissary to get it for me. 'What in the world do you want with that' he asked. 'I want it to bake bread in,' I replied. Well, he laughed, and some of the boys standing around laughed also, but I got the iron cuspidor and an old furnace door with one hinge broken off and smooth on one side. Now I was fixed. I put the spittoon on the fire and got it red hot. Of course, that made it clean, as far as dirt was concerned. I then took a brick and scoured and cleaned it until it was bright. The furnace door I also scoured and cleaned in the same way. Now, I was just made. I had money; I could buy flour; I had salt and soda, and Mr. Simpson gave us meal. I also bought pork and bacon. I made bread of flour and meal in loaves. I would grease the now new Dutch oven, heat the furnace door and put it over it, and bake just as nice a loaf as one would wish to have. Sometimes I worked all day and baked a lot of bread for the boys. The cooking utensils we had were those brought from Macon, and were not half enough to supply our wants.

> The greatest trouble I had was cooking. I had no special qualifications for that work, and could not boil dish-water without burning it on; but according to our rule, I must cook for our mess once in three days. My feet were bare, and the rice or mush would boil over on them, and as I jumped back I was sure to land in some other fellow's fire. [24]

From A.O. Abbott's *Prison Life in the South*:

> Some of the men found the plates to the oven, and had broken them up, and were using the doors and

pieces of the front for "griddles," upon which they baked their corn meal.

HOW SOME WHITE UNION PRISONERS WERE TREATED

The treatment of POWs ranged from cruel to kind. Examples of both were recorded by 28-year-old Frank Bennett of the 55th Pennsylvania Volunteers, captured March 16, 1862 and locked in the Charleston Jail two days later. According to his experience as preserved by the Historical Society of Pennsylvania:

> He described his first few days in Charleston Jail as not unpleasant. He was in better spirits than some of his comrades, although he acknowledged that "a glass of whiskey kindly given us by Captain Sage may have had much to do with this." Although he was aghast at 'this narrow cell, the nail studded door doubly locked and padlocked upon us and the strangely barred windows,' he was hopeful that the situation would be temporary and was generally impressed with the kind treatment he received upon arrival.
>
> When Bennett again picked up his diary on May 1, he revealed that the five weeks since his last entry had not been as pleasant as the first few days. The brutal monotony of prison life had dampened his spirits, and he found that the visits of Sheriff Dingle, "a gentlemanly man" who visited on Sundays, were a unique pleasure. Bennett reflected that the half hour spent with Sheriff Dingle passed more quickly than a minute on other days. Prison life was a never-ending cycle: 'eat, sleep and smoke, then sleep, smoke and eat.'
>
> He was soon moved to Columbia where he found confinement even more unpleasant." [25]

As might be expected, those with the upper hand tended to turn to intimidation, perhaps as a way to vent frustration. Dr. John McGregor in his "Reminiscences" recalled a chilling visit by city officials.

> We were not long in our new quarters before we were called upon by some of the dignitaries of Charleston. At first, they seemed pleased to form our acquaintance, and said that they would do all they could to make our visit pleasant. Very soon, one of the party went to a window, and called our attention to an object which was in the prison yard. On looking out, we saw the same number of ropes suspended, with loops at the ends, that there were of the pirates which the North had just taken. Turning to us, with a leer such as none but a Southerner can express, he said, "Gentlemen, if your Northern friends hang those privateers, just so many of you will hang there." Col. Corcoran straightened himself up, and, with defiance flashing in his eyes, made this reply: "We all realize that we are in your power, at present, and we know that you can do with us as you please. It is the duty of the North to hang those men, and I hope that they will not shirk their duty." And many of the prisoners said, "Amen!" Those brazen faced men soon left the cell, and we saw them no more. [26]

Samuel Harris said his treatment in the jail yard by Rebels was even-handed:

> Our rations were fair, and the officers and men on guard over us were generally kind. We were kept in Charleston about three weeks, when we were taken by cars to Columbia, S.C... [27]

Acts of kindness from townsfolk were also noted. Captain John Adams recalled a particularly poignant example as he and some other prisoners were to be moved from the jail:

October 1 the yellow fever broke out. Our guards were the first taken down, the captain and some of his men dying; then it struck the officers in the prison, and it was not thought safe to remain longer in Charleston, so October 5 we were ordered to pack up and informed that we were to be removed to Columbia. Our squad did not go until the 6th, but they started us so early that we had no time to cook our rice. As we left the prison I bought an apple dumpling off an old colored woman, and am ashamed to say that in my haste I forgot to return the spoon she loaned me to eat it with. If she will send me her address I will send her a dozen as good as the one she lost. [28]

Jail-yard life frequently proved as monotonous for guards as for prisoners. Sometimes the POWs could use this to their advantage, as revealed in this surprisingly light-hearted account in *Prisoners of War and Military Prisons* by Isham, Davidson and Furness:

We were always ready to avail ourselves of any chances to provide for our present and future necessities. Two prisoners in the jail-yard were about shirtless when, upon the morning of the 5th of October, we were ordered to be ready to move to Columbia, S.C. in the evening. The "A" tent we occupied was nearly new, and we saw in it material not only for shirts, but also for shelter in a possible and highly probable emergency. How to become possessed of it was a matter which puzzled us, as the guard was constantly patrolling just back of the tent, between it and the wall. But the genius to accomplish was not wanting. As the light of day began to wane, we cut every other stitch throughout two widths clear across the tent. Then, as the shades of evening fell, we began to hurl choice billingsgate at each other with voices which continually waxed louder and louder. This attracted the guard to the spot, and, the audience thus secured, the show promptly commenced, to his great delight. We buckled to it like prize-fighters, clinched and fell, gouged and bit, kicked the tent poles out, and were covered up in the general wreck.

From Isham's "Prisoners of War and Military Prisons"

"We buckled to it like prize-fighters..." Isham wrote

As we emerged from the ruins each one called upon the guard to witness that the other fellow did it. The guard was unable to decide who did it, and he did not care; he was only sorry that such an untoward 'accident' had ended his enjoyment of an interesting combat. He marched off to the other end of his beat, and we improved the absence to disengage the loose tent widths, roll them up in our blankets, and spread out the rest of the tent over the ground so that no loss of canvass would be apparent. When the order came to

**move out we felt as rich as lords, staggering under all
we could carry. It proved valuable to us at Columbia as
a roof for our "dug out," and as a sort to shelter until
this dwelling-placed was completed.** [29]

HOW SOME BLACK UNION PRISONERS WERE TREATED

As the war progressed, Union officers and war strategists
found they needed more troops and eventually recruited blacks.
Previously, they had resisted placing weapons in their hands, in
part because they were unconvinced they could be made disci-
plined soldiers. Instances of bravery by black regiments would
prove them wrong but blacks captured by the Rebels were often
subjected to abuses even more severe than those accorded whites.

In his book *A Brave Black Regiment,* Luis Emilio said scorn for
black Union soldiers who were captured during the failed assault
on Fort Wagner on July 18, 1863 began even on their march to
the jail.

**The next morning, that of July 19, the Fifty-fourth pris-
oners, numbering twenty-nine, hereinbefore named,
and possibly others reported as missing, of whom no
other record is found, were taken by their guards to
the city of Charleston, where, upon their arrival, they
were greeted by the jeers and taunts of the populace as
they passed to the provost-marshal.** [30]

Under South Carolina law, reimbursement to counties for
the dieting (feeding) of imprisoned blacks was at a cost less than
the cost to feed whites. Among the papers of the late Emmett
Robinson at the South Carolina Historical Society was an excerpt
he apparently found in the 1863 South Carolina Statutes at
Large. On Page 13 of Volume 13 is found the daily allowance
for county jail prisoners, "...Sheriffs shall...be entitled to charge
and receive, for dieting white persons confined in jail, $1 per day
each; and for dieting slaves or free persons of color, 80 cents per
day each." [31]

Capt. Jack Adams refers to captured blacks:

The jail was filled with all classes of criminals, male and female, and, with the exception of the women, all were allowed in the yard during some portion of the day. There were also several soldiers of the "Maryland line" who had refused to do duty longer for the Confederacy, and several negroes belonging to the 54th Massachusetts, captured at the siege of Fort Wagner. The negroes were not held as prisoners of war but rather as slaves. Their captors did not know exactly what to do with them. They were brave fellows, and at night we could hear them singing in their cells. I remember a part of one song. It was a parody on "When this cruel war is over," and ran as follows:

"Weeping, sad and lonely

O, how bad I feel

Down in Charleston, South Carolina,

Praying for a good square meal"

Adams wrote that the prison's black prisoners were not the only African Americans singing sorrowful songs:

Negroes passed the prison nearly every day on the way to Fort Sumter to restore the works which were being knocked to pieces by our batteries and gun-boats. They were collected from the plantations in the country and were a frightened looking set. They knew that their chances for life were small, and they sang mournful songs as they marched along. [32]

Emilio's book includes numerous accounts of the horrendous conditions for black prisoners at the Charleston District Jail. Members of the 54th were among those captured during the failed assault on Fort Wagner July 18, 1863. Of twenty-nine delivered to the jail, some were so badly injured they immediately were taken to Roper Hospital on nearby Queen Street where the plight of patients both black and white was gruesome. Emilio quotes from a Charleston Courier article published July 23:

A chief point of attraction in the city yesterday was the Yankee hospital in Queen Street, where the principal portion of the Federal wounded, negroes and whites, have been conveyed. Crowds of men, women, and boys congregated in front of the building to speculate on the novel scenes being enacted within, or to catch glimpses through the doorways of the long rows of maimed and groaning beings who lined the floors of the two edifices, but this was all they could see. The operations were performed in the rear of the hospital, where half a dozen or more tables were constantly occupied throughout the day with the mutilated subjects. The wounds generally are of a severe character, owing to the short distance at which they were inflicted, so that amputations were almost the only operations performed. Probably not less than seventy or eighty legs and arms; were taken off yesterday, and more are to follow to-day. The writer saw eleven removed in less than an hour. Yankee blood leaks out by the bucketful. . . [33]

Back at the jail, the remaining of the 54th were "… compelled to do menial and often repulsive work about the prison, or elsewhere about Charleston whither some were sent." [34]

In the meantime, the governor of South Carolina, M.L. Bonham, and Confederate States of America Secretary of War James A. Seddon debated the disposition of the blacks since some were believed to be slaves and others free. Should the former be returned to their masters and the latter remain prisoners of war? Ultimately they couldn't decide and left the fate of all in the hands of Confederate officers. All the while the confined blacks, Emilio said, "suffered and fretted in the jail yard."

From the time of their capture, therefore, until December, 1864, when Governor Bonham turned them

over to the military authorities again, these poor prisoners were in constant uncertainty regarding their fate, with the gallows standing in the jail-yard as a reminder of what that fate was to be. They did not know, as appears herein, that action was suspended in their case, for the statements (of prisoners who testified after the war) indicate that they believed their trial, or at least their liability to be tried, extended over many months. [35]

A white Union officer confined in the jail and later exchanged was given a list of black prisoners and urged newspapers to circulate it. The list appeared in an August edition of The New York Tribune, with the accompanying note written by one of the blacks:

I do in behalf of my fellow-prisoners earnestly hope and pray that this may be the means, through you, sir, of procuring our release. The privations of the white soldiers are nothing in comparison to ours and in our destitute condition, being as it were, without friends, and in the enemy's hands, with an almost hopelessness of being released, and not having heard from our families or friends since we were captured. [36]

Captain H.A. Coats, Eighty-fifth N.Y. Infantry, confined in the jail yard with 400 others, told a Congressional Committee appointed to investigate prison abuses of blacks:

Later in his testimony, Captain Coats says that there were about twenty-five colored prisoners in the jail. They had nothing to eat but a small loaf of corn bread. They were compelled to clean out the jail and carry out all the filth from the prisoners, a work the whites were never made to do. [37]

Emilio then presented a series of accounts provided by prisoners who offered observations of District Jail prison life, particularly as it affected the blacks there:

Capt. Frank E. Moran, Seventy-third N. Y. Infantry, was there in July, 1864, and testifies that there was a number of colored prisoners there. They were allowed to come into the yard once a day for water. One of them was murdered by the guard while coming for water.

Lieut. Harvey G. Dodge, Second Penn. Cavalry, was taken there in August, 1864, and says that the water was miserable. There was a double row of tents then, extending around three sides of the yard, and four in a tent. It was almost impossible to keep clean; everything must be laid in the dirt; not a stone or piece of wood to lay anything on. Says there were about forty of the Fifty-fourth there, and some felons and convicts confined in the jail for desertion and other crimes. The captured colored soldiers had been there about a year, and were kept in close confinement, except two or three who were made to do the work of the prison.

Capt. Samuel C. Timson, Ninety-fifth New York infantry, was taken there Sept. 13, 1864. He says: — "There were twenty-one negro soldiers, most of them belonging to Colonel Shaw's Fifty-fourth Mass. regiment of immortal memory, among the number. They were never to be exchanged, but were to be reduced to slavery. They were all that were left of the colored troops captured at Wagner. The rest were bayoneted and shot after they surrendered. Their rations were bread and water; still they would sing Union songs, pouring their melody through their prison bars for the entertainment of the Union officers in the prison and below."

He says there was no shelter for these officers. Filth, garbage, and urine were all about. The gallows were still in the jail-yard. Shells exploded about the jail. On Sept. 16 there was a great bombardment, but only two were injured, and slightly. No cooking utensils were provided. A lot of lean beef was brought in and thrown down to divide. Sept. 17 the yard was so foul that no resting-place could be found. There was no shade. Night was welcome. Only salts were given as medicine. Sept. 20 the yard was submerged in consequence of two days rain, and the filth was intolerable. Colonel Jones, the commandant, did not reply to remonstrances for three days, and a second application brought answer that it was the best they could do. Capt. Timson's statement is to be found in the New York Tribune of March 15, 1865.[38]

Emilio said only one contemporaneous statement of a "colored" prisoner has been found. "It is a letter of Sergeant Johnson of the Fifty-fifth Mass., previously referred to, published in the Boston 'Liberator' of Oct. 7, 1864. He says: —"

I was captured by Confederate cavalry, Nov. 12, 1863, and have been a prisoner-of-war ever since... My treatment has been very humane considering the circumstances of the case. The Confederate authorities show a disposition to release all free men, and as we come under that head, we hope a movement in that direction will be soon made. About fifty of the colored troops are at the jail in Charleston. They are not confined in cells, but volunteering to work they are permitted to go into the yard. Most of the men have hardly enough clothing to cover them. Their food consists of one pint of meal each day. They receive nothing else from the Confederate authorities but this meal, and some of them say they never have enough to eat. Others do cooking for persons confined in the jail, and in this way get more to eat. The men speak of the treatment in other respects as not very harsh compared with the treatment they expected.

Emilio seemed to regard this account with a degree of suspicion:

> **It will be observed that the sergeant's statement
> of their treatment indicates less harshness towards
> them than has been gleaned from others' statements
> embodied herein. This may be explained by the fact
> that the 'Liberator,' or rather the extract in our posses-
> sion, does not give the source or means by which this
> letter was received, and if it came through the enemy's
> hands, subject to their scrutiny, possibly its statements
> were tempered to pass the Confederate authorities.** [39]

Emilio said that after the siege of Charleston and the city's surrender in 1865, black soldiers had heard much about the District jail and sought to tour it:

> **Opportunities were given officers and men to visit the
> city, where they wandered about, deeply interested in
> sight-seeing. Several Fifty-fourth officers were detailed
> there, and always entertained visiting associates. The
> most interesting building to us of the Fifty-fourth was
> the jail, - a brick structure where the prisoners of the
> regiment were confined many months with black and
> white criminals as well as other Union soldiers.** [40]

THE BIZARRE STORY OF ABRAHAM LINCOLN'S BROTHER-IN-LAW AND THE CHARLESTON DISTRICT JAIL

Sometimes, treatment of prisoners bordered on the bizarre. Particular disgust was recorded by more than one veteran for alleged abuses by Dr. George Rogers Clarke Todd, the brother of Mary Todd who was the wife of President Abraham Lincoln. How President Lincoln's brother-in-law came to serve the Confederacy was an anomalous product of the very nature of a civil war - some families were split in two by political allegiances.

According to historian Terrance Strater who maintains an Internet web page about Dr. Todd and the Todd family, the doctor sided with other family members vowing loyalty to the Confederacy.

Dr. George R.C. Todd accepted an appointment as a Confederate surgeon and reported to the medical service in Virginia. He joined half bother Captain David Todd, in charge of prison camps. Both brothers were accused of harsh treatment of union prisoners after the battle of Bull Run in summer of 1861. George was alleged to have been so brutal that he would kick the dead bodies of union soldiers, calling them "Dammed abolitionists". (Ross 1973) Several officers complained to Jefferson Davis, Confederate president, and Dr. George Todd was later assigned as surgeon to the 10th Georgia Volunteer infantry, part of the Kershaw Brigade.

Later on, Todd was put in charge of the First South Carolina Hospital at Rikersville, about four miles from Charleston. Strater said his research suggests Todd's abusive manner continued.

At Rikersville, Dr. George Todd was alleged to have abused union prisoners in his care at the Hospital. A Union Lieutenant from his home state of Kentucky was said to have infuriated him so that he threw him from his hospital bunk and ordered him bucked and gagged for more than an hour. The Lieutenant died the next day. [41]

Todd's duties apparently included the treatment of prisoners at the Charleston District Jail. In his "Brave Black Regiment" about all-black 54th Regiment prisoners at the jail, Emilio identifies Todd as the jail's surgeon and notes additional testimony by Captain H.A. Coats who was a witness at a Congressional investigation after the war:

The rebel surgeon in charge at Charleston was Todd (Mrs. Lincoln's brother). He acted badly towards them. The officers said he would come around among the men and kick and abuse them without trying to benefit their condition in the least. Later in his testimony, Captain Coats says that there were about twenty-five colored prisoners in the jail. They had nothing to eat but a small loaf of corn bread. They were compelled to clean out the jail and carry

out all the filth from the prisoners, a work the whites were never made to do. One negro had charge of a ward where our officers were. Each ward had a kind of wash basin. One of our deserters confined there took out the basin, although the negro told him the doctor would not permit it. But the deserter took it out nevertheless. Later the deserter abused the negro who replied: 'You have no right to talk in that way, — a man who deserted from the United States Service.' Said he, 'I am a soldier in the United States service, and you are a deserter.' The deserter told Doctor Todd, who called up the negro, and he having told his story, it was corroborated by some of the officers. Doctor Todd said he did not care a damn, and had the negro taken out and given forty lashes. When the negro came back he said: 'For God's sake, how long has this thing got to last?' This Todd was considered the most degraded of all the rebels the prisoners had to do with. [42]

Emilio included another Todd-related incident in his book:

Capt. C. W. Brunt, First N. Y. Cavalry, was confined in hospital at Rykersville, four miles from Charleston, in September, 1864. He testifies that Dr. George R. C. Todd was in charge, and claimed to be a brother of Mrs. Lincoln. He states that Todd was a profane, obscene, and brutal man. In his madness he would pound and kick the Union officers, and caused some to be bucked and gagged for spitting on the floor. Brunt testifies later as follows: —

'One of the colored nurses (a soldier captured at Wagner) stopped to talk to me. Todd saw him and ordered the guard to have him whipped. Soon the screams of the poor fellow convinced me the order was being executed.' [43]

PRISONERS' PASTIMES INCLUDED SONG

When not preoccupied with basic survival, prisoners often found time weighed heavily on their hands, particularly in the Charleston jail. One unidentified writer of a New York Times article headlined "Under the Union Guns" article in 1891 said:

> One may ask, what did the prisoners do! Many things. They cooked and ate, performed their daily ablutions, washed their clothes, went on the "skirmish line" hunted for gray backs (lice), and, when all these were done, they went from room to room, chatted, played cards, or checkers, or chess; made rings out of bones, or chairs out of barrels, etc., etc.

> In Libby there was always something going on. Men were carving bones or holding mock courts or playing checkers or discussing exchange, but here in Charleston there seemed to be nothing left us but to mope by day and sleep by night. It was evident that the stoutest was losing strength, if not heart, and it required hard work to combat the apathy and indifference that at times settled down on one like a wet, impenetrable cloud. [44]

But many remember taking comfort in singing and listening to songs. In his book "The Capture, the Prison Pen and the Escape", Capt. Willard Glazier wrote :

> At the close of day the negro prisoners made a practice of getting together in the jail, and singing their plaintive melodies till late in the evening. The character of their songs was unusually mournful; and it was often affecting to listen to them - always embodying, as they did, those simple, child-like emotions and sentiments for which the negro is so justly celebrated. The harmony and rich melody of their voices are rarely surpassed. Indeed, this seems a special gift to them. This very

fact gives the surest promise of their future elevation and refinement. No race so delicately sensitive to the emotional can be essentially coarse and barbarous.

One song, which appeared to be a special favorite with them, was written by Sergeant Johnson, whom I have before mentioned. He intended it as a parody on 'When this cruel war is over.' I give the song as it was furnished to me.

> 'When I enlisted in the army,
>   Then I thought 'twas grand,
> Marching through the streets of Boston
>   Behind a regimental band.
> When a Wagner I was captured,
>   Then my courage failed;
> Now I'm lousy, hungry, naked,
>   Here in Charleston jail.
> CHORUS
> Weeping, sad and lonely -
>   Oh! how bad I feel;
> Down in Charleston, South Carolina
>   Praying for a good 'square meal'

The negroes sang this song with a great deal of zest, as it related to their present sufferings, and was just mournful enough to excite our sympathy. [45]

In "Prisoners of War and Military Prisons", Isham, Davidson and Furness also described singing:

The jail was filled with union colored soldiers, deserters from both armies, thieves, prostitutes, and murderers. This horde was turned out to mix with us for a few hours every evening. Each of these classes - colored soldiers, deserters, and jail-birds - had their distinctive songs, which, in the early evening, they were accustomed to sing alternately. This was rather enlivening, and we could stand a little of it very well. When, however, they all vociferated at the top of their bent, it was as though pandemonium were let loose. Not infrequently, they kept up the infernal discord all night.

There was some melody in the negro voices, and they touched the ear very pleasantly. The deserters drawled out their airs in a rich Irish brogue. There was rather too much sameness of sentiment in the different verses and monotony in the measure. When the ear had to submit to the same strain a dozen times repeated, nearly every night, it may not appear astounding that it came to be considered on of the great discomforts of the jail-yard. But the jail-birds' singing was a rasping jingle which harrowed up the soul and set a man to hunting up brickbats, and longing for dynamite and earthquake. [46]

And in "Gun and Caisson," published in the New York Times, an inmate named other tunes he heard fellow captives sing:

Some of the prisoners slept in the rear wing of the jail, and many a night we who lay in the tents below listened to the voices at the open windows singing "Tramp Tramp", "John Brown's Body", "The Red, White, and Blue" and all the other patriotic songs. [47]

Still captive late in the war, Captain "Jack" B. Adams said that the singing eventually ceased:

The life in the jail yard began to tell on us…groups would get together, sing old army songs, and merry laughter would be heard as some wit told his story, but now we heard no songs; the men walked about sullen and silent; it required little provocation to bring on a fight, as all were nervous and irritable. Our quarters grew worse each day, as nothing was done to change the sanitary condition of the yard, and six hundred men, each doing his best, could not keep it clean unless assisted from the outside. [48]

A SECRET SOCIETY PRODUCES DRAWINGS OF THE JAIL THAT REACH PRESIDENT LINCOLN

In an effort to bolster morale, Dr. John McGregor used his time in the jail yard to rally his comrades into a "secret" society. As Jeremy McGregor wrote in a biography of his father:

> The thought becomes almost unbearable, when our minds go back to December 31, 1861, and resurrect the scenes which were then taking place in that loathsome prison. Two hundred of our most valiant and patriotic men were huddled together within those walls. Men of unblemished character, whose minds soared above rebellion, whose intellects were of the highest order, were suffering for want of bread ad many of the necessaries which sustain life. Men who would never knowingly do a wrong thing, whose minds were as unbending as the forest oak, were by fever and famine brought to a premature grave. But amid all their sufferings and hardships, their minds were at work. You can imprison the body but you cannot confine the mind within prison walls. The mind must be free, or it will desert its throne. Many of our noble soldier boys became idiotic, and died by being deprived of food and water while in those prisons.
>
> The doctor knew that the mind must be employed in some way, to keep it from their terrible situation, or death would ensue; so he went to work and formed a secret organization with these brother prisoners. It was more for the purpose of keeping their minds from their sufferings than anything else, and I have heard him say that he believed that it saved his own life and many other lives.
>
> Among those prisoners was an artist of the highest reputation. As they were moved from one prison to another, he would sketch everything within his view appertaining to the prisons. In some mysterious way

his sketchings (sic) found their way within our lines, and were forwarded to Washington. President Lincoln by some means or other got hold of them. He had them enlarged, and they made a very interesting picture for those who belonged to that organization which was formed at Charleston Jail, and who were lucky enough to get once more within our lines. [49]

Courtesy of the Library of Congress

**Detail from a Union Prisoners Association poster
shows jail yard 's pump**

This poster and another made later include several rare drawings of the jail yard. One includes a view that shows the octagon and a water pump that once stood just behind it in the eastern portion of the space. Depicted are several prisoners and a guard with shouldered rifle. Next to the guard is some sort of fowl, probably a chicken.

COMMERCE AT THE JAIL - CURRENCY EXCHANGES AND THE SUTLERS

Even behind bars, some Union soldiers had cash that they used to ameliorate their plight, however modestly. Jailers sometimes permitted limited commerce among POWs and "sutlers," a breed of traveling salesmen that followed armies and gained access to prisoners being held. Wares consisted mostly of food and small, personal items for mending clothing or grooming.

The trick for captives was either to avoid confiscation or somehow obtain cash once jailed. Incredibly, some inmates successfully had funds sent to them by relatives or friends. Equally astonishing were those able to retrieve money taken from them by their captors.

Then, there was the problem of how to spend it. Sutlers were compelled by those in charge to accept only Confederate tender, thus necessitating an exchange of Northern "greenbacks" for Confederate paper. These transactions were effected by a number of enterprising Southerners who somehow found their ways into the prison population. Typically, a single Union dollar would fetch many times that number in Confederate script. Consequently, inflation meant a single sweet potato could cost two dollars and a simple comb, ten dollars.

This jail economy could create temptations that the penniless — which included many inmates — found difficult to resist. Given that all felt their interments were wholly unjust and that sutlers were simply taking advantage of them, some resorted to thievery. Isham, Davidson and Furness in *Prisoners and Prisons*, with tongues planted firmly in cheeks, cited an example in which a robbed merchant found no sympathy among prisoners nor the jailers :

There was a sutler in the jail with a little stock of bacon, flour, beans, bread, soda, etc., in all worth perhaps about fifteen dollars in greenbacks. The sight of these things to famishing men who had no means with which to purchase but intensified their longing for them, and five or six officers, most of whom belong to the regular army, decided that if possession consti-

> **tuted nine points of the law the other point...might be waived as not being applicable under the statute to hungry prisoners of war, since only civil humanity had been comprehended in the purview.**

The account says the soldiers drew up a list of resolutions declaring "that Union offers who would rob a sutler were unworthy of the name, a disgrace to the uniform they wore" and were "a stench in the nostrils of those with whom fate had associated them, then promptly took his goods "in the dusk of the evening."

The jailer, upon learning of the theft, assigned the task of investigation the crime to the prisoners, themselves. Of course, they found no culprits. All were exonerated by the jailer. The account concludes:

> **The only other party interested in the issue was the sutler. What loss there was, of course, fell to him. But an increment of experience accredited to him which is beyond estimate, though enough probably to save him in the future from the waste of a large aggregate capital and thus much more than counter-balance the temporary loss. The report was accepted as exhaustive, and further proceedings were not deemed necessary in the premises.** [50]

Surviving "Friendly Fire" - Union Prisoners Under Bombardment by Union Guns

Besides the life-threatening neglect and deprivation prisoners suffered at the jail, Union prisoners were also in peril from another, peculiar menace - the continuous shelling by their own cannon from Morris Island. While Confederate strategists had placed them in harms way in hopes the bombardment would be stopped, many inmates reported the barrage actually cheered them up, giving evidence that the struggle continued.

This phenomenon is described in *A Life in Prison* by T.B. Helm:

While at Charleston, S. C., the bodies of prisoners were put into the old "jail yard," and, after-ward, into the "Roper Hospital," both under fire of the Federal batteries. I suppose notice was given to the Union officers, as movement seemed intended as a protection to the city of Charleston. It had no effect however, for the Federal Guns boomed away just as before. They shot beyond us, and no shells ever harmed a single man, except one, by a fragment. That hospital had been struck by a ball that had gone through two walls and the floor, into the basement. But none came near it while we were there.

As has been stated, the rebel authorities put the prisoners under the fire (from) Federal batteries. Instead, however, of receiving any harm there from, they thoroughly enjoyed the situation. It was an agreeable relief from the tedious monotony of ignorance, which so for so many months had been suffered. Before this time, we had been wholly cut off from the world and especially from our friends, and from the operations of the Union army. Now we were in sight and hearing of our fort and guns.

Night after night we stood and watched the shells as they sped their way from the batteries, flying in their shining arch of light above our heads, to carry new terrors to the hearts of the forlorn dwellers in the wretched city so long under siege. And the new situation was decidedly one of comparative pleasure and satisfaction. The prisoners were, considering all things; an orderly and well-behaved set of men, fully as much so as could reasonably be expected. [51]

From a writer in the New York Times "Under the Union Guns" article in 1891:

I recall now, as a curious psychological phenomenon, the fact that the booming of our guns over on Morris

Island, and the shrieking of the shells that went circling overhead and frequently fell close by, affected me like a generous stimulant. They were not intended to hurt me or my friends, and so I entirely lost sight of the terror they were so well calculated to inspire. As a rule, the moral effect of shells, particularly on green men, is far greater than their destructive power, and if the moral effect be proportioned to the size of the shell, and I am inclined to think it is, those sent into Charleston by Gilmour's (NOTE: Probably "Gilmore") Swamp Angel, six miles away, were enough to ruin the steadiest nerves in the city. Yet they made music for me, and I loved to listen to them in their flight, and to catch the downward rush and deafening crash of their explosion, for they seemed, not like missiles of destruction, but messages from near-by friends who would gladly brave death if there was a chance that the effort would result in our rescue.

From sixty to a hundred shells were thrown into the city every day and not a few at night, and as a result fires were of frequent occurrence, and frequently persons were killed, principally negroes, perhaps because the population at this time was principally of that color. Curiously, no shell fell in or about the prison, though now and then a fragment struck the outside of the wall. Many of us wanted to have the shells come nearer, not that we were bloodthirsty or wished to see men killed, but for the sake of the promised excitement. We were in the mood of savages, and would have hailed with a shout of joy the news that Charleston was burning from limit to centre, and that the jail, the poorhouse, and the gallows were going up in the conflagration.

I am very sure the shelling had a beneficial effect on the other prisoners. It was a species of kite flying that amused and exhilarated the most apathetic, and stirred up a spirit of speculation and curiosity as to "where the next one would bust." As the shell flew faster than the sound of the concussion that projected it, it usually exploded in Charleston before we heard the roar of the gun from Morris Island. Every twenty minutes, sometimes less, someone would shout out: "Watch out, boys! here she comes!"

On hearing this no matter how often it was repeated, the most indifferent assumed an attitude of interest and, shading his eyes, looked off to the east. A streak of silvery smoke sweeping up like a quickly-drawn and quickly-obliterated white line against the amethyst blue of the sky. Up, up till a black speck like a far-off bird can be seen. It balances in midheaven, apparently so directly overhead that it must inevitably fall straight down on the beholder. Then a shrill, tortured cry comes down from the sky, increasing into a blood curdling roar that sounds as if an aerial locomotive is about to make a landing with the throttle valve open and the whistle at its loudest. Down, down, then the black mass vanishes behind the prison wall; the earth shakes under the impact and explosion, a column of dust shoots into the air, and, feeling quite exhilarated, we lie down in the stifling shade of the tent to await the next one.

The Swamp Angel usually rested at night, but now and then, and particularly on Sunday nights, when of all times the people in the city prayed for quiet, a few messengers would be sure to arrive. At Vicksburg and Chattanooga I had seen a good deal of night shelling, but the missiles at both place were insignificant compared with Foster's 200-pound shells. The flight of these shells, as marked in an arc of carmine fire against the black wall of the night, was indescribably fine, and the unearthly shrieking seemed to be intensified till all the air trembled in alarm. Then the crash, the fountain of fire, illuminating all the surroundings for an instant like a flash of lightning, and after it shrieks and curses

in the distance, followed by darkness and a silence that
was absolutely thrilling. [52]

From the comparative safety of nearby Roper Hospital,
Adjutant S.H.M. Byers saw a Union shell strike the jail:

> Yesterday there was a large fire in the vicinity of the
> prison: all the fire-companies — black, white and
> yellow — were out and labored till dark with the fire,
> and all the night with whisky. Gen. Foster cannonaded
> the city at a terrible rate, while the fire lasted, and as
> the shells were thrown at the firemen, many of them
> came in close proximity to the prison. One shell struck
> the building, passed trough the rooms, and slightly
> injured one prisoner. Many pieces of shell fell in the
> yard.

> During the conflagration the white and black firemen -
> who were pumping in front of the prison, drank whisky,
> from the same bottle, and got "gloriously drunk,"
> together. What a people to talk of abolitionism, and
> sneer at negro equality. [53]

While watching rounds aimed at their captors might have
been invigorating to some inmates, these events were tempered
by concern for one's own safety: Sam Harris recalled:

> Few shells were fired into the city during the daytime,
> but as soon as it came night, they would begin firing,
> and many times there would be three or four in sight
> at one time. Most of them were fuse shells and each
> would leave a streak of sparks behind it similar to a
> large sky-rocket. They were a beautiful sight. The
> shells were from eight to twelve inches in diameter
> and about two feet long. They were fired at an angle
> of more than twenty-two degrees. They would be fully
> one mile high before they would turn to come down.
> One starlight night I lay on my back watching them,
> when one looked as though it was coming directly at

me. I jumped up and ran several feet, when I stopped and thought, "What a fool I am to try to get out of the way in so small a place." I looked up and saw the shell go directly over us, yet high up in the air. It struck over a mile beyond us. I went back and laid down on my side so I could not see them, and then went to sleep.

One day several of us were sitting under a small locust tree in one corner of the yard playing cards, when a shell came over a little to our left, but the fuse being cut several seconds too short, it exploded when it was about three hundred feet in the air. A piece of it about as large as two hands come over and cut the body of the tree off just above our heads. We scratched out on all fours to get out of the way. [54]

The shelling was of great interest to those outside the jail, as well. Amazingly, townsfolk hoped to profit from those that didn't detonate. From *A Strange Career being the Autobiography of a Convict*:

They sounded like a heavy wagon-wheel going over a rough pavement. Next would be a heavy thud, and, in a few seconds more, a terrible explosion. At first, percussion shells were used, but quite a large percentage of them would turn in their flight through the air, and as they would not strike fuse first, no explosion would take place. A lot of men were always watching for such shells to strike. With shovels and pickaxes they would dig them out of the ground. The rebel ordnance department paid one hundred dollars in Confederate currency for every unexploded shell delivered. The next move was for the Yankees to change from percussion to time fuses. The first shell did not explode on striking, so a crowd, as usual, started to unearth it.

Quite a number of spectators were watching the fun. Suddenly the operations were suspended. The time fuse exploded the shell, killing several persons and

wounding a number more. Of course the Yankees were loudly cursed for playing such a mean trick, but the ordnance department got no more of our shells.

The second day after our arrival a shell passed over the jail and landed in a frame building only a block distant. When it exploded, timbers and boards flew in all directions. We could see the dust and splinters in the air quite plainly from our window. Somehow, I felt pleased whenever one of those missiles came along, although we were liable to be killed at any time by one of them. [55]

Fires were feared by all of Charleston but it didn't always take shells from Morris Island to start them. Closely packed wooden buildings were constantly vulnerable to fires fanned and encouraged by winds from the Cooper River. A particularly devastating one began in a sash factory near Hasell Street on December 11, 1861. It raged westward for blocks and threatened the inmates of the Charleston Jail. As transcribed in a biography of captive Dr. John McGregor by his son:

We were confined in an upper room, the windows of which were barred, and closed with iron shutters, except one very small one, overlooking a very narrow street in the rear of the building...we heard the cry of "Fire! Fire!" and our prison cell, for the first time since we arrived, was illuminated. As nearly as we could judge, the fire broke out in a gas house, next door to a sash and blind factory. The fire spread with great rapidity. Great efforts were made to extinguish it, without the slightest effect. The engines, worked by negroes, seemed utterly powerless, and the flames spread, finally to the jail. The roof soon took fire, No movement was made to let the prisoners out. We could hear the guards making the doors more secure. At first we not alarmed, for we expected, in case the fire should reach the jail, we should be let out; but when we heard the cry, "The jail is on fire!" and heard

the guards making the door more secure, we were dismayed. At that time our room was so filled with smoke that we expected very soon to be suffocated. We formed ourselves into a circle and commenced marching around, and as we passed by the window we would take a breath and than pass on. The heat was becoming intense; but at last the fire was subdued and we were saved, for what purpose we know not. At this time our allowance of food was one pint of oatmeal and one quart of stagnant water a day. [56]

The fire, one of the most devastating in Charleston's history, reportedly destroyed 600 homes.

LEAVING THE CHARLESTON JAIL BEHIND

While the war raged, the flow of prisoners into the Charleston Jail was continuous. However, all of them would eventually depart, one way or another.

Typical was Graham McCamant Meadville, who wrote of his departure from the jail:

We remained in Charleston Jail until July 14th, when we signed a separate parole sheet of which they kept a copy. We were ordered to get ready to go home and we received rations - nine circular hard tack, a good sized piece of razor back, sow meat - and marched to the railroad station in charge of a Home Guard Company, nearly all Jewish Merchants in the City of Charleston, accompanied by their negro servants, as the Barons of old were, by their armed vassals. [57]

In some cases, disease caused the transfer of prisoners from Charleston prisoners. Capt. "Jack" Adams' stay was thus interrupted, as he later wrote:

October 1 (1864) the yellow fever broke out. Our guards were the first taken down, the captain and some of his men dying; then it struck the officers in the prison, and it was not thought safe to remain longer in Charleston, so October 5 we were ordered to pack up and informed that we were to be removed to Columbia.

We were sorry to leave Charleston. While it was called the "hot-bed of secession," we had received the best treatment there of any place in the South. Our guards were kind, and we were seldom taunted by the citizens. We marched through the city, taking our baggage, and, as no two were dressed alike, were a queer-looking procession. There were many Germans in the city, and as we had several officers in our party from that land, they were anxious to do them favors. One had a bottle of whiskey and gave it to one of his countrymen when the guard was not looking. Our comrade had on a rebel jacket, and as he indulged quite freely in the whiskey soon got returns and was fairly full, but the guard, thinking that he was a citizen, said, "You get out of the ranks," and he got. Assisted by his friends, he was soon passed through the lines, and we afterwards heard from him with Sheridan in the Shenandoah Valley.

Arriving at the depot, we were placed in box-cars, and, as usual on the southern railroads, the train ran off the track in a half-hour after we started, which delayed us several hours. The night was dark and rainy, and several escaped, among them Lieutenant Parker of the 1st Vermont heavy artillery. He was pursued by bloodhounds, and when we arrived at Columbia was brought in so terribly torn and bitten by them that he died before night. [58]

Courtesy of the Special Collections and Archives Division, USMA Library

This may be the earliest photograph (possibly 1865) of the jail

Most surviving graphic depictions of the Charleston District jail are from old maps, drawings and etchings, the latter mostly from Civil War-era publications, and sketches prepared by inmates. But a picture said to have been taken in November 1865 could be the earliest, surviving photograph of the jail. (Actually, the author has seen two, slightly different versions of this shot.)

By the time they were made, the rectangular brick structure that had been the Magazine Street jail for 63 years had been expanded and remodeled. Added were the front Gothic facade and towers as well as an octagon of cellblocks to the rear.

The photos consist of a crystal-clear representation of the jail and include a portion of its infamous neighbor to the east, the Work House, (by then, the "colored" hospital). The photos were taken from the northwest corner of Franklin and Magazine Streets. The changing location of shadows on the portion of the western wall visible in both shots suggest they were taken in the late afternoon, one just after the other. A pair of figures caught in the corner of one of the shots stare directly into the camera.

Whether or not the two images actually were captured in 1865, as existing attribution suggests, they certainly were taken prior to 1886. The shots depict an intact jail of four stories and with ventilation tower atop the octagon. This tower and the entire top floor were destined to be removed after damage incurred in a great earthquake.

CHAPTER 7

BAD FOOD, BAD BLOOD AND AN EARTHQUAKE: THE JAIL'S FINAL 75 YEARS

With the end of the Civil War in the spring of 1865 came the release of Union prisoners, including those confined in the Charleston District Jail. The conflict had left much of the South in shambles, and this was particularly the case in Charleston. Many of the city's public buildings had been pocked, pounded and knocked down by shot and shell. Fires had destroyed entire city blocks. The economy was decimated and hope was in short supply.

The city and its inhabitants had been vanquished. Individual attempts to regain a semblance of stability were played out in a post-war landscape of radical change to what had been the old order. The conflict had produced deep and prolonged resentment on both sides and so the transition often was difficult.

Presumably, however, life at the Charleston District Jail returned to something like it had been before the conflict had so dramatically altered its routine. As so often seems the case when tracing the jail's history through surviving records, great gaps in time separate one account from another. Of the jail 20 years after the war, little is known. But an event in the waning days of the summer of 1886 literally shook the building to its foundation and ultimately cost it its entire upper story.

1886-GreatEarthquake"...LikeThegrowlofawild beast swiftly approaching its prey..."

At precisely 9:51 p.m., on August 31 of that year, the earth in the region began to heave. Charlestonians were caught completely unaware and in minutes whatever normalcy they had achieved in the previous two decades was horrifically shattered. Although the Richter Scale of seismic energy measurement wouldn't be developed for another 49 years, some experts estimate that Charleston's quake would have registered between 7 and 8. Put another way, some say, the energy released by such force might approximate that of the largest thermonuclear bomb ever tested. [1]

Carlyle McKinley, a Charleston News and Courier editorial writer was on duty that night on the second floor of the newspaper office on Broad Street when the first tremor hit. His astonishingly detailed account of the event appeared on the paper's front page three days after the quake. Here are excerpts:

> The streets of the city were silent and nearly deserted. Overhead, the stars twinkled with unwonted brilliancy in a moonless, unclouded sky. The waters of the wide harbor were unruffled by even a passing breeze. Around the horizon the dark woodlands hung like purple curtains shutting out the world beyond, as though nature itself guarded the ancient city hidden within the charmed circle. Earth and sea alike seemed wrapped in a spell of hushed and profound repose, that reflected, as in a mirror, the quiet of the blue eternal heavens bending over all.
>
> It was upon such a scene of calm and silence that the shock of the great earthquake fell, with the suddenness of a thunderbolt launched from the starlit skies; with the might of ten thousand thunderbolts falling together; with a force so far surpassing all other forces known to men, that no similitude can truly be found for it. The firm foundation upon which every home had been built in unquestioning faith in its stability for all time, was giving way; the barriers of the great deep were breaking up. To the ignorant mind, it seemed, in truth, that God had laid his hand in anger upon His

creation. The great and the wise, knowing little more, fearing little less than the humblest of their wretched fellow creatures, bowed themselves in awe as before the face of the Destroying Angel. For a few moments all the inhabitants of the city stood together in the presence of death, in its most terrible form, and perhaps scarcely one doubted that all would be swallowed together and at once, in one wide yawning grave...

McKinley said he and others spilled into the streets and that cries of pain and fear could be heard from all directions.

The air was everywhere filled, to the height of the houses, with a whitish cloud of dry, stifling dust arising from the lime and mortar of the shattered masonry which, falling upon the pavement and stone roadway, had been reduced to powder. Through this cloud, dense as a fog, the gas-jets flickered feebly, shedding but little light, so that you stumbled at every step over the piles of bricks, or became entangled in the telegraph wires that depended in every direction from their broken supports. On every side were hurrying forms of men and women, bareheaded, partially dressed, some almost nude, and all nearly crazed with fear and excitement.

Aftershocks continued, some as terrifying as the first. As dazed victims struggled to cope with what had befallen them, the horror continued, according to McKinley:

A sudden light flares through a window overlooking the street. It becomes momentarily brighter, and a cry of "Fire!" resounds from the multitude. A rush is made towards the spot; a man is seen lying doubled up silent and helpless, against the wall; but at this moment, somewhere - out at sea - overhead - deep in the ground - is heard again the low, ominous roll which is already too well known to be mistaken. It grows louder and nearer, like the growl of a wild beast

swiftly approaching its prey, and all is forgotten in the frenzied rush for the open space, where alone there is hope of security, faint though that be. [2]

There were over a hundred quake-related deaths and destruction was widespread. The most severe damage in Charleston occurred in the swampy neighborhood of the Charleston District Jail. Researcher Christine Trebellas' quoted geologist Clarence Edward Dutton who, in his paper "The Charleston Earthquake of August 31, 1886," said the buildings on the block sustained "unusual injury" since they had been erected on "made" (fill) ground. [3]

An article in the September 1, 1886 edition of the Courier told of the terror experienced by inmates at the jail:

The scene at the Jail beggars description. When the building began to shake the prisoners made a dash for the door. Capt. Kelly, however, stood at the door, pistol in hand, and firing a half dozen shots kept the crowd back. Their shrieks could be heard for squares and many of the inmates dashed themselves madly against the bars in their efforts to escape. They were kept within doors, however, and although the building was badly shattered none of them escaped. [4]

However, Capt. Kelly told a News and Courier reporter later that 38 of the prisoners he had taken down into the jail yard had managed to escape.

According to Richard Côté, in his astonishingly detailed book "City of Heroes - The Great Charleston Earthquake of 1886," the jail's walls had been cracked:

It was soon clear that many of the prisoners fled chiefly from the fear of being crushed to death in their cells. These inmates soon returned voluntarily to custody, knowing that it would be better to serve out their relatively short remaining terms than to be recaptured later

and given much longer sentences. Such was the case of James Goff, an accused murderer, whose family asked for bail for him but had been turned down. His family promised the court that he would voluntarily surrender himself "… as soon as the earthquake shocks cease." Those who remained at large consisted chiefly of hardened criminals, who faced long terms. "The cream of the gang - the prisoners charged with capital crimes, and the accomplished burglars were among the forty-two who decamped [in the initial jailbreak] on Tuesday night," the newspaper reported. [5]

After several days, Côté said, prisoners who hadn't fled were moved to improvised holding areas at the Citadel and its square but following an aftershock, two more escaped, leaving ten in custody. Ultimately, said Cote, a stockade was built on Franklin Street to house prisoners until repairs to the damaged jail could be made:

The escaped prisoners — and criminals in general — seemed to have caused the city more fear than actual harm. Whether through efficient law enforcement or because criminals had more important things — such as survival — on their minds, crime was low in the weeks after the earthquake. There were no reports of looting and only scattered accounts of thievery. [6]

It is not clear when the jail was re-opened but the earthquake had inflicted so much damage on the block where it sat that many buildings, including the massive Work House on its east side, eventually would be demolished.

Courtesy of the US Geological Survey

The Work House (City Hospital by the time of the earthquake); towers, crenellations were damaged

Sometime during the 1890s, the jail itself was lowered by one entire floor. Besides the wall, the quake had severely damaged the jailer's quarters in and around the facade towers, caved in the octagon roof, left the ventilation tower in shambles and opened gaping cracks in the octagon's foundation.

The damage was so extensive that the entire top floor of the original building and the rear octagon were removed. As part of repairs, crenellations along the roof line were added to make the remaining three-story building look just like the old one.

Also removed was the 40-foot tower that had been perched atop the octagon roof. A photograph made just after the quake shows the extent of damage to it and other depicts the jail after the tower was razed.

Courtesy of the Charleston Library Society

Octagon tower badly damaged

Courtesy of the Charleston Library Society

The ventilation tower had been removed from the jail (left) by the time this photo was taken; the Work House is on the right had yet to be demolished

According to Christine Trebellas, "From this event through the 1920s, the public function of the block was systematically reduced. The "Colored" Hospital (formerly the Work House) was razed, Roper Hospital was moved in 1904 and the Medical College abandoned its site at Queen and Franklin in 1914." [7]

The down-sized jail, however, would continue to function as the District's primary repository of lawbreakers for another half century.

1912-Assistant Jailer Shoots City Chain Gang Chief- from the Jail!

Political differences among some Charleston city officials occasionally grew passionate and, in more than one case, involved bullets. Late in the summer of 1912, the city superintendent of chain gangs was shot while walking towards the front of the jail. His assailant apparently drew a bead while standing just inside the jail's front door and witnesses said that even more shots were fired from windows of the jail's upper stories.

Photo by author

Assistant jailer was shot by the city chain gang chief from the front entrance

While the Charleston District Jail was supervised by the county, city prisoners were held there, too. These inmates were clad in stripes and routinely taken from the jail to toil at various work projects both public and private. Typically a city guard arrived at the jail in the morning to escort prisoners to the work sites.

This routine was dramatically interrupted on a hot Saturday morning. The August 18 edition of the Charleston Sunday News reported:

> **William E. Wingate, superintendent of the city chain gang, was shot and wounded by Clarence Levy, assistant jailer at the County Jail on Magazine street, between the hours of 6 and 7 o'clock yesterday morning. The shooting is said to have been the outcome of political differences between the two men. Wingate's wound was at first thought to be only a slight one, but later more serious symptoms developed.**

The article noted that assistant jailer Levy, subject to a warrant charging him with assault and battery, was being held in the very jail in which he was employed. Meanwhile, there appeared to be several versions of the chronology of the altercation and subsequent gunplay:

> **Accounts of the shooting are conflicting. It appears, however, that Wingate went to the Jail yesterday morning early according to his custom to take the chain gang out for their day's work. Levy, when seen by a reporter yesterday, stated that Wingate approached the gate of the Jail and said, "Well, I put it all over you last night," referring to the county campaign meeting at the Hibernian Hall on Friday night. Levy stated that he replied, "You didn't put it over me," and that Wingate then said, "Come out in the street, – – you, and I'll put it over you." With that, according to Levy, Wingate threw his hand to his right hip pocket. Levy stated that he had been holding the key of the Jail in his right hand and that his gun was in his left hip-pocket. He stated that when he saw Wingate throw**

his hand towards his right hip-pocket, he (Levy) drew his revolver and fired before Wingate could get his weapon out. Levy stated that Wingate then ran around the corner of the building, but that in a few minutes he returned with his gun in his hand. Levy said he then fired again and that he thought that was the shot which hit Wingate. Levy stated that a few minutes later he heard someone blow a whistle on Magazine street towards Logan, and that he was informed that it was Wingate.

The piece said the victim was unable to make a statement to a reporter but an associate and eyewitness offered another version of what happened:

W.H. Churchill, a member of the chain gang guard, who acts as captain of the guards in the absence of Wingate, stated...that at the time of the shooting he was approaching the Jail in company with a Mr. Laffan. Churchill stated that when they were opposite the Behlmer grocery store near the Jail they heard two shots, a great deal of screaming and the faint blowing of a whistle. They then ran on to the corner, said Churchill, and as they approached the Jail door, they saw Wingate standing in front of the door outside. Churchill stated that Wingate said, "I'm shot. Levy shot me," and that he told them to bring his bicycle, which was leaning against the wall. Churchill stated... as (Wingate) turned around to go for the bicycle five shots were fired from a window on the third story of the Jail.

Levy denied emphatically Churchill's statement that five shots had been fired from an upper story of the Jail.

Jailer William J. Bennett told the reporter that he arrived at the jail after the shooting and asked Levy to hand over his gun, a .25 calibre Colt. The article continued:

> Wingate's wound is in the left chest. The bullet was removed shortly after the wounded man's arrival at the Infirmary… The trouble between Levy and Wingate is said to have had its root in the charges made by A.W. Perry, candidate for sheriff, at the county campaign meeting concerning rations given the prisoners at the Jail. [8]

This dispatch was published in a newspaper the day after the incident, bearing the headline:

Exciting Shooting Affair Occurred Yesterday

Political Enemies Meet

Clarence Levy, Assistant Jailer, Shoots

William E. Wingate, Superintendent

of Chaingang Guards

> Special to The State - Charleston, Aug. 17, 1912 - A shooting affair here this morning at the county jail, in which Assistant Jailer Clarence Levy shot and wounded William E. Wingate in the side, caused tremendous excitement, because of the fact that the two men are of warring political factions, the Martin and Perry supporters. Wingate is superintendent of the city chaingang guards, and is the man who procured for A.W. Perry the famous bucket containing a sample of chaingang dinner.

> Mayor Grace declared today that the shooting of Wingate was a premeditated plot. Jailer Levy claims that Wingate this morning, after an altercation, advanced upon him with a drawn pistol, and he shot in self-defense. Wingate claims that he was about to enter the jail in performance of his duties, and that he

was fired upon without notice from the jail. He is not thought to be fatally wounded.

Sheriff Martin denies all knowledge of the affair, beyond what Levy told him. The assistant jailer was arrested after the shooting and kept at the jail under the guard of a policeman, since it was not practicable for him to leave at the time. Later he was arrested on a warrant of Magistrate Williams, charging him with assault and battery, and held at the jail pending a hearing.

The two men had a difficulty last night at the campaign meeting, and the shooting today is believed to be the outcome. [9]

The city police chief said he believes his chain gang guard was ambushed without provocation. He added that the shooting was the second of a city policeman by a county officer within several months and that he intended to "…use every means to get the facts of the case for the prosecution of the assistant jailer." [10]

By August 20, the chain gang chief was said to be recovering and the Sheriff issued an opinion, as reported by the newspaper:

Capt. William E. Wingate of the city chain gang, who was shot by Assistant Jailer Clarence Levy on Saturday, has probably passed the danger mark. It will be, however, some days before the preliminary examination can be held before Magistrate Williams. The police investigation into the affair continues, and Chief Cantwell says that he will be able to prove that Wingate was shot from ambush. Sheriff Martin stated today that he has also been investigating the matter and he feels sure that Levy shot in self-defense, even if he was on the inside of the jail. [11]

In January, Levy was tried for assault and battery with intent to kill and about a month later, the verdict was rendered:

> **Charleston, February 21 - Clarence Levy, assistant jailer, was acquitted of the charge of assault and battery upon W.E. Wingate today in the court of general sessions. Wingate is the superintendent of the city chain gang, and last summer, when the feeling of the county campaign was running high, Wingate was shot one morning, as he approached the county jail to take the city prisoners out to their task. Levy was charged with having shot Wingate from within the barred sallyport. Levy's defense was that he had fired in self-defense. The jury was out only about 20 minutes. [12]**

Victim Wingate's fortunes, however, continued to go poorly. Eight months after Levy's acquittal, he was again wounded by gunfire in an even more spectacular example of campaign politics run amok. Newspaper readers awoke on the morning of October 16, 1915 to the following:

> **Political Row Ends**
> **In Shooting of Six**
> **Men in Charleston**
>
> —
>
> **Newspaper Reporter is Killed and Four**
> **Others Wounded in Pistol Battle - Entire**
> **Regiment of Militia Called**
>
> —
>
> **Charleston's turbulent municipal campaign resulting in the Democratic primaries last Tuesday being held while seven units of the State Guard was held ready to do police duties, reached a crisis today in a pistol battle in a room where the Democratic Executive Committee was about to meet to canvass the returns. When the smoke of the fight had cleared from the**

room on the second floor of a three-story building at King and George Streets, five men had been shot and others were nursing various bruises.

Sidney J. Cohen, a reporter for The Charleston Evening Post, was shot through a lung and died soon afterward. W.A. Turner, an insurance agent, also was shot in a lung and is in a serious condition, as is W.E. Wingate, superintendent of the city chain gang, who is suffering from a bullet wound in the scalp. H. L. Wilensky, a city meter inspector, was hit in an arm and Jeremiah O'Brien, inspector of weights and measures and member of the Executive Committee, was shot in the ankle. All the wounded were expected to recover.

The article said that others involved included a marine engineer, an ice wagon driver and a stevedore (both former policemen), a deputy sheriff and a keeper of a cemetery. No charges had been brought against any of them. It continued:

Bitterness engendered by a campaign in which personalities seemed to have overshadowed real issues, the presence of the militia on primary day and the closeness of the vote created such a threatening atmosphere that many extra policemen were detailed in and in front of the building where the meeting was to be held. The building was crowded and a good sized crowd in front was held in check by the officers.

Just as the meeting was to be called to order someone started a fight in a hallway adjoining the committee room. During the scuffling, shouting and jamming in the hallway, someone in the committee room fired a shot and the real fight was on. Policemen in the hallway and committee room seemed powerless. Several pistols were brought into play and as the firing continued amid the scramble to escape, yelling and cries of the wounded, someone threw three ballot boxes out of the window.

Cohen was struck as he was making for a window to escape. A pistol for which two men were fighting was discharged and the bullet gave him his mortal wound. Whether any of the wounded were really participating in the fight had not been made known tonight.

The melee caused the governor to send military troops to restore order. The newspaper reported that ballot boxes had been tossed from the windows of the building but were recovered and that an executive committee would count the ballots the following day. [13]

1918 - CHARLESTON JAIL CALLED A "PURGATORY"

One of the most detailed, post-Civil War accounts of life in the Charleston District Jail was published in 1918. Businesman Paul Wierse titled his story "Eighty-Eight Weeks in Purgatory." Held on an unnamed charge, Wierse was critical of jail sanitation, jail food and his exposure to evangelists permitted access to the jail and its inmates.

A Prehistoric Jail

After a long and unsuccessful fight in the courts for liberty I was arrested on Saturday, December 21st... I soon was lodged in the Charleston County Jail. There I was confined until December 26th.

I was put into the "best room we have to offer," to use Capt. Bennet's (sic) words. It was a large room of solid masonry, small windows admitting some light. The "room" had already four inmates, one of whom, a merchant from Columbia, anxiously awaited his transportation to Atlanta which had been delayed, pending my arrival. Capt. Bennet was as good to his guests as was consistent with his duties. His apology for the poor accommodations was undoubtedly sincere. "The best room in the house" contained five cots, a table on which the meals were served, and a privy bowl

that could not be flushed but into which a tiny stream of water could be discharged by opening a faucet.

The room did NOT contain the least facility for ablution (Editor's Note: hand washing) or artificial light of any description. Cracks in the masonry gave egress (sic) to countless ants, and the first night a centipede dropped on my neck. I crushed it sleepily with my fingers, became wide awake, struck a match and ascertained the cause of the smarting. I had a sore on my neck many weeks after reaching Atlanta. But our room was heaven compared with some of the cells I had the opportunity to inspect, and we had certain privileges denied to others. The room containing a lot of chain gang prisoners was much worse. And the poor devils could not remove the chains from their ankles by day or night.

Surprisingly, Wierse said there were over two hundred women in the jail, the majority of them black. He said they were kept unseen behind "stout oaken doors..." and were "...packed like herrings." That observation he derived from a trustee whose duties he described:

In the morning he passed by my cell with a bucket so revolting and evil smelling that the stench lingered for a long time in the close atmosphere. Two more buckets followed, leaving consternation in their wake. After I got my breath back I interrogated the trustee concerning these buckets and he told me they were placed in the women's room for their private "convenience." It is too revolting a subject to be discussed, but think of it, oh, reader, to what horrid, shameless and unsanitary methods the women had to submit. And white women at that! Useless to say that the negroes enjoyed similar "conveniences."

Wierse said food was poor was prepared by inmates forced to work in the kitchen. "... it made me shudder," he wrote.

"Luckily prison terms in any county jail are short, as a rule; otherwise they would be equivalent to death sentences." He said some prisoners were fortunate enough to receive meals from the outside.

Wierse reserved particularly harsh criticism for the jailer's practice of permitting evangelists access to the jail's captive audience:

> I refer to the particular brand of religion handed out in prisons. The average prison preacher is a self-righteous man of the "better than thou" type who appeals to the imagination of ignorant prisoners in an effort to make them think little of the wrong perpetrated on them by exaggerating the wrong they have been guilty of. Fire and brimstone are abundantly employed in their pyrotechnic word pictures and the shivering wretches are told that they will be saved if only they meekly submit to their lot and kiss the hand that smites them.
>
> Such a gospel sharp entered our cell on Christmas eve. Telling us of his own sinless life, he begged us to bear our punishment with meekness and to be thankful for it, because it were necessary for the salvation of our souls. He unctuously held out the promise that even for such black sinners as we, salvation could be achieved under certain restraints and conditions.
>
> I listened to the man's self-glorification and condemnation of all others as long as I could stand it, but finally interrupted him. I told him to pray for those who had been instrumental in putting us in our predicament, as they needed salvation at least as much as we - if not more so. This seemed to rattle him. He went off on another tangent, telling us we should and must have faith in our mothers. Our mothers believed in Jesus, why then should we refuse to believe in the Savior? This was clearly adding insult to injury, and I told him that a few hours prior to his coming we had discussed religion very seriously and agreed on the infinite

mercy and love of God. "One of us," I continued, "is a Jew. His mother never did believe in Jesus, nor does he. What right have you to take advantage of his helplessness and try to ram your own religious views down his throat, contrary to the principle of religious liberty proclaimed by our fathers?"

He became very pale, and kneeling down, begged God to show us the error of our ways and to make us "good again." I concluded the prayer for him: "And, oh Merciful Father," I prayed, "make that conceited preacher aware of the fact that self-righteousness is one of the blackest sins, practiced by the Pharisees and condemned by our Savior - Amen."

That preacher went away a wiser if not a better man. He returned the next day, but never came near us, confining his efforts to terrorizing the negro prisoners. [14]

Wierse's opinion notwithstanding, it is likely that at least some of the prisoners welcomed visits by clergy. In fact, no telling of the Charleston District Jail story is complete without mention of evangelical pursuits there by the Reverend Obadiah Dugan for The Star Gospel Mission. For many years, the Mission, which still exists today, conducted Sunday morning religious services in the cellblocks.

Courtesy of the South Carolina Historical Society

**Star Gospel Mission's Rev. Obadiah Dugan and
chaingang inmate inside the jail**

According to its own web site, the organization was born in 1904 inside the Star Vaudeville Theater that had been closed down by the city "...because of the undesirable element associated with it." Dugan petitioned Charleston's mayor to permit him to use the old theater as a shelter for homeless persons. The request was granted and the first worship service on April 24, 1904 attracted 500 attendees. By 1920, Dugan had moved Star Gospel to an abandoned church building at 474 Meeting Street, where it still operates today. [15]

Star Mission archives preserved by the South Carolina Historical Society are inconclusive as to when jail visits started, but one newspaper clipping there is dated Sunday, February 20, 1927 and announces "The Star Gospel Mission will hold services at the county jail this morning at 10 o'clock, at the mission at 3 o'clock in the afternoon and at 7:45 o'cock in the evening, and at St. Andrew's convict camp at 5 o'clock in the afternoon."

Courtesy of the South Carolina Historical Society

Chain gang inmate spreads Mission gospel

Another, undated item in the archive probably appeared in a religious publication rather than a commercial newspaper. It is an unabashedly upbeat counterpoint to Wierse's derision. Headed "SERVICES AT THE JAIL - Star Gospel Mission Visits the Unfortunates and Offers Spiritual Comfort," it said:

> **If there is one hour in the week the prisoners serving time in the County Jail look forward to it is 10 o'clock Sunday morning, when the weary monotony is broken by the entrance of those versed and fitted to teach the Gospel of truth and life to the unfortunates forced to serve time for some crime they have committed against society. White and colored prisoners alike are eager to listen and hear the visiting people, and all of them stand as near as the cold bars surrounding them will permit.**

A Reporter took the opportunity recently to note the work done by officers of the Star Gospel Mission among the prisoners, and was much impressed with the earnestness and zeal displayed in endeavoring to show them the best way in deriving even some contentment in their present situation and how to again regain their self-respect after their release.

It was interesting to note the varied way in which two boys nearby behaved during the simple services. One of them evidently had underwent enough of the unpleasant Jail life and eagerly listened to the gentlemen and sang heartily in the selections, accompanied by Mr. Dugan on a little portable melodeon. The other, locked up for some unsuccessful venture in the petty thievery line, sat in a corner with sullenness written all over his face, and reminded one of the proverbial ex-convict who leaves prison with a fierce and undying hatred towards all mankind, and only lives to pay it back for the fancied wrongs it has exposed him to. He could not be drawn into the services, but instead ate with evident relish the food which at that time had been brought to the cell by the keepers.

The piece then lapsed into stereotypical and condescending vernacular that was common at that time:

Probably the most fruitful field of work is the colored woman's department of the Jail for the workers of the Mission, and the fervent ejaculations of the damsels during prayer and the hearty interest they displayed in the singing is altogether a novel sight. The present members of the chain gang were treated to several songs by the visitors, after which hymns were rendered by all. Whatever may be the failures of the individual darkies comprising the dreaded chain gang, it must be said that each and every one is a born singer, and while their interpretation of the songs was not of the most classic origin, the general harmony was there, and the bassos and tenors vied with each other in getting all the changes and combinations of chords there were to be gotten out of the hymn under treatment. [16]

1922 - JAIL "REPORT CARD": NOT THE WORST BUT NOT THE BEST, EITHER

The South Carolina Board of Public Welfare rated the Charleston District Jail fourth in the state, according to a story published March 5, 1922, in the State newspaper:

Newberry county boasts the best jail in the state, according to the grading of the state board of public welfare, this jail being given 943 points out of a possible 1,000. The Greenville jail came next with 915 points, Richland with 893, Charleston 869 and Chester 855. The five lowest scores were given as follows: Colleton with 535, Oconee, 525, Laurens 500, Calhoun 499 and Clarendon 493.

The report explained that points were allocated on a scale evaluating "permanent plant and equipment," management, personnel and repairs. It noted that a score below 650 points was classed as "...poor and is said to be unsuitable for the confinement of human beings." Though criticism of the Charleston jail continued unabated in other quarters, its score in this case seemed respectable. [17]

1930S-JAIL NEIGHBORHOOD FESTERS WITH DISEASE, CRIME

The neighborhood surrounding the Charleston District Jail was among the worst in the city. The blocks near the jail consisted of dilapidated residences and tenements. The area was described as the worst disease-breeding spot in the lower section of the city, as being rife with police problems and was a fire hazard. [18]

1931 - Feuding Checkers Players Resort to Razors

The tedium of routine jail life was occasionally disturbed enough to warrant mention in the local press. In a Post and Courier article published September 20, 1931, a game of checkers at the jail led to a razor slashing.

As a result of a quarrel in the Charleston county jail about a game of checkers, one negro prisoner was in Roper hospital last night and another was nursing wounds at the jail. According to jail authorities, they cut each other with safety razors when a charge of cheating passed at a checker game at 8:15 a.m. yesterday.

Drawing by Sam Wilson

Checker players resort to razors

James Smith, of Edisto Island, suffered severe lacerations of the forearm and both hands in the fight. He was a patient last night at Roper, and was in good condition. His release today or tomorrow is expected.

Ezekiel Green, of Union Heights, was cut on the temple, ear and hand. Green was given emergency treatment at the hospital and was returned to the jail.

John A. Gleason, assistant jailer, who is in charge of the jail in the absence of Captain William Bennett, jailer, who is on a vacation, said that the two men, held for minor offenses, were quartered in the same cage with fifteen other negroes. Green and Smith were playing checkers, and a dispute arose, being terminated when each grabbed a safety razor and started to work on the other.

The two negroes finally were separated and were taken to the hospital in a police patrol for treatment. Assistant Jailer Gleason said that men charged with minor offenses are permitted to have razors, so that they may shave themselves. Both negroes were being held for illegally using automobiles. [19]

1931 - 160 Inmates Too Many, Says Jailer

Periodic overcrowding continued to plague the jail. In a January 19, 1931 Post and Courier article headlined "Peak Load" Being Carried – Emphasizes Need of Prison Farm," the jailer issued a plea for relief:

The county jail population Tuesday noon was at its highest peak in over a year when the roster showed 160 on the list, approximately (illegible) more than the normal of capacity of the prison.

The jail, built for the accommodation of between 90 and 100 prisoners, has been overcrowded almost the entire past several years and according to Capt. W. J. Bennett, it has been fortunate for the inmates that no epidemic of some sort has broken out to endanger the health of the prisoners and citizens of the community.

Repeated efforts have been made for an annex but without avail. Some days ago Jailer Bennett suggested a farm prison, built near the city, where the city prisoners could be kept and at the same time made to perform farm work and in the production of vegetables and be almost self-sustaining since these supplies could be furnished the Charleston Home, Old Folks Home, orphan houses and such county and city institutions.

Capt. Bennett feels that it is just a matter of time when either the annex will have to be built or the prison farm established.

The unusually large number of prisoners at this time is increased with the current term of the federal court. Many of these defendants are kept in the county jail, the government pays the county for their lodging... [20]

1931 - JAIL'S "EATING UTENSILS COULD BE MADE MORE ATTRACTIVE"

Over the years, the Charleston County Grand Jury regularly submitted to the state its recommendations pertaining to the jail. These were based on visits it made during each of its sessions.

One citing health and disease issues was released in September 1931:

Saying it saw no reason why Charleston county should lend assistance toward the tuberculosis sanatorium at Pinehaven if it had to breed tuberculosis in its county jail, a Charleston county grand jury, in its third presentment to the court of general sessions yesterday severely criticized the county penal institution.

"We found the premises to be kept as well as they can be under existing conditions" it said, "but we feel that with the expenditure of not more than $50 the interior walls of the jail could be painted a light color by the prisoners."

The grand jury as a body visited the jail having made certain recommendations at the last term of court.

"We find that one of our recommendations, that with regard to white women prisoners, has been carried out," it reported (Editor's Note: Specifics of that recommendation were not given in the article). "We find the kitchen to be in slightly better condition but there is still much room for improvements."

The kitchen, the report specified, should be held to the same standards as commercial restaurants including the addition of screening and regular inspections by county health authorities. Also, it recommended that a full-time cook should be on duty and "...eating utensils could be made more attractive." (A description of the current utensils was not provided.)

Issues pertaining to recreation, exercise and communicable disease rounded out the report's suggestions:

On inspecting the upper floors and cages we find a very outstanding lack of natural light. In some instances the window panes have been colored in order to keep out the light. In one section we find that the windows had not been raised so as to let in fresh air.

On questioning some of the prisoners we find it is almost impossible for them to read, if they have anything to read, by the daylight which is given them. They are given very little light at night.

We further recommend that each and every prisoner be given the benefit of natural sunlight and some exercise at least two or three times a week by permitting them the privileges of the jail yard under proper guard.

We understand that the expense in connection with this will not be excessive and we can see no reason for the county to lend assistance in supporting Pinehaven if we are to breed tuberculosis in our jail. [21]

Specific action taken as a result of this report — or, for that matter, most of the jail-related recommendations made by Grand Juries over the years — is undiscovered. Typically, however, little was done, mostly due to costs. By most accounts, local officials responsible for the jail's operation did what they could with the meager resources provided them.

Two months after the Grand Jury report cited above, a group made up of local clergy toured the jail and some of their suggestions mirrored those offered by the Grand Jury. Here, in part, is how the Post and Courier reported it:

Sixteen members of the Charleston Ministerial Union yesterday visited and inspected the Charleston County jail. Their visit resulted in recommendations for the employment of a full time cook instead of depending upon prisoners to do the cooking for the jail inmates; provision of additional guards in order that the prisoners may be taken into air and sunshine at stated periods, and the construction of a new kitchen with sanitary equipment.

...The visiting ministers were met at the jail by Sheriff Joseph M. Pulnot and W. J. Bennett, jailer, who accompanied the committee on its tour of inspection. All parts of the jail were visited and in several instances the ministers conversed with the inmates. This population of the jail yesterday was given at 118, slightly lower than the average because recent courts have cleared the institution to some extent.

Bennett who advocated building a new facility to replace "...
the oldest jail in America..." said the interior was badly in need of
repainting. His suggestion that the work be done by "jail labor" at
no cost met objection from local unions, even though sufficient
funds to pay them had not been appropriated.

On the plus side, Bennett said, was the fact that offensive
smells no longer plagued the jail:

> **By a system of ventilation, he said, the jail is now virtu-
> ally odorless. Due to the cleanliness, Captain Bennett
> pointed out the health of inmates at the jail has been
> remarkably good. In its report the committee found
> that the jail "is well kept, sanitary and efficiently
> managed as could be expected with equipment at
> hand. We recommend that Sheriff Poulnot, Captain
> Bennett, the jailer, and their assistants, be commended
> for their humane interest in the task and for efficiency
> in the service rendered. [22]**

At the end of the day, however, the ministers recognized that
their suggestions were unlikely to be implemented because funds
did not appear to be forthcoming. Therefore, like a great many
well-intended committees before them and those still to come, they
recommended "... that the whole problem be given further study...
(Note: Eight years later the jail was permanently closed because of
the same issues raised by the ministers and the grand jury.)

Some hope was provided by the county appropriation of
several thousand dollars for repairing and enlarging the jail, a
newspaper article published in May of that year said. The work
was scheduled to begin within 30 days and by August, the jail had
a brand new annex. A newspaper article gave details:

> **The new annex to the Charleston county jail went
> into use yesterday afternoon when Captain William J.
> Bennett, county jailer, and his assistants transferred
> thirty-one negroes and twelve white prisoners into the
> new quarters. Practically all of the inmates of the annex
> are prisoners convicted in the Charleston police court.**

With the completion of the new annex, the jail now can handle comfortably approximately 200 prisoners. There are now 153 inmates in the jail. The new annex accommodates seventy-five prisoners. And the old building, while constructed to accommodate approximately 140 has housed as many as 160. At such times, however, it was greatly overcrowded.

The transfer of the prisoners was made at 3:30 o'clock yesterday afternoon. The new annex, which is two stories high, and is joined to the old jail by corridors, was made possible through an appropriation of $3,500 made in the 1932 county supply bill. Plans were prepared by David H. Hyer and construction was done by the Simons-Mayrant company.

In the new annex all prisoners will sleep in two large rooms in hammocks, instead of on the cots provided in the cells of the old structure. The main jail building also has been improved, principally in the kitchen. The jail, however, still uses prisoners as cooks. There also are no provisions made for the handling of women prisoners, who will be lodged at the Charleston police station and in other jails as heretofore. [23]

But despite the new annex and the ongoing transfer of prisoners to the farm outside of town, congestion remained a problem. In September, Bennett blamed equipment shortages. While the annex could theoretically accommodate 75 inmates, he had cells, bedding and other gear for only 50. He said he would be forced to refuse to accept any more. [24]

1933 -- City Prisoners Forced to Wear Stripes but not County Inmates

City prisoners were kept with County inmates at the jail but the two groups were treated differently. Unlike county prisoners, city prisoners were required to serve on "chain gangs" and wear uniforms. In order to more readily spot escapees from city work details, officials resorted to dressing those prisoners in stripes. The Courier published the following article on February 19, 1933:

> Because too many prisoners were escaping from city chain gangs which were worked in the open, the use of striped suits for some of the city convicts has been resumed recently. A few city convicts employed in cleaning the police station, however, do not wear the striped suits, and none of the prisoners who work at the county jail use them. There is no chain gang for county prisoners.
>
> The striped suits are useful in identifying the convicts when they work in places where they are likely to mingle with others. The suits also enable the guards, working with large groups of prisoners, to keep an eye on those who are staying to the edge of the gang. Because all of the city prisoners are in jail for only minor offenses, the escape of one of them entails no great menace to the public.
>
> A group of five or six prisoners are used to clean the cells and lobby at the Charleston police station. Every day when they finish their labors, they are searched before they are taken back to the county jail. At the present time, the city gangs working in the open are employed on the golf course, cutting wood for city relief work, and in doing ditching and other work in various sections of the city. [25]

Prisoners apparently had occasional contact with residents of the neighborhood surrounding the jail. Retired South Carolina Senator Herbert Fielding, whose father owned a funeral business in the neighborhood, recalls fetching cigarettes for inmates at a penny each.

"I must have been seven or eight years old at the time," said Sen. Fielding. "We used to go around there, the front part, I guess. The prisoners would lower a big matchbox with a string tied on it. The pennies would be in the matchbox and they'd let it down. I'd go to Frasier's grocery store at Beaufain and Wilson and buy the cigarettes. Probably got two or three for a penny."

Sen. Fielding said he would then return to the front of the jail, place the cigarettes in the lowered matchbox and they'd be pulled up and into a barred window.

Photo by author

Drawing by Sam Wilson

"...prisoners would lower a matchbox..."

"I'd go around there at a certain time almost every day," he said. "It was in the afternoon. That front part of the jail projects out and I'd see'em up in there. What I was dealing with, though, might have been trustees."

Sen. Fielding said he remembers his father retrieved at least one body from the jail. Since the last person hanged in its jail yard was in 1911, deaths after that would have been due to natural causes or unofficial violence like suicide or fights among prisoners.

"I don't know how the heck he died but I damn sure remember daddy getting a body from there about 1933."

Ralph McLaughlin of Charleston remembers the jail well and was actually inside it on several occasions.

"Back in those days, I used to, well, roam a bit and one time I went into a cellblock - not that I was supposed to be in there."

McLaughlin said what he saw inside was pathetic that he'll never forget it.

"Some of the decrepit-looking young people that was in there - I guess they picked them up for stealin' or rape or somethin' like that," he said.

One he saw was a young girl.

"I just couldn't believe they could put women in those cells," he said. "There was this girl - 18 or 19 or maybe younger - and she looked so bad being in there in a big old cell all by herself. She was miserable looking, dirty and wearing an old dark dress that looked like it was made out of bags. After that, I didn't do too much roaming in other parts."

Once, McLaughlin recalls, officials lost some keys to the jail and he found them.

"A man there – his name was Gleason – was a guard and we used to go see him at night," he said. "Once I went over there and they had lost the keys to the jail. Must have dropped them somewhere and they was hunting all around. Being a young boy, I went and found them."

He said he remembers two occasions when would-be escapees afraid of heights had to be plucked from atop the wall by the fire department.

McLaughlin said his family knew Jailer Captain William J. Bennett's family and that he knew Bennett's son, Harold, "pretty well." In fact, his first-hand experiences with the jail probably occurred during the months after Capt. Bennett's retirement and while son Harold oversaw the place, all just before the jail closed in 1939.

After that, he said, the city took out most of the jail "equipment" and moved it to the new jail at the base of the Cooper River Bridge. It was called the Seabreeze.

"After it was vacated, I went in there again." he said. "It looked horrible. Much later, my brother put in new bathrooms for the jail. When the project (Robert Mills Manor) came in 1939, the city wanted us to move. My uncles decided my grandmother could do good by getting rid of the property, so she took what they offered and got out, 'stead of getting in an argument with them about more money."

1933 - Feds Complain Jail "Unfit Place"

By 1933, poor conditions at the jail were attracting Federal attention. U.S. Government prisoners awaiting transfer or trial were regular residents there and so the facility was subject to federal inspection. A report prepared by a Bureau of Prisons official compiled a list of faults with which many local jail officials disagreed. According to a newspaper story:

> The jail was described last week by a government inspector as an unfit place for the housing of federal prisoners. In a complaint by Sanford Bates, director of the (Federal) Bureau of Prisons of the Department of Justice, filed with Sheriff Poulnot, who has jurisdiction over the jail, it was charged that the jail fails to meet the requirements of sanitation and health, and that proper precautions for keeping the prisoners are not observed.

> Sheriff Poulnot denied the charges generally last night and declared that the jail is the best in the state. It is said to be the oldest jail in the country, in the point of continuous service.

> The sheriff said that the prisoners are given good food and good attention. The Bates complaint declared that the jail has a lack of proper refrigeration for foods and that new bedding and mattress slips are needed.

Other points of contention pertained to inmates' mail and meals:

> The government officer's complaint charged that jail authorities do not inspect all incoming mail with a view to preventing the importation of contraband. Sheriff Poulnot declared that neither he nor the jailers have any authority to open a prisoner's private mail. In regard to packages, however, the sheriff said that these were opened by an official in the presence of another official.

> Letters and private mail of this type, he said, are carried to the prisoner, who is required to open and read them in the presence of the jailer or a guard, in order that "dope" and other contraband may not be contained in them.

> In regard to the charge that federal prisoners are being allowed to secret their meals from outside sources, the county officer declared that as long as any man had money of his own and desired to buy better food than the jail could provide, this would be allowed. The government pays seventy cents per day per federal prisoner for meals.

There was unfortunate agreement, though, on one point: The jail's ever-present vermin:

> Sheriff Poulnot admitted a government charge that the jail contains vermin, but said that all public institutions of this kind are subject to invasions of vermin. The local jail, he declared, is in no worse condition in this respect than any other jail in the country and is in much better condition than many.

> Poulnot indicated that the government threat to cease using the jail for federal prisoners was not a matter of great weight. He said that the report was probably a routine matter. [26]

Despite official complaints, recommendations, suggestions and pleas, there is little evidence to suggest that much was done, other than building the annex, to improve the jail during these last years. All concerned finally gave up any hope of its reformation. When urban planners announced in 1937 a major cleanup of the deplorable slum in whose midst it sat, it was generally agreed the jail would be closed.

The same year, the building caught the eye of famed female photographer Frances Benjamin Johnston, who was fascinated by the architecture of old buildings that had fallen into disrepair. Two of her pictures are in the Library of Congress Prints and Photographs archive. The remarkable thing about old jail photographs — from the 1800s through today – is how little the facade has changed.

Courtesy of the Library of Congress

Courtesy of the Library of Congress

The appearance of the jail today is virtually the same as in these photos shot 73 years ago

The End Finally Comes

Twenty-eight years after the jail gallows took its last victim, the life of the prison itself was snuffed out.

One hundred and thirty-seven years of steady deterioration, failed renovation and mounting pressure from both citizens and public officials caused state and county authorities to put an end to the Magazine Street facility's service as a prison. The fact that it had taken so long to get it done probably was a combination of lack of funds and bureaucratic inertia.

No one inside or outside of government had ever championed the warehousing of convicts there. Rather, the jail's longevity seemed more the result of a dearth of good options. But by the latter part of the 1930s, the building's woeful condition was deemed even worse by the fact that it stood in the center of an ugly slum that badly needed cleaning up.

According to the "Year Book 1938 City of Charleston," the blocks surrounding the jail contained a large number of dilapidated residences and tenements. It deemed the area "...the worst disease breeding spot in the lower section of the city. Its existence was a constant police problem and fire hazard. It's crowded, poorly lighted, evil-smelling tenements depreciated the entire section of the city." [27]

The last nail in the jail's coffin was the winning by city officials of a federal grant to build a low income housing project in the neighborhood. The development was to be called "Robert Mills Manor," after the famed architect who had once designed a long-gone wing of the jail. [28]

Public squabbles among developers and preservationists as to the fate of the empty jail played out in meetings and the newspaper. In the end, the building itself was granted a reprieve from the wrecking ball but its wall was not so fortunate. Most of it was shaved down to a height of four feet so that sunlight could reach a playground planned for the jail yard.

Moving day for the last prisoners was September 15, 1939. A newspaper story noting the event was accompanied by a photo of inmates lined up to board a city patrol wagon for their trip to a county prison farm. They were to be kept there until completion of their new home, the remodeled immigration station on the Cooper River. It became known as "The Seabreeze Hotel."

Courtesy of the Post and Courier

Jail's last prisoners line up at entrance for move

An accompanying story headlined "Today is Moving Day for Convicts" said:

> **Thirty-nine prisoners will be transferred from the Charleston county jail today to the state penitentiary in Columbia and the remainder of the local prisoners will be moved to the county prison farm, seven miles from the city on the North Charleston boulevard.**
>
> **A truck is expected to arrive here about 11 a.m. from the state penitentiary to return there with six white men, thirty negro men and three negro women, sentenced at the March term of the court of general sessions.**

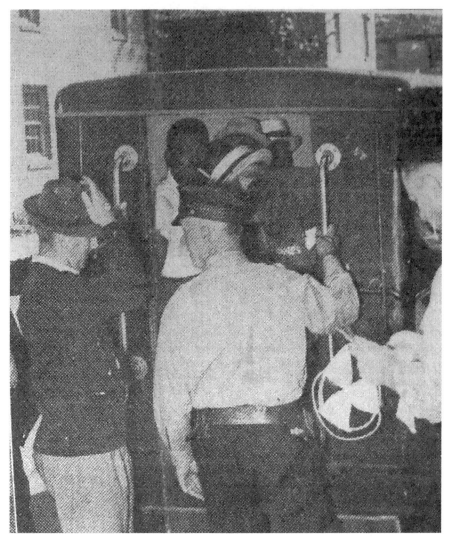

Courtesy of the Post and Courier

Loading up inmates for transfer

Sheriff Joseph M. Poulnot plans to be ready to turn over the jail building tomorrow at noon to the Charleston housing authority, which will include part of the jail building in the Robert Mills manor low-cost housing project.

Considerable equipment such as mattresses, blankets, cups, cooking utensils, buckets, coal, light bulbs and so forth is needed at the prison camp for housing prisoners properly, Sheriff Poulnot said... [29]

And with that, after 137 years of incarcerations, executions, hardships, escape attempts, inmate uprisings and threats from fire, disease and earthquake, 21 Magazine Street quietly went out of service as a jail.

By the time the first Mills Manor homes were built, the block bounded by Franklin, Magazine, Logan and Queen and its adjoining neighborhoods had totally been repurposed. All that remained as reminders of the past were the Old Marine Hospital (by then the offices of the Housing Authority) and the Charleston District Jail building.

The jail itself was locked up and, for the next several decades, its only use was for storage.

SECTION II

THE DEVIL IS IN THE DETAILS

Courtesy of the Historic American Building Survey

(Third floor holding cell photographed in 1995 by Jack Boucher)

CHAPTER 8

WRETCHED TENANTS – A GALLERY OF PRISONERS AND WHY THEY WERE LOCKED UP

The identities of most persons once held at the Charleston District Jail will never be known. Logs and related official records appear to have been lost or tossed. Some were documented in hand-written listings in a few musty grand jury ledgers that have survived.

Of course, there were well-publicized exceptions. Individuals involved in particularly sensational cases received wide notoriety and we know their names through newspaper accounts, journals and passages in books. Those involved in "lesser" crimes might show up in the press if the offenses were sufficiently unusual of if they involved a person of prominence. A few names were scratched into the plaster of the jail's cellblocks by the inmates, themselves. Some of this graffiti still exists, although it is disappearing as the walls crumble with age (See Chapter 12).

Names notwithstanding, more is known about the kinds of crime that could lead to imprisonment. While petty offenses could be forgiven by the prompt payment of small fines, those unable to pay could be locked up. They usually were segregated from the harder cases. Simply witnessing a crime could lead to imprisonment, too. The courts wanted all those with relevant testimony readily available for trials, so witnesses were sometimes held in the jail along with the alleged criminal.

Most prisoners, however, were jailed for serious charges. Examples, in no particular order, might include drunkenness, deception, illegal sale of liquor, wife beating, robbery, assault,

"Negro stealing," rape, manslaughter or murder. Sentence length could vary from a few days to a year or longer but six months seems to have been the most common maximum stay. Longer terms were served out at the state penitentiary in Columbia.

The vignettes that follow pertain to specific prisoners known to have been confined on Magazine Street in what many called "a pest hole without compare." [1] These glimpses give a sense of the variety of offenses that landed miscreants in the jail.

1819-Martin Toohey: "Wanton and Inhuman Murder"

Charleston Courier, March 20 - It gives us pleasure to state that the murderer, Martin Toohey is once more confined within the walls of the jail of this District. He was discovered yesterday forenoon, in the woods in the vicinity of the four mile house, by a detachment of the Charleston Riflemen, who were scouring the woods. [2]

Months earlier, twenty-five year old Toohey, in the company of his older brother Michael, had been convicted of brutally stabbing to death James W. Gadsden, Esq., father of eight who was, according to newspaper reports, "a citizen of the most mild and amiable deportment." The brothers, on their way home from a military parade, reportedly had been intoxicated.

Arrested almost immediately on the day of the murder, Monday, December 21, the Tooheys were confined in the Charleston District Jail. A two-day trial ended January 30. Martin was convicted of murder; his brother of manslaughter. The two were then returned to the jail to await sentencing.

But on the evening of March 17, jail "turn-key" Thomas H. Eyre, in exchange for $600 and two silver watches, unlocked Martin's cell and accompanied the accused murderer out the front door of the jail. An alarm was sounded, launching a search by citizens and the City Guard:

About 1 o'clock, a party of the guard came up with two men on one horse in Meeting Street. The guard

were much exhausted, but one of them got hold of the reins of the Horse, and another stuck a blow with his sword at (as he declares, and he knows him) **Martin Toohey** - the riders lashed the horse, and being a high spirited animal, he dragged the guardman about ten paces, who had then to give way... [3]

The next morning, South Carolina Governor John Geddes offered a reward of $1,000 "...to any person or persons who shall apprehend the said Martin Toohey, and lodge him in any gaol of the state." Geddes' proclamation included a highly detailed description of both Toohey and the jail employee who had made the escape possible:

Martin Toohey is about 25 years of age, about 5 feet 10 inches high, stout made, full faced, dark complexion, black hair and beard, a little knockneed, with large and flat feet, thick lips, very slightly pitted with the small-pox, and down-cast look; a carpenter by trade.

He went off with Thomas H. Eyre (the turn-key) who was in the employment of the Gaoler, and it is said they were seen both on the same horse last night.

Thomas H. Eyre about 24 years of age has resided in New York, and been some time in this city. He is about 5 feet 10 inches high, stout and well made, hazel eyes, and has a light red circle under his right eye, black hair and beard, with large flat feet, has rather a down-cast look, but in other respects a good countenance. [4]

Two days later, on March 20, the Charleston Courier reported that Toohey was back in jail.

He was discovered yesterday forenoon, in the woods in the vicinity of the four mile house, by a detachment of the Charleston Riflemen, who were scouring the woods. A member of that corps, Mr. Edward Morris, a young gentleman of 19 years of age, and a relative

of the deceased Mr. Gadsden, who was murdered by Toohey, had the good fortune first to come up with him…in the top of a fallen tree, where he was reading a book.

The discovered Toohey fled, though, in a hail of bullets and fired one of his own at one of his pursuers.

One ball, or slug, passed through Mr. Morris's coat, and slightly wounded his breast, another went through his sleeve and passed off under his arm, without doing further injury. Mr. Morris instantly made a blow at (Toohey's) head, with his sword, which brought him to the the ground; when others of the corps coming up the murderer was secured. The wound which the prisoner received, is severe, but not dangerous. Notwithstanding there had been much rain through the night, Toohey's clothes were perfectly dry; from which it is inferred that he had been sheltered in some neighboring building the night. [5]

Eyre, the turn-key accomplice, was soon captured nearby and "…they were escorted in to town, the one in and the other tied to the tail of a cart, and committed to jail."

On May 19, the Constitutional Court refused a motion for a new trial and sentenced Martin Toohey to death on May 28, along with a man named Hardy Miles, who had been convicted of "negro stealing" in an unrelated case.

At 1 o'clock on the fateful day, Martin Toohey was hanged "…on the Meeting street road, near the Lines", according to the Courier.

The unhappy man was attended by the Rev. Mr. Fenwick, who administered those consolations most soothing in a dying hour. He made a short address to the spectators, declaring that he died in peace with all men; and we learned that he had previously avowed that he was prepared to meet his fate, in the hope of another and a better world. After hanging about 25 minutes, his

body was cut down and delivered to his friends. Some attempts were made to resuscitate it, but the "vital spark" had fled, the blood had congealed in his veins, and his "mortal had put on immortality."[6]

As it turned out, Hardy Miles had not accompanied Toohey into eternity, having been pardoned by the governor.

The murder of Gadsden by Toohey was widely reported and followed with great interest all over the east. A copy of the complete trial proceeding was offered for one dollar in Charleston book-stores, such was the interest in the apparently random slaying.

1820-John Fisher, His Wife and Their "Day Laborer of Death"

Among the more infamous of the jail's inmates were John and Lavinia Fisher. They were arrested, confined at the jail and later hanged (but not at the jail) for the crime of highway robbery. Probably because the offenses of which they were accused were committed in the context of matrimony, the Fishers remain marquee subjects for tellers of Charleston's history to this very day.

Stories about the Fishers are highly entertaining. They allude to serial killing, bodies unearthed and profane defiance by a ravishing beauty who was hanged while wearing her wedding dress. It is claimed that Lavinia Fisher tried to cheat death by exploiting a legal loophole that prevented a widow from being executed. Supposedly, though, a judge cleverly ordered that she die moments before her husband, thus negating the ploy. Also, she is said to have to have mocked the huge crowd that had gathered to watch her execution by boldly offering to deliver in person whatever messages they might have for the devil.

If any of these colorful details actually occurred, they went unreported at the time by the Charleston Courier. In fact, the Fishers went unidentified in the press until just before they were executed. Furthermore, there is no mention of murder or corpses by the newspaper or the writer of a lengthy essay who visited them in jail and witnessed their executions. The origin of the more sensational claims remains, at least to this author, a mystery.

Given these differences, it may be useful to recount here what actually was written about the events at the time they occurred. Nine Courier articles about the incidents in which the Fishers were allegedly involved were published over the course of a year, beginning February 20, 1819. Also, an account of the Fisher's confinement and subsequent execution can be found in John Blake White's "The Dungeon and the Gallows," an essay published in "The Charleston Book: A Miscellany in Prose and Verse." A man named "John Blake White," prominent Charleston attorney and artist, lived from 1781 to 1859 7 and may have created the piece.

The first mention of crimes which later were associated with the Fishers appeared in the February 20, 1819 edition of the Courier. The article reported that a "gang of desperadoes" had been preying on "wagoneers" and others, "...practising (sic) every deception upon the unwary, and frequently committing robberies upon defenceless (sic) travellers." Fed up with this serious mischief, a band of citizens surprised them at two buildings — one called the Five-Mile House — routed them and burned both structures to the ground. No names of suspects were provided. 8

The next article, published in the Courier two days later, said the gang had reappeared, beat a man "in almost inhuman manner," and robbed another. This time, the Sheriff organized a posse and arrested three men and two women (still unnamed) and locked them in the jail.

Although the gang was said to be armed with muskets and a keg of powder, members were taken without incident. While allusions to robbery and assault were made in the articles, neither murder nor human corpses were mentioned. However, one death was reported:

> **The posse found in an outhouse, the hide of a cow, which had recently been killed, and which was identified to be the property of one our citizens. She had been missing for several days. This accounts for the manner in which the cows are disposed of, which are so frequently stolen and never afterwards heard of. 9**

After the gang was imprisoned, several articles specifically identified some of the alleged gang members — but not the Fishers. One newspaper piece said the case of the jailed offenders was to be heard during the May Court of Sessions but a serious search of all of the Courier editions published that year failed to turn up an account of the trial. [10]

The Fishers were first named in the one-paragraph announcement of their impending execution in the Tuesday Morning, January 18, 1820 edition of the Courier:

> **John Fisher, and Lavinia, his wife, who were convicted of highway robbery at the last Court of Sessions, were yesterday brought before the Constitutional Court, and (a motion for a new trial having been rejected,) received the sentence of the law... the unhappy criminals were condemned to be hung, on Friday, 4th February next. [11]**

Three more short articles alluded to the actual execution but even they, like those that had previously appeared, made no mention of murder, bodies or clever loopholes involving the order of hanging. Rather, "Highway-Robbery" is named as the charge that led to capital punishment. [12]

Essayist White corroborated these newspaper accounts and offered considerably more detail, including a visit he made to see the Fishers at the jail.

> **We were called to the prison, on professional business, the evening previous to the execution. At the instance of the jailer, we went down with him to the ground cells of the prison, where he unlocked a door, which opened into an extensive apartment. The furniture of this gloomy chamber, illumined only by a lantern, which our guide carried in his hand, consisted of several...coffins, a gallows pole, whose disjointed parts lay lumbering against the wall, some fragments of rope, a spade, a pick-axe, and a few like implements of death and the grave. The jailer proceeded to**

examine the machine, and to ascertain that all its parts
were complete, and fit and ready for the morrow...

White said that after two coffins of appropriate size to accommodate the Fishers had been selected, he was led by the jailer to
a remote corner of the building. After several calls, he said, a
noise was heard from the darkness:

The door being unbarred and opened, we beheld,
stretched upon the floor, a being that appeared to be
rather than human. Haggard, pale, emaciated, it began,
slowly, to rise from the floor, growling like some glutted
hyena at being roused from his lair. It stood, at length,
erect before us, resembling more anatomical preparation than a true and living man. 'Thus am I served,'
muttered he, "whenever you want my work. But give
me something to drink. I must have drink, and I will be
contented." This was the executioner! Yes, we stood
in the awful presence of a minister of justice, and we
shrunk with reverential horror at his glance!

... Here, then, stood before us, in unsophisticated
reality, the murderer of state, the pensioned cut-throat,
the day-laborer of death, one who did his work for
pay with fidelity and skill, and all by virtue of law and
under the sacred sanction of justice. This miserable
man, being extremely intemperate, it became necessary (sic) to confine closely when his services were
about to be required. Again and again, he entreated to
be supplied with liquor, which was positively refused,
though with the assurance that, after the execution,
if well performed, he should have as much drink as
he desired. A transient, but ghastly smile flickered for
an instant on his cheek, when the door of his cell was
again closed and bolted. [13]

The Fishers actually had been scheduled to die two weeks
prior, on February 4, but had petitioned the governor for "an
opportunity for repentance, and asking but for time to prepare

to meet their God." [14] The request had been granted but once the time had elapsed, they were understandably distressed. White wrote that he went to the jail the following day and could hear the Fishers:

> From their cell, sighs, sobs, and moans were heard, and sometimes loud and lengthened lamentations; then all was silent, and now frantic shrieks broke upon the ear... In the lobby, silently awaited the sheriff and his attendants. At the farthest end of the gallery stood the executioner, arranging, with professional skill, the slip-knot and the noose, and stretching to their utmost length the fatal cords. The moment at length arrived, and the order was given to prepare the convicts. The door was thrown open, and what a scene was then exhibited! The miserable man and his wretched wife were both before us. Two finer forms the sculptor's fancy has seldom sketched; tall, graceful, we might almost add, majestic; but, alas! Fallen, helpless, degraded to the very dust!

> As the door opened, the eyes of the hapless woman fell upon the ghost-like apparition of the executioner, when she sent forth a shriek that chilled every heart with horror. After a long parley and much difficulty, and even resistance on her part, the jack-ketch (Note: hangman) adjusted the cords and pinioned his victims. His task was performed with indifference the most cold, and with skill the most perfect.

White described the pair as attired in "loose white garments" they had purchased for themselves and wore them over their clothing. He said they embraced and "...bade each other an eternal adieu."

The unhappy victims descended the stairs, arm-in-arm, to a coach in waiting at the prison door, and the procession slowly moved forward, flanked by a company of cavalry. It was a melancholy, though novel sight, to

behold a female led out to execution, and it attracted an immense concourse of spectators, wonderful to add, of both sexes, and of all ages and conditions!

Both White and the newspaper article reporting the execution agreed that John Fisher stoically faced his fate but that Lavinia, believing to the end that she would be spared, was frantic. White said constables were forced to nearly drag her to the scaffold and, once there, "... she called upon the multitude to rescue her, and stretched forth her trembling arms, imploring pity." At times, White said, her screams were "truly demoniacal."

At just past two o'clock, the two stood together on the trap door. White described what happened next:

"... The executioner we beheld, mounted aloft, on a ladder, hovering like a vampire, over these devoted beings, engaged in making fast the cords, and adjusting the caps over their faces... A private signal passed from the sheriff — the platform gave way — they fell – all was hushed and still — their loose white garments only floated on the breeze." [15]

The newspaper account said Lavinia "died without a struggle or a groan" but that it was some minutes before John stopped moving. Afterward, their bodies were taken down and conveyed to Potter's Field, where they were buried. The article concluded:

The concourse that attended the execution was immense. May the awful example strike deep into their hearts; and may it have the effect intended, by deterring others from pursuing those vicious paths, which end in infamy and death. [16]

Perhaps there are facts in some of the detail larded onto the Fisher story but until proof is forthcoming, they remain suspect.

Incidentally, the accounts of the hanging suggest the method used differed from that employed at the jail. Although the couple had been kept there for a year, they were taken to "... the lines, on the Meeting-Street Road..." where they mounted a scaffold and simultaneously dropped through a trap door. Those hung at the jail stood on the bare ground and were jerked into the air when a heavy weight was dropped into a hole beside the gallows pole.

1820 - James Collier "...fell in with the wrong crowd..."

In a newspaper report headlined "Citizens Beware!," a newcomer to the city apparently fell in with the wrong crowd and paid a price. James Collier of Savannah was locked up after he apparently attempted to force open a door at a residence on Legare Street. The owner was away but two neighbors subdued Collier while two accomplices escaped by scaling a garden fence. The newspaper warned its readers:

> These circumstances admonish us to be on the alert. This man, when taken, was not in the dress which he is said to wear in common, but had disguised himself in a sailor's pea-jacket and an old straw hat. His associates are supposed to belong to a gang of rogues, who support themselves entirely by depredating upon the property of others. It is also supposed that he had just been initiated into the fraternity, as he arrived in the city but a few days since. [17]

1835 - Mr. Carroll Tarred, "Cottoned" and Jailed

A "Mr. Carroll," thought to be a thief, was escorted by citizen vigilantes to the Charleston jail, but not before they subjected him to a variation of an old, particularly public punishment. The Charleston Journal on August, 21, 1835, reported:

> Lynch Law was exhibited this morning on the person of a Mr. Carroll who has been carrying on the business of a Barber, but who has attended more to the purchase of Stolen cotton, it is Said he has shipped in a Season as much as 75 bales. He was taken from his house to Lathrop's loft, there tried and rec'd 20 lashes, then

tarred and Stuck with Cotton, marched up the Bay, thru' the Market and thence to the Jail. It is said Some of the principle Actors were I L Wilson, R Harnett & England. On the 29 He was put on board of a Vessel & sent to New York. [18]

1889 - Dr. Thomas McDow Jailed After Gunning Down a Newspaper Editor

A doctor who shot dead the editor and publisher of the Charleston News and Courier spent many days in the District Jail as an outraged community followed the sensational progress of his trial.

The deadly assault occurred over improper attentions allegedly directed by the doctor toward a young Frenchwoman employed by the editor as a servant.

Based on accounts published at the time, Dr. Thomas Ballard McDow killed Capt. Francis Warrington Dawson in the basement office of McDow's home. It was said that the newspaperman felt responsible for the well-being of his charge and, responding to rumors regarding the doctor's advances, decided to call on him and admonish the doctor for his conduct.

The result of the meeting was a killing the newspaper called "...the most brutal and atrocious ever committed in Charleston. The popular indignation is intense; all classes in the community stand aghast at the assassination and would lynch the murderer if they could get him out of jail." Its report said:

> "Captain Dawson left the News and Courier office at 3:30 o'clock. Some time ago it had been brought to his attention that one of his domestics, a stranger in America, and one for whose conduct, being employed in an educational and fiduciary capacity, he was responsible, was conducting herself in a manner that demanded his immediate attention. As will appear elsewhere, Captain Dawson had the best of reasons for calling on Dr. McDow, which he did at probably about 3:40 o'clock yesterday afternoon. Captain Dawson, on reaching the

office of Dr. McDow alighted from the street car and entered. He never returned alive. The whole truth of the history of what really occurred in that office, and in the few fateful moments of the tragedy, will be buried in the grave of Captain Dawson. [19]

The evening of the killing, McDow surrendered to police and was "...immediately transferred to the county jail." A reporter who interviewed him there wrote that the doctor "...bore all the evidences of a man affrighted by the consciousness of a crime without an excuse. He was ashen pale, troubled visibly, and the perspiration was thick upon his forehead and face."

The newspaper account continued:

A drenching rain and wind storm which has prevailed since the night of the murder prevented the gathering of a crowd and probably saved the murderer from lynching. He was brought out of the jail about 11 a.m. and placed in a police patrol wagon. A guard of four policemen and three special deputy sheriffs accompanied him. At his request he was first driven to the office of his counsel, Governor A. G. Magrath, the last secession governor of South Carolina. His counsel, however, did not accompany him to the inquest. The inquest did not develop anything startling. Only three witnesses were examined." [20]

The trial provided plenty of lurid revelation, including accusations that McDow had tried to bury the body in his back yard and that he was a serial philanderer. Ultimately, the jury acquitted him, presumably on the basis that he was defending himself in his own home against a probable physical attack by Dawson.

1908 - Gracie Tonsey "...could not resist the 'call of the wild'..."

Not all jail dramas involved thievery or mayhem. Most, in fact, were the result of offenses more pedestrian in nature, like the item that about Gracie Tonsey that appeared in a Charleston newspaper on the first day of December, 1908:

> **Gracie Tonsey, white, was given a fine of $15 or sentenced to thirty days at hard labor in the County Jail for being drunk and disorderly on Queen street Sunday afternoon. Gracie is an old offender and has appeared before the Police Judge dozens of times. Although under 20 years of age, she has been here for several years without a home. Gracie stated that her folks lived in Baltimore and that she had run away at the age of 13. After that event her story is identical with that of thousands of girls in a similar situation, in which fast company and drink play a principal part.**

In the article, Gracie's plight had been noted at the end of a list of cases disposed of the morning before in the Police Court. William Green was to serve 30 days for disorderly conduct. William Doctor was assessed the same penalty for the same crime but earned an additional 30 days "…on account of carrying a razor in his pocket". Others named had been arrested for assault and battery, indecent conduct and cursing.

But Gracie received more attention in the sotry than the others, including a level of judgment by the writer unlikely to see print today. The item continued:

> **Gracie is apparently stricken with remorse over her conduct after each spree and her condition has been so pitiful that no less than a half dozen people have offered to help her and bring her back to the straight and narrow path. Money has been raised several times to send her back to her relatives, but the girl either refused point blank to go at the eleventh hour or else switched off on the way home. About a month ago the officers of the Star Gospel Mission became interested in her and secured employment for her in a respectable home, but she could not resist the 'call of the wild' and was recently arrested and again sent to Jail yesterday morning.**

An intriguing reference in the report mentions that jail sentences in several of the cases, including Gracie's, included "hard labor". For example, Robert Williams was sentenced to a fine of $15 or ten days "...at hard labor on the chain gang" for swearing and disorderly conduct on Meeting and Columbus streets. Research suggests only "city" prisoners were made to wear stripes and transported to labor details outside the jail. Since there is no record of such physical penalties inside the walls of the jail, it begs the question as to whether women like Gracie Tonsey were forced onto chain gangs. [21]

1910 - Bloody Arrests of William Howard, Maggie Goodley and John Temper

Several newspaper items in 1910 pertain to a variety of alleged crimes. In one, an suspected killer was unsuccessful in explaining to authorities the whereabouts of a women with whom he lived:

> **August 2 - William Howard a negro of John's Island, was lodged in jail today on a warrant, taken out before Magistrate Royall, charging him with the killing of L.M. Smith, a woman with whom he lived on the island. It appears that the woman has been missing for some time but Howard gave some reasonable explanation of her absence of more than a week, and nothing was thought of the matter. A few days ago, Howard was with several negroes boating in a creek, when some of the party thought that they saw a woman floating on the water and when they started in the direction of the body, Howard said that it was only a mattress. The negroes made the investigation and established the fact that the Smith woman had been killed.**

The day before Howard's confinement, Maggie Goodley had been jailed on the charge of the murder of Thomas Maxell. According to a newspaper account, "She admitted the killing of the man saying that she had used the negro's own pistol in the act." [22]

Then, on August 12, a man was jailed on a burglary charge but not before both he and another man were bloodied:

John Temper was committed to jail today for trial on the charge of burglary, having had a desperate encounter last night with Henry Hutchemacher, as the latter entered his residence about midnight. The young man had hardly closed the door after him when the negro set upon him in the hallway and with a glass bottle, which changed hands during the mixup. Both men were profusely bleeding from cuts in the head when assistance reached Hutchemacher, enabling him to turn the negro over to a police officer, who had been summoned.

Reports on the punishments of Howard, Goodley and Temper remain undiscovered.

On the same day as the report on the Temper-Hutchemacher fight with a broken bottle, was the following account:

Two small white boys were arrested today and held for trial on the charge of burglary, in forcibly breaking a lock on a small grocery store on Church Street. [23]

While the report does not specify that the youths were held on Magazine Street, it is likely that they were. Research reveals that children regularly were confined at the Charleston District Jail. By 1911, no separate provision had yet been made in the criminal justice system to accommodate youthful offenders. It appears that sixteen was the demarcation age of adult versus juvenile. Officials at the time were quoted as saying that sometimes they had no alternative but to incarcerate youngsters in the only available facility - the Magazine Street jail. An example follows.

1911 - ALONZO SMALL, AGED 10, "ADMITTED TO JAIL"

A story appearing in the News and Courier on December 5 was headlined: "Runaway Car Claims Victim, Capt. Thomas Symmes Meets Horrible Death. It said:

As the result of one of the most peculiar accidents that have ever taken place in Charleston, Capt. Thomas Symmes, for nearly thirty years a conductor on the old South Carolina and Georgia Railroad and a well known man in this section of the state died yesterday afternoon at the Roper Hospital, only three hours after he had been taken there in the automobile patrol. Capt. Symmes was struck while getting off of Car No. 36, at the corner of Reid and Meeting streets, by Consolidated Car. 35, which was stolen from the Consolidated car barns by some very small colored boys.

The story said the run-away vehicle hit Symmes, 66, just as he alighted from another trolley car. The run-away car "...struck him fairly, nearly severing both of his legs from his body." An investigation by police revealed that several youngsters had been playing in the trolley car barn. It continued:

Officer Redell hastened to the spot, the police automobile having been summoned. The wounded man was rushed to the Hospital, losing much blood meanwhile. The police arrested three little colored boys, Gus Washington, Alonzo John and Robert Pinckney, the oldest of whom cannot be more than ten or twelve ears of age. One of the boys went out with Special Officer Fults and helped to locate John Hutson, another one implicated, making four arrests in all. These four boys are charged with malicious mischief in taking a car from the Consolidated barns and causing it to run wild down Meeting Street and collide with another car.

The little fellows seemed scared out of their wits when questioned, except John Hutson, who stated that he had nothing to do with actually starting the car, but admitted that he was with the other boys when the thing occurred. Gus Washington, a small, black negro, is accused of having started the car. [24]

It was not known how the youngsters managed to start the car but some of the blame was assigned to the Consolidated Company for permitting them to play in the barn.

Several days later, another story appeared that said that a 10-year-old had been jailed in connection with the incident:

> **Small (Editor's Note: Alonzo's surname was listed as "John" in the original story), 10-years-old, a negro boy, was admitted to jail today, charged with the responsibility for the death of Capt. T.H. Symmes, who was killed by a run-away car of the Consolidated company, the boy having started the car, it is alleged, out of the car shed. The boy is held on the statement of several other negro children that he started the car. The coroner refused this morning to accept bond for the boy's appearance at the term of the court. The criticism is mainly directed against the company for permitting children to play about the car shed, rather than against the child, who scarcely realized what he was doing. [25]**

So far as can be determined by a search of newspaper files, no follow-up story appeared to trace the fate of Alonzo Small or any of the children involved. It's a safe bet, though, that his time in the Charleston District Jail was unforgettable.

1911 - SOPHIE REED: "PROMISCUOUS FIRING OF PISTOLS"

It was only two days past the Christmas of 1911 when gunfire shattered the calm and a man lay dead. Samuel Waring, according to a Charleston newspaper, had been shot in the head by Sophie Reed "...following the very general and promiscuous firing of pistols...":

> **Trouble between Waring and the woman seems to have resulted from too excessive use of liquor. A rough house ensued on the premises of the woman, and it is said that the negro had a bottle in his hand and was endeavoring to hit the woman when she shot.**

The woman is held for trial. A number of negroes were sent to jail today on the charge of assault. [26]

1914 - G.B. Perkins: "Murder on the High Seas"

Charleston being a port town, its jail accommodated a fair share of sailors, including one accused of murder. A newspaper account said:

Reports from Roper hospital today stated that G.B. Perkins, detained there under guard awaiting improvement of his physical condition, before he is moved to the county jail and brought to trial on the charge of murder on the high seas in the federal court, is getting along "about the same." Some improvement is said to be noticeable in his physical condition." [27]

1917 - H.L. Koester: "German Merchant" Arrested on "Orders from Washington"

Several inmates of German descent were arrested and kept at the jail during the First World War. In one case, the Federal government requested a man be confined until it could investigate his activities with regard to existing war regulations. The State newspaper reported on July 17, 1917:

H.L. Koester, a well known storekeeper at Three Mile, who for many years was a resident of Charleston, was arrested today by federal authorities, under, it is believed, war proclamation provisions, the officials are not talking much about the case, except to say that the arrest was made on orders from Washington. It is said that secret service men visited Mr. Koester's place recently and found evidence alleged to point to violation of the war regulations. What disposition of the case will be made is not known here apparently as yet. Mr. Koester is said to have already taken out first papers leading to citizenship. The arrest is taken as indication that the authorities are going to tighten up in enforcing the rules as to enemy aliens. Mr. Koester was placed in the county jail pending further orders. [28]

In another case, German sailor prisoners of war apparently indulged in "America's Pastime" while confined. According to The State Newspaper:

It was learned today that five German war prisoners incarcerated in the Charleston county jail, who were reported to be slated for transfer to Richland county, will remain here, as they put up a plea to be allowed to do so. They are well treated here, enjoy considerable latitude and are consequently well satisfied. They particularly enjoy sports in the jail yard, which they are allowed to indulge in freely, and have acquired considerable skill in baseball playing on a limited scale. The five men are interned seamen under control of the immigration authorities. [29]

Whether or not there's a connection, it is interesting to note that an old baseball recently was found by workmen repairing a section of the jail's octagon. Tattered and coming apart at the seams, the ball was found INSIDE brick and mortar that is thought to date at least back to the time when the jail was in operation.

1919 - EUGENE MANLY: "CHLOROFORMED, ROBBED MARY ROBERTS"

Although his age was not stated, Eugene Manly's youth failed to keep him from being returned to Charleston and incarcerated in its jail.

Charleston, Aug. 9 - Calmly admitting that he chloroformed May Roberts and robbed her of four diamond rings, valued at $400, Eugene Manly of Griffin, Ga., a mere stripling, was sent to jail here today in default of bond of $1,000, on a charge of grand larceny. Young Manly was arrested for this crime in Baltimore last week, after the police here had made an extended search for him. He made the mistake of trying to sell the ring too cheaply. [30]

1921 -- "Alleged Murderers" on the Way to the State Penitentiary

Sometimes high profile prisoners who committed crimes elsewhere in the state temporarily were kept in Charleston's jail until tempers cooled. Such was the case of two charged with the brutal murder of a college student near Columbia.

C.O. Fox and Jesse Gappins, both Columbians, who for several weeks have been held in the Charleston county jail charged with the killing of William Brazell, young Columbia taxi driver, were brought to Columbia early yesterday morning and were lodged in the state penitentiary where S.J. Kirby, the third man implicated in the crime, has been held since being brought to South Carolina the day following his arrest August 8 with Fox and Gappins near Waynesboro, Ga... [31]

1932 -- Fort Moultrie Sergeant Held in Hatchet Murder of Family

The Charleston jail cells hosted at least one alleged ax murderer. In the summer of 1932, Sgt. Charles Long of Fort Moutrie (near Charleston) was accused of hacking his wife and children to death with a hatchet.

The deaths occurred in January at the family home on the post. After the killing, Long had attempted suicide by slashing his throat and wrists. He was taken to Walter Reed Hospital in Washington for treatment, where he was quoted as saying that he must have been "crazy" to do what he did.

However, a medical board at the hospital adjudged Long "sane when the homicide was committed and sane now," according to a newspaper account, and Charleston law enforcement authorities had issued a warrant for his arrest. Long was to be delivered to the Charleston jail by US Marshals.

The maximum penalty upon conviction would have been death by hanging but Long's fate, as far as the surviving written record is concerned, remains unknown. However, if he had been executed, it wouldn't have been in the yard of the Charleston jail. Hangings there ceased in 1911 when that task was left to the penitentiary in Columbia. [32]

Courtesy of Robert Grenko

Grenko drawing of jail "The Descent to Hades"

CHAPTER 9

DESPERATE TO GET OUT: ESCAPING FROM THE JAIL

Jail breaks have always been a preoccupation with inmates, as well as with those responsible for keeping them locked up. Convicts with time on their hands are understandably obsessed with freeing themselves by any means possible while their guardians are loathe to admit that escapes are successful.

It is likely that most escape attempts from the Charleston jail were thwarted and never publicized. Authorities were fond of boasting that no one had ever successfully escaped from their jails, although this claim sometimes should have included the phrase "without being recaptured and returned."

Poor structural design, ongoing deterioration and lack of funds for repairs combined to offer daring inmates numerous opportunities to flee. Especially in its early days, the jail's locks, bars and flimsy floors and ceilings were regularly assaulted and some of these efforts even reached the press.

Perhaps the most famous Charleston District Jail escape occurred during the aftermath of the catastrophic earthquake that struck Charleston in 1886. (See Chapter 7 - Bad Food, Bad Blood and an Earthquake) While a pistol-wielding guard prevented frightened inmates from fleeing after the initial shock had subsided, 38 did manage to escape after they had been taken from their cells and into the yard at the rear of the jail. The quake had split the wall. Nearly all were later recaptured.

Here are a few other escapes, culled from newspaper accounts.

1858 - BARS SAWED, LOCK PICKED BY A ONE-EYED BLACKSMITH

"Broke Jail" was the headline of a story published May 3, 1858 in the Charleston Courier that included remarkably detailed descriptions of three escapees who had been awaiting trial on robbery charges. The victims were all of guests at local hotels. George McNairy, A. Butler and Charleston Thompson managed flight in the wee hours of a Sunday morning. The newspaper explained:

> Butler who is a blacksmith and machinist, succeeded in picking the lock of his cell door, and then liberated the other two, and the three escaped from the body of the jail by sawing off two of the bars of a window grating and letting themselves down by a rope made of their blankets, into the jail yard, from which they escaped by climbing the wall, and passing through, as is supposed, the premises of the Marine Hospital.

The account said that "Justice demands that these notorious scoundrels should not go unpunished..." and, to aid their recapture, offered the following descriptions:

> McNairy is about five feet seven inches high, of slight build, and will weigh about 125 to 130 pounds, is about 35 years old, hair very grey, and has lost the first joints of three fingers of his left hand, upon which he usually wears a glove.

> Butler is about five feet eight inches high, rather thick set, and will weigh about 150 pounds; has light hair, is marked with the small pox, and has lost one eye.

> Thompson is about five feet eight or nine inches high and will weigh about 140 pounds, has dark hair and complexion, and looks like a countryman, for which he endeavors to pass himself. He was convicted some four or five years since for larceny, under the name of

Fisher; and broke jail with two others while serving out his sentence, but was recaptured. He is also known to our police as Capt. Savage. [1]

As is so often the case with early newspaper accounts, a conclusive follow-up is missing and we're left to wonder if any of the trio was ever returned to his cell. The answer apparently was "no" two and a half months later when three more inmates tried their own escape — after spending the night on the roof of the jail:

> July 12 - Three prisoners - John Webb, George Long and John Morris - escaped from the Charleston Jail at about 4 o'clock Sunday morning. They were confined in the tower, and after making their way through eight locks reached the roof, whence they let themselves down the front of the building to the street by means of their blankets. Long, who was the last to descend, was arrested by private Donahue of the police, and sent back to jail. He had a large knife on his person when taken. Webb and Morris are still at large.
>
> Long states that the party reached the roof of the building about 11 o'clock on Saturday night, but did not make the descent until 4 o'clock on Sunday morning, as the policeman was on duty. Long had been detained as a witness against McNary, Butler and Thompson, who were confined in jail for an alleged robbery of a boarder at the Charleston Hotel early in May, last, but who subsequently effected their escape.
>
> Morris, the third of the party, has just been found guilty of negro stealing...and...on Saturday was sentenced to be hung on the 27 of August next. [2]

1859 – FINAL ATTEMPT TO FLEE THWARTED

In 1859, an accused murder particularly skilled at freeing himself almost succeeded again but came up short. A newspaper article revealed the facts:

...it was found that Richard J. Foster, now under extreme sentence for burglary - who it will be remembered made an adroit escape from the Guard House after his first arrest - had made considerable progress in preparations for an escape before the day of (his) execution.

By means of a saw, extemporized from a table-knife, and other implements which he had cunningly secreted, he had finished an opening large enough for his person, through the wood and brick work, and was about entering on the task of severing or bending the iron bars.

From his own proficiency in such resources, it is probable that he would soon have made his attempt at escape. [3]

Foster, in fact, was hanged in the jail yard on the day originally scheduled. (For more on Foster's execution, see "Chapter 10 - Very Grim Reaping".)

1864 - Union Army Prisoners Dig Through Jail Yard Wall, 27 Escape

Escape was top of mind for many of the captured Union soldiers kept in the jail and its yard during the Civil War. According to a journal he published after his release, Joseph P. Darling, Company F, First Maine Cavalry, and more than two dozen of his comrades managed to let themselves out by removing bricks from the high walls that surrounded them. According to Darling, whose account was published in the 1897 issue of "The Main Bugle," a large, old door that had been left in the jail yard was leaned against the wall for shelter. "Six or eight men could sleep under it," he said, noting that tents for those confined in the yard were scarce. He wrote:

One day one of the boys under the door began to dig the mortar out from between the bricks and found it very soft. He soon dug out a brick and then another. Then they began to plan an escape. A few of us were let into the secret, and we began to investigate. We discovered that on the other side of the wall was the yard of the penitentiary (Editor's Note: refers to the Work House), inclosed by a high brick wall, and that it was entered by a large, heavy wood gate, and that the gate was not guarded.

The boys commenced work systematically, secretly removing bricks and concealing the breach in the wall by hanging a shirt or some other article over it.

Darling said he and a friend decided a break for them was too risky but they did elect to assist in the plot:

We took a part of a tent, tore in into strips, tied it together and made a long, strong rope, tied a half brick to one end and everything was ready. After dark they opened the hole, and while the rest of us were making a great noise, about thirty of the boys went through the hole.

Everything was still and quiet on the other side. They threw the half brick over the gate, and began to climb over. Twenty-seven of the boys landed in the dark narrow street below, but it could not be done without some noise. On the other side of the street opposite the gate, lived an old Dutchman. His window in the second story went up, and he sang out, "Vat vas de matter ofer tare?" The fugitives scattered in every direction, and those who had not yet scaled the gate, went back through the hole in a hurry, lay down in their accustomed places, and, of course, were fast asleep, - my chum and I among the rest.

Darling said that in less than twenty minutes, thirty Rebel soldiers poured into the yard and, with a lantern, determined 27 prisoners were missing.

There were many Union men and women in the city, and they tried to find the fugitives to hide them away. There was great excitement in the city but the boys managed to avoid recapture until the next day when four of them were brought back. In a week or so thirteen more were brought in, tired, hungry, and almost dead. They were put in the lower cells (Editor's Note: Possibly cells buried in the yard and alluded to in other accounts) for punishment for a few days.

Masons were sent in to fix up the hole, a guard was stationed inside, and peace again reigned in Charleston. [4]

1867 - ESCAPEES WIELD AX, 31 GO FREE

After the war, the Charleston jail's prison population reverted to the collection of civilian offenders it had confined before. The notion of escape, of course, continued to flourish. In one case, the state's failure to replace an inadequate lock was blamed for a break. The story was picked up by The New York Times and published on December 11, 1867:

At 7:30 A.M. yesterday, about 30 prisoners, confined in the jail, were turned into the yard for the purpose of emptying their slops. While there, some of the prisoners managed to steal an ax from the woodhouse, and rushing at the gate, succeeded in forcing the lock and making their escape before Mr. Hazeltine, the jailor, who was present, could interfere. As soon as practical, he closed the gate and secured the yard, but one white and thirty colored prisoners made their escape.

The story said a policeman on guard outside the jail actually saw the escape. Armed with just a club, the guard was able to arrest only one of the escapees, not before, however, a prisoner swung the ax at him which "...fortunately, proved harmless."

Later that night, only two additional inmates had been found and returned to the jail. The article concluded:

> **The gate from which the prisoners escaped was fastened by a padlock alone...Frequent applications have been made by the jailor, Mr. Hazeltine, to the Commissioners to have the gate secured by a stronger and more serviceable lock, but from want of funds this was not done. Most of the prisoners who made their escape were confined for larceny, vagrancy and similar offenses. Some of them had not been brought to trial, and a few were to be sent to the state Penitentiary at an early day. [5]**

CHAPTER 10

VERY GRIM REAPING – WHY SOME NEVER GOT OUT ALIVE

There are those who claim that 40,000 or more prisoners died in the Charleston District Jail, many at the hands of sadistic and violent guards. This extraordinary assertion equates to an average of 292 deaths each of the 137 years the jail was operated. However, there is no reliable evidence to support this. In fact, there are records that suggest that deaths in the jail were not as common as one might assume and that the overwhelming majority of these probably were from natural causes. Furthermore, it is possible that in some years, no one died while confined.

While a definitive list and number of all jail deaths has not been found, there are sources from which implications can be drawn.

For example, mortality in Charleston from 1819 to 1863 is documented in a series of books entitled the *South Carolina Death Records* available at the Charleston County Public Library. [1] Compiled from various sources including original, hand-written index cards, many include the addresses at which bodies were found. The Charleston District Jail is only occasionally named. In some cases, deaths listed can be matched up with newspaper articles in the library's microfilm archive, especially in the rare instances when execution or suicide is given as the cause.

In those books, most jail deaths were blamed on ailments like acute bronchitis, debility (physical weakness), hepatitis, dysentery, gastritis, convulsions, heart rheumatism, inanition (lack of nourishment), nervous prostration, typhoid fever, apoplexy (stroke), scarlet fever and old age. Several infants as young as eight months are listed as having died at the jail — presumably because their mothers were incarcerated and the children had no where else to go. One man was said to have succumbed to a "puncture wound" and another to "a visitation by God." Few jail deaths are listed as executions and after 1911, the practice was moved to the state penitentiary in Columbia.

It appears that executions were relatively rare. A list of felony convictions taken from the Records and Dockets of the Court of Sessions for the Charleston District from 1800 through 1817 includes only eight for the charge of "murder," sixteen for "manslaughter" and five for "negro stealing," three of the listed offenses that might carry the death penalty. [2]

Only a couple dozen references to jail yard hangings have surfaced. Newspapers of the day aggressively covered such events but stories about them number no more than a few in any given year.

The last execution was in 1911, the year Capt. William J. Bennett took over as jailer. He served until just before the jail was closed in 1937. In a 1938 Post and Courier interview, Bennett said, "In the last twenty-seven years, only five prisoners have died at the jail. Two committed suicide and two were sick when brought to the jail. The other died suddenly." [3]

Even several influenza outbreaks that occurred during Captain Bennett's years of service failed to penetrate the walls of the jail and claim lives, he said.

Still, some have argued that thousands of jail deaths went unrecorded because inmates were considered "throwaway" persons about whom no one cared. Another sensational claim is that many bodies were unceremoniously tossed into the Ashley River. It stretches this author's imagination to think corpses bobbing about in a waterway flanking the city would remain a secret or go unreported. Careful reading of the city's newspapers on file at the Charleston County library suggests that newspapers regularly published reports of crimes and disturbances large and small, including many that involved incarceration for those involved. It seems unlikely that the ongoing disposal of numerous corpses would escape notice.

It is likely the majority of jail deaths occurred during the time captured Union troops flowed through the facility from 1861 to

1865. Many were already wounded or ill when they arrived. They were forced to live with little shelter or appropriate clothing and often failed to receive adequate rations or medical treatment. Battlefield wounds were made worse by malnourishment and exposure to the elements. Whether or not POW deaths were officially recorded is not known but some were cited in journals published by the soldiers after the war.

Captured soldier Samuel Harris, in his 1897 memoir, describes one such death:

> ... we were taken by rail to Charleston, S.C. and put in the jail yard. We found that all the other prisoners we had left behind in Macon had been brought direct to Charleston. We were all taken there to keep our folks from firing into the city from the Swamp Angel Battery. Quite a number of our boys thought we were going to be exchanged very soon. They were very much disappointed that we were not. Capt. Sprague, an officer in the First Michigan Cavalry, gave up to a feeling of despondency. One day I was walking by the jail and saw him sitting on the ground leaning against the wall with his face laying on his knees, the worst picture of despair I ever saw. I tried my best to rouse him up; so did others, but all to no use. The second day after this he died. A perfect example of the power of the mind over the body. [4]

In *The Capture, the Prison Pen and the Escape*, William Glazier tells of an officer who tried to comfort a dying comrade:

> One poor fellow, who was lying in the jail-yard when we arrived, recognized in one of our number his former captain. In a feeble voice, he addressed him as such, but the poor prisoner was so tattered and emaciated, and blackened by disease and exposure, that the captain did not recognize him. A faltering, broken explanation located him in his memory, and the look a melancholy pleasure in rehearsing their mutual and individual experiences. The dying man was too far

gone to need assistance had any been possible, and all the captain could do was to lie down by his side during the long, cold night that followed, and close his eyes in the morning. [5]

A suicide in the jail was reported in detail in the June 5, 1867 edition of a Charleston newspaper:

The man Hughey Kerns, who was sent to jail Monday last, for a brutal outrage and deadly assault committed upon the person of a little colored girl, near Happoldt's farm, on the previous day, committed suicide Tuesday night, by strangulation. The manner in which the poor wretch took his life exhibited a determination of purpose that could only have been aroused by an overwhelming consciousness of his guilt, and consequent inability to endure the tortures of conscience. Fastening a leather belt and silk pocket-handkerchief together, he attached one end to the grating of the inner door of his cell and the other around his neck in a a slip-knot, and then threw himself forward and lay in that position, only his head and arms being above the floor, until death ensued. A very considerable length of time must have elapsed before life became extinct. The body was found in the position we have described by a colored employee of the jail between six and seven o'clock yesterday... [6]

EXECUTIONS AND THE CHARLESTON DISTRICT JAIL

Of all the ways one could meet his maker at the Charleston District Jail, it is the act of execution that invariably provokes the most curiosity. In fact, most of what we know about death at the jail comes from newspaper accounts of what, for a time, were rather popular spectator events.

Death by hanging was always the officially sanctioned method employed at the jail but precisely how many occurred remains a mystery. Did jail authorities or the sheriff maintain an official log of executions? If so, it has yet to surface.

There is an interesting list, apparently compiled by the late Emmett Robinson, Charleston theatrical entrepreneur and contributor to the museum project at the jail in the 1970s. Among his papers archived at the South Carolina Historical Society is one labeled "Hangings, Etc." Not all events listed occurred at the jail and it includes a few other punishments, as well. The tabulation without attribution is as follows:

Feb. 8, 1805 -   Richard Dennis, the younger
        Joshua Nettler - back of jail
Jan. 30, 1813 - Pierre Matheseau - front of jail
Feb. 29, 1813 - John E. Baldioiu
Mar. 29, 1819 - Martin Toohey
        (1820 - May 13 Pirates, Aug. 20, pirates)
        1820 - Lavinia Fisher and husband - Boundary Street
Aug. 12, 1820 - William Hayward
        1822 - Denmark Vesey
Sep. 24, 1831 - Negro, jail yard
Oct. 21, 1831 - Negro, jail yard
Aug. 17, 1832 - Irvin - jail yard
        1822 - Whipping in market
Jun. 8, 1828 - Lifo, the Spaniard - jail yard
Jul. 14, 1843 - Thomas McCantz - jail yard
Sep. 3, 1847 - Nicholas (slave)
Jul. 20, 1849 - 2 men - jail yard
        1853 - whipping in market
        1858 - whipping in market
Mar. 25, 1859 - Richard Foster - jail yard, weight system
Nov. 2, 1860 - Abraham - jail yard
        1906 - Marcus - jail yard, weight
        1911 - Duncan - jail yard, last [7]

Some on Robinson's list received much notoriety at the time they occurred and easily are found in newspaper archives. References to others remain elusive. Also, Robinson's list is by no means complete. But given the intense interest in these deaths among many citizens of Charleston, it is unlikely that many escaped notice.

Jail yard hangings, by most accounts, seemed to have been a popular attraction. When permitted, citizens jammed themselves onto the jail property to watch. The overflow was forced to perch on balconies and rooftops of homes and businesses adjacent to the jail, thus providing an unobstructed view over the high wall. From time-to-time authorities closed the jail gates to the general public. One presentment by the Grand Jury of 1818 included an item that decried "…execution of criminals within the city, as a nuisance, and a violation to the feelings of persons dwelling in the vicinity of the gaol, and recommend(s) that the sentences of the law be carried into effect somewhere out of the limits of the city." However, the jail yard seems to have been the site for nearly all officially sanctioned hangings for the next 93 years.

In fact, the most spectacularly detailed accounts of deaths at the jail can be found in lurid newspaper reports describing these hangings. It was the fashion of newspapers to provide readers unable to attend with rich detail.

How the Condemned were Hanged

The historical record is not definitive as to when execution on the jail property began but the method employed has been well-documented. Death came at the end of a rope, but not in the drop-through-the-trap-door manner most often associated with this form of capital punishment. Rather, the condemned stood on the grassless earth of the jail yard, next to a vertical pole some 20 to 25 feet in height whose top had been fitted with a crossbar, forming an inverted "L". The noose rope was threaded through several pulleys and its end was attached to a heavy metal weight hidden from view in a wooden box next to the pole. Under the weight box was a deep hole. Upon the order of the Sheriff, the gallows operator released the weight into the pit, jerking the noosed victim off his feet and into the air. This process either broke the neck or choked the air from the lungs.

This gruesome but effective approach may have been a carry-over from one employed aboard sailing vessels. Convicted of piracy and held for a while at the Charleston District Jail, George Clark and Henry Robert Wolf eventually were moved to the deck of a vessel moored in Charleston Harbor. As reported in a newspaper in 1820:

> **Charleston, May 13 - The Execution of George Clark, and Henry Robert Wolf, convicted of acts of Piracy on board the Buenos Ayrean ship Louisa, fitted out at Baltimore, was carried into effect yesterday, at noon, agreeably to their sentence, on board the United States schooner Tartar, lying in the stream.**
>
> **Preparations having been previously made on board the Tartar, at an early hour, a yellow flag was displayed at the fore-top mast head, the usual signal for an execution. A short time before eleven o'clock, the solemn procession moved from the gaol. Morton A. Waring, Esq. whose province it was, as Marshall of the District, to put the Execution in force, accompanied by Francis G. Deliesseline, esq. the sheriff of Charleston District, with their respective Deputies, mounted on horseback, led the way, they were followed by the two prisoners, with halters about their necks, in a carriage; in which also were the Rev. Mr. Bachman, and the Rev. Mr. Munds, the coach being surrounded on all sides by the City Guard.**

The story said the procession proceeded through the city, to the wharf and then to ship. The condemned mounted the scaffold. Clark maintained his innocence but both seemed resigned to their fate.

> **... The hangman proceeded to make the halters fast to the ropes which had been rove through the blocks at the yard arms, but evincing an ignorance of his business, the prisoners respectively, with their own hands**

affixed them, their eyes were then covered with hand-kerchiefs, & at about ten minutes past 12, the fatal signal gun was fired — and they were run up to the respective yard arms, in the smoke. This operation was not performed as is frequently the case by the seamen; but by heavy weights attached to the other ends of the ropes, by which they were suspended; these had been secured to the sides of the vessel, and on the signal being given, the lashings were cut away, & the weights sinking in the stream, launched the prisoners into eternity.

It was an awful scene — and the mode of execution being entirely new to the great body of our citizens, together with the great interest excited by the nature of their crimes, drew together an immense concourse of people – the wharves, shipping and stores, within view, being filled with spectators, and the harbour covered with boats in all directions. [8]

LOCATION OF THE GALLOWS

It is likely that one gallows pole or another stood in the yard of the jail for nearly all but the last few years the prison was in operation. But its specific location there seems to have varied.

References written years apart place it on both the east side of the property and, during the Civil War, it was described as being near the rear jail yard wall, directly behind the octagon. Drawings and engravings made by imprisoned Union soldiers confirm this.

Courtesy of the Library of Congress

Detail from Union War Prisoners Association engraving shows gallows

After the last man was hanged in 1911, twenty-one years passed when, in 1932, the Grand Jury offered the heavy weights used in the apparatus to the Charleston Museum. The article suggests that the gallows pole and drop box had been dismantled, moved or destroyed sometime between 1911 and 1932. A Post and Courier article published September 20, 1932, and was headlined "Grand Jury Suggests Giving Gallows Weights to Museum":

> **The Charleston county grand jury yesterday recommended that the weights which were used until twenty-five years ago (Editor's Note: probably a math error since the last hanging occurred in 1911, not 1907) in the gallows at the Charleston County Jail be presented to the Charleston Museum. The weights are the only part of the gallows which still remains at the jail.**[9]

Martha Zierden, Curator of Historical Archeology for the museum said that there is no record that the institution accepted the weights. It is possible they still reside in the jail yard, buried in one of the holes into which they regularly dropped while in service.

Following are accounts pertaining to the macabre activity that defined capital punishment at the Charleston District Jail.

1859 - RICHARD J. FOSTER HANGED IN THE JAIL YARD

The Last Penalty… was inflicted on the body of Richard J. Foster, according to due and solemn sentence, on Friday, 25th inst., in the jail yard of this city and District. The convict was attended, in his last moments and in the procession to the place of execution, by his spiritual advisers…The prayers appropriate for the occasion were read with and for the convict by these clergymen, and a crucifix borne by one of them… was frequently applied to the lips of the prisoner.

Thus began the March 26, 1859 newspaper account of the hanging of Richard J. Foster who had been convicted of a burglary during which a death occurred. The reader of "Chapter 9 - Desperate to Get Out" might recall that Foster had a few days earlier been found to have scratched through the wall of his cell in hopes of escaping but was thwarted. His day of reckoning came on schedule and he found found himself standing at death's door:

… under the charge of John E. Carew, Esq., Sheriff, the white cap was fixed on the prisoner's head, the noose adjusted around his neck, and the signal was given. At 3:12 P.M. the iron trigger which supported the heavy weight suspended over the pit, was released by a touch of the official appointed, and the body of the convict was shot upward.

In less than one minute - we believe in about forty seconds - all signs of life and motion and sensation had ceased. … the Clergymen before mentioned performed the short but solemn funeral rites that had

been requested. The body was then taken in charge by the Sheriff and disposed of according to law.

The attendance was large and in some respects on the outside tumultuous, but we heard of no special disorder. Such scenes are rare, and, we trust, will continue rare, and nothing will secure this result so certainly as the rigid, and righteous, and just enforcement of the laws. [10]

The Gallows During the Civil War

It is unclear whether or not any captured Union soldier was hanged in the jail yard but it is doubtful. Post-war writers made many references to the presence of the gallows but none claim to have witnessed an execution by hanging. Such an occurrence would likely have received wide notoriety among prisoners and the Northern press.

However, the gallows stood as a reminder of their plight and was recollected by almost all who wrote of spending time in captivity on Magazine Street. One Union captive eloquently recounted his memory of the gallows in a story that appeared May 10, 1891 in the New York Times. Headlined *From Under the Union Guns*, the unidentified soldier wrote:

If any one were to ask me, "Did you ever stand under the gallows?" I should feel compelled to say "Yes," and to add, "I have slept in the shadow of the gallows for weeks." In most county jails the gallows is a temporary affair, put up the night before an execution and then taken down afterward, so as not to outrage the vision and shock the sensibilities of prisoners whose offenses do not call for capital punishment; but the scaffold in the Charleston jail yard was a permanent fixture. I never looked at it, even on the hottest day, when the sight did not lower the temperature perceptibly. Like the gnomon (projecting piece) of a weird sun dial the shadow of the scaffold marked high noon at the entrance to the ragged tent in which three companions and myself slept. It looked particularly ghostly and aggressive in the uncertain light of the half-clouded moon.

Drawing by Sam Wilson

"In the center of the yard was a gallows…"

And in the darkness, when the sea winds roared in and the rain hissed spitefully down through the many rents in the canvas, the upper arm of the gallows seemed to sway and groan as if a strangling man were hanging from it. It took on its most frightful aspect when seen by a flash of lightning in a dark night. For years afterward I always saw that gallows in dreams induced by late and imprudent dining.

The writer then used dialect to relate a conversation he had with one of his captors:

"Ever anybody hanged on it," repeated a Confederate Sergeant, to whom I had put the question. "Wa'al, I shoud say that there haz been. Befu' the wah more'n twenty men, white and black, but mostly n——s, wuz jerked up thar a livin' and dropped down - ker chunk - dead. Since the wah, more particularly since the jail haz been made a prison for Yankees, things hazn't been quite o brisk in that line. Still thar haz been a right smart of hangin's. Some of your folks say hit's ole fashion and ain't up with kinks they rig on to gallowses up North. But, I tell you, thar's a power of good solid work in that thar old machine yet," and the conservative Confederate looked up at the creaky, weather-beaten scaffold with an expression of actual admiration. [11]

Apparently another gallows was erected in the expectation that 24 blacks — including four former slaves — were to be hanged after their capture as soldiers of the 54th Massachusetts Regiment. They had attempted, and failed, to take Fort Wagner. As Fergus M. Mordewich wrote in an article entitled "A Civil Battle for a Civil War Battlefield" in the July 2005 Smithsonian Magazine, black captures presented Confederate leaders with a political dilemma:

Armed blacks were the South's worst nightmare, conjuring deep-seated fears of slave rebellion and race war. Moreover, to acknowledge blacks as soldiers was to admit that they were equal to whites, which would undermine the whole rationale for slavery, and much of the rationale for secession. According to Confederate law, captured black soldiers were to be disposed of by state law: the punishment in almost all the Southern states for "instigating slave rebellion" was either death or, for free blacks, enslavement.

Mordewich wrote that 24 of the black captives were ordered to stand trial in Charleston and a new gallows was built in the yard, even before the proceeding began.

However, President Lincoln had warned that for every Union soldier executed—black or white—a rebel would be executed, and for any one enslaved, a Rebel prisoner would be put at hard labor. "Our slaves are to be made our equals in our own country, fighting against us," fulminated the Charleston Mercury. "If President Davis submits to this, it will argue that he determines we shall not carry on the war, and adopts the Yankee policy of ending it."

Unexpectedly — probably under pressure from Confederate generals who feared the consequences of the anticipated executions for their own POWs in the North—the court caved in to Lincoln's threat. It quietly ruled that it had no jurisdiction in the case, thus tacitly admitting that black soldiers were prisoners of war like any others, and had to be treated accordingly.

Mordewich said the court's decision was "...so potentially incendiary that the (Charleston) Mercury dared not even report it. Confederate authorities never again dared to put them on trial." [12]

JAIL HANGINGS RESUME AFTER THE WAR

Even if the jail yard gallows stood idle during the war, its function resumed afterward. An execution there in 1872 was described in a New York Times account February 3, 1872, headlined "A Murderer's End." Daniel White had been convicted of the murder of railroad depot agent and sentenced to death.

The horrible spectacle, as usual, seemed to have a strange fascination for the multitude, and the gates of the jail-yard were besieged at an early hour by crowds of men and boys anxious to see the execution. The hanging, however, was, in a measure private, hardly more than 100 persons beside the officials being present. Admittance could be obtained only by a pass from the Sheriff. The weather was dark, damp and cold, and masses of threatening clouds shrouded the

face of the sun, throwing a glow over the faces of the shivering spectators.

The sheriff, the article said, climbed the stairs to the "... tower, where the felons are confined..." and found White in the corridor. White was described as having "...an ashy, sickening hue" and maintained his innocence, explaining that the real killer had gotten away. But when asked for the identity of the culprit, White replied that he was going to die for it and that there was no use in saying any more about it.

> **... the Sheriff and his officers descending to the yard, proceeded with the final preparations. There was little to be done. The heavy weight was on the spring, and a strong one-inch rope was passed through the top-piece, and tied securely to the weight. The other end hung down in the middle between the posts. A small hempen rope, about a third of an inch in diameter, was quickly fashioned into a running noose, and fastened to the longer rope. The weight was then let down once to ascertain whether it would draw the noose to the required height, and having been again replaced, everything awaited the coming of the doomed man.**

The reporter said neighboring piazzas and house-tops were crowded with the curious seeking a view over the wall. Among those few that had been admitted to the jail yard was the murder victim's father-in-law who wanted "to see the thing done." In time, White appeared in the yard. Despite the raw winter chill, he wore not hat or coat.

At the foot of the gallows, the sheriff read the sentence calling for execution and asked White if he had anything to say. White, who had a chew of tobacco in his mouth, cleared his throat, shook his head and said he had "nothing," according to the article.

> **The prisoner now knelt with the priest upon the damp ground, and prayed long and with much apparent fervor, the spectators standing hushed and with uncovered heads. At the end the wretched man arose, and**

taking another chew of tobacco, stood eyeing with apparent defiance the preparations for death. While doing this he continually spoke with the priest, and at length broke forth into a hymn.

He was now made to stand directly under the fatal noose, and while his hands and feet were being secured he addressed himself to various persons present, particularly one of the turnkeys, whom he exhorted to repent and meet him in heaven, and to whom he also gave a chew of tobacco, and asked him to pray for the giver while using it. He then prayed aloud with the priest, and this being ended the Sheriff stepped forward and adjusted a white stockinet cap over the prisoner's head and face. As it came over his mouth, White asked them to stop until he could spit out his tobacco, and having done so the cap was fitted on. The noose was then tightened gradually around the neck, and the knot adjusted with care beneath the left ear.

He stood thus for a moment when the Sheriff gave the signal. The (hangman) gave a quick pull to the rope attached to the iron spring, and while the weight came down with a crash into the deep hole the body of White was jerked violently upward, within a few inches of the cross-piece of the gallows, and then came down with a heavy thud. The rope tightened and cut into the neck as the body swayed from side to side in muscular contortions. For about three minutes, the strong life struggled within the body, and heavy sighs could be heard. Then the limbs grew still, and the widely distended eyes could be seen beneath the stockinet cap as they almost burst from their sockets. A small trace of blood was visible upon the cap, where the latest breath had left the mouth, and the motionless body swung around and faced the vast assemblage on a neighboring piazza, as if in stern rebuke of their idle curiosity.

The body, the article said, hung for thirty minutes and then was cut down. An examination by two doctors confirmed White was dead and his body was turned over to the coroner. It was said his neck had been dislocated but not broken. Eventually, the crowd dispersed. [13]

By 1878, the clamor among those who found public hangings distasteful was heard by the state legislature which passed an act that attempted to discourage such displays. Attendance in the jail yard was limited to the sheriff, his deputy and assistants, the solicitor, attorneys for the defense and "10 discreet persons."

It appears that 11 years passed before an execution was performed under the decree. A court had sentenced Daniel Washington to hang for the death of Allen Collins, whose gunshot wound to the leg had turned to gangrene. Collins, it was said, had been aiding detectives in the capture of members of a gang of horse-thieves. One night, while dining with his family, someone fired a load of buckshot into the house, striking Collins in the leg. He died after several days and Washington, thought to have been a member of the gang, was arrested.

Evidence against Washington was said to be "purely circum-stantial" but his bid for retrial was denied. "Strenuous" efforts by the sheriff to have Washington reprieved seemed so promising until just an hour before the hanging was scheduled. The turn of events apparently caught everyone by surprise. The newspaper report said "…no preparations had been made for the execu-tion, and it required considerable activity after that time to erect and rig the gallows."

> **About 12 o'clock Sheriff Collins entered Washington's cell… and announced that there was no further hope, and advised him to prepare himself for the worst. It was apparent from the heart-rending demonstrations of despair of the unfortunate man which followed this declaration, that hope had still lingered in his breast. He cried bitterly, and over and over declared his inno-cence of this crime.**

After the violence of his grief had somewhat subsided, he... said: "It is so hard to have right and justice denied me. Oh, I hope I won't be long dying."

At 1:15 p.m., the hangman entered the enclosed box next to the gallows and Washington, supported on each side by priests, approached the foot of the gallows. He wore a gray sack coat, black pantaloons fastened around the waist with a red scarf but was shoeless. When asked if he wished to speak, he said "No, I haven't much to say. I am not guilty; but I forgive everybody who helped to get me here.

The cap was then drawn over his eye, the noose was adjusted, his arms and legs were fastened, and at precisely 1:30 o'clock the lever was turned. Washington shot about six feet into the air, and then dropped three feet, in which position he hung motionless until life was pronounced extinct, at 1:45 P.M., when his body was taken down and sent to Potter's Field for interment.

Dr. Bellinger stated that death occurred instantaneously, his neck having been broken when the weights fell. (The priests) said that as far as they were allowed to reveal anything that transpired in the confessional, they could conscientiously declare Washington innocent of the murder...Sheriff Collins and nine-tenths of those present concurred in this declaration and expressed the opinion that Washington's bad reputation had had more to do with his conviction than the evidence in the case... [14]

ICE PICK MURDERER'S HANGING LEAVES CHARLESTON BLACKS IN DISBELIEF

On a beautiful August day in 1906, a former railroad worker may have been the first white man to be executed in Charleston County since the Civil War. William Marcus had been sentenced to death for stabbing his wife 42 times with an ice pick because he believed she was having an affair. Many in Charleston's black community were so astonished that they refused to believe the hanging actually occurred. Their doubts were reinforced by the fact that no blacks were present inside the jail yard. The following day, a newspaper article said:

> **There was a good deal of talk on the streets today in Charleston about the execution of yesterday, because of the fact of the rarity of a hanging in Charleston county, and especially of a white man. The negroes generally in the city refuse to believe that Marcus was hanged at all yesterday. Although there were over 500 men present at the execution, no negroes were admitted, cards being required at the jail gate. The fact that no colored man saw Marcus die and the superstition that because it rained here this morning he was not dead has given rise to the stand taken by the negroes.** [15]

Revelations pertaining to the Marcus case and his execution fanned intense flames of interest throughout Charleston. The newspaper called the murder "...the most brutal in the criminal annals of Charleston County." Marcus apparently was a rover who, it was later discovered, had another wife and five children in Ohio. His relationship with his "wife" in Charleston was mostly on-again, off-again as his frequent travels took him as far away as Seattle and Cincinnati.

According to testimony at his trial, the 44-year-old killed Maggie Stone Marcus on the night before Easter, just after she had returned from confession at a nearby church. Marcus had accused her of having an affair with a man who employed her as a servant. Marcus accused Maggie of passing along to him a sexually transmitted disease. He demanded that she resign from her job. When she refused, the newspaper said, "He then drew the ice pick, which he admitted that he had specially sharpened for the purpose, and began to stab her with the instrument."

Marcus left the woman's body on the beach where he had taken her and, with another man, went to the victim's house and destroyed a picture of himself she had hung on a wall. After a night of drinking, he was found on the home's rear piazza and arrested. He admitted the slaying to a marshal. He was quickly taken to the Charleston County jail since it was feared island residents might do him harm. The article reported that a doctor "… made an examination of the woman, and found nothing to verify Marcus' charge that she was diseased."

A plea of insanity was rejected by the court and, the newspaper said, a jury of white men wasted no time in reaching a verdict of guilty in the first degree:

> **Marcus received the verdict without any emotion, showing an air of absolute indifference, which he maintained through all the time that he was in jail, although recently his manner weakened a little, as the time for the execution drew near.**

After his conviction, Marcus was returned to the Charleston District Jail and kept in solitary confinement. The Evening Post of Charleston of June 14, 1906 said:

> **…The prisoner (William Marcus) is confined on the third floor of the jail, on the Franklin street side, in a section by himself. He is shut up in a cage about eight by six feet in dimensions. The hammock which is usually hung up in the cage for use as a bed was taken down last night in the cage occupied by Marcus and a mattress put on the floor for him to sleep on. There are ropes on the end of the hammock and it was thought that in case Marcus should take a notion to hang himself that it would be well to deprive him of the means.**

Over the following 45 days, Marcus discussed religious affiliation with various visiting ministers, talked easily about his impending fate and exhibited, the paper said, an enormous appetite: "Marcus ate everything that come his way."

It was 10:50 a.m. August 3 when the sheriff went to his cell and read the death warrant. The paper said that when Marcus paused for a last interview with reporters, he "...spoke distinctly and without tremor." He was dressed in a neat, black suit, white shirt and collar and black tie. He was clean-shaven and his hair neatly brushed.

His march to gallows was slow but firm. "Once...he stumbled slightly and Sheriff Martin gripped his left arm," the article said. "He smiled a bit and immediately afterwards asked the sheriff to excuse him for smiling, as he did it with no intention of levity in the solemn moment."

After binding his arms to his sides, Marcus was escorted outside and around the west side of the jail building and into the brightness of the morning. The sheriff unfolded an umbrella and held it above the prisoner's head.

> **The march to the gallows was made through the flower garden of the jailor, and the beauty of the flowers smiling under a bright morning sun cast a sharp contrast on the procession that wended about the south corner of the jail.**

> **The crowd was waiting on the east side of the jail. They were roped off from the gallows, which was inclosed in an open space of about thirty feet square. Just under the east wall of the gloomy jail building the machine of death had been built. In its simplicity it appeared all the more formidable as an instrument of execution. At the south end of the big frame from which dangled the heavy rope with a loop in its end was a box like structure. This was divided into two compartments, one of which held the heavy weight, and the other the ketchman. The gallows frame was painted a light blue.**

The sheriff asked all present to remove their hats. Under the noose and facing the spectators, Marcus offered a last statement begging forgiveness, concluding "...I appeal to pray to God to have mercy on my soul."

> **An officer advanced and tied slender ropes about the knees of Marcus. Then the hangman's noose was**

brought forward with the black cap. The noose rope was made of half-inch hemp and had been soaped and put into condition. It was about seven feet long.

Marcus was drinking in the sunlight and taking a last look at his fellow men when the dread black cap was thrown over his head. His face, in a moment, was hidden from view, and he straightened himself up slightly, a terrible object to behold, bound and capped ready for the execution.

The noose was dropped over his head and the thick firm knot was slipped tight about his neck. Sheriff Martin asked him if the noose choked him and from the black cap the reply came that it was pretty tight. After having set the heavy knot under his left ear the officers attached the rope firmly into the loop of the gallows rope and Marcus was prepared for execution.

The congregated throng was grouped around the western and northern portions of the yard. About the jail the roofs of the houses were thick with people. On the Roper Hospital a number of persons were gathered to witness the work of the law. Even the unoccupied cells that overlooked the gallows were crowded with spectators.

The crowd watched breathlessly as the noose was fastened around Marcus' neck. When the ketch was sprung and the body rose in the air and then shot upward and downward again, a deep stillness filled the place, then a long sigh could distinctly be heard. It was an awesome moment and one that can never be eradicated from the mind of every hushed onlooker. Even some dogs that were about the jail yard seemed to appreciate the solemnity of the occasion and gave vent to dismal howls. Several chickens were seen to look inquiringly up at the man who had paid the penalty for his crimes.

There was no special convulsive movement at first. The hands twitched a little and the legs drew up a bit. Following this movement the body began to tremble sharply from head to foot and then became still.

A stepladder was placed beside the gallows and a doctor in attendance who climbed it detected a faint heartbeat. Nine minutes passed before Marcus was pronounced dead. He later said that the average time of a hanging death was 14 minutes. He went on to speculate that Marcus had gone unconscious at the moment he left the ground and suffered no pain.

After the execution, the paper said, the crowd quietly dispersed. It was noted in a later story that Marcus' legitimate wife had missed a train in Ohio and, consequently, had not been in attendance. [16]

1911 - THE LAST TO BE HANGED AT CHARLESTON DISTRICT JAIL

Charleston, July 6 - Sitting a hammock strung along the top of his cell from where he could look down upon the gallows on which tomorrow he will hang, Daniel Duncan early this afternoon earnestly declared his innocence. He chatted for twenty minutes with a reporter for The Evening Post, and was the least concerned of the group of which he was a party. This afternoon a dispatch from Columbia states that Gov. Blease will not interfere with Duncan's sentence. [17]

This description launched a story in the Charleston Evening Post published July 6, 1911. It was not realized at the time but Duncan's execution was to be the last performed at the Charleston County Jail. After that time, the condemned were sent to the penitentiary in Columbia where sentence was carried out.

Duncan's was another sensational case that received much coverage. The 23-year-old black man had worked since the age of 10 in a Charleston bakery when he was arrested for the murder of a Jewish merchant. Max Lubelsky's skull had been crushed with a board.

In the ensuing investigation, another shopkeeper and a delivery truck driver gave police descriptions of a black man they'd seen at the store. And, perhaps worse, Mrs. Lubelsky, who had been away on the day of her husband's slaying, said Duncan was the man who several weeks afterward, attacked her at the store. Police arrested Duncan and locked him up in the jail.

During his subsequent trial, Duncan swore that at the time Lubelsky was killed, he had been in front of Jacob's Shoe Store on King Street, contemplating the purchase of a pair of patent leathers, "…reduced from $2.50 to $1.98." He said he heard some screams and rushed to their source, Lubelsky's clothing store, also on upper King. Nonetheless, the jury rendered a verdict of "guilty".

The newspaper said public sentiment was divided and that many believed an innocent man had been wrongly convicted on circumstantial evidence.

His execution was scheduled for July 7 and the Charleston Evening Post that day reported that while a relatively small group of witnesses had been permitted inside the jail yard wall, "…roofs in the neighborhood of the jail were crowded with spectators, and the streets running by the jail were thronged."

As Duncan appeared at the south end, women prisoners in the jail set up a blood curdling howl, that was startling, as it fell upon the quiet atmosphere. Duncan did not flinch when he heard this mournful wail. As he came in sight of the gallows and the spectators, he looked about with interest, and glanced up at the grim frame of death calmly. He shook hands with the official in charge of the weight box warmly, and took his place in position under the rope which dangled down from the top of the frame, and which was in a few minutes to bring him death.

Ropes were tied about Duncan's legs, at the ankles, and he was almost ready for the execution. He made his last statement without a tremor or without stuttering, saying in a low voice that only those near him could hear that he would not die with a lie on his lips.

He was innocent, and wanted to meet all in Heaven.
This was all he had to say.

The reporter noted that after a black cap and noose were slipped over Duncan's head, the latter required tightening "... as Duncan's neck was very large in proportion, and there was a danger of the rope slipping were it loosely fixed."

> **Everything was ready for the springing of the weight, when suddenly Duncan swayed and fell to one side. He had fainted, without a sound. Two officials quickly sprang forward to see that the noose rope was clear. It was. An instant later the weight was sprung, and it dropped over five feet, in its wooden box, jerking Duncan's body straight into the air...then dropped precipitately.**

After a few minutes, motion ceased but the body was left hanging for 39 minutes, to ensure life had been extinguished. About 11:50, the account said, the body was lowered to the ground, freed of shackles and placed inside a plain, pine coffin. The newspaper report concluded:

> **The sheriff and his officials were well pleased with the smoothness of this unpleasant duty. Sheriff Martin has hanged eight men since he has been in office, and every hanging has been a model of order and of careful work.**[18]

POSTSCRIPT: GRANDMOTHER SOLD ROPE TO JAIL'S HANGMAN

Ralph McLaughlin of Charleston confirms a story that has circulated for years about how the jail's hangman was a customer at his grandmother's store in the neighborhood. "The man in charge used to come over to the store and buy the rope they were going to use to hang the people," said McLaughlin. "So, one day some smart aleck comes back over afterward and tells my grandmother that she can buy back the rope cheap and sell it again. I think she ran him out of the store."

McLauglin, who retired after operating a plumbing business in Charleston for many years, said that many of his family members, including his brothers and him, were born in the living quarters above the store.

"They used to hang people in the yard on the east side of the jail," said McLaughlin, "and folks used to pay my grandmother to go up to her porch or attic which were high enough for them to look over the wall and see the gallows."

Chapter 11

Keeper of the Keys: The Jail Career of Captain William J. Bennett

"It's not a bed of roses," said Captain William J. Bennett of the Charleston District Jail, shortly before it was closed. [1] His quarter century as "landlord" tied him so closely to the place that local wags deemed it "Bennett's Hotel." Judging by newspaper accounts and the remembrances of his granddaughter, Bennett was even-handed and compassionate, but he once used his fists to knock a man to the sidewalk in front of the county courthouse.

Jailer from 1911 to 1939, Bennett housed both himself and his family in quarters that were part of the jail itself. It appears that he was resolutely dedicated to his job and did his best to keep his inmate charges from suffering any more than was necessary.

By all surviving accounts, he brooked no nonsense in his lockup. Physical abuse of inmates by guards was strictly forbidden. He provided special meals for prisoners at Thanksgiving and Christmas and was extremely proud that he had managed to keep epidemics of diseases like tuberculosis from getting inside, despite meager resources available to him.

And while his jail service understandably included physical encounters with his charges — an undocumented escape attempt left scars — it was said that he '... never really encountered any serious trouble." [2]

Coincidentally, Bennett's career would end at almost the same time as the jail's when both would succumb to the ravages of old age.

Courtesy of the Post and Courier

Capt. William J. Bennett, jailer for 27 years

Born in Charleston in 1871, Bennett worked his way through a variety of city-related jobs, including 16 years as a city fire department call man and chief of the city street cleaning department. He was named jailer at age 40 in 1911. It is unclear when he began using the title "Captain" or where it originated.

It appears that his first nine or ten years on Magazine Street were uneventful — at least as far as the public record is concerned. The jail was very much a Bennett family affair. His first wife Rosa and their children all lived in special, sealed-off quarters in the front of the building. By 1920, Rosa, had been made jail "matron" by a committee of women assigned to fill the position. A report by the group's chairwoman on May 19, 1920 includes confirmation of Mrs. Bennett's appointment as well as some positive observations on jail conditions:

> Our visit to the jail was most gratifying after our past experiences. The improvements show up at a glance: The yellow walls and ceilings, concrete floors, electric lights, plumbing, shower baths, etc., and, above all, the presence of a real matron in the person of Mrs. Bennett, the wife of Captain William J. Bennet, the jailer. Mrs. Bennett is the official matron at the jail and has been employed as matron since February 1, 1920, at a salary of $50 per month.
>
> A special room has been fitted up for the matron's use near the women's cells, and many modern improvements added.
>
> Only eight negro women prisoners were in the jail. In former years we found as many as 25.
>
> The heating plant, big airy kitchen and other improvements showed what the commission under W.K. McDowell is doing in expending that $20,000 appropriated by the legislature at its last session. The whole work will be completed by June 15, when Captain Bennett, the jailer, hopes to invite the public for inspection. [3]

Another mention of Bennett can be found in the oddly whimsical caption of a newspaper photograph of the front of the jail published August 18, 1928 and captioned "THIS LOOKS LIKE THE COUNTY JAIL":

> Thousands of people in this city have never had the experience of occupying a room in the stately hostelry pictured above, while other thousands, besides many visitors to the city, have used its accommodations, involuntary guests of the genial Capt. W.J. Bennett, general manager. Recently this "hotel" has been the subject of much comment because its guests list exceed its space, and lodgers had to be turned away.
>
> This substantial building, located on Magazine street, has some classic architectural lines, as the glimpse shown in the photograph reveals, and it ought to for it was constructed, according to all accounts before the Revolution. It is really one of the show places of the city, a point of interest for tourists to rejoice over, if viewed from the outside, but within the scenery is not so conducive of joy, if one's time of departure is regulated by law. However, Capt. Bennett occasionally has visitors who come and leave at will, friends of the guests, or natives or tourists who wish to go over the property. Like many other Charleston buildings, its yard is surrounded by a very high wall, and due to the staunch protection given the windows and doors, a burglar would have a tough time breaking in, while the only thing that could break out is measles, it is said, and nobody recalls that this has happened. Yes, of course, this building is the county jail, and, as was remarked at the outset of this verbal hike, thousands of Charleston people have never been inside, and moreover thousands here have never even seen it. [4]

Whether or not pre-1911 Charleston District Jail inmates were physically abused by keepers is an unanswered question. But Bennett, in 1932, stated flatly that no prisoner had been beaten or flogged during his watch, at that time 21 years in duration. Several inmates at a prison in Greenville, South Carolina had claimed mistreatment and the Governor had ordered an investigation. The notoriety prompted a Charleston newspaper to question Bennett about the treatment of inmates in the Charleston jail. In response, he declaimed physical abuses and said, "We never allow beating. I do not think there is any more disgusting idea than striking a grown man when he has not chance to retaliate. The guards here study the interests of the prisoners and they seem to appreciate it." The article continued:

> Being placed on the "black list" is practically the only punishment applied to any Charleston county prisoner, Captain Bennett said yesterday. This means that the prisoner is deprived of the right to receive certain luxuries from friends on the outside, such as cigarets, ice cream, or cake. To this sometimes is added "solitary confinement," - as solitary as it can be in the generally crowded Charleston county jail - for several days. The only disadvantage in this is that it deprives the prisoner of the social contacts with the other prisoners in the same cell block. Lights remain on at the jail until 9 p.m. and prisoners in each cell block generally get together and talk or play checkers between supper time and 9 p.m. In extreme cases, a man may be confined to a diet of bread and water for a day only, but his happens only about once a year in the most recalcitrant cases, he said.

The remainder of the article, in explaining the role of the Charleston jail in the state's justice system, provided a remarkably detailed sketch of what the nature of life there had become, albeit from the perspective of those in charge:

> The county jail receives prisoners from the city police court, from magistrates' courts, coroners' commitments, the court of general sessions and federal prisoners. The federal prisoners generally are at the jail for only a few days awaiting trial, or delivery to some other jail to begin sentences. The county prisoners at the jail either are awaiting trial or serving sentences of less than six months. Those who have sentences of more than six months serve their time at the state penitentiary at Columbia.

There is no county chain gang and there has been none since the abolition of the county prison camps two years ago. The city, however, maintains a chain gang for the male prisoners convicted in the city police court, who are lodged at the county jail to serve their terms. Every day the city convict guards report to the jail and get the city prisoners and take them to work on some municipal project. Most of the prisoners now are being employed cutting wood for poor relief in the city of Charleston. Some have worked at the city golf course, and others are used in cleaning the police station and cell blocks there.

None of the prisoners, either city, county or federal, wear stripes or any uniform. They wear their own clothes, and friends are encouraged to bring new clothes to them. The city prisoners generally are transported to their place of work in a police patrol.

Shackles are worn by only the city prisoners who are used on the chain gang. These are body shackles, the purpose of which is to restrict the leg movements of the prisoners, preventing them from taking long steps in the running away. The chains do no interfere with ordinary locomotion. The prisoners are not linked together with a long chain as been done in previous years.

The county prisoners at the jail are employed in keeping the premises clean and preparing their meals. Women and men are kept separate. The job of preparing three meals a day of substantial food for the prisoners is a considerable task. As an example, there were 148 prisoners at the jail yesterday. Forty of these were received on the day before, twenty-eight of them coming from the city police court. Usually, the city prisoners are in jail for short terms, ranging from three to thirty days, though occasionally some prisoner has several terms to serve.

No money is provided for the work in the jail, and the prisoners keep the place in order at no cost to the county. One of their number acts as cook and he has several assistants.

Bennett admitted that some inmates are 16 years of age and even younger but that they are not required to work. Those younger than 16 ordinarily are kept temporarily, until provision can be made to send them to the state reformatory.

As for order in the jail, Bennett was emphatic:

"There is no kangaroo court at the jail. We positively will not allow the prisoners to attempt to control each other. We have very little trouble with our prisoners, much less than might be expected in any group of the types of individuals which they are. We feed them wholesome food. We never allow beating. [5]

In 1934, the Post and Courier interviewed Bennett again and in an article headlined "Prison Has No Good Effect on Criminals". Bennett blamed fast cars and movie tough-guys as corrupters of youth and, he said, his jail only made things worse:

The prisoners of today are much younger than those of 1912, (Bennett) added, the majority ranging between eighteen and twenty-six years of age. Of nineteen persons convicted at the last term of the court of general sessions, most of them were between fourteen and twenty-seven years old.

Love of adventure, good roads, automobiles, hitch-hiking, gangster pictures, with a little influence of the depression, according to Captain Bennett, are the major causes of crime.

Boys - and girls, too - leave home to seek work and decide to hitch-hike their way. They start out intending to be honest, but failure to find work and despon-

dency and hunger force them into crime. They try blackjacking, holdups and automobile thefts and before they know it they are in jail.

Bennett told the reporter that he favors giving a first offender a suspended sentence to shield him from the "influences" he might encounter in the jail. He said Charleston prisoners are kept segregated, as far as possible, by race, age and sex. At the time the article was published, the jail population was 135, although it could handle as many as 200.

Bennett said the repeal of prohibition (in 1933) and legislation enacted regulating opiates had resulted in a drop in the number of federal prisoners in his jail. He said most criminals freed by governmental pardons returned "sooner or later" and that the incidence of drunkenness continued unabated. Criminals in general, he said, are more hardened and "...he shook his head sadly when asked if many persons who had ever served jail sentences ever amounted to much..."

He said that when he began as jailer, 50 to 60 prisoners in jail at a given time was considered a large number while in 1934, there are 125 to 150 behind his bars at all times.

Despite his reservations about the effectiveness of incarceration, Bennett soldiered on in his post, winning the attention and praise on September 22, 1934, of a New York-based business magazine, "The Nation's Commerce" which said "It is of the utmost importance that the criminal institutions of the country be headed by thoroughly capable and experienced men in order that the progress which has been achieved may be continued and Capt. Bennett is a fine example of a capable executive."[6]

An incident involving Bennett that prompted enough amusement to warrant a newspaper story was, apparently, a case of mistaken identity mixed with a healthy serving of liquor. As reported by the Post and Courier November 24, 1934:

There probably is one visitor to Charleston who is scratching his head and wondering what happened to him a few nights ago in Savannah. Yesterday the man approached Captain William J. Bennett, county jailer, on the street with a glad hand.

"When did you come over?" he asked. "I thought you were still in Savannah."

"Me?" asked Captain Bennett. "When have I been in Savannah?" The stranger appeared befuddled, and explained that he had had a "big" time night before last in Savannah with another traveling salesman, and if Captain Bennett wasn't the man, then he was his twin brother.

"I admit I had been drinking," he said. "But my memory never did anything like this to me before." [7]

But a year later, levity was notably absent when Bennett decked a former employee on the steps of the Courthouse. The precise cause of the altercation was not revealed in the account published by the Post and Courier on December 5, 1935:

As a result of fisticuffs in front of the court house early yesterday afternoon between Captain William J. Bennett, county jailer, and Frank M. Wienges, former watchman at the jail, Wienges was taken to Roper hospital for first aid treatment.

Wienges was flattened to the sidewalk by a blow from Captain Bennett. The altercation grew out of a feud of long standing, and there had been an encounter not long before, inside the court house, the two being separated.

Previously there had been differences between the men, apparently settled when Wienges resigned.

In the encounter, Wienges suffered a cut on the back of his head when it connected with the court house wall and the sidewalk. Captain Bennett said he had been informed that Wienges had a knife and had threatened to assault him. He said that he found an open knife in the pocket of Wienges after he had knocked him down, and that he took away the knife, having acted purely in self-defense. [8]

Wienges denied wielding an open knife but admitted a closed one had been on his person:

> "I was standing on the platform on the second floor of the court house outside of Judge Lunz's office. Captain Bennett came up the steps. I had no thought of his attacking me. I thought he would go into the court room. He made a pass at me, and I ducked and held him away with my foot until some men separated us. Deputy Sheriff Frank J. Simmons ordered me out of the court house and when I said that it was a public building, he said that he would put me out, so I went. I was standing on the corner and Policemen Herron and Cox came up, and Herron told me I'd better leave and keep out of trouble. As Herron left, Captain Bennett appeared and drove my head into the wall and knocked me completely out. I had no open knife in my pocket. I had a closed knife, which I carried for cutting my chewing tobacco." [9]

As part of an on-going series of articles about Charlestonians and their occupations, Bennett was profiled in 1938 and the reporter noted his appearance included "several scalp wounds and facial scars…the mementos of a jail mutiny of six years ago." While this author was unable to find published reference to the uprising, it is likely that such a lengthy term of supervision of the jail included its share of such incidents. Certainly prisoners occasionally tried to break free but Bennett appeared equal to the challenge:

> During the twenty-seven years that Mr. Bennett has been custodian of the jail, not one prisoner has escaped and remained free. Seven years ago, four prisoners escaped from the Charleston jail, only to be recaptured after a short lived liberty. One of the four fugitives was a negro charged with murder. Mr.

Bennett knew that the man had relatives living in New York. He went to New York, traced the fugitive to his hideout, and brought him back to Charleston.

Regarding the feeding of prisoners, the article said:

The inmates of the jail receive three substantial meals daily. The victuals consist of bacon, fresh meat, fresh vegetables in season, and fresh bread. Much cornbread is baked in the jail kitchen to please the prisoners who prefer it to wheat bread.

At Thanksgiving and Christmas the county provides a special menu, with roasted pork for dinner. Pork is used in preference to fowl because it can be shared more equally, Mr. Bennett says. If one prisoner should receive the wing of chicken and another a leg, a jealous squabble would very likely result.

In order that the food might be prepared properly, the county hired a regular prison cook on November 15.

Bennett told the reporter that two doctors care for the medical needs of inmates and that he was particularly proud of the fact that over his twenty-seven years of service, only five inmates had died at the jail; two committed suicide, two were very sick when they arrived and one died suddenly, he said. The article continued:

During the World war when Charleston was visited by influenza epidemics, incoming boats carrying prisoners were quarantined, and the prisoners were lodged in the jail for safe-keeping. This brought the number of prisoners to 200, and not a single case of flu broke out among them.

Bennett said that prisoners are given reading matter but that the sensational and "spicy" kind are banned. He said that each Sunday the Star Gospel Mission conducts religious services there.

He said the average yearly population of inmates is 150 but that at the time he was interviewed, the number was 130. [10]

Capt. Bennett's granddaughter remembers the jailer in his latter years, just before he retired. Betty White often visited the jail with her mother who, along with siblings, actually grew up living in the jailer's quarters of the building. She said she was fascinated by the jail and, as a child, envied the fact that her mother had lived there.

Courtesy of Betty White   *Photo by author*

Captain Bennett, and granddaughter Betty White

Ms. White remembers her grandfather as "a real character" who "drove around town in his big Buick with jump seats in the back, looking like a funeral director."

"My mother used to tell me stories about what it was like (living in the jail)," said Ms. White, who still lives in Charleston. "I do remember my mother saying they could hear spirituals being sung, all the voices singing the different parts. She said sometimes babies were delivered in jail and you could hear yelling and screaming from the mothers. They didn't have the luxury of taking them to the hospital."

The jail "mutiny" noted in the newspaper article cited earlier was known to the family, but not in detail.

"He got hit on the head," said Ms. White. The incident apparently occurred in 1932, several years before Ms. White was born. Among family members, there was only slight mention. "All we ever knew was from mama who said they had this jail break and 'papa' (Capt. Bennett) got hit on the head. I do remember (hearing) that prisoners were immediately shipped out to another facility because granddaddy's wife and seven children lived up stairs. He wasn't going to let anyone be in danger due to that altercation. He did get them out of there."

As a toddler, Ms. White and other grandchildren and friends were regular guests in the jail's living quarters. The Bennetts' jail living space was open to all of their children's friends, she said. "We would come in the front door," said Ms. White. "Granddaddy's office was off to the (side), looking out to the street. Visitors were granted entry by a guard posted near the barred alcove in the front.

"Old man Gleason (a guard on duty at the time) was usually sitting on a kitchen chair, right at the front by one of the windows," Ms. White recalled. "I remember he always had the chair tipped back. He had a big turnkey on a rope or string. I remember that after Old Man Gleason let us in, we would go into Granddaddy's office," she said. "Then Granddaddy would open a door and we'd go up some stairs. Suddenly, we'd be in the living quarters. It was just like a house, except for the walls - they were whitewashed and not straight. I remember a piano and there was a kitchen where they did their own cooking up there. I remember sitting at a big black dining room table and it seemed to a kid like me that it had 100 chairs."

Ms. White said no one was permitted inside the cellblock areas and social visitors rarely - if ever - saw prisoners.

"We were always upstairs in the living quarters and they (the inmates) were safely locked up down below," she said. "When we were allowed to play in the jail yard, they were never there." However, she said she did occasionally peek in the ground-floor windows and saw "dishwashers" but had no idea if they were prisoners or not. She said she could hear prisoners, though.

She does recall teasing admonitions from adult relatives regarding the jail's inmates. She said some would caution the kids to be "...good or the prisoners will catch you and cut off your head. They scared children to death in those days."

She said she recalled the high brick wall that surrounded the jail yard (it was dramatically reduced in height after the closing in 1939) and a "paddy wagon" similar to the vehicle that now sits in the jail yard. "The one I remember was smaller." (Editor's note: The convict car currently sitting in the jail yard was moved there in the 1970s when the jail briefly became a museum.)

Ms. White said her recollection of Capt. Bennett during those visits was that he permitted no foolishness among the family's younger members.

"He was a very positive, strong-willed person. If you...sassed back to your parents, he would put you on the ground," she said. "He did not tolerate that sort of thing. I remember sassing my mother once after he retired and he beat me with a razor strap across the leg."

She said they all respected him but "I don't remember him as much of an affectionate person, hugging and all that grandparents do."

By May of 1938, though, ill health forced Capt. Bennett to retire. The official announcement was published in the April 18, 1938 edition of the Post and Courier:

William J. Bennett, county jailer for more than twenty-eight years, yesterday confirmed a report that he will retire May 1. He does within the provisions of the state police pension act. Captain Bennett said that he would send in his formal resignation, to take effect on that date, in a day or so.

His retirement is due to poor health. He plans to enter a hospital soon.

Sheriff Joseph M. Poulnot, who praised Captain Bennett's record of service, said he had not yet decided on a successor. He pointed out that he had

not yet received the resignation..."Many people think that criminals become tame and quiet as soon as they are put in jail, but that isn't so," he said. "Many of them give out of money, have nothing with which to buy tobacco. They are more desperate inside jail than out." [11]

Ms. White said after retiring, Capt. Bennett suffered a stroke and spent much of his time with her aunt and uncle on Folly Beach.

"He would sit on a porch on the second floor and yell at us, correct us," she recalled. He'd say 'You better behave when you go out of this house. I don't want any reports of you misbehaving on this beach.' He was always a disciplinarian but we respected him."

The gruff old Captain apparently had a softer side, especially at his piano.

"When he moved out of the jail (in 1939), he was married for the second time," said Ms. White. They lived on George near King and Meeting - it's now torn down - and he played piano while we all sang. We used to go there every Friday and Saturday, stand around the piano, eating and drinking. His favorite song was 'Roll Me Over in the Clover,' at which point we were sent out of the room." She said there was plenty of singing and dancing and that the children often played the piano, as well. Ms. White's Aunt had played music for silent films in a downtown theater.

Ms. White said that while her memories as a child of the jail are quite good, she has rarely been back.

"Occasionally" she said, "I'll make the circle, not often, and come down Queen Street, look at the jail and get a funny sensa-tion. "As a little kid, I was impressed that my mother grew up in this place. We used to call it 'the castle'."

Capt. Bennett's son, Harold L. Bennett, was chosen to succeed his father as jailer. Harold had been a guard at the jail for 12 years and became assistant jailer when John Gleason, the front door guard remembered by Ms. White, died. The April 30, 1939 newspaper article that announced the change noted that the jailer's yearly salary was $2,700.[12]

Son Succeeds Father as Jailer

(Staff Photo by Peck)

Harold L. Bennett (right), who has been appointed to succeed his father, Capt. William J. Bennett, as county jailer, is shown above re-
...... from his father. who resigned and will end

Courtesy of the Post and Courier

Newspaper noted jailer's job passing from father to son

The younger Bennett would preside over the Magazine Street facility for only several months until its closing in September. He continued to serve as jailer for a number of years at the new jail - the so-called "Seabreeze Hotel" - located at the foot of the Cooper

River Bridge. Ms. White and others visited "Uncle Harold" there and remembers it fondly, too.

"Harold wasn't nearly as strict as granddaddy," she said and "would let us look into the cells. We were older and would say 'let's go down and see if Harold's on today and get a Coke. Harold didn't live at that jail."

At some point, probably in the early 50s, Harold left the jail and became clerk of City Recorder's Court and in 1955, was named director of the City of Charleston Department of Safety Service and custodian of the dog pound. [13]

On February 17, 1953, his father, Capt. William J. Bennett, died at the age of 80. [14]

CHAPTER 12

HIDDEN SURPRISES: THE FLEDGLING ARCHEOLOGY OF THE JAIL

Left behind long ago by the prisoners and their guardians of the Charleston District Jail are bits of evidence that hint at the routine of life there. These range from cryptic words and numbers scored into the plaster of its cell walls to neatly cleaved animal bones hidden by accumulated silt in dark corners of what was once its kitchen.

The graffiti was mostly ignored for years, partly because few persons had access to the inside but mostly because it was rendered more or less invisible in cells lit only by whatever daylight might seep through small, barred windows. Decades of discoloration in the plaster further obscured the markings.

Fragments of crockery and bottles, tarnished metal buttons, a ring and a toothbrush made of ivory are among items discovered during restoration efforts.

It is hoped that soon a systematic and professional exploration of the building and its grounds can be financed so that significantly more of its archeology might be revealed. In the meantime, finds are catalogued and stored after examination by interested parties such as the Charleston Museum.

Preservation of this physical history occasionally has been threatened by unauthorized "bottle chasers" – amateur artifact seekers who, without authorization, attempt to sweep the jail yard with metal detectors in an effort to unearth historical remnants. Plunderers are confronted with legal action and evicted and so far the yard remains intact.

A greater danger may be seeping moisture that, along with old age, is slowly disintegrating the cell wall graffiti.

WALLS THAT SPEAK

Names, dates, outlines of ships and automatic pistols and hash marks denoting time served or time remaining are among the pictographs and markings in the fragile plaster on jail's ancient cell walls. Inmates with time to kill awaiting trails or serving sentences expressed a variety of sentiments, some clearly poignant and others obscure.

Photos by author

**Outlines of two pistols have been enhanced
by the author in the bottom picture**

"A man's ambition must be small to write his name on the jail-house wall" is inscribed in blocky letters near one corner, to the right of the doorway to a cell. There is no indication as to when this bit of jail house wit was etched.

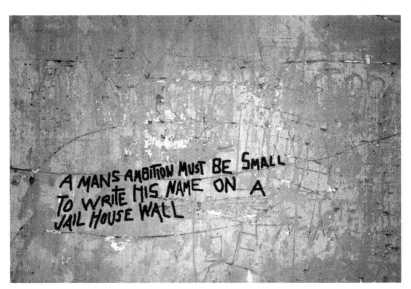

Photos by author

One inmate's sense of humor (enhanced by the author in the second image)

"Housebreaking and Grand Larceny" is scrawled in another spot, unaccompanied by either declaration of innocence or admission of guilt. Only the charge was shared.

Since the jail was effectively sealed up for about thirty years when operations ceased in 1939, vandalism has been minimal. Except for a few splotches of spray paint apparently contributed by some truly persistent trespassers, contemporary graffiti is absent. The walls seem pretty much the same as they would have been when the last prisoners were removed seventy years ago, except for continuing deterioration.

Words and pictures, even when adequately illuminated, are often difficult to make out. Photographing them, then varying contrast and color helps.

The earliest date found so far is included in the inscription "Eqstaquio - 6-Enero - 1927." Eqstaquio is an Hispanic surname and the Spanish word for January is "enero" so it seems appropriate to assume that a prisoner, probably a sailor, named Eqstaquio decided to add his name on the 6th of January, 1927.

Another dated name is "Leif Tor Bjornsen, Fevik, Norway 1936."

Other names include Kelly, Beverly, Henry, Ernest SH, Clarke, M. Fletcher, E-DuBose, H. Morris, A. Hines, Joe, Albert Reynolds, Avelino Varela Cor, Marion and Woodrow Blanchard. One name - Henry Morris - is repeated three time and is accompanied by the phrase "Age #15". Newspaper references confirm that children as young as 10 were jailed. Could Henry Morris have been 15 years old?

Photos by author

**"Henry Morris Age 15" is scratched in several spots
(enhanced in the second shot)**

There are drawings of at least 30 ships, some fairly elaborate and, in at least one case, a ship's name, "SS OABBS."

Photo by author

One of the ships etched in plaster

With only a few exceptions, the kinds of sexually graphic imagery found in many modern-day public buildings is notably absent.

Phrases and words include "Reform School," "Fools," "75 Days," "Intent to Kill," "State," "AME" and, stretching high across the length of one wall, "Communist Party."

The years "1937" and "1938" are also recorded.

And while it is clearly unwise to impart undue significance to what these artists of necessity chose to leave behind, it is interesting to note that one drawing of a heart pierced by an arrow is labeled "Love is Mother."

Much of what remains recently has been covered up by shiny new whiteboards and other classroom paraphernalia as cellblocks have been transformed into classrooms by the jail's owner, the American College of the Building Arts. It has been forced by economic necessity to use its most precious physical asset — the jail — as a working campus. School representatives express regret that these installations are covering up this unique collection of jail "art" but care has been taken to make installations reversible.

Also, it turns out that inmates weren't the only persons to leave behind messages inside the jail. One interesting discovery occurred in 2002 when the project manager for jail restoration was climbing among wooden beams in the building's attic. Her "find" was revealed in a June 25 Post and Courier article by reporter Jason Hardin:

> **On a sizzling summer's day, a day probably much like today, nine men stood atop the roof of the City Jail and reflected on a job well done.**
>
> **That was 114 summers ago. The men who rebuilt the jail's roof after the 1886 Charleston earthquake are long gone, and while their work still stands, they remained for more than a century as nameless contributors to the city's tradition of craftsmanship.**
>
> **Until Lea Cloyd recently found their names painted on the rafters in the jail's attic.**

"I was just shining a light around, and we just started looking and we noticed the names," said Cloyd, project manager for the jail restoration project being done by the School of the Building Arts. "It's magical when I bring the staff up here, and they read each of the names aloud. It's spiritual."

Painted on the rafters are the names T. Baker, D.A. Cameron, Tom Carey, T. Carney, M. Kelly, F. Lord, G.H. Meitzler, M. Walsh and T. Williams.

Photos by author

Workman Cameron's name painted on rafter in 1888 (enhanced by the author in the second photograph)

Signing work has always been a tradition for builders, Cloyd said. "It's the signature on their work. It's an opportunity to be remembered." [1]

OBJECTS FOUND

Locked away inside a storage cabinet in an office at the jail is its growing collection of physical curiosities that reveal themselves from time-to-time as repairs and restoration of the building proceed. A few were found during clean-up efforts and some churned to the surface of the yard of the jail after heavy rains.

Most discoveries have been small, personal items like buttons, a ring, a toothbrush, a cuff link, a change purse and marbles. The latter probably belonged to the children of the jailer and their visiting friends, although, as previously mentioned, some inmates were as young as 10.

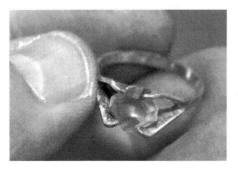 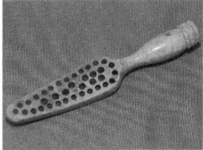

Photos by author

Items found include buttons, a leather change purse, a ring, an ivory toothbrush; braid, rifle ball, cufflink and buckle at bottom

A particularly intriguing find was on old baseball that workmen repairing the brickwork of a barred window found embedded inside the wall. At least one reference has been found to indicate that baseball was played in the jail yard by German prisoners of the World War I who were confined there. [2]

Photo by author

**Was this baseball found in the jail wall used
by German inmates in 1917?**

Recently excavated from a small shaft between floors of the jail was a dumb waiter — a small elevator device that ferried food from the kitchen to the upper stories. Bearing a metal badge reading "James Bates Improved Dumb Waiter, Baltimore, MD," the device appears to have been electrically operated when in use. (A "James Bates" of Baltimore is said to have built the first automatic elevator in the U.S. in 1846. Bates died in 1896 but it is not clear how long his company continued to operate.)

The Bates dumb waiter at the jail was found wedged askew inside a shaft that had long been boarded-up. Since the device had been available beginning in 1846, it is an intriguing possibility that it was knocked off its track during the great earthquake that shook Charleston, and especially its jail, in 1886.

In any case, workmen recently removed the elevator (see photo).

Photo by author

Worker Jay Rice examines the long-hidden dumbwaiter

And then, there are the bones.

Many hundreds of all shapes and sizes have been found - mostly in the area of the kitchen - and all have been examined by Charleston County forensic experts. Rumors to the contrary, none have been identified as human. Rather, they're the remnants of cattle and pigs whose meat was served to inmates. Many bear evidence of the butcher's saw and cleaver. A few are thought to be from squirrels entering the building through its many cracks and openings.

Photo by author

None of the teeth and bones found are human

Interestingly, a number of the bones have been found in crevices, high up the brick walls of the dumb waiter shaft in one corner of the kitchen. It is thought that foraging rats probably carried them there.

Many more have been found in the foot or so of sediment that had accumulated in the bottom of the shaft.

STILL UNDISCOVERED?

It is likely that new finds will be revealed as jail renovation progresses. In fact, some fascinating, jail-related things may lie buried in its yard. These include the heavy gallows weights used for executions and underground cells that may have been used to punish recalcitrant inmates.

As previously mentioned in Chapter 10, the Grand Jury offered the weights to the Charleston Museum in 1932 but there is no record that they were accepted. The metal probably weighed at least three hundred pounds and may have been left in the hole in which they were dropped, when Daniel Duncan — the last person to be hung at the jail — was hanged July 7, 1911.

Buried in the yard with them may also be the remnants of underground cells referenced in several historical texts, including that of Union captive Joseph Darling, as recounted in Chapter 6. [3]

It is hoped that a professional archeological search, perhaps employing "ground radar" techniques, may one day locate these curiosities - if they still exist.

CHAPTER 13

GHOSTLY ENCOUNTERS: IS THE JAIL HAUNTED?

No compilation of facts, secrets and myths about the jail would be complete without touching on perhaps its ultimate mystery: Do spirits of the dead prowl its halls and cells?

Are apparitions occasionally visible in its dimly lit hallways? Do specters suddenly grasp the faces of visitors entering cells? Do they mischievously reveal themselves as circles of light in photographs, create cold spots, make eerie noises and leave footprints on the dusty floors?

Answers clearly vary, depending on your source, but 20,000 persons a year pay Bulldog Tours for the privilege of lingering in a few rooms of the jail as part of the nightly "Charleston Haunted Jail Tour." For many, the price of a ticket includes an expectation that "something" otherworldly might happen — and some say they get what they pay for.

Photo by author

Nightly ghost tours offer a brush with the supernatural

It should be noted that The American College of the Building Arts, current owner of the jail, does not conduct this entertainment but, rather, leases a portion of the jail to the tour operator. As such, it has no official position on the issue of ghosts. However, a portion of tour fees go toward much-needed maintenance and upkeep of the building. For that, College officials are extremely grateful, ghosts or no ghosts.

But is the jail really haunted?

"Well, I don't really know," says John Paul Huguley, founder of the College and an individual who has spent as much time in the building as anyone. "I've never seen anything that I would call a ghost but the place occasionally can produce unsettling feelings — particularly for newcomers."

However, others closely associated with the jail have noted unusual encounters. In a story by Post and Courier reporter Clay Barbour that appeared several days before Halloween 2002, several incidents were covered:

> **It was dark by the time Jay Rice decided to wrap up work at the Old City Jail and head home.**

He had stayed behind to finish a project for a friend, but it was late and he was ready to go.

A blacksmith by trade, Rice was one of the 50 or so craftsmen hired by the School of the Building Arts to help bring the historic landmark back to life — a daunting task considering the building had been vacant since its closing in 1939.

Rice had worked there for close to a year, doing his best to restore the old jail's rusted out ironworks. He had heard the stories about the place; that it was haunted by ghosts of former prisoners. But he was a skeptic.

That all changed after Rice came face to face with something he still can't explain.

He was leaving the jail by the back exit, like he had done a dozen times before. But as he entered a 20-foot stretch of hallway leading to the back door, Rice became aware of a presence.

The other workers had already gone, leaving him to finish his project alone. The jail was quiet, save for the sound of his feet brushing against the cold concrete. But he was not alone.

He stopped and shined his flashlight on the back door. That's when he saw him, a tall, thin man in a dark suit standing to the right of the exit. Rice stared at the man for a long moment.

He seemed off somehow, Rice thought. His eyes were hollow and he had a grayish complexion. When Rice moved toward him the man disappeared, only to reappear on the left side of the door and then disappear again.

Startled and confused, Rice quickly left the building. Once outside he turned to see if the gray man appeared again. But there was nothing.

"I didn't tell anyone for several days," Rice says. "But when I finally did, I found out that I wasn't the only worker to have weird experiences in the jail."

Photo by author

Jay Rice stands at the spot where he said he saw specter appear, then disappear

The article said jail restorers reported "odd" experiences from the beginning. Some said they were tapped on their shoulders. Others felt "hands" on their faces.

"There is something in there," says Lea Cloyd, the project manager. "I really believe that. I don't necessarily think it's evil or anything, but it's there."

"My wife won't go nowhere near that building," says Clay Barnes, who lives in the apartments behind the jail. "There is just something about it."

David Dick, a carpenter working on the preservation project told the reporter that one night he heard noises coming from the second floor:

"You could hear the distinct sounds of heavy footsteps from the main cell room," Dick says. "The problem was that area was locked, and I was the only one in the jail."

Dick says the footsteps stopped once he approached the stairs leading to the room.

Rice, too, has heard similar sounds, the article said, but Cloyd reported a more personal phenomenon. Once, as she entered a cell, she said she felt two hands press the sides of her face.

"Not violently," she says. "It was more like someone just trying to keep me from entering the room. A few weeks later my husband had the exact same experience in the exact same place. He won't go back in the jail now."

Several persons over the years have said they've found the footprints in parts of the jail where no one was supposed to have been. One such incident was reported in the article.

...workers closed (a) section off as they removed lead from the old

building. The work kicked up a lot of dust, forcing the workers to wear protective suits.

One day Cloyd entered the cell room, which had been locked for weeks, and found footprints all over the dusty floor.

"That was surprising in itself, but the really weird thing is whoever made those prints was walking around barefooted," she says. "They were small, fat, bare feet

prints. **Here we are all covered head to toe in these protective suits and in this room, there were bare feet prints. And no one could get in there but us." [1]**

On Halloween day of the same year, the Post and Courier carried another story about the jail — this one written by a reporter who spent the entire night there — along. In a story headlined "Talk About Having a Bad Scare Day," Bryce Donovan, an avowed skeptic to the notion of ghosts, wrote:

Sitting in the main room on the second floor, I began hearing things. First there were a few creaks, and then something that sounded like a door closing. Then footsteps. And were those voices?

Maybe I wasn't alone in the building.

But then I heard a honk followed by some really loud rap music. It was at this moment I realized I had been caught up in all the ghost hysteria. All those sounds had been coming from outside.

It seems all that ghost talk from the workers had my brain working overtime. My mind tricked me into thinking there were people in the building with me. But then I took a deep breath and remembered something.

I don't believe in ghosts.

Then I heard another noise. Only this one came from inside. I took another deep breath and reminded myself once again: I don't believe in ghosts.

But then I remembered something else.

Neither did Rice and Cloyd. [2]

There have been a few somewhat systematic attempts to test the veracity of the jail's reputation as a haven for those roaming the beyond. In 2007, Charleston City Paper reporter Greg Hambrick accompanied representatives of "Southern Paranormal Investigation and Research" as they examined the building. His story noted that no conclusion was reached. [3]

The jail also has enjoyed the attention of L.E.M.U.R., the League of Energy Materialization & Unexplained phenomena Research. It is based, according to its Internet web site (shadowboxent.brinkster.net/lemurhome.html), in Asheville, North Carolina. Content available on-line includes a report said to be written on behalf of L.E.M.U.R. by Joshua P. Warren.

Warren's report, the site says, pertains to an investigation conducted over several days in January 2007. It includes "Some Anomalies Reported at the Old City Jail Through the Years," such as:

> **1. During renovation in 2000, though the building was locked for months to seal off lead paint contamination, bare footprints were found in the dust. Afterward, several workers saw the apparition of a jailer with rifle on the third floor. He passed through bars, heading toward them, before vanishing.**
>
> **2. Sounds of dumbwaiter passing through floors are heard, though it is no longer operational. In particular, this happened April of 2006 by (sic) Rebel Sinclair and guests of a 10pm tour.**
>
> **3. Jewelry and other objects frequently disappear. For example, a woman's ring vanished inside May of 2006. A man's handkerchief (with personal meaning) vanished June of 2006. Neither object has been found to date.**
>
> **4. In the basement, a man had his sunglasses knocked off by a violent, unseen force.**
>
> **5. In the basement, during 90 degree temperatures, breath can be seen as a cloud of fog.**

6. Alarms set/reset themselves frequently.

7. A black man, in ragged clothing, has been clearly seen wandering halls. The first sighting was February of 2002, latest was June, 2006.

8. There are numerous cell phone disruptions, including calls from unknown numbers and batteries draining then charging up again.

9. Doors are found open after being closed. A heavy iron door fell off its hinges for no apparent reason during a tour in February of 2005.

10. The "crane of pain," a torture apparatus repro-duction consisting of ropes, has been found with ropes intertwined without explanation.

11. Many visitors have captured EVP (Electronic Voice Phenomenon) with video cameras.

12. A Charleston police officer investigating an alarm in 2006 found the back door open. He went inside with a gun drawn, and ascended the spiral stair case. Upon reaching the third floor, he reported a strange sensation, as though his "arms were wrapped in plastic wrap."

13. Several guides and visitors have complained of a choking feeling, and shortness of breath, while on the main staircase.

14. Visitors involved in corrections often become queasy and complain of a foul odor.

15. One guide felt a rope "snake" around her ankles.

16. Numerous visitors have been pushed and shoved by unseen forces.

The site says a L.E.M.U.R. Investigation team spent several days with various electronic measuring devices and cameras in hopes of capturing evidence of paranormal activity. After a detailed account of its efforts, it said:

> Though visual manifestations are limited at this location, strong physical forces (perhaps related to the magnetic surges) are prominent. And when anomalies manifest audibly, they are extremely distinct. As a preliminary investigation, we found the experience valuable. We certainly consider the site haunted, meaning it regularly houses/produces a wide range of anomalous activity, and plan to focus our efforts more for future investigations. [4]

A particularly unusual mix of researchers tackled the jail ghost issue later that year, as reported in a Post and Courier article by Jill Coley, published April 4:

> Skeptics and ghost hunters faced off after midnight in the Old City Jail, pitting logic against the paranormal.
>
> On one side sat members of the College of Charleston's Atheist-Humanist Alliance. On the other, two teams of paranormal investigators.
>
> Rick Zender, curator of the college's John Rivers Communications Museum, concocted the strange mix of late-night guests with the help of Bulldog Tours guide Ginger Williams, who roped in the ghost hunters.

The article said the four paranormal investigators employed digital cameras, voice recorders and an electromagnetic field meter in their search for the unusual. Meanwhile, it was reported, the students mostly kept to themselves. At the end of the night:

> Each group left the jail with the same beliefs they came with. The prevailing sentiment, in the end, was politeness. [5]

One controversial phenomenon that many visitors report involves "orbs" of light that appear on flash photos they snap while touring the jail at night. Those inclined to believe are adamant these circles are photographic proof of the presence of spirits. Skeptics maintain these shapes are nothing more than flecks of dust on the electronic sensors of today's digital cameras or out-of-focus insects caught between the lens and the point where the camera is aimed. One jail guide recently told a group that she had seen human faces in the orbs captured in one shot that was shown to her by a tour member. Regrettably, she did not obtain a copy of this astonishing picture.

Arguably, the question of the haunting of the Charleston District Jail remains unproven for many and unresolved for all. For what it's worth, the author of this book has spent many hours in the jail — some of them alone — and failed to encounter a single apparition, an unexpected touch or note any other experience that would suggest a disembodied spirit was responsible. This was somewhat disappointing since a personal experience could have provided a particularly intriguing chapter.

To this day, many jail visitors say they "feel" something ominous there, as though all of the suffering that has taken place in and around the place creates a palpable heaviness of sadness and dread. Knowledge of what went on there and the appearance of the surroundings no doubt contribute to this sensation, perhaps more pronounced in some than others. But a jail aura that manifests itself supernaturally in the form of ghostly sightings, sounds or physical contact has not been experienced by this author — yet.

SECTION III

PRESERVING THE JAIL

Photo by author

CHAPTER 14

DEALING WITH AN EMPTY BUILDING

Preserving the past can be a messy affair.

Nostalgic affection for the decaying, old edifice on Magazine Street likely was in short supply among inmates who got free of it. Likewise, those who lived in the neighborhoods that bounded it probably hoped its closing quickly would be followed by a wrecking ball.

But those concerned with maintaining historically significant buildings made a persuasive case that the jail's unique and lengthy service, unsavory as it was, had earned it status as a landmark worth saving. The problem was that its deplorable physical condition — already bad in 1939 and growing worse all the time — presented a formidable and expensive challenge.

SLUM CLEARANCE

The jail's fate was closely linked with its geography. It stood surrounded by what had become one of the city's worst slums. The area was overrun with tumbledown shacks and tenements. Stores and legitimate businesses kept uneasy company with a tawdry collection of bars and brothels. Poverty was rampant and the crime rate high.

In an effort to reverse decay throughout the city, officials in 1934 formed the "Charleston Housing Authority" and charged it with the improvement of "residential building stock." In 1938 it was restructured to take advantage of new Federal aid for construction of low-income housing and slum clearance.

According to the Post and Courier of January 20, 1938:

Mayor Burnet R. Maybank in person today filed with Nathan Straus, administrator of the federal housing authority, applications for two Charleston housing projects involving an expenditure of $900,000.

One of these projects calls for slum clearance in the heart of the city, including the demolition of the county jail, built about 1820 (sic), and the Jenkins orphanage (that had burned in 1933 and was uninhabitable). The new development will provide 107 housing units and will be bounded by Queen, Logan, Magazine and Franklin streets. The estimated cost is $500,000.

The other project is in the northwest end of the city, at Ninth and Tenth avenues and Grove street. There will be seventy-five units in this development and the cost is estimated at $400,000.

Both projects will be for white tenants. [1]

The part of the plan that included razing the jail building itself was controversial, probably as much due to the cost required as historical preservationists' efforts to keep it intact. In any case, according to an article in the Post and Courier on February 18, 1939, plans were well underway to clear both prisoners and equipment from the building:

State Senator Cotesworth P. Means said yesterday that Charleston county technicians are planning to move cell blocks from the Magazine street jail to the prison farm on the North Charleston boulevard, for housing prisoners who cannot be allowed the comparative liberty of the farm.

"We could move the prisoners today, if necessary," Senator Means said, explaining that the county has no intention of delaying the progress of the Robert Mills Manor slum clearance project. Edward D. Clement,

director of the Charleston Housing authority, has requested that the jail be vacated by March 15. [2]

SAVE THE JAIL

As the project progressed, Charleston groups dedicated to the protection of the city's historical structures mounted campaigns to shield the jail building from destruction or even significant alteration.

For example, in March the "Society for the Preservation of Old Dwellings" went on record as opposed to the destruction of the jail as well as other old buildings in the area of the proposed housing project.

Letters to the editor at that time suggested some members of the community at-large shared the preservationists' sentiment. One contributor said:

To the News and Courier:

When at home last week-end, I enjoyed as usual the Sunday News and Courier, and saw with much interest the pictures illustrating the proposed Magazine street slum clearance. But I was sorry that the magnificent old jail was not included among the pictures. From my earliest childhood, its stern and austere beauty has struck terror to my law-abiding heart, and I have always felt that the immortal Bastille of Paris perhaps had little to offer in architectural competition.

Recently, in checking through the older statutes, I have been surprised to note the frequent and liberal state appropriations for the jail in Charleston. Almost every year from the Revolution to Secession, the jail was being repaired, improved, or rebuilt. In 1805 it received $9,000 for a surrounding wall. In 1821, while Robert Mills was a member of the state board of public works, $10,000 was appropriated for repairs, and Mills added a wing. In 1853,

> $30,000 was appropriated for a new jail, and the next year $10,000 more was added. No doubt the old building lacks some modern conveniences which are yearned for by the inmates and their keepers. But it has passed through fire, war and earthquake, and still looks as though it might be good for centuries to come; and it possesses a priceless advantage in having been placed correctly, with a long southern exposure, upon an amply walled yard. If modern conveniences can be added, why not? [3]

Another writer celebrated the distinctive, battlement-like crenelations of the jail's parapets as reason enough for preservation. While erroneously ascribing them to architect Mills (it was later discovered that they were actually the work of Barbot and Seyle), Eola Willis suggested the jail remain as a repository for historical documents:

> We have all the right we need, to call the large building now used as a jail, THE CASTLE. When the present inmates have been removed, may we not implore the powers that be, to make the castle fireproof and prepare the building to receive such Archives as shall be deemed worthy of the greatest protection now, with space sufficient for a truly fitting structure to receive all such valuable documents now in the city's possession and those that shall accrue later. [4]

The struggle between renovators and preservations was to include another old building in the jail's neighborhood. A deteriorating, wooden house at 2 Magazine Street had confined Revolutionary War hero and 35th governor of South Carolina General William Moultrie. Arrested as a debtor, Moultrie had been held there as per "jail bounds," a colonial notion of confinement that permitted certain "gentleman" prisoners freedom to roam a block or two beyond their cells. In a letter to the editor published in December, 1938, a John Bennett of Charleston wrote:

... If those in authority cannot endure to remember that in this small house General Moultrie dwelt in jail-bounds as an insolvent debtor, they may well pass up that melancholy memory, and stress only the fact that "Here General William Moultrie wrote and completed his Memoirs of the American Revolution"; and let that courageous remembrance obscure the less charitable fact that an honest man, a brave soldier, and an heroic spirit for a time of adversity made this small house his home or dwelling; and that he here ended his days honored by his friends, beloved by the community, and imprisoned by his creditors - what or whosoever they may have been.

What is to be the fate of this house; No. 2, Magazine street? Is it to be preserved with its memories, or torn down through careless neglect of the facts or a false feeling of humiliation that General Moultrie should ever have been compelled to endure here a tedious imprisonment, before imprisonment for debt became a dead letter or moribund law? We should like to know. [5]

Despite Bennett's plea, the wooden structure at 2 Magazine Street was regularly "...stripped for firewood..." according to a Post and Courier article found at the Charleston County Public Library. Although the clip is undated, it probably was published in 1938 or 1939 and included photographs of the Moultrie structure. It reads, in part:

The house still stands there, partly dismantled and in a regrettable state of dilapidation, owing to the habit of the neighbors of removing all detachable wood-work for purposes of fire and warmth in the inclement weather. The small front door steps have gone long ago; the shutters doubtless had followed but that they are shut, boarded fast and nailed up. But the neighbors have begun the removal of the weatherboarding, as is the custom in slum districts. [6]

Eventually, the Moultrie building was completely torn down.

AND SAVE THE WALL, TOO

As for the jail building, officials weighing demolition costs and preservation sentiment decreed it would, in fact, be spared. Not so, however, the high wall that surrounded its yard. That had to go, they said. A feature of the housing project plan was a playground in the yard of the jail. The height of the old wall, designers said, blocked sunlight from reaching the space.

Victorious in their efforts to keep the jail building whole, preservationists turned their attention to the threat to its wall.

At some point during the process, responsibility for the jail, its yard and its wall was transferred to the Housing Authority, the entity coordinating renovation of the neighborhood. When operating, the jail had been the province of state and county officials. Its closing occurred just as the city secured federal funding for clearing the slum surrounding it. This meant that the federal government had a say in its disposition, as well.

The Authority announced its intention regarding the wall in a News and Courier article published in 1939:

> **The Charleston Housing authority has decided to change "to some extent" the appearance of the old brick wall surrounding the county jail, it was said yesterday by E.D. Clement, executive director of the authority.**
>
> **The work should start in the next two weeks, and probably will include lowering the wall, so that more sunlight may reach inside where a children's playground will be established, Mr. Clement said. Other changes to the wall have not been determined, he said. [7]**

The Society for Preservation of Old Dwellings immediately issued a protest, maintaining that "...the jail wall is one of the class of original architectural and historical items that contribute to make Charleston a place of special interest for visitors and thereby constitutes one of the city's principal economic assets..." [8]

Soon the matter of the wall's fate turned political, with then Mayor Henry W. Lockwood rising from his sick bed (with a bad case of the flu) and publicly siding with preservationists.

"Charleston still has ample room for modern development without destroying those things that annually bring many visitors to the city...," he told a newspaper reporter in March. I will do everything in my power to assist in having as much of the wall as possible preserved." [9]

A picketing action was threatened by a group of community women concerned with maintaining the jail's original appearance. The Society for the Preservation of Old Dwellings sought support from Federal housing authorities. In the latter case, its meeting with US Housing Administrator Nathan Straus proved fruitless when, according to Society President William M. Means, Straus "...was very firm in stating that the jail wall would be changed in accordance with existing plans. He got up and the interview ended there." [10]

South Carolina Governor Burnet R. Maybank personally took the preservationists' case to Straus.

Finally, in March, South Carolina Governor Burnet R. Maybank, who previously had been mayor of Charleston, appealed to authorities on behalf his former city constituents. "I started this project as mayor," Governor Maybank said, "and I felt obligated to see that the people of Charleston get what they want," he said. [11]

Letters to the newspapers appeared throughout the controversy. In one, a writer seemed to place the value of the jail wall above social improvement:

> **...it is somewhat shocking that outsiders in some instances regard themselves as more capable of appraising these values. In this instance the federal housing authority has erred in determining its proposed course, to say the least, for anyone at all familiar with conditions here realizes perfectly well that over a period to years the jail and its wall and such other things contributing to the city's unusual atmosphere**

are worth more than any housing center that will ever be constructed here with United States funds. [12]

Another writer seemed to agree:

More than a wall will be torn down when this thing happens to Charleston! That piece of masonry, pronounced by the housing commission and the architects of Charleston (according to Mr. Straus) an ugly thing, is standing today for far more than it ever did as an inclosure for a few criminals. It is standing as a symbol. Will Washington dictate again to Charleston, the historic city? If it comes down from its great height, it will be a wailing wall, so long as one per cent of Charleston live to tell the story. And that one per cent, don't let Mr. Straus forget, is the one per cent capable of telling it. In the arts and letters, they have been a rather important one per cent. [13]

One writer expressed a tour operator's point of view:

To the big majority of people of the city of Charleston the jail wall is a matter of dollars and cents. Will the city's income be increased or decreased by letting the wall stand as it is? That is the question.

In the last analysis, a successful administration of the affairs of the city by our mayor is going to be very much affected by the income of its citizens, which in turn is very much affected by the tourist industry, so that he could come to the city's rescue at this time. [14]

One intriguing Letter to the Editor of the News and Courier appeared in the March 28, 1939 edition. The piece took the form of a poem cleverly written in the vernacular of "Gullah", the Creole language with which the jail's prisoners – particularly the black ones – would have been familiar:

"Dat Ol' Jail Wall"
I knowed dat Ise did neber seed
    Uh wall mak' sich uh trubble.
Hit mak' white folkses fume an' fret
    An' bile an' stew an' bubbel.
Sum folkses say dat hit mus' stay;
    De odders, dey say "No".
Deres sum a-wantin' hit to stan'
    Sum wish to lay hit low.
To me de wall wifout de jail
    Dat 'pear so berry strange
Hit lik' a bran' new kitchen gran'
    complete wifout de range.
Sum folses say hit be antick
    dat mean hit berry ol'
An' dy want for to leb him
    Fur de yankees to behol'
Uh ting ob brick, mota an' san'
    Uh wailin' wall fur which?
Mus' is hit be dat relief man
    Who gwine to wail fur sich?
Lots ob we uns in dis town
    Hab seed de wall - bofe sides.
Hw cum hit mak' de buckra fuss?
    De answer to dat hides.
Poems is writ by sich as me
    But Ise axiin' ob you' all
War at 'cept in Charleston would
    Buckra worry 'bout uh wall?
(Signed) XERXES [15]

Ultimately a victory of sorts was won by the pro-wall factions. Most of the wall would be reduced to four feet in height but two small, sixteen-foot sections flanking the jail's Magazine Street front facade would be allowed to stand. (Editor's note: Various estimates of the wall's height were published over the years. These ranged from 20 to 16 feet.)

The official word on the wall's fate reached the newspaper-reading public in an article published April 21, 1939, headlined

"4-Foot Wall on Franklin St., 16 (feet) on Magazine St., Rest Goes":

> **When the Robert Mills Manor housing project is completed the only section of the sixteen-foot wall that enclosed the county jail property remaining virtually intact will be that on Magazine Street.**

The section on Franklin street will appear as a four-foot-high remnant. The east and south, or interior walls, heretofore unnoticeable from the street, will be obliterated.

This outcome is in accord with plans of the Charleston and United States housing authorities as revealed in a letter from Nathan Straus, U.S.H.A. administrator, to Governor Burnet R. Maybank, who had interceded in Washington in behalf of those desiring to preserve the wall intact, and an announcement of the local authority.

Mr. Straus endorsed the plan for altering the walls as cited with the statement that "to allow a very ugly sixteen-foot-wall to remain in the center of the housing project is completely out of the question."

Bricks removed for the disassembled portions of the wall would be used in the construction of three buildings in the housing project, the article said. [16]

A photograph published April 28, 1939 in the News and Courier showed pickax-wielding workmen in the process of the wall's razing. [17]

Once the actual work of lowering of the wall began, the controversy ebbed and the progress was noted in an undated newspaper clipping, accompanied by a photograph, captioned:

> **Only the Magazine street side of its big wall still standing untouched, the county jail building, claimed to be the oldest in continuous use in America, now presents an unusual view to passers-by.**
>
> **Destruction of the jail wall, despite protests from many Charlestonians desiring its preservation, is a part of the general Robert Mills manor housing project. It**

marks, too, the end ultimately of the use of the jail building as place of confinement.

Men today were "scraping" bricks salvaged from the wall while others were putting them to new use in the construction of the project homes in that section of the development at Queen and Franklin streets. All of the salvaged bricks are to be used in the manor... [18]

WALL'S DEMISE MAKES SHERIFF NERVOUS

The wall was being dismantled — even as prisoners remained inside — and this deeply disturbed authorities charged with keeping criminals securely locked away from the general public.

A News and Courier article expresses concerns that, "outsiders are trespassing on the jail property" who Sheriff Joseph Poulnot believes are passing items to prisoners to whom they're talking at the windows. He feared a jail break and brought the matter to the attention of Mayor Lockwood, since the remaining inmates were "city" prisoners. He suggested a guard be posted throughout the day and night as wall demolition continues. [19]

Lowered jail yard wall worried the sheriff

In another article published April 28, 1939, the sheriff of Charleston County issued a plea for assistance in containing the yet-to-be-transferred prisoners, since the jail would not be vacated for months:

... "I wrote a letter to the mayor and asked for police protection," Sheriff Poulnot said. "I can't be inside and *outside at the same time. I need some help.*"

...Yesterday there were eighty prisoners at the jail. Captain William J. Bennett, jailer, said he could take care of that number without difficulty, but that the absence of the walls presented a dangerous situation.

The jail itself is to be vacated before tenants move into Robert Mills Manor. The prison farm is to be used for most prisoners, but no definite arrangements have been made for those too desperate to be kept at the farm.

> **The county has made application for public works administration aid on a jail project, and it is possible that a cellblock will be put at the (illegible) or in some small building in the vicinity. Officials have opposed building a new jail on the scale of the present facilities within the city.** [20]

Despite the Housing Authority's desire to see the building empty by March, it took another six months for that to occur. A Post and Courier article published September 14 announced that the building was officially "Going Out of Service" as a jail the following day and that it "has been condemned by federal authorities and local grand juries as unit, obsolete and unhealthy." [21]

"IT CAN'T BE LEFT AS IT IS"

September 1939 found the jail empty and shut tight. Controversies associated with its preservation had been resolved: The building was to remain, its wall reduced in size. But the problem of its ongoing upkeep remained.

Its steward was the Charleston Housing Authority and while occasionally using it for storage, did not have sufficient funds to adequately maintain it, let alone mount a serious restoration effort.

Suggestions for use of the building surfaced from time to time. In November 1940, a newspaper article suggested that The National Youth Administration, a federal "New Deal" agency set up to address the problem of unemployment among young persons, had been given use of the second and third floors for unspecified "activities" but there is no surviving evidence that this agency ever used the jail. [22]

Renovation of the surrounding slum continued under the Housing Authority's supervision. As the fortunes of the neighborhood improved, concern over long-term preservation of the jail building continued. As the Housing Authority's Executive Director said at the time, it is "… impossible to purchase old buildings that cannot be fitted into the development program and allow them to remain in ruins." [23]

So virtually nothing was spent on its upkeep and it continued its structural decline.

From 1939 through the mid to late 1970s, it saw occasional use as a repair shop for the city and as a storage area for the Housing Authority, which was headquartered in the renovated Marine Hospital nearby.

Courtesy of the Historic Buildings Survey

The basement was used as a repair shop and for storage; this shot was taken in 1995

In 1951, Miss Marjorie Dukes (later to become Mrs. Lonnie Martin) launched a free kindergarten "upstairs" at the jail, under the auspices of Southside Baptist Church located nearby at 87 Beaufain Street. Church records indicate the school lasted several years before being discontinued. [24]

In the mid-1970s, an idea was hatched to operate a museum in the building. Application was made to the city by two local entrepreneurs, former Charleston County treasurer Bartley J. Riddock and A.A. Burris, Jr., president of Burris Chemical Co.

Their proposal include an authentic restoration of the interior and a gift shop.

Later, a newspaper article said Riddock and Burris had signed a five-year lease, renewable for five years, and that it was hoped the museum would open by the following year. They were assisted by Emmett Robinson, director-manager of the Dock Street Theater, who reportedly costumed a dozen manikins representing jail inmates and staff. [25]

The attraction opened to the public January 5, 1976 - "Monday through Saturday from 8:30 a.m. To 4:30 p.m. And 10 a.m. To 4:30 p.m. On Sundays." [26]

On February 1, The State Newspaper in Columbia published a story about the new museum written by Tom Hamrick:

> **Stealing a cold shudder from some of the world's leading horror museums, two Charlestonians and a theatrical producer have joined forces here to restore a 174-year-old gloomy bastile into the pit of human misery which housed thousands of local prisoners over the years, until 1939.**
>
> **As one of the nation's oldest still-standing penal bastions, the foreboding "Old Charleston-Jail and Museum 1802," as hand-out literature reads, has been peopled with a dozen hauntingly-realistic fiberglass manikins and opened as a pay-to-see attraction which is expected to become one of the Port City's most compelling pieces of tourist bait.**
>
> **Missing is the towering scaffold from which scores of condemned men - and perhaps some women - were killed over the years, into the 20th century. But one star feature available for goose-bump viewing is an imaginary recreation of Charleston's still remembered "drunken hangman" of the early 1800s, who was routinely jailed before every execution just to keep him sober enough to climb the scaffold stairs.**

..."Being in jail around here was short of a picnic, wryly observes manager Mike Haymore, who gave up free-lance writing to glad-hand tourist visitors. And we've tried to preserve it in such a way that visitors who tour the place can get a feel for what it was really like to be in a cell in this place."

...Records keeping at the old jail was for the most part "hit and miss" apparently, and not even a record of hangings exists anymore, reports Haymore. "We can only guess how many people were hanged here," he admits. "Maybe it ran into hundreds."

The article said the lease signed by the co-developers provided renewal options over the following 15 years at $5,000 per year. Five percent of net proceeds were to go to the city, as well. [27]

At some point, though, originators Riddock and Burris apparently sold or turned over their enterprise to C. Harrington Bissell, who was operating a "remodeled" museum in 1978. [28]

But the venture would not survive and the museum had closed its doors by 1980. For the next dozen years, the building mainly reverted to its use as a storage facility but occasionally also served as a set for theatrical productions.

"Swamp Thing," a horror film directed by Wes Craven and starring Louis Jourdan and Adrienne Barbeau, reportedly included a scene filmed inside the jail [29] although a viewing of the DVD version suggests it would difficult to identify precisely where in the building filming took place.

In 1985, according to a story in the News and Courier, "... the building was dusted with manmade snow for a scene in the television movie "North and South" being filmed here for ABC." The same article said the building — still owned by the Housing Authority — was being used for offices and storage and a "haunted house" each Halloween by the city's recreation department.

"The second and third floors are leased to Spoleto USA (a city-wide performing arts festival held each year), which uses the space for storage and workshop areas," the piece said. "And the bottom floor serves as a substation for a city police team and animal control division." [30]

By this time, the Housing Authority was being run by Donald J. Cameron who had joined it 1975 as assistant director and named executive director in 1981. While Cameron's primary job was managing and maintaining the city's public housing residences and related services, he also inherited responsibility for the jail. It was he who agreed to assign the $200-per-month museum lease, unfulfilled when that attraction closed down, to Spoleto for offices and storage. That organization was to occupy the entire second and third floors as well as part of the first floor. [31]

Also in the building were a Charleston's police team and the city's animal control division. And during some Octobers, the city recreation department turned the jail into a Halloween "haunted house."

Then, in 1986, engineers determined the building was unsafe. Less use was made of it while the Housing Authority continued to explore options. According to a newspaper article published in the spring of 1988, a plan to subdivide 2.6 acres of the area and sell portions was discussed - but there was a bureaucratic snag:

Donald J. Cameron, housing authority executive director, said the subdivision restores property lines that were erased 40 years ago by mistake (when the jail was closed and given to the Authority). Without property lines between the different buildings, U.S. Department of Housing and Urban Development guidelines prevented the authority from disposing of a portion of it.

Cameron said the jail has not been used since 1986, when an engineering study determined the structure was not safe for habitation. Another study showed that renovating the building will cost about $1 million, which the authority does not have, he said.

"We think the building should remain in the public domain. This action will free us to possibly give it to the Charleston Museum. I think this will trigger our board to do something about the old jail," he said. [32]

Meanwhile, more studies were done, including one in 1989 that suggested fix-up costs might actually be substantially less than a million dollars. A report prepared for the Housing Authority by Preservation Consultants, Inc., a firm dedicated to "Historic Preservation Planning and Design", said the price tag was closer to a quarter of a million dollars — a figure more in keeping with the Housing Authority's budget. In a February 12, 1990 article by Post and Courier reporter Kerri Morgan, Cameron said:

> **"The housing authority's position is that it is a vital and important treasure not only to the city but to the nation," said Donald J. Cameron, the authority's executive director. "It must be restored and preserved properly and used in a manner that will not adversely affect the preservation."**
>
> **The housing authority is considering using half of the vacant jail in conjunction with the Robert Mills Manor public housing project, which abuts the jail property, and renting the other half for archival storage. Cameron said more archival storage space is needed in the community.**

In the article, Cameron said the new restoration estimate of $260,000 "...is well within our capacity" and that the federal government and historical organizations might contribute to the effort, too. [33]

But a second study revealed that the first had been too optimistic. It was discovered that long-neglected damage and the building's age conspired to elevate repair costs far beyond the hoped-for figure of $260,000. The real number was more like $1.5 million.

The study had been conducted by Charleston design firm Cummings and McCrady. The devastating findings were recounted by engineer Craig Bennett to Post and Courier reporter Robert Behre in an article published August 3, 1998. In part, it said:

(The jail) was appraised at a minus $1.5 million because of the projected cost of putting it in a usable condition," says authority Director Don Cameron.

Bennett found a host of structural problems and recommended replacing the octagon floors with new timber-supported floors, and replacing the jack arch system - which is failing and causing pressure on the outside walls - with a timber system.

"To preserve the building's exterior, you'd have to go in and remove the floors, then just brace the walls," Cameron says. "That's the major catalyst that's threatening the building, but it's not the only one. There are other problems in the walls."

The authority has changed tactics, deciding instead to try to rid itself of the building.

The building attracts suitors, Cameron said, but the structural problems, deterioration and the "bureaucratic nightmare" of jail ownership puts them off.

"To a great degree, the building's interior looks a great deal like it did when it used to have incarcerated prisoners. Just as scary. Definitely a foreboding place," he says.

Many groups know that the building soon may be available, but no one is first in line.

"Every once in a while, somebody comes by and wants to look at it. They think it's just a wonderful old building, which it is. But when they hear about the structural condition and we share with them the cost estimates we've received, they get discouraged. We don't get people coming back a second or third time," he says.

Cameron told the reporter that if ownership hurdles could be overcome, there was hope that the Authority could hand it over to a responsible entity that promised to fix it up. However, he added, any reuse would have to be agreeable to both residents of Robert Mills Manor and nearby neighborhoods.

The clock, though, was ticking. Continued deterioration might render it totally unfit for occupation or even worse, lead to a serious structural collapse.

"It's not (an immediate) danger or a threat, but it can't be left as it is indefinitely," Cameron says."How long indefinitely is is anybody's guess." [34]

CHAPTER 15

A LIVING LABORATORY: HOW A COLLEGE IS SAVING THE JAIL

By the mid to late 1990s, the jail's future looked more precarious than ever. Physically, it was on its last legs and the Charleston Housing Authority had no money to fix it. But as the Authority sought an appropriate new owner, it had to recognize a potential ownership interest held by the U.S. Department of Housing and Urban Development.

The conundrum was formidable: How to find someone willing to spend millions of dollars to rescue a crumbling historical landmark whose ownership lay in a murky no man's land of government complication.

A reprieve for the "most endangered building in the Low Country," as the Historical Charleston Foundation once deemed the jail, began in 1997. That year, a 28-year-old structural preservation engineer with a passion for quality construction paid $1 for a year's lease of the property in exchange for a promise to repair and preserve the building.

John Paul Huguley, only recently in town from Boston, had been one of a number of parties expressing interest in 21 Magazine Street. Craig Bennett, an engineer colleague who worked for local design firm Cummings and McCrady, had sent him pictures of the old jail and something clicked.

"Craig knew I wanted to become involved in a large, structural project," said Huguley. Bennett's firm had, in fact, monitored the jail for years and had previously done a study on it for the Housing Authority.

Huguley moved to Charleston, was hired by Cummings and McCrady and soon found himself circling the jail opportunity and trying to come up with a way to address it. Others were interested, too, he said. "Their ideas ran the gamut from carving it up as condos to tearing it down."

But Huguley was armed with a Masters' degree in engineering and a Certificate of Historic Preservation degree from the University of Virginia. His proposal sought to restore the building as an important landmark and this approach was commensurate with Housing Authority desires.

"The Preservation Community had not paid attention to it for years," said Huguley. "Charleston had revitalized itself but this great, old building had been forgotten and didn't have a home. I took the lease which helped block all others who wanted to do something that wouldn't have preserved it."

Huguley's passions for building craftsmanship and preservation of historically important structures were fostered by his mother. "The best advice my parents ever gave me came in a quote by Thoreau that my mother shared: 'If you have built castles in the air, your work need not be lost; that is where they should be. Now put the foundations under them.'"

Huguley's philosophy developed in his early studies which included travel abroad and through associations with the like-minded founders of the Boston firm for which he worked. It is based on the fundamental belief that architects and designers must acquire an intimate knowledge of the basic materials used in building and how the interaction of those materials affects building quality structures.

"The idea of sitting in a room, designing a building for which you've never touched materials doesn't work," said Huguley.

As Huguley pursued the jail, a previous idea began finally to take shape; that of establishing a school that would graduate expert designers thoroughly versed in the science of materials. Eventually he found support for both of his ideas - the school and the jail - among local influentials including South Carolina State Senator Herbert Fielding, Mayor Joe Riley and preservation leader Jane Hanahan, who was on the board of the National Trust. The latter relationship ultimately would lead to the jail being added to the Save America's Treasures program.

"It was a while before the idea for the school and the restoration of the jail became linked," said Huguley, "but eventually I saw the jail as a kind of living laboratory for the students. It seemed to be a good fit."

While the group pressed forward with plans that ultimately would become the American College for the Building Arts, acquisition of the jail proved to be challenging. First, Huguley needed millions to fulfill his promise of stabilization, then restoration. Even worse was the apparent legal mistake made when the jail was closed in 1939 that entangled it with the Robert Mills Manor Housing project and the Department of Housing and Urban Development (See Chapter 14).

Fundraising was not something with which Huguley had experience but he was confident the money could be found. The issue of the jail's ownership - by HUD, rather than the city of Charleston - turned out to be a nightmare.

"I was ready to tear my hair out," said Huguley of the process. "The school was going but I needed the building released. It would give me a location, a calling card. I'd found that in Charleston, it's all about real estate."

Huguley said an important hurdle was crossed after he met with an Atlanta-based HUD regional director who liked the proposal but resolution remained elusive. He said Cameron generally had been a good steward of the building but the jail was not a priority with the Authority.

"Here was the problem," said Huguley. "For the Housing Authority, the jail was a liability. But it was our core mission. The whole thing played out in the press every month."

In one article published Feburary 16, 1999, Post and Courier reporter Robert Behre wrote:

The School of the Building Arts, a fledgling nonprofit group that hopes to fix up Charleston's Old Jail on Magazine Street, could see its bid fly or fail later this month.

And the decision could hinge on money - not just cash in the bank but the prospects for raising the more than $3 million estimated to rehabilitate the jail.

The Charleston Housing Authority, the public agency that owns the abandoned Gothic-style jail, wants assurances that the school can raise the money to fix up the building before it agrees to hand over the title, Executive Director Don Cameron said.

"We recognize they don't have that ($3 million) in the bank, but we would like to see commitments of some magnitude toward 10 percent of that," he said.

But John Paul Huguley, president of The School of the Building Arts, said its fund-raising ability is hampered by having no assurance of getting the building. The group currently has a short-term lease on the jail and office space in a nearby authority property, the Old Marine Hospital on Franklin Street.

The suspense is expected to end during the authority's Feb. 23 board meeting.

Cameron said the authority board could resolve to ask the U.S. Department of Housing and Urban Development to release the jail from restrictive covenants and to designate The School of the Building Arts as the recipient.

Huguley said if the authority doesn't do that, then his largely self-financed effort will end.

"We have to secure the building in order to raise the funds," he said. "The Charleston Housing Authority wants to know that we have a capable team. It's a chicken and egg kind of thing."

Cameron said Huguley's group has come a long way since its first presentation to the board last August, but the authority must make sure that the group can handle the crumbling building. The jail is nestled in the middle of Robert Mills Manor, the authority's oldest public housing.

"It could turn into more than a white elephant, but a danger," Cameron said of the jail.

Huguley said while the school plans to rehabilitate the old jail, its more important mission is to educate youths and others about carpentry, masonry and iron work and to improve and respect the surrounding neighborhood, including both private homes and public housing.

"I haven't found anyone in this neighborhood that's excited about me fixing that building up. They tell me, `Do something for the kids,' " he said. "This is not about buildings any more. It's about community." [35]

A few weeks later, the HUD issues still not decided, another article appeared that, at least, offered Huguley and his group some encouragement. Post and Courier Ron Menchaca's story said:

A local nonprofit foundation hoping to secure a concrete decision from the Charleston Housing Authority on the foundation's request to renovate the Old City Jail was left still hoping after a Feb. 23 meeting.

"We don't directly want to support it, and we don't indirectly want to support it," Housing Authority Chairman Kenneth Krawcheck said of the foundation's plan to convert the building into a School for the Building Arts.

The foundation currently holds a short-term lease on the property, but the school's president, John Paul Huguley, says that in order to move his foundation's fund-raising efforts along, he needs a more substantial commitment from the housing authority.

The school's purpose would be to provide educational programs and discussion in the field of preservation and the arts for youths and others, according to a proposal submitted to the authority.

An impassioned plea from former state Sen. Herbert Fielding, the foundation's acting board chairman, and a polished slide presentation by some of its members outlining the group's vision were not enough to push the authority into a long-term agreement - yet.

"I hate to sound like the bad guy here, but we are not here tonight to authorize a deed transfer," said authority attorney Marvin I. Oberman. "These people are going to have to prove to us that they are the right people."

The Old City Jail at Franklin and Magazine streets hasn't seen a real use - other than storage - since the last prisoners were shuttled out of there about six decades ago.

Its oldest part - the middle segment - dates back as far as 1802, although it took its present form in 1859.

Authority members told the group, led by architect Huguley, that the decision rests ultimately with the U.S. Department of Housing and Urban Development.

Before a property deed can be signed over, HUD must lift restrictive covenants on the jail.

But the school's backers did receive a verbal commitment from the board.

"It is our intention to transfer this property to the School of the Building Arts," said Oberman.

"We really need to cross our T's and dot our I's on this one," said Krawcheck. "We have to make sure we don't cross HUD."

Krawcheck also floated an idea that would have the property revert to another entity in the event the school fails, thereby protecting the housing authority's interest.

"We want to be rid of this building. Once that's done, we don't want it back," said Krawcheck.

The board did pass a resolution to get the ball rolling on forming a letter of intent, which would set forth specific requirements that Huguley's group would need to meet. The letter also would assist the board in preparing the HUD application.

An optimistic estimate would have issues between the School of the Building Arts board and the authority's board being worked out while awaiting a decision from HUD, expected to take 90 days.

"Maybe it will all just magically come together," said Fielding. [36]

After pressure by the National Trust on HUD, countless meetings to pore over binders of studies and sheer tenacity, the jail was released by the federal government, clearing the way for its "disposition" by the Charleston Housing Authority. [37] But the next obstacle proved to be the Housing Authority and its need for assurance that Huguley could make good on his promises. [38]

More meetings, more presentations and more fundraising ensued. In May 1999, the jail was included on a list of 73 endangered sites and artifacts under the Save America's Treasures program, a public-private partnership between the National Trust for Historic Preservation and the White House Millennium Council, co-chaired by then-First Lady Hillary Clinton. [39]

Finally, the Charleston Housing Authority sold the jail for $3 to the nonprofit "School of the Building Arts," later to become known as the American College of the Building Arts." [40] Acquisition of the deed helped clear the way for a series of state and federal grants that have financed major restoration projects. These have included a massive steel girder system to stabilize the basic structure, replacing the floor system of the Octagon, replacement of the roof, extensive repairs to brick and mortar and the rebuilding of all windows.

Photo by author

Massive girder system prevents collapse

But despite the grants — by 2002 they already had totaled almost $1.5 million — revised estimates pegged the total cost of the job to be $7.5 million so the job of maintaining the jail is ongoing. And, unfortunately, Huguley has found that not everything original to the jail can be saved. A Post and Courier reporter in February 2002 shared the facts with readers:

> **The building originally had floors supported by timbers, but after the 1886 earthquake, the floors were rebuilt with a mixture of concrete and steel. That steel**

is now rusting and expanding, putting potentially fatal pressure on the exterior brick walls.

"It's been known since 1996 that the walls have to have some support," Huguley says. "All the floors are going. They're corroding and placing structural problems on walls."

Huguley says he tried to see if at least one portion of the old concrete and steel flooring could be saved — or if it could be removed and built back, but the structural engineers say no.

So the floors will be removed and built as they were when the jail was first constructed. [41]

Since then, fundraising and repairs have continued. The American College of the Building Arts was granted in 2004 a license by the South Carolina Commission on Higher Education to recruit students and graduated its first class in 2009. Its physical presence in the jail has undergone many iterations, including a plea to the Housing Authority in 2003 to permit construction of additional buildings to accommodate the school. The request was denied, with disruption to the residents of the Robert Mills Manor project cited as the reason. [42]

Photo by author

Jail repairs and restoration are ongoing

Since the building's size and condition preclude its service as a primary campus, classrooms have moved among several Charleston-area properties as the school seeks a permanent home. However, the jail hosts a great deal of instruction and students are part of nearly every restoration effort there. Restoring the jail remains central to the school's mission.

At the time this book was published, the school was under-going accreditation reviews with the expectation of timely receipt of pre-accreditation. Its first commencement was held in May, 2009 with seven graduating students receiving bachelor's degrees in applied science. An eighth student received an associate's degree.

"We want to preserve the irreplaceable," said Huguley. "And I'd add that we want our students to create buildings that are likewise irreplaceable."

Photo by author

SUMMARY TIMELINE OF EVENTS PERTAINING TO THE JAIL AND ITS TIMES

The following chronological list of jail-related events is augmented with a few others of significance to Charleston in general. Dates included are noted in records or known accounts. Some are approximate. Gaps reflect time periods for which records or accounts have not yet surfaced or are unknown to the author.

1685 – Former cemetery for blacks set aside as public land, 200-foot-square plot reserved for "gaol" (near present jail site)

1737 – 1740 City builds circular powder magazine on site of Jail (called at the time the ""New Magazine")

1738 – Workhouse/poorhouse (probably wood) built on the "Burying Ground" facing newly created Mazyck (now Logan) Street

1748 – A second magazine, this one rectangular, is built at Back (now Franklin) and Queen Streets

1768 – New Poorhouse built on Mazyck (Logan) between Queen and Magazine; three stories tall with cupola, two flanking outbuildings, holds almost 1,000; old poorhouse of 1738 becomes place of detention and correction

1769 – Assembly appropriates money for construction of a jail (but it was not built for 11 years)

1775 – The Revolutionary War begins

1775 – British build barracks for 500 men near present jail site

1779 – During Siege of Charleston by the British, the rectangular magazine blows up

1780 – A jail that had been authorized by the assembly in 1769 is built east of where the present structure sits; described as resembling a dwelling, with a central hall and a detached kitchen

1780 – On May 12, Charleston falls to the British; the round powder magazine accidentally explodes, taking with it the old poorhouse, a guard house, barracks and arsenal and, by some estimates, 200 lives

1782 – The British evacuate Charleston

1782 – Assembly orders construction of a "Gaol" (different than the one erected two years earlier)

1783 – City of Charleston Incorporated; given control of 200-foot-square parcel previously set aside for a jail

1787 – Jail-Bounds Act adopted; gives certain "gentleman" prisoners, such as debtors, limited freedom outside the jail proper

1794 – State Assembly appoints jail commissioners; solicits designs for a building to incarcerate debtors separately from criminals

1794 – The jail built in 1769 is deemed dilapidated; problems with it said to be "acute"

1794 – Revolutionary War hero General William Moultrie confined to jail-bounds (see above 1787)

1794 – Traveler Duke de la Rochefoucault describes jail as "spacious and airy" but that all prisoners are "in irons; a dreadful treatment"

1796 – Letter dated Nov. 8 to the Governor reveals much about the jail design process. Due to the lack of funds many of the ideas are not incorporated

1797 – Committee of the State Legislature sets dimensions for a "new" jail at 100 feet by 50 feet (the approximate size of the the extant main cell block of today's building); allocated $15,000 to back stock for projected $45,000 construction cost; commissioners wanted a secure, well-designed building with separate accommodations for debtors; rising cost of labor and material delayed the project; wanted to fashion the building after (probably) the Walnut Street jail in Philadelphia, which was a prototype for many other jails in the U.S.

1799 – Legislature authorized Charleston to sell jail stock

1801 – A Poorhouse is constructed on Logan, at mid-block

1802 – Jail built on Magazine Street; by November, the new, two-story rectangular brick jail building is mostly complete; keys to new "gaol" passed on to Governor Drayton; suggests prisoners be "accepted"; old jail turned into house of corrections (Workhouse for slaves)

1803 – Sometime in January, prisoners are admitted to the new building, even though outbuildings, wall and well have not been finished

1803 – In a November 26 letter, Sheriff Thomas Lehre advises governor on jail "hardships"; complains the windows are without shutters and sashes to keep out rain and wind; lack of the outer jail forces him to confine prisoners together in small apartments with no means of exercise; poor sanitary facilities result in unsatisfactory living conditions.

1803 – Foreign Slave Trade reopens; 40,000 African slaves are imported until the importation of slaves is ended in 1808.

1805 – In May, Grand Jury states that several windows were still without shutters and the jail yard continued to lack an outer wall. The weak structure of the windows and the absent wall had resulted in numerous escapes.

1805 – Grand Jury report notes concern regarding "the practice which is adopted in the Gaol of cooking in apartments with wooden floors, since their are good kitchens with paved floors under the building."

1805 – Richard Dennis, Joshua Nettler hung in back of the jail

1805 – Grand Jury notes that jail is insecure, unhealthy

1805 – In December the state assembly appoints several men to superintend the construction of a brick wall around the jail yard

1811 – Sheriff Nathaniel G. Cleary first notified the state legislature that the slate roof needed repairs; "open and untight" state of the roof allowed water to enter the jail and saturate the upper apartments;   prisoners cut through the ceiling below the roof which consisted of thin pine boards or planks.

1811 – Great cyclone strikes Charleston

1813 – Hurricane comes ashore in the Low Country surrounding Charleston

1813 – Pierre Matheseau hanged in front of jail

1813 – John E. Baldioiu hanged

1817 – Roof in such poor repair the Grand Jury feared for the lives of inmates; slate roof repaired; another roof was requested over the steps leading to the front door of the Jail;

1817 – Double flight of stone steps added; jail whitewashed; ironwork repaired

1817 – A sum not to exceed $3,000 was allocated by the Committee on Public Buildings by March and work began only months later.

1819 – Front railing started two years earlier finally finished

1819 – Convicted murder Martin Toohey escapes on May 16, is recaptured and hung in jail yard on May 18

1820 – Lavinia Fisher and husband, after year's confinement in the jail, are hanged December 12 on Boundary Street

1820 – Pirates hanged (not at jail) on May 12

1820 – William Hayward hanged on August 11

1820 – Pirates hanged (not at jail) on August 19

1820 – Grand Jury recommended a cistern for gathering rainwater on October 6; Jury will continue recommending a cistern until 1826. (Not known if the present cisterns are a result of this effort.)

1821 – Jail deemed too small for needs of District; addition planned

1821 – Bidders sought for modifications to Jail

1821 – Man publicly whipped in market

1821 – White Denmark Vesey conspirators jailed on Magazine Street; (Vesey confined next door in the Work House; Vesey and others hanged at Work House near the jail)

1821 – Per internal reports, the jail had been deemed as too small

1822 – Architect Robert Mills advertises for bids to remodel jail based on his design of three story, 18-foot x 51-foot fireproof annex with individual cells; arranged windows for "free circulation or air" Mills paid $1,000 for his involvement

1824 – Overseen by Sheriff Nathaniel Cleary, main jail plaster repaired; interior painted; garden enclosure added to Jail yard

1825 – Jail described by author and traveler Karl Bernhard: "upon the whole it left an unfavourable impression on me."

1825 – Two cisterns may have been built in the attic

1826 – Piazza (approx. 9 ft.) added to the rear of the jail

1826 – Medical College of South Carolina, designed by Frederick Wesner, is constructed at corner of Queen and Franklin

1828 – Jail described by Captain Basil Hall: "…in the court-yard of the jail, there were scattered about no fewer than 300 slaves, mostly brought from the country for sale…"

1828 – Lifo, the Spaniard, hanged in jail yard

1830 – Marine Hospital (for sick and disabled seamen) constructed; designed by

Robert Mills

1831 – Unnamed slave or freedman hanged

1832 – Irvin hanged in jail yard

1838 – Fire rages across 145 acres of Charleston; destroyed 1,000 buildings eastward from King Street to Ansonborough.

1842 – The Citadel is established in Charleston

1843 – Thomas McCantz hanged in jail yard

1847 – Nichols (slave) hanged in jail yard

1849 – Two men hanged in jail yard

1849 – Roper Hospital Built

1849 – New workhouse constructed

1850 – Grand Jury faults old jail; proposes new one

1851 -Grand Jury complains jail is badly ventilated, poorly arranged and insecure; Jury states conditions are result of "radical errors in the original plan and construction of the building." Jury wants to build new building incorporating " enlightened experience and modern improvement."

1853 – On 20 December the state legislature appropriates $30,000 for a new jail.

1852 – Novel "Manuel Pereira" by F.C. Adams describes jail

1854 – Jail renovation planned by Barbot and Seyle

1854 – Grand Jury asked for S10,000 additional; adopts new building plan, decides to build a jail in the same location using existing materials.

1855 – Charleston Daily Courier publishes request for proposals for jail construction. Plans and specification available at the office of architects Barbot and Seyle

1855 – Inmates of the Poorhouse moved; poorhouse becomes "House of Correction"

1855 – Grand Jury presentment implies new jail plan and style follow current fashion and would "present a building both useful and ornamental.

1855 – Jail expanded, redesigned as per Barbot and Seyle's design (gothic front, towers and octagon still present today)

1857 – Illustration of redesigned jail appears in Ballou's Pictorial Drawing-Room Companion

1858 – Two thieves escape from jail

1858 – Three Prisoners escape from jail

1859 – A fray in Jail reported

1859 – Richard Foster hanged in jail yard

1859 – Jail renovation is completed

1859 – Grand Jury asks for the addition of a stove or some other mode of heating

1860 – Stove added to heat the building

1860 – On 20 December at Institute Hall, South Carolinians sign the Ordinance of Secession. Six days later U.S. Army Major Robert Anderson moves his troops from Fort Moultrie to Fort Sumter.

1860 – Man named Abraham hanged in jail yard

1861 – February Harper's New Monthly Magazine includes engraving of octagon

1861 – April 12 Confederate batteries fire upon federal forces at Fort Sumter starting the Civil War

1861 – On 11 December, a devastating fire extends in a diagonal direction from the Cooper to the Ashley Rivers; General Ripley blows up houses to stop a raging fire threatening jail and the surrounding area

1861 – Union prisoners begin arriving at Charleston Jail

1861 – Union captive Samuel Harris describes Rebel guard shooting black youth in jail

1862 – Union shells sail over jail yard

1863 – Gallows built (but not used) in jail yard for 54th Massachusetts black soldiers

1863 – Jail described by black Union captive; says Abraham Lincoln's brother-in-law a surgeon at jail

1865 – Federal troops occupy Charleston

1865 – In July Harper's New Monthly Magazine again depicts the rear of the jail, similar to 1861.

1868 – Photograph of jail shows a four story jail with a large tower atop the octagon

1872 – Samuel White hanged in jail yard

1885 – Great cyclone hits Charleston

1886 – Catastrophic earthquake hits Charleston in August and kills ninety-two people; greatest damage from the earthquake is claimed to be in the block containing the jail

1886 – As earthquake rends jail wall, prisoners escape

1886 – Damage to jail requires prisoners be moved to the Citadel in Marion Square, some escape

1886 – New stockade built on Franklin while repairs to jail considered

1887 – Jail still four stories but needs repairs

1889 – Daniel Washington hanged in jail yard

1889 – Jail's fourth floor removed due to damage from earthquake

1893 – Hurricane hits Charleston

1906 – Executions in jail yard said performed "as needed"

1906 – Marcus hanged in jail yard

1911 – Hurricane hits Charleston with record winds (94 to 106 mph)

1911 – Daniel Duncan last man hanged in jail yard

1911 – Newspaper reports 10-year-old jailed after trolley accident

1911 – Capt. William J. Bennett appointed jailer

1912 – Assistant jailer shoots from jail doorway, wounds city chain gang chief

1916 – Prisoner dieting fee system called "a relic"

1919 – Governor vows he'll never punish lynchers of black men that have assaulted white women

1920 – The Society for the Preservation of Old Dwellings (now the Preservation Society) founded by Susan Pringle Frost

1920 – Jail matrons named, including jailer William Bennett's wife

1922 – Charleston Jail "Fourth Best" in state

1925 – DuBose Heyward describe jail in novel "Porgy"

1920 – Area around jail deemed slum

1931 – Jail population said to number 160

1931 – Peak load emphasizes need for annex or farm

1931 – Altercation in jail over game of checkers reported

1931 – Grand Jury calls jail "disease trap"

1931 – Ministers inspect jail

1931 – Jail kitchen remodeling estimate described

1932 – Jailer Bennett suggests "Convict Farm" could solve overcrowding

1932 – Jail repairs sought

1932 – Commission agrees to build annex

1932 – Jail accepts 18 city police station prisoners

1932 – 23 jail Prisoners transferred to county camp

1932 – Annex Construction Begins

1932 – Grand Jurors suggest city jail farm

1932 – Jail receives hatchet murderer

1932 – 43 prisoners moved to newly constructed jail annex in jail yard but doesn't alleviate "congestion"

1932 – Six more prisoners moved to annex

1932 – Gallows weights offered to Charleston Museum (no record of acceptance)

1933 – "Beating" of jail convicts is officially outlawed but never happened anyway, jailer says

1934 – City chain gang to wear striped suits (other jail prisoners do not)

1934 – Sheriff lists jail needs

1934 – Prison "No Good Effect on Criminals" says jailer Bennett in newspaper

1934 – Jailer Bennett warmly praised by New York business magazine

1935 – Jailer Bennett, former watchman fight in front of the court house

1938 – Two tornadoes hit Charleston the same day, devastate City Market

1938 – City of Charleston plans "slum clearance project" (to become known as Robert Mills Manor) and discontinued use of jail building. In return for title to jail, City Council of Charleston gives County Board of Commissioners prison farm located seven miles north of the city

1938 – Ownership of jail "mistakenly packaged" with Robert Mills Manor project

1938 – Jail "No Bed of Roses" Says Jailer Bennett to newspaper

1938 – Jail, Jenkins Orphanage to be razed as part of slum renovation

1938 – Mayor opposes presence of a jail in city

1938 – "Save the Jail" campaign includes letters to the editor

1938 – Robert Mills Manor project measures 315,000 square feet

1938 – Jail renovation grant to go to prison farm

1938 – Plans for a new jail drawn up

1938 – Sheriff opposes farm jail

1938 – Jail area termed "City's Worst Slum"

1939 – Jail goes out of service; is closed September 14, 1939

1939 – Wall demolition may be picketed

1939 – Governors steps in to save wall

1939 – Charleston Housing Authority buys jail for $5

1939 – Jail wall mostly demolished; some sections left at four feet high

1939 – Jail cellblocks to be moved

1939 – Brick Annex Razed to make way for Robert Mills Manor

1939 – Jailer Bennett confirms he'll retire May 1

1939- Jail walls down, police aid requested by sheriff to secure prisoners

1939 – W.J. Bennett retires as Jailer

1939 – Son Succeeds W.J. Bennett as Jailer

1939 – Prisoners Vacate Jail

1940 – Jail building proposed to house National Youth Administration offices (probably never realized)

1940 – Hurricane hits Charleston

1940 – Jail used as a Housing Authority maintenance headquarters

1941 – World War II begins

1941 – New jail (Seabreeze) at foot of bridge boasts modern facilities

1951 – Kindergarten run by local church on upper level of jail

1952 – Jailer W.J. Bennett Dies

1975 – The Housing Authority leases jail building to Bartley Riddock and A.A. Burns, Jr. for the use of a museum.

1976 – Jail Museum Opens

1978 – Error in crediting jail design to Robert Mills discovered (his wing had been torn down in 1855)

1980 – Jail museum closes (approximate)

1985 – Jail dusted with man-made snow as location for "North and South" TV miniseries

1986 – Engineering study determines jail structurally "unsafe"; separate study estimates cost of renovation at $1,000,000

1988 – Panel clears Way for jail disposal (but it doesn't happen)

1989 – Hurricane Hugo causes extensive damage to Charleston

1989 – Another study pegs renovation price tag at $260,000; "…well within our capacity," says Housing Authority's Cameron but second phase of study reveals cost actually is $1.5 million

1991 – Spoleto Festival USA sites installation art in the jail for ""Places with a Past."

1994 – Historic American Buildings conducts survey (HABS)

1998 – Clemson Architecture students make measured drawing and models of the existing jail and Marine Hospital

1998 – Preliminary proposal by the Huguley Group submitted

1999 – Jail named to Save America's Treasures program of the National Trust for Historic Preservation

1999 – HUD public hearing on plan for sale of jail to School of the Building Arts

1999 – In January, the School of the Building Arts incorporated as a non-profit school with the mission to train in the building arts. The existing Steering Committee became the Board of Directors.

2000 – School of the Building Arts acquires Jail for $3 and promises to stabilize, then renovate it, use for good of the preservation community and to make it an education center for the larger community

2002 – Structural stabilization construction performed plans by Simpson Gumpertz & Heger, Inc. 2002-09-01

2002 – Jail worker tells newspaper he's seen ghost inside

2002 – Grants to College to renovate jail total $1.5 million but revised estimates put cost at $7 million

2004 – American College of the Building Arts officially granted license by state Commission on Higher Education to recruit students

2009 – College graduates its first class of students

2009 – American College of the Building Arts moves its primary classroom campus to the jail

ACKNOWLEDGEMENTS

The "Acknowledgements" section of a given book probably is of interest only to those acknowledged. Nonetheless, I would be remiss if I didn't publicly state my gratitude to some persons and institutions that helped greatly in the process of producing this book.

The patience that my wife, Debbie, demonstrated throughout has been remarkable and very much appreciated. She also read the first drafts, as did friends Gary Arnold and Jennifer Arnold, and they provided corrections, good suggestions and encouragement.

The bulk of the editing was done by my long-time mentor and good friend, David Easterly. A fellow "ink-stained newspaper wretch," David doggedly hacked his way through tangles of super-fluous words and phrases, dispelled clouds of unclear expression and counseled me with regard to the organization and presentation of material. He did all of this as a favor and I owe him.

However, despite the best efforts of those above, I had the temerity to change a few things during the final stages of preparation for print. I apologize to them and note that if something herein is amiss, it is not their fault.

Of course, it is doubtful that this book would have been created had it not been for the cooperation and support of John Paul Huguley, founder of the American College of the Building Arts, the institution that has owned the jail since 1997. Its leaders and supporters are responsible for obtaining grants and assistance to shore up the physical structure of the jail and oversee its ongoing preservation. John Paul made available to me every scrap of jail-related material his teams had previously collected and these have proven invaluable. He also read the various drafts, despite enormous demands on his time. Becca Walton, also with the College, read the final draft and provided necessary corrections and welcome suggestions.

Thanks to the Post and Courier for permission to excerpt its stories, both old and recent and I especially appreciate the help given to me by the newspaper's librarian, Libby Wallace.

In the course of my research, I have met and have been assisted in matters large and small by many persons. They include, in no particular order, Walterboro artist Robert Grenko; Rev. William K. Christian, Executive Director of the Star Gospel Mission; Charleston County Chief Deputy Coroner Judy Koelpin and Deputy Corner Bobbi O'Neal; Post and Courier Librarian Libby Wallace; Betty White, granddaughter of long-time jailer William J. Bennett; Nick Butler, Special Collections Manager for the Charleston County Library; Don Cameron, president and chief executive officer of the Charleston Housing Authority; retired Senator Herbert Fielding; Harlan Greene, author and Project Director at the Avery Research Center; John Laverne of Bulldog Tours; Ralph McLaughlin; Bill Merton; Ron Reuger, Charleston County Clerk of Courts; Karen Stokes, Processing Archivist and Mary Joe Fairchild, Archivist, both of the South Carolina Historical Society; Janice Knight and Joyce Baker, both with the Charleston Library Society; Katherine Saunders, Associate Director of Preservation for the Historic Charleston Foundation; Christina Shedlock of the Charleston County Public Library; distinguished authors Richard Côté, Robert Stockton, Warren Ripley, Jack Thomson and Gene Waddell; Charleston Police Major Herb Wetzel; publisher Charles Wyrick; Martha Zierden, Curator of Historical Archeology at The Charleston Museum and Judson Manley, Manley Jail Works.

Thanks to American College of the Building Arts student Sam Wilson for his drawings, photographer Jack Alterman for the use of his bucket truck and Jay Rice, who is darned convincing when he says that he actually saw a ghost in the basement of the jail.

Source Notes

Epigraphs

[1] Willard W. Glazier, The Capture, the Prison Pen, and the Escape, Giving a Complete History of Prison Life in the South (Hartford, Conn: H.E. Goodwin, Publisher, 1869), p. 159

[2] The Mudcat Cafe, "Down in Charleston Jail," Composed by Sergeant Johnson of the 54 Massachussetts (colored) Infantry while prisoners in a Charleston military prison. Parody of When this Cruel War is Over., http://www.mudcat.org/@displaysong.cfm?SongID=1683 (tune available)

Introduction

[1] Samuel Harris, The Personal Reminiscences of Samuel Harris (Chicago, IL: The Rogerson Press, 1897), p. 128.

Chapter 2

[1] Alan Taylor, American Colonies (USA: Viking Penguin, 2002), p. 224

[2] "Stede Bonnnet," Wikipedia. 2010. http://en.wikipedia.org/wiki/Stede_Bonnet

[3] Lawrence Friedman, Crime and Punishment in American History (New York: BasicBooks, 1993), p. 48

[4] Friedman, Crime and Punishment in American History, p. 43

[5] Taylor, American Colonies, p. 213

6. Frederick Howard Wines, Punishment and Reformation – A Study of the Penitentiary System (New York: Thoms Y. Crowell Company, Publishers, 1919) p. 117

7. Friedman, Crime and Punishment in American History, p. 81

8. Charles Woodmason, Carolina Backcountry on the Eve of the Revolution (North Carolina: University of North Carolina Press, 1953), p. 219

9. Francois Alexandre Frederic, Duke de la Rochefoucault Liancourt, Travels Through the United States of North in the Years 1795, 1796, and 1797, (London: for R. Phillips, 1800), p. 392

10. John Bennett, "City's Jail Problem Was Acute in 1794," News and Courier, March 28, 1939.

Chapter 3

1. Jonathan H. Poston, The Buildings of Charleston – a Guide to the City's Architecture, (South Carolina: University of South Carolina Press, 1997), p. 392

2. Christine Trebellas, Historic American Buildings Survey – Charleston County Jail (Charleston District Jail), (Washington, DC: Historic American Buildings Survey [HABS], 1995), p. 24

3. Trebellas, Historic American Buildings Survey – Charleston County Jail (Charleston District Jail), p. 24

4. Trebellas, Historic American Buildings Survey – Charleston County Jail (Charleston District Jail), p. 22

5. Bernhard, Karl (Duke of Saxe-Weimar Eisenach), Travels Through North America, During the Years 1825 and 1826, Vol.2, (Philadelphia: Carey, Lea & Carey, 1828), p. 10

6. John Lambery, Travels Through Lower Canada, and the United States of North American in the Years 1806, 1807, and 1808, Vo. 2 (London: C. Cradock and W. Joy, 1814), p. 173

7. Berhard, Travels Through North America, During the Years 1825 and 1826, Vol. 2, p. 9

8. Berhard, Travels Through North America, During the Years 1825 and 1826, Vol. 2, p. 9

9. Berhard, Travels Through North America, During the Years 1825 and 1826, Vol. 2, p. 9-10

[10.] Robert Mills, Statistics of South Carolina, including a view of its Natural, Civil, and Military History, General and Particular, (Charleston: Hurlbut and Lloyd, 1826) p. 214

[11.] F.C. Adams, Manuel Pereira or, The Soverign Rule of South Carolina with Views of Southern Laws, Life, and Hospitality, (Washington, DC: Buell & Blanchard, 1853), p. 129

[12.] Trebellas, Historic American Buildings Survey – Charleston County Jail (Charleston District Jail), p. 32

[13.] Trebellas, Historic American Buildings Survey – Charleston County Jail (Charleston District Jail), p. 19

[14.] Trebellas, Historic American Buildings Survey – Charleston County Jail (Charleston District Jail), p. 33

[15.] Trebellas, Historic American Buildings Survey – Charleston County Jail (Charleston District Jail), p. 34

[16.] Trebellas, Historic American Buildings Survey – Charleston County Jail (Charleston District Jail), p. 35

[17.] Francois Alexandre Frederic, Duke de la Rochefoucault Liancourt, Travels Through the United States of North in the Years 1795, 1796, and 1797, p. 565

[18.] Trebellas, Historic American Buildings Survey – Charleston County Jail (Charleston District Jail), p. 36

[19.] Trebellas, Historic American Buildings Survey – Charleston County Jail (Charleston District Jail), p. 2

[20.] Trebellas, Historic American Buildings Survey – Charleston County Jail (Charleston District Jail), p. 3-6

[21.] Trebellas, Historic American Buildings Survey – Charleston County Jail (Charleston District Jail), p. 5-6

[22.] Trebellas, Historic American Buildings Survey – Charleston County Jail (Charleston District Jail), p. 6

Chapter 4

[1.] Trebellas, Historic American Buildings Survey – Charleston County Jail (Charleston District Jail), p. 9

[2.] Receipt "for Repairing Charleston Gaol," Emmett Robinson Papers, South Carolina Historical Society

[3.] Trebellas, Historic American Buildings Survey – Charleston County Jail (Charleston District Jail), p. 10

[4.] Mills, Statistics of South Carolina, p. 240

[5] Trebellas, Historic American Buildings Survey – Charleston County Jail (Charleston District Jail), p. 13

[6] SoBA Facility Master Plan, Glen Keyes, Architect in collaboration with Robert Miller, Architect, 2003, p. 2-13

[7] Basil Hall, Travels in North America, in the Years 1827 and 1828, Vol. III (Edinburgh: Printed for Cadell and Co., 1830), p. 169-170

[8] Trebellas, Historic American Buildings Survey – Charleston County Jail (Charleston District Jail), p. 15

[9] Berhard, Travels Through North America, During the Years 1825 and 1826, Vol. 2, p. 178

[10] Adams, Manuel Pereira or, The Soverign Rule of South Carolina with Views of Southern Laws, Life, and Hospitality, p. 137

[11] A.O. Abbott, Prison Life in the South at Richmond, Macon, Savannah, Charleston, Columba, Charlotte, Raleigh, Goldsborough, and Andersonville During the Years 1864 and 1865, New Yrok: Harper & Brothers, 1865, p. 102

[12] SoBA Facility Master Plan, Glen Keyes, Architect in collaboration with Robert Miller, Architect, 2003, p. 2-43

[13] Kenneth Severens, Charleston Antebellum Architecture and Civic Destiny, University of Tennessee Press, Knoxville, 1988, p. 157

[14] SoBA Facility Master Plan, Glen Keyes, Architect in collaboration with Robert Miller, Architect, p. 2-25

[15] "The County Jail," News and Courier, September 4, 1886

[16] Trebellas, Historic American Buildings Survey – Charleston County Jail (Charleston District Jail), p. 20

[17] "Commission Lets Prison Contract," Charleston newspaper article, June 1, 1932 (found in the Post and Courier morgue)

[18] "43 Prisoners in New Jail Annex," Charleston newspaper article, August 28, 1932 (Post and Courier archive)

[19] City of Charleston Yearbook, 1939, (Charleston County Public Library) p.173

[20] "Wall on Franklin Will be Reduced," Charleston newspaper, 1939 (Post and Courier archive)

[21] "Today is MovingDay for Convicts," Charleston newspaper, September 16, 1939 (Post and Courier archive)

[22] "New Charleston County Jail Boasts of Modern Facilities," Charleston newspaper, August 1, 1941 (Post and Courier archive)

Chapter 5

1. Letter to Governor John Drayton from "Commissioners for Building a Gaol in Charleston," November 11, 1802, (from Emmett Robinson papers, South Carolina Historical Society)

2. Letter to Governor John Drayton from Sheriff Thomas Lehre, November 13, 1802, (from Emmett Robinson papers, South Carolina Historical Society)

3. SoBA Facility Master Plan, Glen Keyes, Architect in collaboration with Robert Miller, Architect, 2003, p. 2-13

4. Engraving, Union War Prisoners Association, organized in Charleston jail, Dec. 31st, 1861, New York: Published by Goupil & Col, M. Knoedler successor, July 1862

5. "Sentence Day," The Courier, July 12, 1825 and "Hangings, Etc.," Emmett Robinson papers, South Carolina Historical Society

6. "Brandings", Emmett Robinson papers, South Carolina Historical Society

7. Court of Sessions, The (Charleston) Courier, Feburary 13, 1819

8. Digital Library on American Slavery, "Sheriff Nathaniel Cleary," http://library.uncg.edu/slavery/details.aspx?pid=1439

9. Berhard, Travels Through North America, During the Years 1825 and 1826, Vol. 2, p. 178

10. Committee Report on Petition Above – 1828 – Penal System, Petitions, 1829 Charleston District, Emmett Robinson papers, South Carolina Historic Society

11. S.G.B., Reminiscences of Charleston, SC, The Monthly Religious Magazine, Volume XV, Cambridge: University Press, p. 116

12. Crockett, Hasan, The Incendiary Pamphlet: David Walker's Appeal in Georgia, Association for the Study of African-American Life and History, Inc., 2001, p. 305

13. F.C. Adams, Manuel Pereira: Washington, DC, Buell & Blanchard, 1853, p. 129-137

14. Bancroft, Frederic,Slave Trading in the Old South, 1831, University of South Carolina Press, 1996, p. 178

15. Ballou's Pictorial Drawing Room Companion, August 8, 1957, clipping in (Charleston) Post and Courier archive

16. "Affray in Jail," The Courier, March 21, 1859, Emmett Robinson Papers, South Carolina Historical Society

Chapter 6

1. Abbott, Prison Life in the South, p. 104
2. SoBA Facility Master Plan, Glenn Keyes, Architect in collaboration with Robert Miller, Architect, 2003, p. 2-25
3. Abbott, Prison Life in the South, p. 103-104
4. McGregor, Jeremiah S., Life and Deeds of Dr. John McGregor, "Union War Prisoners Association" engraving, Foster: Press of Fry Brothers, 1886, p. 50
5. "The Prisoners at Charleston; They are Committed to the City Jail," New York Times October 3, 1861, from the Charleston Mercury, September 14, 1861
6. Meadville, Graham McCamant, Sixteen Months in Rebel Prisons by the First Prisoner in Andersonville, provided by Betty Lee Meadville, p. 3
7. Glazier, The Capture, the Prison Pen, and the Escape, p. 115-116
8. Shurtleff, George W., A Year with the Rebels, Itinerary of the Seventh Ohio Volunteer Infantry, 1861-1864, edited by Lawrence Wilson, p. 318-319
9. Adams, John G.B., Reminiscences of the Nineteenth Massachusetts Regiment, Boston: Wright, Potter Printing Company, 1899, Chapter XIII
10. Meadville, Sixteen Months in Rebel Prisons by the First Prisoner in Andersonville, p. 3-4
11. "The Prisoners at Charleston; They are Committed to the City Jail," New York Times October 3, 1861
12. "Under the Union Guns," New York Times, May 10, 1891
13. Anonymous, "The Story of a Strange Career being the Autobiography of a Convict," Edited by Stanley Wateroo, New York: D. Appleton and Company, p. 265, 269-270
14. Asa Brainerd Isham; Henry Davidson, M., Henry B. Furness, Prisoners of War and Military Prisons: Personal Narratives of Experience in the Prisons at Richmond, Danville, Macon, Andersonville, Savannah, Millen, Charleston, and Columbia with A General Account of Prison Life and Prisons in the South

during the War of the Rebellion, including Statistical Information Pertaining to Prisoners of War; together with a List of Officers who were Prisoners of War from January 1, 1864., p. 67

15. Alonzo. Cooper, In and Out of Rebel Prisons, Swego, N.Y.: R.J. Oliphant, 1888, p. 258 - 260

16. Adams, Reminiscences of the Nineteenth Massachusetts Regiment, Chapter XIII

17. Glazier, The Capture, the Prison Pen, and the Escape, p. 155-156

18. Adams, Reminiscences of the Nineteenth Massachusetts Regiment, Chapter XIII

19. Isham, Davidson, Furness; Prisoners of War and Military Prisons, p. 67-68

20. "Under the Union Guns," New York Times, May 10, 1891

21. "With Gun and Caisson; Scraps from the Notebook of an Artilleryman. Headed for Antietam – Passing Through Washington on a Sunday Morning – How the Capital Looked in War Times. IV.", New York Times, March 15, 1891, P. 19

22. Abbott, Prison Life in the South, p. 112

23. Helm, T.B., Prison Life Part 1, History of Delaware County, Lora Radiches, p. 112

24. Darling, Joseph T., Nine Months in a Rebel Prison, The Main Bugle, 1898, p. 9-13

25. Bennett, Frank, Frank Bennett's Diary, The Historical Society of Pennyslvania, (http://www2.hsp.org/collections/manuscripts/b/bennett3041.htm)

26. McGregor, Life and Deeds of Dr. John McGregor, p. 50

27. Harris, The Personal Reminiscences of Samuel Harris, p. 130

28. Adams, Reminiscences of the Nineteenth Massachusetts Regiment, Chapter XIII

29. Isham, Davidson, Furness; Prisoners of War and Military Prisons, p. 72

30. Luis F. Emilio, A Brave Black Regiment, The History of the 54th Massachusetts, 1863-1865, p. 400

31. 1863 South Carolina Statutes at Large, Volume 13, p. 13, Emmett Robinson papers, South Carolina Historical Society

32. Adams, Reminiscences of the Nineteenth Massachusetts Regiment, Chapter XIII

33. Emilio, A Brave Black Regiment, p. 401

34. Emilio, A Brave Black Regiment, p. 403

35. Emilio, A Brave Black Regiment, p. 411

36. Emilio, A Brave Black Regiment, p. 411-412

37. Emilio, A Brave Black Regiment, p. 414

38. Emilio, A Brave Black Regiment, p. 415-416

39. Emilio, A Brave Black Regiment, p. 418-419

40. Emilio, A Brave Black Regiment, p. 285

41. Strater, Terrance, The Life and Times of a Rebel Surgeon, Dr. George Rodgers Clark Todd

42. Emilio, A Brave Black Regiment, p. 414

43. Emilio, A Brave Black Regiment, p. 416

44. "Under the Union Guns," New York Times, May 10, 1891

45. Glazier, The Capture, the Prison Pen, and the Escape, p. 152-153

46. Isham, Davidson, Furness; Prisoners of War and Military Prisons, p. 68-69

47. With Gun and Caisson; Scraps from the Notebook of an Artilleryman

48. Adams, Reminiscences of the Nineteenth Massachusetts Regiment, Chapter XIII

49. McGregor, Life and Deeds of Dr. John McGregor, p. 137-139

50. Isham, Davidson, Furness; Prisoners of War and Military Prisons, p. 170-172

51. Helm, T.B., Prison Life Part 1, p. 112

52. "Under the Union Guns," New York Times, May 10, 1891

53. S.H.M. Byers, What I Saw in Dixie or Sixteen Months in Rebel Prisons, New York: Robbin's and Poore, 1868, p. 58

54. Harris, The Personal Reminiscences of Samuel Harris, p. 128-129

55. Unknown, "The Story of a Strange Career being the Autobiography of a Convict, p. 268-269

56. McGregor, Life and Deeds of Dr. John McGregor, p. 53-54

57. Meadville, Sixteen Months in Rebel Prisons by the First Prisoner in Andersonville, p. 3

58. Adams, Reminiscences of the Nineteenth Massachusetts Regiment, Chapter XIII

Chapter 7

1. Richter magnitude scale, Wikipedia, http://en.wikipedia.org/wiki/Richter_scale

2. Carlyle McKinley, The Charleston Earthquake, August 31, 1886, Prepared Expressly for the City Year Book, 1886, Charleston, 1886

3. Trebellas, Historic American Buildings Survey – Charleston County Jail (Charleston District Jail), p. 19

4. (Charleston) Courier, September 1, 1886

5. Richard N. Côté, City of Heroes, Mt. Pleasant, SC: Corinthian Books, 2006, 9. 189-199

6. Richard N. Côté, City of Heroes, Mt. Pleasant, SC: Corinthian Books, 2006, 9. 201

7. 134. Trebellas, Historic American Buildings Survey – Charleston County Jail (Charleston District Jail), p. 18

8. "Shooting at the County Jail," Sunday News, August 18, 1912

9. "Exciting Shooting Affair Occurred Yesterday," State Newspaper, Columbia, SC

10. "Wingate Slightly Better," State Newspaper, August 20, 1912

11. "Charleston News Gathered in a Day," The State Newspaper, August 21, 1912

12. "Charleston News Gathered in a Day," The State Newspaper, February 21, 1913

13. "Political Row Ends in Shooting of Six Men in Charleston," Associated Press, October 16, 1915

14. Paul Wierse, Eighty-Eight Weeks in Purgatory, Charleston, SC: Farlane Printing and Publishing Company, 1920

15. Star Gospel Mission, http://www.stargospelmission.com/

16. Star Gospel Mission, Emmett Robinson papers, South Carolina Historical Society

17. "Newberry County Boasts Best Jail," The State Newspaper, March 5, 1922

18. Preservation Consultants, Inc. "Plan for the Adaptive Use of the Old Jail"; prepared for The Housing Authority of the City of Charleston, 1989, Plan for the Adaptive Use of the Old Jail, Phase 2, p. 10

19. "Checker Players, in Jail, Use Razor Blades in Row," Courier, Sept. 20, 1931

20. "'160 Prisoners Now in Jail," Courier, Jan. 19, 1931

21. "Grand Jury Finds Jail Disease Trap," Courier, September 20, 1931

22. "Ministers of City Inspect Charleston County Prison," Courier, November 3, 1931

23. "43 Prisoners in New Jail Annex," Courier, August 28, 1932

24. "Six Prisoners Removed," Courier, September 8, 1932

25. "City Chain Gang Prisoners Wear Striped Suits Again," Courier, February 19, 1933

26. "Beating Convict Outlawed at Charleston County Jail," Courier, January 27, 1933

27. Yearbook City of Charleston 1938 (Charleston County Public Library), p.

28. "Going Out of Service as Charleston County Jail," Courier, September 14, 1939

29. "Today is Moving Day for Convicts," Courier, September 16, 1939

Chapter 8

1. "Jail Cell Blocks to be Moved," Courier, February 18, 1939 (Post and Courier archive)

2. "Martin Toohey Jailed," Courier, March 20, 1819 Emmett Robinson papers, South Carolina Historical Society

3. "Escape of Martin Toohey," Franklin, Pa Gazette, March 27, 1819

4. "State of South Carolina – A Proclamation by his Excellency, John Geddes, Governor and Commander in Chief," Miller's Weekly Messenger, April 7, 1819

5. "Martin Toohey Jailed," Courier, March 20, 1819 Emmett Robinson papers, South Carolina Historical Society

6. "Martin Toohey Executed," Courier, May 29, 1819, Emmett Robinson papers, South Carolina Historical Society

7. John Blake White, from http://www.famousamericans.net/johnblakewhite/

8. CHARLESTON, SATURDAY MORNING, FEB. 20, 1819, Charleston County Public Library

9. CHARLESTON, MONDAY MORNING, FEB. 22, 1819, Charleston County Public Library

10. CHARLESTON, FRIDAY MORNING, FEB. 26, 1819 and FRIDAY MORNING, MARCH. 26, 1819, Charleston County Public Library

11. CHARLESTON, TUESDAY MORNING, JAN. 18, 1820, Charleston County Public Library

12. CHARLESTON, TUESDAY MORNING, JAN. 18, 1820 AND FRIDAY MORNING, FEB. 18, 1820 and SATURDAY MORNING, FEB. 19, 1820, Charleston County Public Library

13. John White Blake, The Dungeon and the Gallows, The Charleston Book, Charleston: Published by Samuel Hart, Sen., King Street, 1845, p. 125-127

14. CHARLESTON, TUESDAY MORNING, JANUARY 18, 1820, Charleston County Public Library

15. White, The Dungeon and the Gallows, p. 127-131

16. CHARLESTON, SATURDAY MORNING, FEB. 19, 1820, Charleston County Public Library

17. "Citizens Beware!," Courier, February 17, 1820, Charleston County Public Library

18. "Lynch Law was exhibited," Emmett Robinson papers, South Carolina Historical Society

19. "The Dawson Murder," Philadelphia Enquirer, March 14, 1889

20. An Accomplice of McDow," Macon Telegraph, March 15, 1889

21. "In the Police Court," newspaper clipping, Star Gospel Mission files, South Carolina Historical Society

22. Negro Accused of Murder," The State Newspaper, August 2, 1910

23. "Charleston News Gather in a Day," The State Newspaper, August 13, 1910

24. "Runaway Car Claims Victim," Courier, December 5, 1911, Charleston County Public Library

25. "Negro Boy Responsible," The State Newspaper, December 7, 1911

26. "Charleston News Gathered in a Day," The State Newspaper, December 27, 1911

27. "Charleston News Gathered in a Day," The State Newspaper, November 19, 1914

[28.] "German Merchant Arrested by Federal Officers," The State Newspaper, July 17, 1917

[29.] Charleston News Gathered in a Day," The State Newspaper, July 17, 1917

[30.] "Manly Admits Drugging and Robbing Woman," The State Newspaper, August 10, 1912

[31.] "Fox and Gappins Placed in Prison," The State Newspaper, September 9, 1921

[32.] "Kills His Children and Attacks Wife," Sunday Times-Advertiser, Trenton, N.Y., January 3, 1932

Chapter 9

[1.] "Broke Jail," Courier, May 3, 1858, Emmett Robinson papers, South Carolina Historical Society

[2.] "Escape from Jail," Courier, July 12, 1858, Emmett Robinson papers, South Carolina Historical Society

[3.] "Affray in the Jail," Courier, March 21, 1859, Emmett Robinson papers, South Carolina Historical Society

4. Darling, Joseph T., Nine Months in a Rebel Prison, The Main Bugle, 1898, p. 13, 115-116

[5.] "A General Delivery at Charleston," New York Times, December 15, 18

Chapter 10

[1.] Charleston, South Carolina Death Records, 1819-1845, Compiled by Geo. K. Bonnoitt

[2.] Convictions taken from the Records and Dockets of the Court of Sessions, for Charleston, Emmett Robinson papers, South Carolina Historical Society

[3.] "27 Years Custodian of the Jail, Bennett Finds Life No Bed of Roses," Courier, Post and Courier archive

[4.] Harris, The Personal Reminiscences of Samuel Harris, p. 128

[5.] Glazier, The Capture, the Prison Pen, and the Escape, p. 155

[6.] "Suicide in Jail," Courier, June 6, 1867, Charleston County Public Library

[7.] "Hangings, Etc.," Emmett Robinson papers, South Carolina Historical Society

[8.] "The Execution," Easton Gazette, May 27, 1820

[9.] "Grand Jury Suggests Giving Gallows Weights to Museum," Courier, September 20, 1932

[10.] "The Last Penalty," Courier, March 26, 1859

[11.] "Under the Union Guns," New York Times, May 10, 1891, Post and Courier archive

[12.] Fergus Bordewich, The Battle The Battle for Morris Island, originally from A Civil Battle for a Civil War Battlefield, Smithsonia Magazine, July, 2005, from http://www.fergusbordewich.com/PAGESjournalism/FBmorris.shtml

[13.] "A Murderer's End: Execution of a Negro Man in Charleston, S.C.," New York Times, February 10, 1872

[14.] "The Penalty for Murder,; Daniel Washington's Death on the Gallows," New York Times, July 10, 1880

[15.] "Negroes Don't Believe Marcus was Hanged," The State Newspaper, August 5, 1906

[16.] "Big Crowd Saw Marcus Hanged," The Evening Post, August 3, 1906, Emmett Robinson papers, South Carolina Historical Society

[17.] "Duncan to Hang Here Tomorrow," Evening Post, July 6, 1911, South Carolina Historical Society

[18.] "Daniel Duncan Hanged at Jail," Evening Post, July 7, 1911, Emmett Robinson papers, South Carolina Historical Society

Chapter 11

[1.] "27 Years Custodian of the Jail, Bennett Finds Life No Bed of Roses," Courier, Post and Courier archive

[2.] "Son Succeeds W.J. Bennett," April 29, 1939, Post and Courier archive

[3.] "Charleston Jail Matrons Procured," The State Newspaper, July 4, 1920

[4.] "This Looks Like the County Jail," Evening Post, August 18, 1928, Charleston County Public Library

[5.] "Beating Convict Outlawed at Charleston County Jail," Courier, January 27, 1933

[6] "Prison Has No Good Effect on Criminals, Jailer Finds," August 11, 1934, Post and Courier archive

[7] "Visitor Mistakes Jailer for Buddy," November 24, 1934, Post and Courier archive

[8] "Jailer and Former Watchman in Fight," December 5, 1935, Post and Courier archive

[9] "Denies Knife Was Open," December 5, 1935, Post and Courier archive

[10] "27 Years Custodian of the Jail, Bennett Finds Life No Bed of Roses," Courier, Post and Courier archive

[11] "Bennett Retires as Jailer May 1," April 18, 1939, Post and Courier archive

[12] "H.L. Bennett Named Charleston's Jailer," April 30, 1939, Post and Courier archive

[13] "Harold L. Bennett to Direct City's Safety Service," January 1, 1955, Post and Courier archive

[14] "W.J. Bennett, Former County Jailer, Dies," February 18, 1952, Post and Courier archive

Chapter 12

[1] "Workers Sign Off on Jail Repairs," by Jason Hardin, Post and Courier, June 25, 2002

[2] "It was learned today," The State Newspaper, July 17, 1917

[3] Darling, Joseph T., Nine Months in a Rebel Prison, The Main Bugle, 1898, p. 10

Chapter 13

[1] "Eerie, Dark History Haunts Old City Jail," by Clay Barbor, Post and Courier, October 27, 2002

[2] "Talk About Having a Bad Scare Day," by Bryce Donovan, Post and Courier, October 31, 2002

[3] "Ghost Hunting at Charleston's Old Jail," by Greg Hambrick, Charleston City Paper, August 29, 2007

[4] Report on Investigation of the Charleston, SC Old City Jail, Conducted January 18-20, 2007, by Joshua P. Warren on behalf of L.E.M.U.R. (League of Energy Materialization & Unexplained

phenomena Research, Asheville, North Crolina, http://shadow-boxent.brinkster.net/LEMUR/charlestonoldcityjail.html

[5] "Scary Idea: Ghost Seekers, Skeptics Explore Creepy Jail," by Jill Coley, Post and Courier, April 4, 2007

Chapter 14

[1] Jail, Orphanage Will Be Razed," January 20, 1938, Post and Courier archive

[2] "Jail Cell Blocks Due to be Moved," February 18, 1939, Post and Courier Archive

[3] "Preserve the Jail," Letter to the Editor, February 4, 1938, Post and Courier archive

[4] "Robert Mills, Architect," Letter to the Editor, April 14, 1939, Post and Courier archive

[5] "It Should be Saved," Letter to the Editor, December, 1938, Charleston County Public Library

[6] "Wooden House Where General Moultrie, Jailbound for Debt, Wrote His Memoirs, is Being Stripped for Firewood," undated, Charleston County Public Library

[7] "Wall to be Cut to Admit Light," January 17, 1939, Post and Courier archive

[8] "Society for the Preservation of Old Dwellings," 1939, (clip torn) Post and Courier archive

[9] "Save the Old, Mayor Urges," March 24, 1939, Post and Courier archive

[10] "County Jail Wall May be Picketed," March 19, 1939, Post and Courier archive

[11] "Governor Steps in to Save Jail Wall from Demolition," March 30, 1939, Post and Courier archive

[12] "Battle for the Wall," Letter to the Editor, 1939, Charleston County Public Library

[13] "More Than a Wall," Letter to the Editor, 1939, Charleston County Public Library

[14] "Letter to the Editor," 1939, Charleston County Public Library

[15] "Letter to the Editor," March 28, 1939, Charleston County Public Library

16. "4-Foot Wall on Franklin St., 16 on Magazine St., Rest Goes," April 21, 1939, Post and Courier archive

17. "Eastern Section of Jail Wall Being Razed," photo with caption, April 28, 1939, Post and Courier archive

18. "County Jail, Much of Wall Gone, Now Presents Unusual Appearance," undated newspaper clipping, Charleston County Public Library

19. "County Jail, Much of Wall Gone, Now Presents Unusual Appearance," undated newspaper clipping, Charleston County Public Library

20. "Jail Walls Down, Police Aid Asked," April 28, 1939, Post and Courier archive

21. "Going Out of Service," Evening Post, September 14, 1939

22. "New Use Found for Old County Jail Building," photo with caption, November 29, 1940, Charleston County Public Library

23. 149. Preservation Consultants, Inc. "Plan for the Adaptive Use of the Old Jail"; prepared for The Housing Authority of the City of Charleston, 1989, Plan for the Adaptive Use of the Old Jail, Phase 2, p. 12

24. History of Southside Baptist Church, http://www.southsideincharleston.com/about_us.html

25. "Old Jail Restoration as Museum Proposed," May 20, 1975, Charleston County Public Library

26. "Old Charleston Jail Museum to Open," December 27, 1975, Charleston County Public Library

27. "Old Charleston Jail Refurbished," by Tom Hamrick, picked up by The State Newspaper, February 1, 1976, Charleston County Public Library

28. "Atmosphere Important to Old Jail Museum," Evening Post, March 20, 1978, Charleston County Public Library

29. "May be Renovated," May 25, 1980, Charleston County Public Library

30. "Charleston Trying to Unlock Old Jail's Future," by Robert Behre, Post and Courier, August 3, 1998

31. "Spoleto Officials Eye Lease of Old Jail," by Mary A. Glass, June 12, 1981, Charleston County Library

32. "Panel Clears Way for Jail Disposal," by Kerri Morgan, Post and Courier, April 21, 1988

[33.] "Old Jail Restoration Planned," by Kerri Morgan, Post and Courier, February 12, 1990

[34.] "Charleston Trying to Unlock Old Jail's Future," by Robert Behre, Post and Courier, August 3, 1998

[35.] "Bid for Old Jail Awaiting Decision," by Robert Behre, Post and Courier, February 16, 1999

[36.] "School Plans for Old Jail Hinge on HUD," by Ron Menchaca, Post and Courier, March 4, 1999

[37.] "School's Plans Coming Together at the Old Jail," by Robert Behre, Post and Courier, January 24, 2000

[38.] "Bid for Old Jail Awaiting Decision," by Robert Behre, Post and Courier, February 16, 1999

[39.] "Old City Jail Now a National Treasure," by Robert Behre, Post and Courier, May 28, 1999

[40.] "School's Plans Coming Together at the Old Jail," by Robert Behre, Post and Courier, January 24, 2000

[41.] "Old City Jail Firmed Up as Rebuilding Continues," by Robert Behre, Post and Courier, February 25, 2002

[42.] "Arts School Encounters Roadblock," by Jason Hardin, Post and Courier, December 20, 2003

Interviews

Visited grandfather at the jail, Interview with Betty White, June 5, 2008

As a child, sold Cigarettes to Inmates, Interview with Herbert Fielding, March 24, 2008

Grandmother sold rope to hangman, Interview with Ralph McLaughlin June 5, 2008

BIBLIOGRAPHY

Abbott, A.O., Prison Life in the South at Richmond, Macon, Savannah, Charleston, Columba, Charlotte, Raleigh, Goldsborough, and Andersonville During the Years 1864 and 1865, New Yrok: Harper & Brothers, 1865

Adams, F.C., Manuel Pereira: Washington, DC, Buell & Blanchard, 1853

Adams, John G.B., Reminiscences of the Nineteenth Massachusetts Regiment, Boston: Wright, Potter Printing Company, 1899 (National Library of Australia, transcribed by Kerry Webb, http://sunsite.utk.edu/civil-war/Mass19.html)

Bancroft, Frederic, Slave Trading in the Old South, 1831, University of South Carolina Press, 1996

Bennett, Frank, Frank Bennett's Diary, The Historical Society of Pennsylvania (http://www2.hsp.org/collections/manuscripts/b/bennett3041.htm)

Bennett, John. "City's Jail Problem Was Acute in 1794." News and Courier, March 28, 1939.

Bernhard, Karl (Duke of Saxe-Weimar Eisenach), Travels Through North America, During the Years 1825 and 1826, Vol. 2, Philadelphia: Carey, Lea & Carey, 1828

Blake, John White, The Dungeon and the Gallows, The Charleston Book, Charleston: Published by Samuel Hart, Sen., King Street, 1845

Byers, S.H.M., What I Saw in Dixie or Sixteen Months in Rebel Prisons, New York: Robbin's and Poore, 1868

City of Charleston Yearbook, 1939 (Charleston County Public Library)

Cooper, Alonzo., In and Out of Rebel Prisons, Swego, NY.: R.J. Oliphant, 1888

Cote, Richard N., City of Heroes, Mt. Pleasant, SC: Corinthian Books, 2006

Crockett, Hasan, The Incendiary Pamphlet: David Walker's Appeal in Georgia, Association for the Study of African-American Life and History, Inc., 2001

Darling, Joseph T., Nine Months in a Rebel Prison, The Main Bugle, 1898

Death Records, Charleston, South Carolina 1819-1845, Compiled by Geo. K. Bonnoitt

Emilio, Luis F., A Brave Black Regiment, The History of the 54th Massachusetts, 1863-1865, Da Capo Press

Frederic, Francois Alexandre, Duke de la Rochefoucault Liancourt, Travels Through the United States of North in the Years 1795, 1796, and 1797, London: for R. Phillips, 1800

Friedman, Lawrence. Crime and Punishment in American History. New York: Basic Books.

Grenko, Bob. Old City Jail. Walterboro, SC: Self-published, 2001.

Glazier, Willard W. The Capture, the Prison Pen, and the Escape, Giving a Complete History of Prison Life in the South. Hartford, Conn: H.E. Goodwin, Publisher, 1869.

Hall, Basil, Travels in North America, in the Years 1827 and 1828, Edinburgh: Printed for Cadell and Co., 1830

Harris, Samuel. The Personal Reminiscences of Samuel Harris. Chicago, IL: The Rogerson Press, 1897.

Helm, T.B., Prison Life Part 1, 1881 (HIstory of Delaware County, p. 112-117, http://boards.ancestry.com/localities.northam.usa. states.indiana.counties.delaware/1236/mb.ashx?pnt=1)

Isham, Asa Brainerd; Davidson, Henry M., Furness, H.B., Prisoners of War and Miliary Prisons: Personal Narratives of Experience in the Prisons at Richmond, Danville, Macon, Andersonville, Savannah, Millen,

Charleston, and Columbia with A General Account of Prison Life and Prisons in the South during the War of the Rebellion, including Statistical Information Pertaining to Prisoners of War; together with a List of Officers who were Prisoners of War from January 1, 1864, Cincinnati: Lyman & Cusing, 1890, p. 67-73

Johnson, Charles. A General History of the Pyrates, from their First Rise and Settlement in the Island of Providence, to the Present Time. London: T. Warner,

Lambert, John, Travels Through Lower Canada, and the United States of North American in the Years 1806, 1807, and 1808, Vo. 2, London: C. Cradock and W. Joy, 1814

Meadville, Graham McCamant, Sixteen Months in Rebel Prisons by the First Prisoner in Andersonville, provided by Betty Lee Meadville

McGregor, Jeremiah S., Life and Deeds of Dr. John McGregor, Foster: Press of Fry Brothers, 1886

McKinley, Carlyle, The Charleston Earthquake, August 31, 1886, Prepared Expressly for the City Year Book, 1886, Charleston, 1886

Mills, Robert, Statistics of South Carolina, including a view of its Natural, Civil, and Military History, General and Particular, Charleston: Hurlbut and Lloyd, 1826

Poston, Jonathan H., The Buildings of Charleston – a Guide to the City's Architecture, South Carolina: University of South Carolina Press, 1997

S.G.B., Reminiscences of Charleston, SC, The Monthly Religious Magazine, Volume XV, Cambridge: University Press

Severens, Kenneth, Charleston Antebellum Architecture and Civic Destiny, University of Tennessee Press, Knoxville, 1988

Shurtleff, George W. A., Year with the Rebels, Itinerary of the Seventh Ohio Volunteer Infantry, 1861-1864, edited by Lawrence Wilson, New York: The Neale Publishing Company, 1907

Taylor, Alan and eric Foner. American Colonies. Viking Penguin, 2002

Wierse, Paul, Eighty-Eight Weeks in Purgatory, Charleston, SC: Farlane Printing and Publishing Company, 1920

Wines, Frederick Howard. Punishment and Reformation – A Study of the Penitentiary System, New York: Thomas Y. Crowell Company, Publishers, 1919

Woodmason, Charles. Carolina Backcountry on the Eve of the Revolution, North Carolina: University of North Carolina Press, 1953

Yearbook City of Charleston 1938 (Charleston County Public Library)

Anonymous, The Story of a Strange Career being The Autobiography of a Convict, Edited by Stanley Waterloo, New York: D. Appleton and Company

Emmett Robinson papers, South Carolina Historical Association

Letter to Governor John Drayton from Commissioners for Building a Gaol in Charleston," November 11, 1802 (from Emmett Robinson papers, South Carolina Historical Society)

Letter to Governor John Drayton from Sheriff Thomas Lehre, November 13, 1802, (from Emmett Robinson papers, South Carolina Historical Society)

Committee Report on Petition Above – 1828 – Penal System, Petitions, 1829 Charleston District, Emmett Robinson papers, South Carolina Historic Society

Convictions taken from the Records and Dockets of the Court of Sessions, for Charleston, Emmett Robinson papers, South Carolina Historical Society

Newspaper Articles

"A General Delivery at Charleston," New York Times, December 15, 1867

"A Murderer's End: Execution of a Negro Man in Charleston, S.C.," New York Times, February 10, 1872

"Affray in the Jail," Courier, March 21, 1859, Emmett Robinson papers, South Carolina Historical Society

"An Accomplice of McDow," Macon Telegraph, March 15, 1889

"Arts School Encounters Roadblock," by Jason Hardin, Post and Courier, December 20, 2003

"Atmosphere Important to Old Jail Museum," Evening Post, March 20, 1978, Charleston County Public Library

"Battle for the Wall," Letter to the Editor, 1939, Charleston County Public Library

"Beating Convict Outlawed at Charleston County Jail," Courier, January 27, 1933

"Bid for Old Jail Awaiting Decision," by Robert Behre, Post and Courier, February 16, 1999

"Big Crowd Saw Marcus Hanged," The Evening Post, August 3, 1906, Emmett Robinson papers, South Carolina Historical Society

"Broke Jail," Courier, May 3, 1858, Emmett Robinson papers, South Carolina Historical Society

"Charleston Jail Matrons Procured," The State Newspaper, July 4, 1920

"Charleston News Gathered in a Day," The State Newspaper, August 21, 1912

"Charleston News Gathered in a Day," The State Newspaper, February 21, 1913

"Charleston, Saturday Morning, Feb. 20, 1819," Charleston County Public Library

"Charleston, Monday Morning, Feb. 22, 1819," Charleston County Public Library

"Charleston, Friday Morning, Feb. 26, 1819," Charleston County Public Library

"Charleston, Friday Morning, March 26, 1819," Charleston County Public Library

"Charleston, Tuesday Morning, Jan. 18," 1820; Charleston, Friday Morning, Feb. 18, 1820 and Charleston, Saturday Morning, Feb. 19, 1820 Charleston County Public Library

"Charleston News Gathered in a Day," The State Newspaper, August 13, 1910

"Charleston News Gathered in a Day," The State Newspaper, December 27, 1911

"Charleston News Gathered in a Day," The State Newspaper, November 19, 1914

"Charleston News Gathered in a Day," The State Newspaper, July 17, 1917

"Charleston Trying to Unlock Old Jail's Future," by Robert Behre, Post and Courier, August 3, 1998

"Citizens Beware!," Courier, February 17, 1820, Charleston County Public Library

"Checker Players, in Jail, Use Razor Blades in Row," Courier, Sept. 20, 1931

"City Chain Gang Prisoners Wear Striped Suits Again," Courier, February 19, 1933

"County Jail Wall May be Picketed," March 19, 1939, Post and Courier archive

"Daniel Duncan Hanged at Jail," Evening Post, July 7, 1911, Emmett Robinson papers, South Carolina Historical Society

"Denies Knife Was Open," December 5, 1935, Post and Courier archive

"Duncan to Hang Here Tomorrow," Evening Post, July 6, 1911, Emmett Robinson papers, South Carolina Historical Society

"Eerie, Dark History Haunts Old City Jail," by Clay Barbor, Post and Courier, October 27, 2002

"Escape from Jail," Courier, July 12, 1858, Emmett Robinson papers, South Carolina Historical Society

"Escape of Martin Toohey," Franklin, Pa Gazette, March 27, 1819

"Exciting Shooting Affair Occurred Yesterday," State Newspaper, Columbia, SC

"Fox and Gappins Placed in Prison," The State Newspaper, September 9, 1921

"German Merchant Arrested by Federal Officers," The State Newspaper, July 17, 1917

"Ghost Hunting at Charleston's Old Jail," by Greg Hambrick, Charleston City Paper, August 29, 2007

"Going Out of Service as Charleston County Jail," Courier, September 14, 1939

"Going Out of Service," Evening Post, September 14, 1939

"Governor Steps in to Save Jail Wall from Demolition," March 30, 1939, Post and Courier archive

"Grand Jury Finds Jail Disease Trap," Courier, September 20, 1931

"Grand Jury Suggests Giving Gallows Weights to Museum," Courier, September 20, 1932

"Harold L. Bennett to Direct City's Safety Service," January 1, 1955, Post and Courier archive

"H.L. Bennett Named Charleston's Jailer," April 30, 1939, Post and Courier archive

"In the Police Court," newspaper clipping, Star Gospel Mission files, South Carolina Historical Society

"It was learned today," The State Newspaper, July 17, 1917

"Jail Cell Blocks Due to be Moved," February 18, 1939, Post and Courier Archive

"Jail, Orphanage Will Be Razed," January 20, 1938, Post and Courier archive

"Jail Walls Down, Police Aid Asked," April 28, 1939, Post and Courier archive

"It Should be Saved," Letter to the Editor, December, 1938, Charleston County Public Library

"Jail Cell Blocks to be Moved," Courier, February 18, 1939

"Jailer and Former Watchman in Fight," December 5, 1935, Post and Courier archive

"Kills His Children and Attacks Wife," Sunday Times-Advertiser, Trenton, N.Y., January 3, 1932

"Letter to the Editor," 1939, Charleston County Public Library

"Letter to the Editor," March 28, 1939, Charleston County Public Library

"Lynch Law was exhibited," Emmett Robinson papers, South Carolina Historical Society

"Manly Admits Drugging and Robbing Woman," The State Newspaper, August 10, 1912

"Martin Toohey Executed," Courier, May 29, 1819, Emmett Robinson papers, South Carolina Historical Society

"Martin Toohey Jailed," Courier, March 20, 1819, Emmett Robinson papers, South Carolina Historical Society

"May be Renovated," May 25, 1980, Charleston County Public Library

"Ministers of City Inspect Charleston County Prison," Courier, November 3, 1931

"More Than a Wall," Letter to the Editor, 1939, Charleston County Public Library

"Negro Accused of Murder," The State Newspaper, August 2, 1910

"Negro Boy Responsible," The State Newspaper, December 7, 1911

"Negroes Don't Believe Marcus was Hanged," The State Newspaper, August 5, 1906

"New Charleston County Jail Boasts of Modern Facilities," Charleston newspaper, August 1, 1941 (Post and Courier archive)

"New Use Found for Old County Jail Building," photo with caption, November 29, 1940, Charleston County Public Library

"Newberry County Boasts Best Jail," The State Newspaper, March 5, 1922

"Nobody who watched...," Worcester Daily Spy, July 1 1889

"Old Charleston Jail Museum to Open," December 27, 1975, Charleston County Public Library

"Old Charleston Jail Refurbished," by Tom Hamrick, picked up by The State Newspaper, February 1, 1976, Charleston County Public Library

"Old City Jail Firmed Up as Rebuilding Continues," by Robert Behre, Post and Courier, February 25, 2002

"Old City Jail Now a National Treasure," by Robert Behre, Post and Courier, May 28, 1999

"Old Jail Restoration as Museum Proposed," May 20, 1975, Charleston

"Old Jail Restoration Planned," by Kerri Morgan, Post and Courier, February 12, 1990County Public Library

"Panel Clears Way for Jail Disposal," by Kerri Morgan, Post and Courier, April 21, 1988

"Political Row Ends in Shooting of Six Men in Charleston," Associated Press, October 16, 1915

"Preserve the Jail," Letter to the Editor, February 4, 1938, Post and Courier archive

"Prison Has No Good Effect on Criminals, Jailer Finds," August 11, 1934, Post and Courier archive

"Robert Mills, Architect," Letter to the Editor, April 14, 1939, Post and Courier archive

"Runaway Car Claims Victim," Courier, December 5, 1911, Charleston County Public Library

"Save the Old, Mayor Urges," March 24, 1939, Post and Courier archive

"Scary Idea: Ghost Seekers, Skeptics Explore Creepy Jail," by Jill Coley, Post and Courier, April 4, 2007

"School Plans for Old Jail Hinge on HUD," by Ron Menchaca, Post and Courier, March 4, 1999

"School's Plans Coming Together at the Old Jail," by Robert Behre, Post and Courier, January 24, 2000

"Shooting at the County Jail," Sunday News, August 18, 1912

"Six Prisoners Removed," Courier, September 8, 1932

"Society for the Preservation of Old Dwellings," 1939, (clip torn) Post and Courier archive

"Son Succeeds W.J. Bennett," April 29, 1939, Post and Courier archive

"Spoleto Officials Eye Lease of Old Jail," by Mary A. Glass, June 12, 1981, Charleston County Library

"State of South Carolina – A Proclamation by his Excellency, John Geddes, Governor and Commander in Chief," Miller's Weekly Messenger, April 7, 1819

"Suicide in Jail," Courier, June 6, 1867, Charleston County Public Library

"Talk About Having a Bad Scare Day," by Bryce Donovan, Post and Courier, October 31, 2002

"The County Jail," News and Courier, September 4, 1886

"The Dawson Murder," Philadelphia Enquirer, March 14, 1889

"The Execution," Easton Gazette, May 27, 1820

"The Last Penalty," Courier, March 26, 1859

"The Penalty for Murder,; Daniel Washington's Death on the Gallows," New York Times, July 10, 1880

"The Prisoners at Charleston; They are Committed to the City Jail," New York Times from the Charleston Mercury, September 14, 1861

"With Gun and Caisson; Scraps from the Notebook of an Artilleryman. Headed for Antietam – Passing Through Washington on a Sunday Morning – How the Capital Looked in War Times. IV.", New York Times, March 15, 1891

"This Looks Like the County Jail," Evening Post, August 18, 1928, Charleston County Public Library

"Today is MovingDay for Convicts," Charleston newspaper, September 16, 1939 (Post and Courier archive)

"Under the Union Guns," New York Times, May 10, 1891, Post and Courier archive

"Visitor Mistakes Jailer for Buddy," November 24, 1934, Post and Courier archive

"Wall on Franklin Will be Reduced," Charleston newspaper, 1939 (Post and Courier archive)

"Wall to be Cut to Admit Light," January 17, 1939, Post and Courier archive

"Wingate Slightly Better," State Newspaper, August 20, 1912

"W.J. Bennett, Former County Jailer, Dies," February 18, 1952, Post and Courier archive

Wooden House Where General Moultrie, Jailbound for Debt, Wrote His Memoirs, is Being Stripped for Firewood," undated, Charleston County Public Library

"Workers Sign Off on Jail Repairs," by Jason Hardin, Post and Courier, June 25, 2002

"160 Prisoners Now in Jail," Courier, Jan. 19, 1931

"27 Years Custodian of the Jail, Bennett Finds Life No Bed of Roses," Courier, Post and Courier archive

"4-Foot Wall on Franklin St., 16 on Magazine St., Rest Goes," April 21, 1939, Post and Courier archive

"43 Prisoners in New Jail Annex," Courier, August 28, 1932

Internet Sites

Bordewich, Fergus, The Battle for Morris Island, originally from A Civil Battle for a Civil War Battlefield, Smithsonia Magazine, July, 2005, from http://www.fergusbordewich.com/PAGESjournalism/FBmorris.shtml

Digital Library on American Slavery, "Sheriff Nathaniel Cleary," http://library.uncg.edu/slavery/details.aspx?pid=1439

History of Southside Baptist Church, http://www.southsideincharleston.com/about_us.html

White, John Blake, from from http://www.famousamericans.net/johnblakewhite/from from http://www.famousamericans.net/johnblakewhite/

Report on Investigation of the Charleston, SC Old City Jail, Conducted January 18-20, 2007, by Joshua P. Warren on behalf of L.E.M.U.R. (League of Energy Materialization & Unexplained phenomena Research, Asheville, North Crolina, http://shadowboxent.brinkster.net/LEMUR/charlestonoldcityjail.html

Star Gospel Mission, http://www.stargospelmission.com/

Strater, Terrance, The Life and Times of a Rebel Surgeon, Dr. George Rodgers Clark Todd, Brother of Mary Todd Lincoln, (http://colquitt.k12.ga.us/gspurloc/Cobbslegion/gasca/letters/todd_biography.htm)

Union War Prisoners Association, prints, Library of Congress Prints & Photographs, http://www.loc.gov/pictures/search/?q=Union%20Prisoners%20Association

Periodicals

Ballou's Pictorial Drawing Room Companion, August 8, 1957

Ellis, Rev. Rufus (editor, with E.H. Sears). "The Monthly Religious Magazine, Volume XV. University Press, Cambridge: Welch, Bigelow and Company.

Studies

Preservation Consultants, Inc. "Plan for the Adaptive Use of the Old Jail"; prepared for The Housing Authority of the City of Charleston, 1989, Plan for the Adaptive Use of the Old Jail, Phase 2

SoBA Facility Master Plan, Glenn Keyes, Architect in collaboration with Robert Miller, Architect, 2003

Trebellas, Christine, Historic American Buildings Survey – Charleston County Jail (Charleston District Jail), Washington, DC: Historic American Buildings Survey (HABS), 1995

33546347R00210

Made in the USA
Middletown, DE
17 July 2016